Lex Fa

PROLOGUE

5:29:21 AM. JULY 16, 1945 - TRINITY SITE, NEW MEXICO

In an instant, blinding white light bloomed out from the new man-made sun in the Jornada del Muerto desert about 56 km southeast of the town of Socorro, New Mexico. At 'Point Zero', at the top of a 100-foot-tall steel tower, had been sitting the result of several years of work under the codename The Manhattan Project. It was a spherical device roughly two metres in diameter nicknamed *the Gadget*.

The searing light from the explosion was unlike anything ever witnessed on Earth before, and it enveloped the entire desert plain and lit up every peak, crevasse and ridge of the nearby mountain range. The device released almost unimaginable amounts of energy, stretching the laws of physics to their extreme and threatening to tear open the very fabric of reality. No one present on that day would have been able to look directly at the explosion without suffering serious and lasting damage to their retinas, and so every one of the 425 people at the nuclear test site who were observing the detonation from a safe distance, were wearing heavily tinted welding goggles issued by the U.S. Army before the test.

One of the observers was nuclear physicist Robert Oppenheimer who was the director of the Manhattan Project, and whose Los Alamos Laboratory designed the bomb itself. Having started as a small operation in 1939, the project eventually grew to employ as many as 130,000 people.

The Gadget was a so-called plutonium implosion fission device, which works by arranging conventional explosives in a spherical shape around an inner core of plutonium. When the explosives are detonated at precisely the same time, the plutonium is compressed toward the centre of the device with such force that it triggers a nuclear fission chain reaction that releases enormous amounts of energy, mainly in the form of heat.

Oppenheimer was later haunted by witnessing the awesome and terrifying power of the weapon he had helped create. Two years later, and after similar devices had obliterated the Japanese cities of Hiroshima and Nagasaki killing upwards of a quarter of a million people, he would relay his thoughts to fellow physicists.

"This weapon has dramatized so mercilessly the inhumanity and evil of modern war. In some sort of crude sense which no vulgarity, no humour, no overstatements can quite extinguish, the physicists have known sin, and this is a knowledge which they cannot lose."

After the initial brilliant flash of light as the Gadget exploded, a powerful shockwave raced out from where the now completely vapourised steel tower had stood. As the shockwave travelled outward at just over 1000 kilometres per hour or 300 metres per second, it also punched upwards in a rapidly expanding dome that seemed to evaporate and clear away the few wispy clouds that had been floating above the Trinity Test site on that day. A few seconds later the intense heat at the centre of the explosion caused the dust-filled air and the water vapour created by the explosion to start roiling violently upwards into the characteristic mushroom shape. Mushroom clouds are not unique to nuclear explosions. Any explosion large enough and which develops enough heat will produce the same atmospheric phenomenon. However, nuclear explosions just happen to be so extraordinarily powerful that they have become firmly associated with this shape. The destructive power of nuclear weapons is measured in thousands of TNT equivalents, or so-called 'kilotons'. A one-kiloton nuclear explosion is the equivalent of detonating 1000 tonnes of TNT.

The device named 'the Gadget' contained less than ten kilograms of plutonium but was estimated to have produced a 25-kiloton explosion. It was the first nuclear explosion to happen on planet Earth and it was by far the largest explosion in human history.

Where the steel tower had been there was now a circular area 600 metres across where the sand had been turned into a thick but brittle layer of greenish glass. The shockwave which was reportedly felt as much as 100 miles away, took just under 40 seconds to reach the observers who were around 9 kilometres away, and they reported the heat from the explosion as being as hot as an oven. The towering mushroom cloud eventually reached a height of 7.5 miles or 12 kilometres.

As Oppenheimer watched the terrifying power of the first nuclear explosion in history, he began to understand the magnitude of destruction and potential suffering that it had opened the door to. More than a decade earlier he had begun to develop an interest in Hinduism, and as he watched the mushroom cloud towering over the New Mexico desert, a phrase from the ancient Hindu sacred text, the Bhagavad-Gita, ran through his mind.

Now I am become Death, the destroyer of worlds.

ONE

PRESENT DAY - THE NORTH ATLANTIC

The nuclear submarine USS Tennessee belonging to the U.S. Navy's Submarine Squadron 20, had made its way south from the ongoing NATO winter exercise in the North Atlantic towards Scotland. Still submerged, it was now slowly proceeding south-east through the North Channel between Ireland and Scotland, in the direction of the wide inlet called the Firth of Clyde some 50 kilometres south-west of Glasgow as the crow flies.

Operating out of Naval Submarine Base Kings Bay in Georgia as part of the Atlantic Fleet, the vessel is officially designated the SSBN-734, where SS denotes *submersible*, B denotes *ballistic missile*, and N denotes *nuclear powered*. The submarine had spent the past four days taking part in a large exercise involving both naval and air forces from the US, the UK, Norway,

France, Germany and a number of smaller NATO allies.

Its role had been to simulate a retaliatory response to a nuclear missile launch carried out by the Russian Federation, by attempting to launch two nuclear missiles at strategic targets near Nizhny Novgorod Oblast deep inside Russia where the 6th Tank Brigade of the Russian Ground Forces is located.

Navy ships from several NATO countries, including surface vessels and so-called attack or hunter-killer submarines from the US and the UK, were then tasked with hunting down and destroying the USS Tennessee either using simulated depth charges or torpedoes fired from the hunter-killers.

The USS Tennessee's mission had been a success. Using so-called *silent running*, it had been able to make its way undetected to its designated launch location on the abyssal plain located 35 kilometres west of the Shetland Islands.

In this stealth mode of operation, which is designed to evade enemy passive sonar or any other form of remote detection, the vessel had remained submerged at depths of several hundred feet with all non-essential systems shut down. At the same time, the crew had been instructed to rest and refrain from making any unnecessary noise, and the active cooling of the nuclear reactor had been turned off with the boat relying solely on natural convection cooling.

Most importantly, the speed of the submarine was significantly reduced, eliminating the so-called propeller cavitation. This phenomenon occurs when the rapid movement of a propeller blade through water causes a sufficiently low pressure just behind the edge of the blades to create small vapour-filled cavities or bubbles immediately behind it. When these cavities are once again subjected to the higher ambient pressure of the deep ocean, they collapse causing sound waves that can be detected by other submarines or listening stations.

All of these noise-suppressing measures allowed the USS Tennessee to glide almost silently through the water and arrive undetected at its launch location, where it had then moved up to a depth of 100 feet or around 30 metres. Here, despite being hunted by numerous surface ships, attack submarines and air assets belonging to fellow NATO countries, it had successfully performed the simulated launch of two of its nuclear missiles, after which it had again descended back down to around 500 feet near the relatively shallow ocean floor west of the Shetland Islands.

Oceans cover more than 70 percent of the Earth's surface, which equates to 361 million square kilometres or 140 million square miles. The average depth is 3.7 kilometres or 2.3 miles and combined all the world's oceans contain 1,370 million cubic kilometres of water. That is the amount of water that would fit inside a cube measuring over 1,100 kilometres on all three sides. Another way of visualising this is to imagine the states of Texas and California, both with one thousand kilometres of water covering their entire areas.

Compared with such an unfathomably large haystack, the needle that was the nuclear submarine USS Tennessee was vanishingly small and almost impossible to find once it was submerged. By design, the ballistic missile-carrying submarine was made to be silent and extremely difficult to detect, either by surface vessels or by enemy hunter-killer submarines.

One of eighteen Ohio-class submarines built since 1981, the USS Tennessee was conceived as a mobile launch platform for both conventional and nuclear missiles. Most of these vessels carry nuclear missiles, and as such have served as a deterrent against a nuclear first strike mainly from the now long-dead Soviet Union.

The logic behind their conception was simple. Even if against all odds the Soviet Union should manage to successfully carry out a first strike against the United States, potentially knocking out the land-based intercontinental ballistic missiles or ICBMs, subsequent nuclear strikes from a fleet of submerged US submarines were regarded as a sufficiently large threat to effectively nullify any first strike advantage the Soviets might initially be able to obtain.

The SSBN fleet is thus considered a so-called assured second-strike capability since it is a survivable system for carrying out retaliatory nuclear attacks even if full-scale nuclear war was to break out. It is also sometimes referred to as CASD or Continuous At Sea Deterrent, and it was part of the strategic thinking that resulted in a military doctrine with what is possibly the most appropriate acronym ever devised. Mutually Assured Destruction, or MAD.

It was a cold, grey and foggy day as the submarine slowly surfaced a few kilometres from shore. As its periscopes and communications antennae broke the surface followed by the submarine's sail and hydroplanes, the water went from seemingly still to frothy and roiling as the hulking steel beast gradually appeared from the deep. Then the long hull of the vessel appeared and the submarine began to slow down gradually as it approached the inlet.

Making its way smoothly across the calm waters of the Firth of Clyde towards the lochs of southwestern Scotland, the submarine's relatively small size belied its destructive capabilities. An Ohio-class SSBN can carry up to 24 Trident II ballistic nuclear missiles each armed with several warheads. Together they represent devastation on an almost unimaginable scale, particularly when considering that they can be launched from just a single vessel. Eighteen such vessels is generally viewed as a guarantee that no other state will ever contemplate launching a first strike against the United States.

The same deterrent applies to an attack on its NATO allies since the founding principle of NATO is the notion of 'collective defence'. This is written into the NATO treaty's Article 5, whereby an attack on a single member country shall be regarded as an attack on all member countries of the alliance.

Through the decades of the Cold War, this implicit understanding of the calamitous consequences of any first strike was enough to keep the world from descending into nuclear war, despite tensions reaching nerve-racking levels on several occasions, not least during the Cuban Missile Crisis in 1962. Since the end of the Soviet Union and the subsequent increasing assertiveness and belligerence of the Russian Federation, the same nuclear doctrine has persisted with both sides able to field numerous nuclear-capable submarines. The same deterrence dynamics also apply to other nuclear powers such as China and

North Korea, or at least that is the prevailing military dogma. The USS Tennessee was a small but important part of that dynamic.

As it made its way into the 7-kilometre-long Gare Loch and approached Faslane Bay where HMNB Clyde is located, the hatch at the top of the submarine's sail opened and an enlisted sailor appeared wearing a dark blue waterproof coat with the name of the submarine emblazoned on its back. A few moments later the boat's captain appeared and stood at the front of the sail looking ahead across the bow of the vessel as it cut through the shallow waves and parted the waters in front of it. A few metres below him two huge hydroplanes extended around four metres from the sail on either side. These control the pitch of the submarine when submerged. Below and in front of him about five metres away from the sail on the top of the bow was the forward escape hatch. A similar hatch is located at the back of the submarine, and both are intended as a last resort escape option for submariners trapped in a disabled vessel.

The escape procedure on a modern submarine involves the use of so-called Submarine Escape Immersion Equipment, or SEIE-suits, and the Ohio-class is equipped with the Beaufort Mark 11, which is the latest iteration. Each of these suits is an all-in-one whole-body insulated suit and life raft for just one person, and they can be used from depths of around 180 metres.

Thankfully the captain of the USS Tennessee and his crew had never needed to employ these units during anything other than a drill. As effective as they are having been developed since the 1950s, they are the very last piece of equipment any submariner would ever want to use.

A group of vehicles and service personnel were lined up and patiently awaiting the arrival of the USS Tennessee on the docks of HMNB Clyde. The naval base in western Scotland, also known as Faslane, is the United Kingdom's naval base serving as the home of the UK's nuclear submarine deterrent force. The Royal Navy operates 4 Vanguard-class nuclear submarines from here, and just like their US counterparts, they also carry the Trident II missile. One of the Vanguard-class submarines was moored to one side of the service pier, leaving the other side open for the U.S. Navy vessel coming in from Gare Loch. At either end of the pier sat two tall swivelled gantries for transporting supplies and weapons in and out of the submarines.

As the contingent of UK and US personnel waited for the submarine to be towed the final stretch to the quayside, its true size began to become apparent. The vessel suddenly did not look so small anymore. Measuring 170 metres in length, 13 metres at the widest point of its hull, and displacing 18,750 tons of water, the Ohio-class submarine is almost three times as long as a Boeing-747, and more than twice as wide. The internal layout contains what is effectively a large four-storey building wrapped inside two hulls. The non-watertight outer hull provides a hydrodynamically efficient shape, and the inner pressure hull is designed to shield the submarine and its crew of 15 officers and 140 enlisted sailors against the immense pressures of the deep.

As the towropes became taut and the imposing vessel was nudged the final few metres towards the pier, another car arrived at the docks carrying the HMNB Clyde base commander Commodore Mark Harrington who had arrived to greet the United States Navy submarine. This was the first time a U.S. Navy boat had entered the complex at Faslane, and the base commander was keen to welcome it and get the new joint weapons interoperability initiative off to a smooth start.

Harrington was a well-groomed man in his sixties with neatly trimmed brown hair and a thin moustache. As he walked from the car towards the pier, a mobile articulated gangway was moved to the side of it where it was extended and lowered to settle on top of the submarine's hull allowing the crew to disembark.

First off the boat was its 'CO' or Commanding Officer Captain Conrad Vandenberg, followed by his 'XO' or Executive Officer and 2nd in command John Chisholm. Remaining in charge on the submarine was 3rd in command, the 'COB' or Chief of the Boat Tom Payne, who served as the most senior enlisted advisor to both the Commanding Officer and the Executive Officer.

Captain Vandenberg was a tall and lean man with a chiselled face and short black hair. His steely eyes were light blue and conveyed an air of intelligence and calm. His XO was shorter and stockier but appeared to be physically very fit. He had brown hair and keen eyes, and he moved with the physical self-assuredness of a man who had received special operations training.

Both of the two commissioned officers disembarking the boat were wearing the almost black dark-blue SDB or Service Dress Blue uniforms, consisting of a suit coat and trousers, white shirt, black necktie and a white cap with black shade upon which were affixed their rank insignia. On the left side of their chests were the various medals and commendations they had each been awarded during their Navy service.

On the sleeves and shoulders of his suit coat, Vandenberg had four medium gold stripes with one star placed above them, indicating his rank as U.S. Navy Captain. Chisholm's insignia were two medium gold stripes with one small stripe in between, indicating his rank as a Lieutenant Commander.

'Captain Vandenberg,' smiled Harrington holding out his hand to greet the commander.

He had the typical accent of a member of the British ruling classes often found amongst the highest ranks of the military's officer core.

'And Lieutenant Commander Chisholm,' he continued. 'Welcome to HMNB Clyde. Very glad to have you here.'

'Commodore Harrington,' responded Vandenberg in his slow drawn-out Virginia accent as he took the commodore's hand and gave it a firm shake. 'Happy to be here. This here is my XO, John Chisholm.'

'Commodore,' said Chisholm and shook the commodore's hand.

'Pleasure to meet you,' replied Harrington politely, shaking the XO's hand.

'So,' said Captain Vandenberg, placing his hands on his hips and looking around the pier. 'I assume the torpedo is ready to be taken aboard my boat?'

'It is indeed,' said Harrington, gesturing towards a large truck parked on the pier. 'It arrived early yesterday morning, and the loader team has been preparing to bring it aboard your vessel so hopefully, everything will go smoothly.'

'Outstanding,' replied Vandenberg with a smile as the three men began walking towards the waiting car. 'Well, I guess we'll find out if it works tomorrow.'

'I am sure it will,' said Harrington confidently. 'I am told the torpedo underwent several rounds of extensive testing and simulated firings before being shipped and everything went as expected. Anyway, let's go to my office and sit down for a cup of tea. My car is this way.'

'Do you have coffee?' asked Vandenberg.

'I am sure we can find you some,' replied Harrington.

'Good. I prefer coffee,' said Vandenberg dryly. 'And as strong as you can make it. I don't like being able to see the bottom.'

The torpedo the men had been referring to was one of the UK's Spearfish heavy torpedoes used by all of its submarines including the Vanguard-class. With a maximum speed of 110 kilometres or almost 70 miles per hour, it is an extremely fast torpedo that is used as a self-defence weapon against both enemy submarines and surface ships. The Spearfish is slightly longer and heavier than the U.S. Navy's standard Mark 48 heavy torpedo, but both types are launched from a 21-inch torpedo tube at the front of a submarine.

The specific torpedo mentioned by the two men was a standard Spearfish that had undergone slight modifications to its electronic interface with the submarine carrying it. In theory, this should allow it to also be fired by a U.S. Navy submarine. However, this was the first time such a modified torpedo was going to be loaded into a torpedo tube on an Ohio-class SSBN, and the live-fire exercise planned for the following day was intended to test whether this relatively small modification would allow true weapons interoperability between the U.S. Navy and the Royal Navy for these types of weapons.

If successful, the modified Spearfish could potentially be used by all U.S. Navy submarines, and if a similar test with a Mark 48 torpedo fired by a Vanguard submarine scheduled for a few days later proved successful it would allow for significantly increased flexibility for the two navies with regards to weapons re-supply options in the future.

The group entered the black Range Rover and left the pier just as the loading team were manoeuvring the specially designed truck carrying the torpedo closer to the submarine. Chief of the Boat, Tom Payne appeared at the top of the sail to oversee the opening of the munitions loading hatch and the transfer of the torpedo into the lower front section of the vessel where the torpedo room was located. Out of its 18 secure storage racks, only one was currently empty in anticipation of the arrival of the modified Spearfish torpedo.

The huge pier gantry swung around slowly until its crane was directly above the truck carrying the Spearfish. As the crane operator lowered the hook towards the truck, a team of loaders prepared the seven-metre long and almost two-tonne heavy missile for being lifted onto the submarine. Tom Payne was holding a walkie-talkie which allowed him to communicate directly with the crane operator. After less than an hour, the torpedo had been taken aboard the USS Tennessee and placed securely in the torpedo storage room from where it could be loaded quickly into one of the submarine's four torpedo tubes.

Harrington, Vandenberg and Chisholm entered the base commander's office on the hillside overlooking Gare Loch.

'Beautiful view,' said Vandenberg looking out of the window at the loch and the tall headland on the opposite side of it. 'It's peaceful here. Not many people around these parts.'

'Yes,' replied Harrington. 'It is a very sparsely populated area in this part of the country.'

'That's how I like it,' mused Vandenberg.

'Oh,' said Harrington awkwardly. 'My deepest condolences about your wife.'

Vandenberg blinked a couple of times as if uncomfortable with the sudden reminder.

'Yeah,' he said slowly, his voice taut. 'Cancer can take a life faster than you might think.'

'I can only imagine the terrible loss that must have been,' said Harrington sympathetically.

'It was rough, that's for sure,' replied Vandenberg. 'A thing like that changes your perspective on a lot of things. Life's just not the same after that.'

'Do you have children?' asked Harrington cautiously.

'No,' replied Vandenberg flatly. 'Carrie couldn't. I was ok with that, but I don't think she ever really accepted it.'

'I am so sorry,' mumbled Harrington apologetically. 'I really shouldn't pry. None of my business.'

'That's alright,' smiled Vandenberg sadly and glanced at the commodore. 'I've met a lot worse. Some people just don't know when to quit.'

'Right. Anyway,' said Harrington, keen to move on to another topic. 'If you look over to the other side of the loch, you might be interested to know that on the other side of that ridge is RNAD Coulport where we store this base's nuclear warheads. Eighteen separate bunkers with Trident II missiles. Enough to keep us going for a while.'

'Unless war breaks out,' said Vandenberg dryly, squinting to look at the far side of the loch.

'Well,' smiled Harrington and spread his hands out wide as if gesturing to the whole naval base. 'Hopefully, it doesn't come to that, but arguably that is why there are all here. It is called a nuclear deterrent for a reason. But anyway, all of that is up to the politicians.'

'I know,' said Vandenberg ruefully. 'And there's a fresh bunch of those in the White House every four years.'

He paused for a moment as if pondering how to phrase something, but then seemed to decide not to elaborate any further.

'Anyhow,' he finally continued. 'I'd be much obliged if you'd show us the files on the Spearfish torp. My chief of the boat is going to perform a visual inspection himself as soon as it has been brought aboard, but I need to make sure everything is as expected as far as the paperwork is concerned.'

'Certainly,' said Harrington, retrieving a leather folder from a drawer in his desk. 'It should all be here. I received all the details from BAE Systems in Portsmouth yesterday but you are welcome to inspect them.'

Harrington handed the folder to Vandenberg who placed it on a table in Harrington's office and then spent a couple of minutes meticulously going through all of the specs of the torpedo, not least the highlighted section concerning the nature of the changes to its electronics system.

'Everything looks fine,' he finally said. 'Thank you.'

'My pleasure,' said Harrington. 'Now, let's sit down and get to know each other a bit better. I have a feeling these visits are going to become a regular occurrence here at Clyde.'

★ ★ ★

A couple of hours later Commodore Harrington escorted Vandenberg and Chisholm back down to the pier where the USS Tennessee's 3rd in command Tom Payne was waiting for them.

'All set?' asked Vandenberg.

'Yes sir,' replied Payne. 'The torpedo is safely stored. Boat's ready to go.'

'Good,' said Vandenberg and turned to face Harrington. 'Commodore. Thank you for your hospitality and for making our little pitstop here as quick as possible. No doubt, we'll be seeing each other again soon.'

'It was our pleasure,' smiled Harrington. 'I look forward to reading about the test firing tomorrow. Weapons interoperability between our two navies has been in the works for many years so it is excellent to finally see it come to fruition. Good luck out there.'

'Thank you,' replied Vandenberg, giving a quick salute and then turning to walk back towards the gangway extending out to the submarine.

Chisholm shook the commodore's hand and then followed a moment later. As the two officers mounted the sail to re-enter the submarine, the towropes were untied and the last remaining crew were busy completing the final preparations for the submarine to leave port. Payne was the last crew member to enter the vessel, and after he had closed the hatch he turned the levers to lock it tightly.

'Last man down. Hatch secure!' he announced loudly as he climbed down the ladder to the Command & Control Centre where the two senior officers were taking up their stations for departure.

Half an hour later the USS Tennessee was heading back out of the narrow Gare Loch into the Firth of Clyde, after which it slowly turned north towards the North Channel. A few hours after that it eventually passed back out into the inhospitable North Atlantic where strong arctic winds were coming down from a northerly direction creating high waves with white caps, also known as white horses. Combined with the low grey clouds moving swiftly overhead it made for a beautiful but eerie vista.

However, none of this was noticeable inside the submarine which had submerged as soon as it had passed out through the North Channel. Now at a depth of 100 feet or around 30 metres, it was entirely unaffected by the powerful ocean swells on the surface above it.

It was becoming dark as the submarine had disappeared beneath the waves, and inside it the crew now slipped quietly into their new normal - the underwater routine. Everyone had a well-defined job to do and often a series of precise individual tasks that needed to be carried out in a particular way and in a particular order, and in conjunction with other tasks carried out by other crewmembers. Together they formed a disciplined and well-oiled machine under the firm leadership of Captain Vandenberg whom the crew trusted implicitly. His leadership abilities and natural authority had made him a well-respected captain both by the officers and by the enlisted men. He was known to be stern but fair, cultivating a strong and loyal chain of command, and his management style was very much one of 'my way or the highway.'

Such an approach might not have endeared him to the crew of a surface vessel, but down here at the sharp end of potential nuclear warfare and with millions of tonnes of water always ready to squash the submarine like a tin can, everyone understood that there could be no room for sloppiness or a lax attitude to the running of the boat. A single mistake down here could cost 165 people their lives in just a couple of minutes, and in that scenario, it was best to have someone with a zero-tolerance attitude to failure at the helm. Autocratic leadership was more or less built into the system aboard an SSBN, and everyone on the USS Tennessee fully understood and accepted that fact.

★ ★ ★

The next morning XO John Chisholm took care of his regular duties in the Command & Control Centre. He also paid a visit to the radio room which is adjacent to and just ahead of C&C, and also to the sonar room which is the last room on the top deck near the bow of the ship just before the forward bulkhead ends. Further forward is a large void between the pressurised hull and the spherical sonar array that sits at the very tip of the submarine's bow.

On the deck below just under the radio and sonar rooms were the officer's quarters. They were quite small rooms, and even the captain's quarters were modest by surface standards. However, compared with what most of the crew had available they were positively palatial. Only officers had private quarters and the vast majority of the crew only had a bunk bed to call their own. However, those bunk beds were often so tightly squeezed together that they could only be entered through a feat of gymnastics worthy of the Olympics, and they were nowhere near large enough to sit up in.

Chisholm knocked on the door to Captain Vandenberg's private quarters and waited for a reply.

'Come,' said Vandenberg almost immediately.

He was sitting at his desk in the sparsely furnished room waiting for Chisholm to arrive. On his desk were a couple of folders and a pen along with a laptop and his ball cap carrying the USS Tennessee's insignia. On the wall in front of him under a set of shallow cabinets was a picture of his deceased wife. Near the corner of the desk was a small bust of what looked like a Greek or Roman figure, and on a small gold plaque mounted on its base at the front was engraved the words *Magister Equitum*. Vandenberg was well known to be an avid reader of the military history of his own country as well as those of empires of the distant past. The small bust was a gift from a close friend.

The XO opened the door carefully and checked to make sure he was not disturbing the captain, and then he walked inside.

'Close it,' said Vandenberg, and nodded at the door.

Chisholm closed the door behind him and turned around to stand to attention.

'Sir, we are coming up on the firing location in about fifteen minutes,' he said. 'VLF indicates that our mock target is in position and ready.'

VLF stands for Very Low Frequency radio waves, which is what the land-based command structure uses to communicate with submerged submarines. High-frequency radio waves cannot penetrate the oceans and so submarines with hundreds of feet of water above them are not able to receive communications via regular radio waves from surface ships or satellites. Instead, they rely on very low frequency and very low energy radio waves, which are long and slow enough not to bounce off the ocean. The drawback to this is that these communications are also very low in bandwidth, so only short messages can be received by the vessel. Because a submerged submarine does not itself carry a high-strength VLF transmitter it is unable to respond unless it surfaces and uses its own high-frequency antennae mounted on the sail.

'Very well,' replied the captain. 'Is the torpedo room ready?'

'Yes sir,' said the executive officer. 'They are all set. And I inspected the torp myself just now. Everything is ready. It has already been loaded into Launch Tube 1.'

'Good,' said Vandenberg and rose, casting his eyes on the picture of his wife and putting the cap on his head. 'Let's make this count.'

A couple of minutes later the two of them were in the Command & Control Center, Vandenberg in his captain's chair in the middle of the room and Chisholm standing by his side to the left. Surrounding the chair and arrayed on both of its sides and in front of it were control stations and crew, allowing the captain complete control over the entire vessel and its many functions.

'Helmsman, make your depth 150 feet,' Vandenberg called out.

'Ay-ay sir. Making depth 150 feet,' replied the helmsman.

Seated directly in front of the captain's chair the helmsman was gripping the controls that allowed him, using powerful hydraulic systems, to manipulate the hydroplanes on the submarine's sail. Pushing forward on the controls rotated the hydroplanes and tilted the leading edges of them down thus pushing the front of the submarine downwards and taking the vessel to a lower depth.

'Adjust heading Zero-Seven-Five. Silent running,' ordered Captain Vandenberg.

'Silent running,' repeated Chisholm, and immediately several of the crewmembers in the Command & Control Center began flicking switches and typing commands into their consoles.

These actions quickly rippled through the vessel, as non-essential systems were turned off and the crew was made aware that the submarine was now endeavouring to operate silently.

The submarine's speed was reduced substantially and as the propeller was spun down to very low RPMs in order to avoid cavitation, the vessel's audio signature in the water was reduced dramatically, now making it extremely challenging for both friend and foe to locate it.

'Sonar, report,' said Vandenberg.

'One surface contact, bearing Zero-Zero-Six. 6,300 yards,' said the sonar operator.

'That's our target,' said Chisholm.

'Target acquired,' said the weapons operator. 'Coordinates locked.'

'Open Launch Tube 1, outer shutters,' said Captain Vandenberg 'Set torpedo to autonomous operating mode. Active sonar.'

Spearfish torpedoes can be guided by wire and controlled directly from the launching submarine, or they can operate autonomously using either active or passive sonar. When operating autonomously the torpedo uses its sonar and its onboard processor to classify targets and discriminate between actual targets and background noise including various acoustic countermeasures dropped by other submarines.

'Autonomous operation. Active sonar,' repeated the weapons operator and flicked the Master Arm switch. 'Ready to launch torpedo.'

Vandenberg paused for a moment. Standing next to him Chisholm glanced briefly at his commanding officer. Then he gave a small nod.

'Launch torpedo!' ordered Vandenberg.

The weapons operator pressed the glowing red button on his console, and immediately the faint swoosh of the torpedo leaving the launch tube could be heard from the bow of the vessel. Then came the explosion.

Two

At the bottom of the Atlantic Ocean, spread out over thousands of square kilometres of seabed, are a large number of listening devices. During the Cold War, the US intelligence services constructed a huge network of underwater listening stations, particularly in the North Atlantic Ocean. The aim of this effort was to use sensitive hydrophones to listen for Russian submarines operating in the North Atlantic as they manoeuvred to and from their bases in northern Russia, primarily the Northern Fleet's main base in Severomorsk in the Murmansk Oblast region also known as the Kola Peninsula, which borders northern Norway and Finland.

The first such network was called the Sound Surveillance System or SOSUS, and it operated for several decades with thousands of hydrophones placed near choke points in the ocean, especially in the waters between Greenland, Iceland, and Scotland in the so-called GIUK Gap. The huge volumes of data collected from these networks were fed back to dozens of listening stations in the U.S. and in Europe where they were processed and analysed.

As the Cold War came to an end, the network was paired down and increasingly used for civilian scientific purposes such as acoustic tomography, which involves measuring temperatures and currents, as well as the monitoring of tectonic activity and tracking of whale populations.

However, with the emergence of an increasingly belligerent Russia reasserting itself on the global stage, as well as the rapidly rising naval power of China, there is again a growing demand for high-fidelity underwater monitoring systems on the part of the U.S. Navy and its NATO allies. For this reason, a large amount of military funding has been directed towards rebuilding and refining the network, most recently through the Deep Reliable Acoustic Path Exploitation System, or DRAPES, which will significantly enhance the existing system. In addition, NATO naval forces rely on a system called Surveillance Towed Array Sensor System or SURTASS, which consists of civilian crewed ships towing highly sensitive passive sonar arrays at a distance of around one mile or 1.5 kilometres from the ship. These systems are capable of potentially picking up noises produced by a submarine several hundred miles away.

The DRAPES network of hydrophones closest to the USS Tennessee's position had been able to pinpoint the submarine's position since its arrival near its designated launch position some 300 kilometres north of Ireland and around 270 kilometres due west of the Scottish mainland. It had picked up and recorded the sound of the submarine most of the way from when it left the North Channel, but as expected, it had barely been able to maintain its track of the vessel once it had entered silent running. Most of the time there was nothing to suggest that a submarine was moving through that part of the North Atlantic, and on the few occasions when there had appeared to be a signal, it had been extremely weak and difficult to locate precisely. It was like a faint shadow moving across the walls of a large room lit only by a single candle. Like a person grasping in vain for something barely visible and just out of reach during the twilight.

However, when the USS Tennessee finally reached its designated launch location, the hypersensitive surveillance network clearly picked up the sound of the torpedo launch tube shutters retracting. The noise showed up like a bright beacon in a dark night. A few seconds later the network registered the sound of a torpedo being launched and then immediately thereafter the characteristic noise from the powerful Sundstrand gas-turbine pump-jet on a Spearfish torpedo, as well as cavitation noises that could only have come from the type of propeller fitted to that particular type of torpedo.

Less than two seconds after the torpedo launched, there was the muffled but unmistakable sound of a powerful underwater explosion. Then silence.

★ ★ ★

TWO DAYS EARLIER - PORTSMOUTH, ENGLAND

The Royal Navy transport vehicle left the BAE Systems assembly facility on Broad Oak in Portsmouth on the south coast of England exactly on schedule at 1 am. The heavy eighteen-wheeler was carrying a single object about seven metres long and just over half a metre in diameter. The driver had been told that it weighed just under two tonnes and it was inside a long specially made metal box that was painted a dull grey and covered by a large single piece of black tarpaulin.

As it left the facility, a civilian escort vehicle with two armed police officers slipped in behind it. The officers, who were usually attached to the Civil Nuclear Constabulary and tasked with escorting vehicles used to transport nuclear material to and from nuclear power stations in England and Scotland, had been assigned to what was an extraordinary one-off shipment of an item from BAE Systems at Broad Oak to HMNB Clyde in Faslane, Scotland.

It was pitch black and quiet as the truck pulled out from the assembly facility and onto the main road. It snaked its way through the deserted streets of the industrial area, and soon it was driving along the M27 towards Southampton. There it joined the motorway going north with the escort vehicle following it at a short distance.

After about two hours, the two vehicles were on the M40 and approaching the village of Ardley when a motorcycle came to a stop on the bridge crossing the motorway up ahead just outside of the village. The rider took off his backpack, pulled out a laptop and placed it on the fuel tank between his legs. Then he extracted a small black plastic box from a pocket in the backpack and attached it to the laptop via a short cable.

Opening a tracking app and typing in a few commands brought up a map of the immediate area that also showed the approaching truck as a small red dot slowly moving north along the motorway towards the rider's position. After a couple of minutes, he could see the truck in the distance.

He then selected a unique code from a dropdown menu and activated the small device. It immediately established a connection to the microprocessor inside the escort vehicle and showed an icon on the laptop's screen to indicate that it now had access to the car's onboard electronics. Then the device pushed a hacked firmware update to the car that reset its onboard computer. Since a firmware update is never meant to be performed while the car's engine is on and the car is in motion, the ignition-control system that manages the timing of the sparkplugs immediately shut down, and the vehicle's engine started sputtering to a halt.

The driver immediately put the car into neutral, first thinking that it had run out of fuel and trying to conserve momentum, but the fuel gauge showed that the tank was three-quarters full. As he approached the slip road leading up to the bridge where the motorcycle had stopped, he made a quick decision to get off the motorway. There were large lit-up signs for a service station, so he decided to try to make it up there before the engine died completely.

When the motorcycle rider saw the escort vehicle limp up the ramp from the slip road towards the bridge, he disconnected the electronic interference device, closed his laptop and shoved it back into the backpack. Then he started the engine and drove off into the night.

As the escort vehicle made its way up the ramp, the driver's partner, who was sitting in the passenger seat next to him, picked up the radio and informed the truck driver up ahead that they had engine trouble and would be stopping to assess what the problem was. The two officers then briefly discussed calling in assistance from another escort unit but concluded that it was likely to be several hours away in this part of the country. Instead, they decided to initially pull into the service station and investigate the problem for themselves.

As soon as the truck driver could no longer see the escort vehicle in his rear-view mirror, he sped up dramatically in order to give himself a sufficient time buffer for the upcoming operation. The truck continued along the M40 for another eight minutes until it reached the town of Banbury where it took the slip road off the motorway, crossed the bridge over to the town and turned right into a sprawling industrial estate dotted with large warehouses. It turned down Wildmere Road which runs the full circuit of the industrial area and then proceeded swiftly to a plot with a non-descript medium-sized warehouse. The warehouse had been sitting disused for several years until it had been bought eighteen months ago by a commercial property development firm owned by a holding company in Singapore.

As the truck pulled in, the large double doors of the warehouse slid open and two men appeared. They were both members of a small cadre of individuals, mostly men, who after a careful and lengthy selection process taking several years of deep vetting and gradual advancement, had been inducted into an organisation that was simply known as The Order. It was known only by its insignia, which was a laurel wreath and a vertical dagger at its centre with the tip pointing downward. The main bulk of its membership, who were not permitted to exchange any personal details with each other whatsoever, were known as *Praetorians*.

The two men inside the warehouse were both wearing black leather jackets and dark trousers, and they only communicated with each other when necessary. One of them signalled for the truck to continue forward and enter the warehouse. As soon as it was inside, the doors were closed and locked behind it.

At the service station outside of Ardley around ten kilometres away, the escort vehicle's computer system had finished its firmware update. The two officers had opened the hood and had been inspecting the car's engine, but they had been unable to find any problems. When the driver got back in and turned the ignition, the engine immediately sprang to life and then hummed happily. Taking another couple of minutes to make sure that everything was alright, the two perplexed officers then got back into the car and drove out towards the ramp leading back down to the motorway.

In the warehouse in Banbury, the tarpaulin had been removed and the large metal box had been opened. Hooks had been attached to the 7-metre-long Spearfish torpedo, and one of the two men was operating a crane and lifting the torpedo out of the box. As soon as it was out and placed safely on a specially made storage rack, the other man swapped the hooks onto an identical-looking torpedo sitting right next to it. Then he fed a small engraving machine instructions to copy the serial number from the original torpedo onto a metal plate affixed to the side of the replica. Once complete, the plate looked exactly like the real thing.

After another couple of minutes, the replica torpedo had been lifted up and into the metal box, and the box was then resealed and the tarpaulin replaced. When the praetorians opened the warehouse doors again the truck had been inside for less than six minutes. About a minute later it languidly re-joined the northbound traffic on the M40, and another few minutes after that the escort vehicle caught up and then slowed down to take up its position behind the truck once again. After a quick check with the driver of the truck via the two-way radio, the officers were satisfied that everything was fine and that the journey to Scotland could continue as planned.

The truck driver breathed a sigh of relief. Everything had gone as he had hoped, and as long as he made it safely to Faslane he would stand to receive a substantial payment in cryptocurrency for his services. He had no idea as to what the torpedo swap had been all about or who the two men in the warehouse were, and he did not care either. He had held menial jobs for most of his life and spent the past four years driving trucks for BAE Systems. It was not a particularly well-paid job and he had felt permanently underappreciated considering how the global arms manufacturer, which was also the largest supplier to the UK military, was raking in billions every year. When the chance to suddenly make a life-changing sum of untraceable money had presented itself, he had leapt at the opportunity. He figured it was his turn to make some serious cash.

Six hours later the truck arrived at HMNB Clyde in Faslane, where it underwent a quick inspection before being allowed to enter the naval base. Its cargo was transferred to another truck which was driven off to a secure storage location in anticipation of the arrival of the USS Tennessee the next day.

★   ★   ★

When the truck driver arrived at his home in a small cul-de-sac on the outskirts of the city of Salisbury in the south of England, he felt exhausted. He had only had a short nap in the back of the cab of his truck before heading back down south from Faslane in Scotland, and he really needed to catch up on his sleep now.

Walking up the path of his modest front garden, he looked up at the small house he was renting and felt a pang of excitement for what he would be able to buy with the money about to come his way. No one in his family had ever had wealth like this, and he was determined to make the most of it and not squander it on expensive holidays and fast cars, and had also promised himself not to blow it all on booze and women, fast or otherwise. He was going to buy himself a cottage on the rocky and picturesque Welsh coast where he was planning to open a vegetarian food shop. Having dropped meat from his own diet a couple of years earlier he had become convinced that this was the way things would be going in the future.

He unlocked the front door and stepped inside the hallway where he dropped his bag on the floor and flung his coat on the hook by the door. Then he walked into the kitchen, grabbed a sandwich and a beer from the fridge and sat down at the kitchen table. He wolfed down the sandwich and drank half of the beer before getting up and carrying it upstairs where he slumped down on the bed and watched some TV. When he had finished the beer, he got up to go to the bathroom.

As soon as he exited the bedroom out onto the landing and turned towards the bathroom, the man who had been waiting patiently in the small guest bedroom suddenly appeared behind him and wrapped his powerful right arm around his neck. He moved so quickly and silently that the truck driver barely had time to react.

'Hey!' he shouted, but almost instantly his attacker squeezed so tightly that he was unable to speak or breathe.

Grabbing onto the railing on the landing and trying to wrestle himself free, the truck driver felt himself being hauled sideways towards the stairs. He clawed desperately at the arms of the assailant, managing only to rip the left sleeve of his black shirt, and as he did so he vaguely registered a tattoo on the man's arm. It was a scorpion.

At that moment, the attacker placed his left hand on the side of the truck driver's head and pushed as hard as he could. Before the truck driver realised what was happening, there was a dry crack as his neck snapped. Still conscious but suddenly going limp and feeling a complete loss of sensation throughout his whole body, he then found himself being dragged the last few paces towards the top of the stairs. There his attacker let go of him, and the last thing he experienced was tumbling down the stairs and ending up in a crumbled-up heap at the bottom, his breathing and heartbeat now having stopped. Then slowly, darkness closed in.

* * *

Through the CCTV system, the hooded figure sitting in the elevated throne-like chair could watch the BMW park in its designated spot in the secure carpark under the 58-storey steel and glass high-rise in downtown Manhattan. Sitting in a large darkened room and wearing a long black robe, he watched the screen as the driver got out and headed for an ordinary-looking elevator in the wall next to the car. The driver, who was wearing an elegant dark blue suit and looked like a lawyer or a financier, entered a code on a keypad and allowed a biometric scanner to analyse the structure of his retinas. Then the elevator door opened and he stepped inside. There were only two buttons. One for the car park, and one that read 'S' for *Sanctum*.

After a couple of seconds, the doors closed and the elevator, which was inaccessible to anyone else in the building, began its non-stop journey up to the 58th floor. Most of that floor was taken up by a huge penthouse overlooking Central Park, and access to that normally happened via the private elevator from the lobby where other residents and office workers entered to make their way up to the apartments and offices on the lower floors. Floors 56 and 57 were utility floors with pumps, generators and general storage for building maintenance, and there was no access from those up to the top floor.

The Sanctum could therefore only be reached using the dedicated elevator from the carpark, or through a secret door behind a large false wall in the library of the penthouse, and both of those entrances required biometric authentication.

As the man stood waiting for the elevator to make its way all the way to the top, he checked his wristwatch, slicked back his hair and adjusted his tie. He had come here several times before but he was never relaxed when he did so. His host was intimidating, to say the least, and the setting was equally unnerving. Some people might even call it slightly theatrical, but not him. This was serious business, and the great man deserved respect and loyalty, reverence even, for what he was about to accomplish. For his own part, this was the suited man's ticket to the new world they were creating. The day of the great schism was coming, and he wanted to make sure that he was on the right side when it finally happened.

He exited the elevator into a softly lit anteroom roughly the size of most people's living rooms, where he stopped at a designated spot on the dark mahogany floor a couple of meters into the room. It took his eyes several seconds to adapt to the darkness.

The walls were covered in dark wood panelling and the coffered ceiling overhead was lit by a very faint

LED strip around its internal edges. Hung at regular intervals along the roughly six-metre-long walls were large red silk banners with the insignia of various Roman legions embroidered onto them. Each legion's banner had embroidered upon it the Roman numerals designating its number, along with an emblem of the animal associated with that legion. There was a capricorn, a boar, a lion, a pegasus, a griffin and many others, each one meticulously reproduced to look like the original banners that used to be hung from each legion's standard as they were carried at the front of those army units during ancient times.

Although they were replicas, they had been made to be faithful copies of the originals by another senior member of the organisation, who happened to be a well-known professor of history at Princeton University. Since the organisation modelled itself on the ancient Roman military in terms of its structure, it had been decided that its various chapters that were spread across the world would have these ancient military emblems assigned to them.

At the dim far end of the anteroom by a solid oak door was the barely visible stand-out blue banner of the *Cohortes Praetorianae* or Praetorian Guard. This was an elite unit of bodyguards and intelligence agents in the Imperial Roman army who were tasked with protecting the emperor and providing intel on the strength and movements of the enemies of the empire. Its emblem was a scorpion.

A couple of seconds later a long mechanical arm with sensor equipment extended from an opening in the ceiling, and amid the faint whirring of electrical motors, it began to move swiftly up and down the front and back of the man in the dark blue suit at a distance of about thirty centimetres. Once the AI-controlled security system had determined that he was carrying no lethal weapons metal-based or otherwise, the arm retracted back into the ceiling and a series of soft lights came on, leading the way towards the solid oak door that was set into the wall at the other end of the room, and which had until then been almost completely concealed by the darkness.

The man then walked calmly across the anteroom to the oak door, taking the opportunity to admire the Roman emblems the way he always did. When he arrived in front of the door he glanced up. On the architrave above the solid oak door was written a Latin phrase in gilded letters. *Novus Ordo Invictum*, meaning 'New Invincible Order.'

He reached out for the door handle, hesitated for a moment but then gripped the handle firmly and opened the door. What greeted him on the other side never ceased to impress. It was a large space with a raised area at the far end, and along the walls were colonnades of Roman Doric columns with their typical ribbed features running from top to bottom. The floor was made of veined marble, and from the ceiling hung two large ornate chandeliers. At the centre of the raised area was the throne-like seat, and in it sat the great man himself flanked by two large uniformed guards on either side of him. Praetorians. Wearing intimidating black helmets that were entirely covering their faces in order to conceal their identity, they had been hand-picked and given the ultimate responsibility of protecting the organisation's supreme leader.

The throne itself was sitting on a raised platform made of black marble, and behind it stretching across much of the wide black marble wall hung a red banner similar to those in the anteroom. However, this one was much larger and it had embroidered on it the image of a laurel wreath and a dagger with its tip pointing downward. While most of the impressive space was dimly lit, the platform and the throne were in almost complete darkness with only two candelabras on either side of the large banner providing a small amount of ambient light. It had the effect of placing the throne in a dark silhouette for anyone approaching it from the front, and the face of the seated and hooded figure was shrouded in almost complete darkness making it impossible to see his face.

The entire space had been constructed to emulate a great Roman temple, and it took up almost one-fifth of the entire 58th floor of the glass and steel high-rise building. However, none of the building contractors who had been brought in to build it knew what it was or even where it was. The entire space had been sealed off from the outside during construction, the windows having been painted black on the inside and teams of workers being transported in through the underground garage every morning in vans with no windows and then monitored by guards throughout the day. As far as any of them knew, the site could have been located in any of the hundreds of high-rise buildings in New York City.

The man walked briskly towards the tall hooded figure, sensing his master's impatience even down here at the other end of the enormous room. When he was a couple of meters away, he stopped and knelt down on one knee.

'Centurion,' said the cloaked figure in a deep gravelly voice as he loomed over the man, using the term for the commander of a Roman Legion unit. 'Report.'

'Imperator,' said the man deferentially, bowing his head. He, in turn, used the term for a senior Roman military commander which eventually became the term employed for Roman emperors.

'The two Praetorians completed their mission,' the man in the suit continued. 'The torpedo was delivered safely to the base and it should be taken aboard in a matter of hours. Our source there tells me that everything is still on schedule for the arrival of the USS Tennessee.'

'Excellent,' said the imposing cloaked figure slowly. 'Our plan is finally coming to fruition.'

'Yes, Imperator,' replied the man obsequiously. 'It will be glorious.'

'And the driver?' asked the Imperator probingly.

'He has been dealt with by one of the Praetorians in London,' replied the kneeling man. 'I just received word that he suffered an unfortunate fall in his home. The coroner will rule it an accident.'

'Very good,' said the Imperator, sounding pleased. 'You will be rewarded, as will we all. The time of a new beginning is drawing near.'

★ ★ ★

PRESENT DAY - ARIZONA

Landing at Tucson International Airport just before 2 pm, Aaron Purnell made a point of carrying as little luggage as he could get away with. He had flown in on American Airlines flight 2926 from New York's LaGuardia Airport via Dallas Fort Worth, and he felt pleased to have been able to catch an hour's sleep on the four-hour flight. He had left his small but comfortable apartment on Willow Street in Brooklyn Heights in New York early that morning and had not slept well the night before. He blamed anticipation of his upcoming trip.

Working the features desk at the New York-based online investigative magazine Bad Apples, Aaron had been under pressure to come up with a significant scoop for several months since his exposé on a Catholic priest from Newark who was hosting parties in his basement for local drug dealers, including one connected to the trafficking of underage girls.

Aaron's boss Caroline Walters had sung his praises for his investigative efforts as the pastor had been led away in handcuffs following the exclusive publication of the story in Bad Apples, but now she was growing impatient for more. Aaron was beginning to think that her appetite for headline-grabbing exclusives was insatiable, and his previous successes meant that she was increasingly looking to him to provide more.

Getting the keys for the white Chevrolet Blazer he had rented from Enterprise Rent-A-Car on South Tucson Boulevard, he drove north on the boulevard and then turned left onto Valencia Road. Here he continued in an almost straight line due west for 14 miles, mostly through the southern suburbs of Tucson. Only after about 6 miles did the highway exit the city and begin to make its way west across the dry Sonoran Desert. After another 8 miles, he joined Highway 86 at the small civilian Ryan Airfield and then proceeded west-southwest towards the small sleepy town of Three Points.

The pale desert landscape was barren but beautiful. It seemed dry as a bone, and although there was some vegetation it was sparse, and none of it seemed to grow above two metres or about six feet. In the distance towards the west, Aaron could see the Coyote Mountains which form part of the Quinlan Mountain Range, as well as Kitt Peak which reaches up more than seven thousand feet into the air.

Another six miles later, his satellite navigation informed him that he had reached his destination, but he almost missed it since there was barely any sign of it. As Highway 86 cut through the flat arid landscape sparsely covered with pale-green bushes, a small concrete road stretched away due north. Aaron only just had time to brake and turn off the highway, and as soon as he was on the small road, he stopped to double-check the location. There were no signs anywhere, but the satellite navigation system indicated that this was definitely the right location.

He drove about a hundred metres down the road and stopped the car. If this was the correct spot, then there should be the remains of a large concrete foundation about thirty metres to his right. He left the engine running and got out. Having spent the past hour in the airconditioned car, the dry heat hit him like a sledgehammer, and he could feel his chest tightening.

With the sun on his back, he walked in amongst the bushes and continued walking until he suddenly found himself standing on the foundation of what used to be a building. He was not sure if this had been a guardhouse during the heyday of the operation of the complex or if it had served another purpose, but what he did know was that he was in the right place.

He jogged back to the car and hurried back inside its cool interior. Then he slowly proceeded further along the road. It now curved slightly to the right which meant that soon he was unable to see Highway 86 in his rear-view mirror, and anyone on the highway would now be unable to see his vehicle. After another two hundred metres he let the car slowly roll to a stop.

Ahead of him, he could see the plot which used to belong to the United States government, specifically the US Airforce's Strategic Air Command. He turned off the engine and got out of his car, walking slowly to the tall metal gate. Through it, he could see several buildings that had not shown up on the satellite images he had been studying, but this was definitely it. This was the location of the now-defunct Titan II Missile Silo No. 570-2 launch complex.

A part of the 390th Strategic Missile Wing, the site was activated on May 1st 1962 and remained operational until the 2nd of December 1983. During that entire time, it was on permanent alert status ready for launch of the thirty-one-metre tall LGM-25C Titan II intercontinental ballistic missile sitting in its huge launch silo. This 155-ton missile, and 17 others in similar siloes dotted across the Arizona desert, carried a 9-megaton nuclear warhead that was more than 350 times more powerful than the *Gadget* that was detonated at the Trinity Test Site in 1945.

Its two-stage rocket propulsion system would carry the nuclear payload up through the atmosphere to low earth orbit around 1,100 kilometres or 700 miles up into space, and at its maximum velocity the missile would travel at 15,000 miles, or about 24,000 kilometres per hour, towards its target. With a range of up to 10,000 miles or 16,000 kilometres, a Titan II launched from the United States would take no more than 40 minutes to hit its intended target deep inside the Soviet Union.

At its maximum extent in 1960, the U.S. Airforce had 60 operational and permanently manned Titan II missile silos spread across Arizona, Arkansas, Kansas and California, ready to launch at a moment's notice.

The Titan II launch sites were decommissioned in the mid-1980s when much of the US nuclear arsenal was transferred to the expanding fleet of SSBN submarines. The silos and command bunkers were stripped of equipment and abandoned until about a decade ago when the Air Force began to sell off the plots to private individuals. Some people found the prospect of building a house on the plot where a nuclear weapon launch site used to be, entertaining. Others wanted to restore the silos and command bunkers and open them up as museums. And then there was the buyer of the Silo No. 570-2 complex, who never even showed up to view the site in person.

The entire transaction was carried out remotely, and the real estate agent selling it on behalf of the government only ever dealt with a company in

Delaware - a state widely known for its low tax rates and lax attitude to regulation and oversight of corporate entities, not least of which was the ease with which a shell company can be established to launder criminal proceeds.

This was why Aaron was here. For a few weeks now he had been working on a story about the so-called 'prepper community'. These were groups of individuals who spent virtually all of their time and money on preparing for the end of the world. Most of them existed on the fringes of society, and, some would also argue, sanity, and they often swore by conspiracy theories about secret government programs designed to exert control over the civilian population, or worse. Often much worse.

Aaron's intention had been to write an exposé about the most outrageously paranoid and militant prepper he could find, and it turned out that there was an abundance of people to choose from. One of Aaron's sources had put him in touch with an employee at the City of Tucson Planning & Development Services Department who, for a small fee, had provided him with indications that a community of paranoid conspiracy theory-peddling doomsday preppers might have purchased a plot of land in Arizona that was the former site of a launch complex for one of the most powerful nuclear missiles the United States has ever developed.

The plot had been bought six years ago by a Delaware-registered company called Three Points Realty Holdings LLC. Aaron had looked into the company and discovered that it had no apparent business activities, no turnover, no offices and no employees.

Aaron had decided to pursue it since the involvement of a group of crazies hiding in a former nuclear missile silo was almost guaranteed to be sufficiently enticing to attract those all-important clicks and advertisement dollars. Now that he was finally here, the truth was that he wasn't sure what he would find or what he would do with it.

As he approached the gate, he could see that a tall metal chain-link fence seemed to run the entire circumference of the plot. At the top of the fence were rolls of barbed wire, much like during the two decades when the plot was an active Air Force missile launch site. The square plot itself seemed about the size of two football fields or perhaps a bit smaller, and near the middle of it sat a single white-painted building which appeared to be some sort of mobile office set up inside a converted shipping container. Just beyond it, he could see a low concrete structure with a ramp leading down into the ground.

Aaron had spent less than a minute outside the gate when the door to the building opened and a man wearing a white hardhat and a white boilersuit came out and began walking towards him.

As he approached, Aaron could see that he appeared well-groomed and more like an office manager than a construction worker. He raised his hand in greeting and smiled.

'Hey there,' he called. 'Can I help you, sir?'

Aaron gave a small wave and smiled back, suddenly feeling self-conscious at having turned up unannounced at the site of a bunch of supposed conspiracy theorists, only to be met by someone who looked like a friendly and perfectly normal building site manager. As the man came up close to the other side of the gate and stopped, Aaron noticed the small stitched gold logo on the left side of his chest. It was a simple laurel wreath, and inside it was written the letters A.R.K.

'How's it going?' asked Aaron cheerfully. 'Sorry to bother you, but do you mind if I ask what you guys are building here? This used to be a missile silo, right?'

'Uhm. Well,' replied than man, looking like he was considering his response for a moment. 'We're converting the silo into a luxury home for a Hollywood actor,' came the reply, in what somehow seemed like a rehearsed manner.

'Really?' said Aaron, pretending to be impressed and curious. 'Who is it? Is it one of those nutty Scientology types?' he grinned.

'I am really not at liberty to say,' replied the man. 'Who are you, if you don't mind my asking?'

'Oh, I was just passing by and spotted your mobile office there,' replied Aaron and jerked his head towards the converted shipping container. 'I am pretty sure I didn't see it the last time I came this way, so I guess I just got curious.'

'Well, I don't mean to be rude,' said the man, 'but you are kind of on private property now. And this site is off-limits to anyone that isn't working here, so…'

'Oh,' exclaimed Aaron disarmingly. 'Yeah. Sure man. I guess curiosity just got the better of me. Sorry to bother you.'

'That's no problem,' smiled the man and nodded.

'I'll be on my way then,' said Aaron and took a couple of steps backwards before raising his hands and giving the man a small wave goodbye. 'You have a nice evening now.'

'You too,' replied the man. 'Take care.'

Aaron returned to his car, got in and began reversing towards a spot on the small road where he could easily turn the car around. As he did so he watched the man walk back towards the office building. When he got there, he proceeded up the three steps to the office door and opened it. Then he seemed to stop and hold it open for a brief moment whilst glancing in the direction of Aaron's car, but then he went inside.

Aaron swung the car around and began driving it slowly back south towards Highway 86. Glancing up at his rear-view mirror he watched the office building as he drove slowly away, but something inside him made him decide that there was more to this than met the eye. The site manager, or whoever he had been, had seemed perfectly nice and friendly but there was just something about the whole thing that seemed odd. For one thing, if it was an active building site then where was everyone? There were no vehicles there and no sign of anyone working anywhere. Sure, it was supposedly a conversion of an underground missile complex, but he would still have expected to see other people there and perhaps some accommodation for construction workers or at the very least a few cars or minivans to transport them back to town after the end of the workday.

The sun was now disappearing behind the mountains to the west, and when he got back to

Highway 86 Aaron made a swift decision. He pulled out onto the now almost deserted highway, proceeded a couple of hundred metres further west, and then pulled off the road again. Driving slowly and carefully he then steered the car further in amongst the bushes until he was around fifty metres in, now feeling confident that he would no longer be visible from the road. Then he got out carrying only a small backpack, locked the car and then headed further into the bushes before bearing due east and heading back towards the former missile launch site.

Three

LONDON, ENGLAND

Fiona Keane was walking across the lobby of the British Museum with Marlene Phillips, the head of the Board of Trustees. Marlene was in her late sixties but was often mistaken for being much younger. Her long slightly greying brown hair was put up in a bun skewered by two hair chopsticks, and she was wearing a loose white silk shirt, a red and black flannel tartan skirt and black high-gloss shoes.

'Now, remember to make sure he feels welcome here,' she said to Fiona as they approached the door to the outside. 'Mr Dietrich has donated extremely generously to us over the years, and we do rely on private contributions on top of our government grants.'

'Yes, of course,' replied Fiona. 'You did remind me already.'

As a historian and an archaeologist, Fiona did not particularly like sucking up to the private donors who liked to come and visit the museum from time to time. But as Marlene had pointed out, her employer the British Museum always welcomed donations from private individuals, particularly from people as immensely wealthy as Peter Dietrich.

As far as Fiona understood it, Dietrich had made his money in the burgeoning fintech industry, most notably founding an app-based international payment service that had more or less out-competed conventional banks with regard to international money transfers for retail customers. The company had been listed on the NASDAQ stock exchange in New York six years earlier and was now supposedly valued at 132 billion dollars. According to Forbes Magazine, Dietrich still owned 80 percent of the shares putting his personal net worth just above 100 billion dollars.

Dietrich was known to be a generous donor to many causes around the world, but he seemed to have a special place in his heart for museums to which he donated significant sums of money every year. One of those museums was the British Museum on Great Russell Street in central London where Fiona had worked for a number of years now.

Today's visit had been requested by Dietrich a few weeks earlier, and Marlene Phillips had jumped at the opportunity to welcome one of the most generous billionaire philanthropists in the world. Dietrich had contributed a significant proportion of the funding for a large new exhibition of ancient Roman artefacts in the museum, and Marlene had convinced Fiona to give him a private tour before the exhibition opened to the public.

Fiona and Marlene exited the building and stood outside on the steps of a side entrance on Montague Street. It was a sunny but slightly chilly day. They had been told that Dietrich's car was a couple of minutes away, and as they waited, they both absentmindedly adjusted their clothing and checked that their hair was arranged just so.

Suddenly a black Range Rover with tinted windows came around the corner of Great Russell Street and drove swiftly towards them. Then followed another Ranger Rover and then another. The cortege pulled up next to the pavement directly across from the entrance, and two teams of three men exited the front and rear cars. They quickly fanned out while another person exited the middle vehicle's front passenger seat and then opened the rear door.

A tall dapper man in his mid-fifties stepped out onto the pavement and quickly adjusted his grey pinstriped suit. He had a remarkably youthful appearance with a healthy complexion, smooth skin and a full dark head of hair. His stature hinted at someone who spent time in the gym at least a couple of times per week, and as he began striding purposefully towards the entrance to the museum he briefly glanced at his wristwatch.

'Handsome,' said Phillips quietly, leaning slightly towards Fiona and smiling.

As the man walked along briskly, half of his security team followed a few steps behind him, each one of them occasionally looking around to make sure that nothing looked suspicious. As soon as Dietrich spotted the two women waiting for him on the steps, his face lit up with a wide and affable smile.

'Good morning,' he called, as he closed the distance to them. 'I hope I am not late. I hate keeping other people waiting.'

'It's quite alright Mr Dietrich,' smiled Marlene. 'London traffic can ruin even the best-laid plans. Hello, sir. I am Marlene Phillips. We spoke on the phone.'

'Lovely to meet you,' smiled Dietrich in ever so faintly accented English and shook her hand.

'And this is Miss Fiona Keane,' said Marlene, gesturing briefly to Fiona. 'She will be showing you around today. She is an excellent historian and archaeologist so I am sure she will be able to answer any questions you may have.'

Fiona took his hand and smiled with a slightly embarrassed look on her face. She wasn't used to hearing Marlene singing her praises, or those of anyone else for that matter.

'Mr Dietrich,' said Fiona. 'Pleased to meet you.'

'Please call me Peter,' said Dietrich, giving her hand a gentle squeeze.

'Alright then. Peter,' smiled Fiona.

'Shall we?' said Marlene, motioning towards the museum's interior.

'It's alright, Jason,' said Dietrich, turning back briefly to a man from his security team. 'I can manage from here. I should be back in twenty minutes.'

'Very good sir,' said the bodyguard and began making his way back towards the cars.

The three of them entered the building after which Marlene whisked them past the ticket barriers and down a long corridor towards one of the large exhibition halls in the south-eastern corner of the enormous and sprawling building. The rooms in that part of the museum had historically been the home of Greco-Roman exhibitions, but the latest exhibition funded almost exclusively by Dietrich contained only Roman artefacts, particularly those related to the period around the time of the reign of Julius Caesar.

'Here we are,' announced Marlene proudly and stopped. 'I wish I could stay, but I have a meeting I need to attend. However, you are in good hands with Fiona here. I do hope you enjoy your inaugural visit to this exhibition. We are very excited about it.'

'Excellent,' replied Dietrich and gave a small bow.

Then Marlene walked away briskly along the corridor, the sound of her heels against the marble floors echoing as she went.

'Well,' said Dietrich as he clasped his hands together and turned to face Fiona with an expectant smile. 'Show me everything. I am dying to see it.'

Alright then,' replied Fiona, returning his smile and beckoning him into the large hall where the exhibition had been set up.

She spent the next fifteen minutes or so showing Dietrich the exhibition's most interesting artefacts, including large intact pottery used for storing wine, the famous Portland Vase from around 20 BCE, dozens of coins minted by various Roman rulers and a large separate section devoted to a plethora of well-preserved statues and busts.

'And you'll obviously recognise this statue,' smiled Fiona, gesturing to a life-sized statue of Julius Caesar who through both force and cunning had managed to go from provincial magistrate to Roman emperor, dispensing with the elected Senate in the process. 'I believe this one is from your own private collection, isn't it?'

'Yes, it is,' said Dietrich. 'A great man, or a villain, depending on who you ask.'

'I guess that depends on whether you think democracy is worthwhile,' said Fiona, taking a moment to look at the statue.

'I am not sure if you are aware,' said Dietrich, 'but there is a famous quote by the Roman historian Lucius Cassius Dio, who was wary of giving power to the masses. When discussing different forms of government, he said something like this:'

"Democracy, indeed, has a fair-appearing name and conveys the impression of bringing equal rights to all through equal laws, but its results are seen not to agree at all with its title. Monarchy, on the contrary, has an unpleasant sound, but is a most practical form of government to live under."

'That would probably not go down too well these days,' smiled Fiona. 'He was effectively advocating abolishing Roman democracy and going back to a dictatorship.'

'Well,' laughed Dietrich. 'When looking at the people who end up running most countries these days, you could be forgiven for thinking he was on to something. And you Brits seem very fond of your Royal family.'

'I am Irish,' said Fiona, deadpan.

'Oh, I do apologise,' said Dietrich and smiled apologetically, placing a hand gently on her arm. 'I didn't realise. You don't have a strong accent.'

'It's alright,' Fiona demurred. 'We Irish have a bit of a thing about being mistaken for the English.'

'I understand,' said Dietrich, smiling disarmingly. 'We Austrians have a similar issue with being mistaken for Germans. Anyway, I need to confess something to you. I am afraid I had a slightly ulterior motive for coming today, aside from just seeing the exhibition.'

'Oh?' said Fiona surprised, not sure what to make of it.

'I wanted to speak to you privately,' he said.

'Me?' asked Fiona, sounding perplexed. 'Alright. How can I help you?' she continued hesitantly.

'Well,' said Dietrich. 'I assume that you are familiar with the Corona Civica?'

'The Civic Crown?' replied Fiona. 'Yes, of course. It was a laurel wreath worn by Roman emperors. Or rather, it was actually made from leaves from a Bay tree, but most people don't realise that.'

'Was it really?' said Dietrich inquisitively. 'I did not know that either. Anyway, as far as I am concerned, this exhibition is one of the most impressive anywhere in the world, at least when it comes to the period during the life of Julius Caesar. But the crown is the one thing that I have always wondered about, and it is an item that would quite literally be the crowning jewel of an exhibition like this.'

'*The* crown?' said Fiona, sounding intrigued. 'Do you mean, Caesar's actual crown?'

'Yes,' smiled Dietrich.

'But that has never been found,' said Fiona.

'Precisely,' said Dietrich eagerly. 'Which is where you come in. I want you to try to find it.'

Dietrich's words hung in the air for a couple of seconds during which Fiona was unsure whether he was joking or not. The whereabouts of the golden bay-leaf crown of Julius Caesar had been lost to history for more than two thousand years. Fiona gently blew out her cheeks and then looked at Dietrich uncertainly.

'I don't know,' she said. 'That is a tall order. I have never seen a reference to it after Caesar's death. As far as anyone knows it could have been melted down and sold for next to nothing just a couple of days after his death. I wouldn't even know where to start.'

Dietrich smiled and spread out his hands.

'I have made inquiries about you,' said Dietrich, 'and from what I have heard you have quite a track record when it comes to finding lost artefacts. I am sure you will come up with some ideas for how to do this. I should say that I am not actually *expecting* you to find it, but if anyone can do it, I believe you can. And I really do think that it is worth a shot. Can you imagine what it would do for this museum if you managed to bring it here? Not to mention your own career…'

Dietrich paused for a moment, allowing her to consider his proposal.

'Needless to say,' he continued. 'You will have all the resources you need. I will arrange for you to be on a retainer, and you will be free to access any funds you need for this effort as long as they are properly logged and accounted for.'

'Well, of course,' said Fiona, still sounding reticent. 'I wouldn't dream of misusing funds like that.'

'Great,' beamed Dietrich. 'So, you'll do it?'

'That wasn't quite what I meant,' said Fiona haltingly, feeling herself somehow being pulled along into agreeing to the proposition by Dietrich's infectious charm, enthusiasm and persistence.

'But you'll at least think about it, right?' smiled Dietrich winningly.

'Well, yes,' Fiona heard herself say. 'I will think about it. When do you need an answer?'

'As soon as you have one,' said Dietrich, reaching into his suit pocket for a business card. 'This is my private number. Feel free to call me any time.'

Fiona took the card and held it close to her chest whilst inspecting it. It was matt black with gold lettering and showed contact details for Dietrich's New York Office.

'Alright,' said Fiona, suddenly feeling very self-conscious. 'I will come back to you as soon as I have an answer. I just need to think it through.'

'That is very sensible,' said Dietrich. 'I wouldn't have it any other way. Excellent. Well, I must be going. As I said, call me any time. I am quite keen to get this underway. I will see myself out.'

'Great,' said Fiona, slightly surprised by his sudden departure. 'I hope you enjoyed the tour.'

'It was great,' said Dietrich, taking a few steps backwards towards the door whilst holding up his hand to give a small wave goodbye. 'I hope to hear from you soon, Fiona. Take care.'

'Goodbye, and thank you for coming,' called Fiona, as Dietrich turned and began walking briskly and purposefully back towards the side entrance and back out to Montague Street.

'Crikey,' said Fiona quietly to herself. 'Didn't see that one coming.'

★   ★   ★

Across town, Andrew Sterling arrived in the lobby of the unremarkable office building on Sheldrake Place which houses the special investigative unit of the SAS that deals with possible terrorist threats in the realm of chemical, biological and nuclear weapons. He had driven there from his new home in London's Notting Hill, which he shared with his girlfriend Fiona.

Andrew and Fiona had found themselves working together on a number of investigations in the past, several of which had significant archaeological aspects to them, and when it came to teaming up with someone who had their head screwed on straight and who was not afraid to take the initiative in difficult or even dangerous situations, Andrew could think of few other people he trusted as much as her.

When he got up early that morning, he had planned to remain at home to read a recent intelligence report about Iran's Al Quds Force. It is one of five branches of Iran's Islamic Revolutionary Guard Corps, and it specialises in unconventional warfare and military intelligence operations. Recently there had been indications that they were cultivating relationships with a small number of tribal leaders near Libya's southern border with Niger.

Wearing only his dressing gown, he was just about to sit down with his laptop and a cup of coffee when an email arrived on his phone and his laptop simultaneously. It was from Colonel Strickland, the head of his department, and the message simply read:

Andrew
Please attend urgent meeting.
Sheldrake Place at 09:00.
Emergency briefing by Royal Navy.
Gordon

Andrew frowned. It was very unlike Strickland to be this brief and cryptic in his messages, so he had to assume that things were busy at HQ and that Strickland was short on time. But why was the briefing to be conducted by the Royal Navy? He glanced at the clock on his phone. 7:58 am.

'Shit,' he mumbled, gulping down some coffee and putting the laptop back on the coffee table.

He hurried upstairs to have a quick shower, and then he changed into a charcoal-coloured suit and a white shirt. Quickly scanning his tie rack, he selected a deep blue one. Then he threw on his long dark coat and grabbed his bag from the console table in the hallway, snatched the car keys off the small hook by the door and left the house.

Outside it was only just become light, and it had apparently been raining in the night because the path to the pavement was wet. Or perhaps it was the rain from yesterday that was still there. It could be hard to tell in London during December. Pressing the button on his car key before he reached the pavement he heard the short chirp from his metallic-grey Aston Martin DB9 as it unlocked. He slid down into the driver's seat and pressed the button for the ignition. The engine sprang to life and settled into a throaty growl as he put on his seat belt and turned on the radio. Ten minutes later he pulled into Sheldrake Place and proceeded to the car park, and a few minutes after that he walked through the lobby towards the elevators.

So far so normal, he thought to himself.

There was nothing to indicate that anything was out of the ordinary as he exited the lift and went to his office. Here he hung up his coat, put his bag next to his desk and then he walked down the corridor to Colonel Strickland's office. But before he could knock on the door Strickland's secretary rose and told him that the colonel was in the large conference room expecting Andrew's arrival.

'Good morning, Andrew,' said Strickland as he walked in. 'Thank you for coming, and sorry about the short notice. Seems we have a real problem on our hands.'

'That's alright, sir,' replied Andrew. 'What's going on?'

'The Americans have lost a submarine in the North Atlantic,' he said, shaking his head as if he himself was having trouble believing what he was saying.

'What?' said Andrew incredulously. 'They *lost* a submarine?'

'I know,' replied Strickland ruefully. 'It's a bloody mess. An Ohio-class vessel carrying nuclear warheads. Anyway, the reason we're involved is simply that this incident involves nuclear weapons that have gone missing in UK territorial waters, and until we can establish precisely what happened we have to keep an open mind.'

'By which you mean to say that it might be terrorism?' asked Andrew, looking both concerned and slightly sceptical.

'Who knows,' said Strickland rhetorically, shrugging and shaking his head. 'Anyway, I think it is best if I let the Commodore explain the details. The meeting is about to start. Let's go and take our seats.'

They filed into the conference room with the other attendees, who were largely military types, most of whom Andrew had never met before. Already in the room was a senior naval officer standing at the end of a long table. Andrew could not place him, but he knew that he had seen a picture of him somewhere.

'Gentlemen, please be seated,' said the officer. 'My name is Hugh Spencer, and I am the Royal Navy's Commodore Submarine Service. Thank you all for coming.'

The commodore paused for a few moments, seemingly gathering his thoughts as the group took their seat around the large oval-shaped mahogany table. Then he sat down at the far end of it and opened a folder with a single document inside.

'I'll come straight to the point. As some of you already know, yesterday afternoon the U.S. Navy's Atlantic Fleet lost contact with the nuclear submarine SSBN-734, the USS Tennessee. The vessel is an Ohio-class ballistic missile submarine based at Naval Submarine Base Kings Bay in Georgia. At the time of its disappearance, it was carrying 24 Trident II D5 ballistic nuclear missiles. This is an unusually high number, but the boat had been taking part in an exercise that involved an accurate simulation of a real-world scenario in which three nuclear missiles would be launched at targets inside the Russian Federation. As of a couple of hours ago, the submarine was officially designated by the U.S. Navy as DISSUB or 'distressed submarine', which basically means they believe it has sunk and is unable to surface under its own power. Whether it is still structurally intact is unknown at this time.'

Andrew sat immobile during the briefing and decided not to take notes. He wasn't sure if he was even allowed to bring written notes out from the briefing, and he also felt confident that he would be able to remember anything important. As it turned out, all of it turned out to be important and it was unlike anything he and his unit had dealt with before.

Looking around the room as the commodore spoke, Andrew could see the concern edged into the faces of the attendees. There were eight of them, five being senior military officers in various types of uniforms, and one of them clearly from the U.S. Navy. In addition to Andrew himself, two others were wearing civilian clothing. They looked like they were intelligence types, one probably military intelligence and the other most likely from GCHQ, the UK's main hub for providing so-called signals intelligence or SIGINT to the UK government and its armed forces.

'The U.S. Navy is obviously attempting to find out what occurred here, but since this event took place in UK territorial waters our military and intelligence services are working closely with the Americans on this.'

The commodore looked down at his one-page document and paused for a moment as if reading it again, although Andrew suspected he knew it by heart already. Then he looked back up at the group and continued.

'The submarine was conducting a test firing of a Spearfish torpedo, which as I am sure you know is the standard UK torpedo for both anti-submarine and anti-surface warfare. The aim was to test the interoperability of US and UK weapons systems. As far as we can tell, everything went as planned until immediately after the torpedo left the launch tube. The U.S. underwater network of hydrophones known as DRAPES picked up the distinct audio signature of a Spearfish leaving the torpedo launch tube followed by the sound of an explosion. This was at 14:47 pm yesterday afternoon.'

Several of the attendees shifted uncomfortably in their seats and looked at each other with concerned expressions on their faces. No Ohio-class submarine had ever been lost, but there have been two other losses of nuclear-powered submarines, namely the attack submarine USS Thresher in 1963 which sank with 129 crew, and the Russian attack submarine Kursk, which was lost in 2000 with 118 sailors aboard. Few military accidents evoke such dread as the prospect of dropping to the bottom of the ocean inside a cramped steel tube that can only resist a certain amount of pressure before it finally buckles and implodes.

'At the moment,' continued the commodore, 'and as our friend here from U.S. Naval Intelligence can affirm, both we and the Americans are leaning towards the conclusion that there was some sort of malfunction in the torpedo and that it detonated as soon as it sensed the presence of the USS Tennessee immediately after launch.'

The officer in the U.S. Navy uniform nodded his agreement.

'This, of course, should never happen since torpedoes are designed so that they are incapable of arming until after a set amount of time has passed from the time of launch. But as I said, we are currently left with the most likely conclusion that some sort of malfunction took place either in the arming mechanism or in the warhead itself. At the moment we have no hard evidence yet of this or any other hypothesis about what might have happened. As you can imagine, ascertaining precisely what went wrong will be extremely challenging but that is something for another day. For now, our efforts are focused on locating the USS Tennessee and attempting to rescue the crew if possible.'

Commodore Spencer glanced at an aide who was standing by the closed double doors and nodded. The aide walked swiftly to a laptop that was sitting on a large dark wooden console table by the wall opposite the windows.

'Allow me to play you a recording of what DRAPES picked up,' said Spencer. 'This will give you a sense of what we have to work with at the moment.'

Spencer nodded at the aide again, and he then began replaying the recording on the conference room's speaker system.

At first, there was just a very faint fizzing and crackling noise, almost like static on a radio. Then there was the eerie far-off sound of a whale call, which can often be heard as much as 800 kilometres or 500 miles away. A few seconds later what emanated from the speaker system was distinctly man-made. It was the metallic sound of launch tube shutters opening, sliding aside and then slotting into place in their recesses with a dull clonk. A couple of seconds after that there was the muffled sound of the Spearfish torpedo being ejected from the launch tube using air pressure and then the much louder high-pitched sound of engine noise and a propeller spinning. It was accompanied by what sounded like hissing as the torpedo's propeller generated cavitation in the water as it spun at very high RPMs. About a second later they heard the dull but loud sound of an explosion which seemed to reverberate around that part of the ocean for several seconds as the sound waves travelled through the water and bounced off the sea bottom and underwater ridges before finally trailing off to nothing.

The aide stopped the play-back of the recording and returned to his position by the door.

There was silence in the room for several seconds as the group took in what they had just heard and pondered their ramifications. The worst-case scenario would be that the submarine had been lost and was already lying at the bottom of the ocean. A steel tomb that, depending on the depth of that part of the ocean, might never be recovered.

'Commodore Spencer, if I may,' said Colonel Strickland. 'How many sailors were aboard the vessel?'

'165 souls,' replied Spencer ruefully.

There was another long silence as everyone in the room contemplated the true implications of that number.

'But,' continued the commodore. 'The one saving grace in all of this is that the submarine was over what is called the Anton Dohrn Seamount, which is a large flat-topped undersea mountain in the North Atlantic. It rises almost two kilometres from the much deeper Rockall Through, which means that the depth of the ocean at that point is as little as 500 metres. That still sounds like a lot I am sure, but just a couple of hundred kilometres to the south-west the ocean is almost four kilometres or thirteen thousand feet deep.'

'I am sure this is probably classified information,' said Andrew, leaning forward with his hands clasped in front of him on the table, 'but how deep can an Ohio-class submarine go before it implodes.'

'Unless I am mistaken,' replied Commodore Spencer, 'the Ohio-class routinely operates at around 300 metres or 1000 feet, but perhaps Captain Jack Lynch from U.S. Naval Intelligence here can enlighten us?'

Spencer looked at the man in the smart dark blue inform sitting directly across from Andrew. He looked to be in his late thirties, with short black hair, chiselled features and piercing blue eyes.

'Yes sir,' he said calmly and sat up straight. 'That's correct. Ohio-class subs typically operate at depths between 100 and 300 feet, but they have been certified for regular operations down to 1,000 feet. The absolute maximum diving depth in emergencies is around 1,550 feet. As far as so-called crush-depth is concerned, that can obviously only be estimated since we're not going to destroy a 3-billion-dollar boat just to see how deep it can go. But most of our estimates are in the region of between 2,000 and 2,500 feet.'

'In other words,' said Andrew. 'If the explosion has rendered the USS Tennessee unable to surface and sitting at the bottom of that part of the ocean, it might be able to withstand the pressure at the top of the Anton Dohrn Seamount, correct?'

'That is correct, sir,' replied Lynch, nodding. 'If that is where it is currently located, it should be able to survive. Unless of course there is structural damage to the internal pressure hull, in which case all bets are off.'

'We are in the process of getting a remotely operated vehicle or ROV to the location now,' said Spencer. 'This should hopefully happen shortly, and then we ought to be able to establish quite quickly if our worst fears are borne out and the vessel has sunk.'

'Do we have any telemetry data from the submarine or from the torpedo itself?' asked one of the other men wearing civilian clothes.

'No,' replied Commodore Spencer. 'The USS Tennessee would have been submerged at a depth of about 100 feet around the time of the launch of the Spearfish torpedo, and there is no ability for it to communicate anything to surface ships or satellites at that point. It can receive communications from land-based command and control structures, but it can't send anything itself because of the amounts of water above it and its lack of an antenna with that capacity.'

'On the assumption that it was indeed an accident,' said Strickland, 'there is a good chance that the vessel was damaged and that it is unable to surface. However, in this scenario, should it not have launched a buoy with a distress signal?'

'Yes, I believe that is standard operating procedure for submarines of both of our navies,' said Spencer and looked at Lynch.

Lynch nodded. 'That is correct, sir. Normally in a situation like this, the captain would order the launch of a buoy with a brief message including the sub's location. This buoy would then float to the surface and begin broadcasting the message on a dedicated frequency which would be picked up by nearby surface ships or even satellites. But this has not happened.'

'So, I guess that either means that the buoy system was inoperable for some reason, possibly damaged, or that the vessel is in fact lost?' said Andrew, looking at Captain Lynch.

'Those are both reasonable conclusions,' replied Lynch.

'Sir,' said one of the senior officers in the group. 'We have to assume that the Russians already know about this from their own underwater listening networks. Is there a risk that they could get to the submarine before us? And could it even be possible that they might have caused this?'

'Gentlemen,' said Spencer after hesitating briefly. 'We can't rule anything out at this point. As we all know, the Russian Federation has become increasingly aggressive in its interactions with NATO assets over the past several years both in the air and at sea, so it is certainly a possibility. And yes, if they really are behind it for whatever purpose, it is reasonable to assume that they would have assets in place to take advantage of the situation.'

'How so?' asked another officer. 'And what do you mean by taking advantage?'

'Given the circumstances,' said Spencer, 'I believe we need to keep an open mind about what happened to the USS Tennessee. This includes considering whether it might somehow have been boarded and captured by Russian special forces.'

An unsettled murmur went through the assembled officers.

'Is that even possible?' asked the man whom Andrew had guessed was from GCHQ.

'It is, at least in theory,' said Spencer. 'The submarine has a so-called SDV hangar on top of its hull. SDV is short for SEAL Delivery Vehicle. This is a small underwater vehicle just large enough to fit a SEAL team inside and to allow it to deploy on covert operations from a submerged Ohio-class submarine. Hypothetically speaking, the sub could have been boarded from the hatch connected to that hangar.'

Several of the senior officers were now frowning in dismay at the prospect of that scenario actually having occurred.

'But,' said Spencer, holding up one hand placatingly with his palm facing the group. 'It would require a specially built submarine to manage those depths, and it absolutely would have required someone on the inside to operate the hangar doors and also unlock the access hatch from the hangar to the Tennessee's interior.'

'I'm sorry, are you saying this was an inside job?' said the senior officer, now looking both upset and appalled. 'Are you seriously suggesting that someone allowed a hostile force to board a United States nuclear submarine and hijack it?'

'Like I said,' replied Spencer calmly. 'We should not rule anything out, however unlikely or unpalatable it might sound. If it was not an accident, then we need to consider the remote possibility that it was a non-state actor.'

'You mean terrorists?' asked Strickland.

'I think that would probably also be an accurate description, yes,' replied Commodore Spencer. 'Anyway Gentlemen, I understand why this issue might elicit strong emotions, but it is absolutely imperative that we remain calm and focused and that we explore all possible scenarios, including those that might seem fanciful at this stage. To that end, I would like to ask Captain Lynch of U.S. Naval Intelligence and Captain Andrew Sterling of the SAS's counter-terrorism unit, to head up a joint task force. As I said, both the U.S. Navy and the Royal Navy are hard at work examining all the evidence they have available, but I believe a joint intelligence effort could yield valuable results as well. The two of you should have a chat after this briefing to coordinate your efforts. You will of course have access to any resources you might deem necessary to carry out this investigation on this side of the pond, and I believe the same will be true for the Americans. I will liaise with Downing Street and Washington to ensure this goes smoothly.'

Andrew and Lynch looked at each other across the table and nodded their mutual approval. From what Andrew had seen and heard so far, Lynch seemed like a man he work with. Bright, professional and to-the-point, he came across as both resourceful and calm which was exactly what was needed in these circumstances.

'Needless to say,' continued Spencer. 'All of the information provided to you this morning has been marked Top Secret. For obvious reasons, we can't have any of this come out in the press, and the less information the Russian Federation is able to obtain about what has happened the better. So, we are trying to keep all of this under wraps for as long as possible.'

Spencer looked around the table.

'Alright Gentlemen. If there are no further questions, I think we should adjourn. I am sure you all have full schedules for several days from now on. I suggest we meet again in the near future. I will be in touch.'

And with that, the attendees got up and began to leave the conference room. Andrew and Colonel Strickland filed out together and waited in the corridor for Captain Lynch. As he exited the conference room, he came over towards them with his hand out.

'Captain Sterling,' he said. 'Nice to meet you properly. I am Jack Lynch'

Andrew took his hand and gave it a firm shake.

'Captain Lynch,' he said. 'Please call me Andrew.'

'Sure thing,' replied Lynch. 'And you call me Jack.'

'Deal,' smiled Andrew. 'This is my superior officer, Colonel Strickland. He heads up an SAS unit tasked with investigating possible terror threats in the context of non-conventional weapons.'

'Nice to meet you,' said Lynch and shook Strickland's hand.

'A pleasure,' replied Strickland. 'You two should get to know each other. Why don't you pop into Andrew's office and sit down over a cup of tea? We need to get the ball rolling on our joint task force as soon as possible.'

'Good idea. This way please,' said Andrew. 'I will swing by your office later,' he then said to Strickland as they proceeded down the corridor towards Andrew's office. 'Hopefully, we can make some progress soon.'

'Perfect,' said Strickland. 'I will get on the phone immediately to our counterparts in America to help speed things up for you two.'

Four

It was dusk as Aaron Purnell moved east through the sparse bushes in the desert around 10 miles southwest of Tucson. Arriving at the chain-link fence surrounding the large plot of the former launch complex of Silo No. 570-2 belonging to the 390th Strategic Missile Wing, he crept up to it and knelt down. As night fell the desert air was now cooling rapidly after the sun had sunk beneath the mountains to the west. Unpolluted by either smog or light from the big city to the east, the clear skies allowed the stars to shine and twinkle overhead.

A light breeze was making the leaves on the surrounding bushes rustle gently, and from various locations in the vicinity could be heard the gentle sound of crickets attempting to attract a mate.

Born and bred in New York, Aaron had never been much of an outdoorsman. He had never gone camping out in the wild, but sitting here in the quiet of the desert night he began to think that perhaps he had been missing out. It was extremely peaceful, and he could well imagine coming here with a couple of friends and sitting around the fire with a six-pack of Buds.

This evening, however, was not a pleasure trip. In front of him on the other side of the fence was the white make-shift office building set up inside a converted shipping container, and he could see that the lights were still on the inside. At one point he thought he spotted some movement behind the horizontal Venetian blinds.

Before leaving for Arizona, Aaron had researched how the missile silos were originally constructed, and he had studied old de-classified schematics for Silo 570-2, including the orientation of the entire decommissioned underground facility. He wanted to be prepared for what he might find in case he actually managed to get inside the missile complex.

He had learned that the entire project involved a multitude of major companies, and it began with the digging out of a large deep pit called a 'bathtub' because of its shape. At the bottom of this pit were built the reinforced concrete structures of the complex, including the five-storey access stairwell and the central section with its four 30-centimetre-thick steel blast doors each weighing almost three tons.

From the central section ran a 30-metre-long tunnel towards the east called the 'cableway' because it contained all the power and control cables in the complex. This tunnel led to the missile silo itself, where the 30-metre-tall Titan II missile was continuously kept ready to launch at a moment's notice for more than two decades. The silo was around 45 metres or 150 feet deep, and it had a giant retractable steel-reinforced cover on the surface that would slide away on rails before launch.

A second shorter tunnel ran from the central section towards the west where a cylindrical three-storey structure contained sleeping quarters, a kitchen and a bathroom on Level 1. The complex's missile launch control room was one level down on Level 2, from where the Titan II could be launched in as little as 58 seconds from the time of the crew receiving the order from the President. Finally, on Level 3 was an engineering room containing air and water pumps, air filtration systems and other utilities.

From the control room, there was access to an emergency escape hatch that led into the missile complex's cramped vertical air intake shaft, which was constructed a couple of metres from the large cylindrical structure. A ladder bolted to the inside of the shaft led all the way up to the surface. A similar hatch was located on the engineering level below.

Once the entire complex had been built and completed, all of the excavated soil was then used to bury it all the way up to the top of the central access stairwell, so that the entrance was level with the ground above, and the bottom of the missile silo was almost 50 metres below the surface. The entire complex cost the equivalent of around two billion dollars in today's money, and it had been duplicated sixty times across four states.

Looking at the orientation of the site and his location on the eastern edge of it, Aaron knew that the air intake shaft would be near the northern edge of the site, so he slipped a few metres back into cover and made his way quietly along the eastern side of the fence and then around to the northern side of it where he stopped near its midpoint. He had decided that the main access point through the central stairwell would almost certainly be locked and possibly even manned, so he had decided to go for the air intake shaft instead. He could not see the topside hatch of the shaft from where he was, but he felt confident that it was less than twenty metres away.

Having come prepared, Aaron extracted a sturdy wire cutter from his backpack and quickly snipped a number of links in the fence, creating an opening he could just squeeze through. Once on the other side, he reached back through the opening, grabbed his backpack and pulled it through. He turned towards where he thought the access hatch would be, and crouching down he then made his way carefully between the dry bushes in that direction.

Sure enough, the heavy square steel hatch turned out to be just where he thought it would be, and there appeared to be no lock on it. The hatch in front of him was not the original hatch from 1962 since the entire complex was being refurbished and turned into a habitable space, but as far as he could see it was identical to the original that used to be there back when the launch complex was operational.

Aaron gripped the metal handle and pulled the hatch open. It was much heavier than he had expected, and he had to strain the muscles in both of his arms to open it fully. It produced a metallic squeak as he did so, making him worried that he might be discovered. Once it was opened, he crabbed sideways whilst scouting in the direction of the office building for a few moments. He could see no movement either inside or outside, so he got out his torch and quickly shone it down the shaft, making sure to hold it below the rim so that the torchlight could not be seen from the office building.

Along the side of the shaft furthest away from the centre of the complex were rungs of metal bars extending all the way down to the bottom of the shaft. He swung his legs down into the hole and lowered himself in, grabbing onto the top rung with one hand and tucking the torch under his belt with the light shining down. Leaving the hatch open, he then began to descend.

After what Aaron estimated was around 25 metres and with his arms aching, he finally reached the point where the emergency escape hatch from the launch control room was located. He reached across to the hatch and gripped its handle tightly, but it wouldn't budge. Suddenly concerned that he would be unable to enter the silo complex and might instead have to climb all the way back up again, he became worried that he would end up becoming too tired, slip and then fall to the bottom of the shaft.

Hooking an arm around one of the metal rungs and calming himself down by taking a couple of deep slow breaths, he then climbed down another three metres to where the escape hatch from the engineering level was located. To his immense relief, this one turned out to already be open just a crack. He switched his torch off and pushed open the hatch. A faint light was coming through from the other side.

He slipped through the hatch and found that the space beyond contained various machines arranged neatly in rows across the floor. The room was circular and roughly 15 metres in diameter, and at first he thought he was looking at a reconstructed space that had been intended to replicate the way this level had looked when it was in active use by the U.S. Airforce. Everything looked new and the floor and the walls seemed freshly painted.

However, it quickly became clear that he was looking at modern machinery and that some of the cabinets contained computer servers. The room was lit by faint lights in the ceiling and there was no sign of anyone else being there.

About five metres away were the stairs leading up to what used to be the launch control centre, and as he tiptoed closer he listened out for voices or footsteps above him. However, the only sound he could hear was the hum of machinery, most likely the air filtration systems.

As he ascended the stairs to Level 2, he was taken aback by what he found. The entire floor space of the launch control centre was taken up by a large bar area, complete with plush velvet seating, thick carpets and expensive-looking pendant lamps over small white marble tables. Along roughly a third of the circular wall was a curved bar with row upon row of liquor, wine and other beverages.

Damn, he thought. *They weren't kidding about this being an underground luxury house.*

He snuck through the bar area half expecting an alarm to go off at any moment, but nothing happened. Before heading through the exit towards the facility's central section, he decided to take the stairs up to what used to be the sleeping and eating quarters of the complex. As he emerged on Level 1, he could see that the original vaulted ceiling was still in place. But that was the only thing that was unchanged from the 1960s. The entire space had been converted into a huge bedroom with an artificial starry night sky made from tiny lights on the dome that was the ceiling. Roughly one-third of the level had been turned into a luxurious black marble bathroom with frosted glass walls to the bedroom itself.

Aaron shook his head. This was not what he had been expecting. Looking around the room, it suddenly occurred to him that everything looked immaculate as if no one had ever used either the bedroom, the bathroom or the bar area. If this underground house was still in the process of being built then that would make sense. But then why were there bedding and duvets on the bed if this whole complex was still under construction? And why was the bar downstairs fully stocked, if no one lived here? Was this some sort of show home that was still in the process of being built? A prototype for other similar luxury homes spread across the Arizona desert?

He carefully walked downstairs and through the short tunnel to the central section of the complex. The floor in the tunnel and in the central section was covered by dark and very expensive-looking wood flooring. The central section itself still contained the four enormous original and neatly restored and painted blast doors.

The space was open and did not seem like it was being used for anything other than a thoroughfare to the two main sections of the complex. On the other side of the central section, he could see through to the cableway which ran all the way to the missile silo. The wood flooring extended to the other end around 30 metres away, and there seemed to have been more habitable space created at the end of it. The cableway was only a couple of metres wide, so because of its length and the visible joins between the wide wooden floorboards, it appeared to narrow to a small point at the far end.

Still seeing no one else there, Aaron considered whether to risk walking along the cableway to what used to be the missile silo. There was nowhere to hide along there, so if anyone was going to catch him then this would probably be when it happened. He decided to risk it.

Mildly surprised to make it to the end of the cableway without hearing someone shout "Halt", he found himself standing on the edge of a huge glass floor supported by an elegant black-painted steel structure, which extended all the way across the entire missile silo. The silo seemed slightly smaller in circumference than the launch control centre, and it was perhaps thirteen metres in diameter.

The circular room with the thick glass floor directly in front of him contained what looked like an office. But what really stunned him was that when he looked up, he could see another glass floor above him with an expensive-looking bathroom. And below him, there were at least three more floors also made of glass with different types of rooms including a kitchen. At the very top of the silo was a large skylight almost as big as the silo itself, so the entire space would be lit up brightly by the powerful Arizona sun during the day. As had been the case during the heyday of the launch complex, stairs inside the walls of the silo allowed movement between floors.

Millions, he thought to himself as he gawped at the spectacle in front, above and below him. *This must have cost millions and millions of dollars. This place is insane.*

Looking down through the floors of the 'house', he was unable to spot any movement anywhere. Once again, he wondered why this place was pristine but empty, especially when this was meant to be an active building site. Where was everyone?

He turned around, looking back through the long cableway to the central section and decided to head back. When he was about two metres from the end of the cableway, he suddenly heard the sound of hydraulics operating one of the enormous blast doors. Since he could see the two blast doors that were meant to close off access to the launch control section and to the missile silo, it had to be one of the other two doors that connected the central section to the stairwell and the main access point. Someone was coming through from the surface.

Suddenly feeling panicky, he hurried up to the corner and peeked around it to the inner blast door. It was still closed, so what he had heard opening had to have been the outer door to the stairwell. Right now, whoever was coming through would be entering the small room between the inner and outer blast doors, and in just a few seconds they would begin operating the hydraulic machinery to open the inner door. This meant he had a few more seconds to hide before the inner door would open.

His eyes darted anxiously around the space as he tried to spot a place to hide. He considered running across the central section and through the short corridor to hide inside the launch control centre, but the sound of his feet on the wood flooring would be bound to alert whoever was entering to his presence, once the blast door swung fully open. Then he spotted what looked like a set of tall utility lockers built into the wall just next to the blast door, so he dashed for the nearest one. Opening it he saw that there was plenty of space, so he slipped inside, turned around and closed the door. Just below eye level was a narrow slit in the locker door that allowed him to see out if he bent down slightly.

No sooner had he closed the door before the clang of the metal bolts unlocking the inner blast door sounded. Then he heard the whirring of the hydraulics as they laboured to swing the almost three-tonne steel door aside. As it was opening, Aaron realised that the enormous finely balanced block of steel designed to withstand a direct nuclear hit was opening towards him. He momentarily felt the blood drain from his face at the prospect of the blast door remaining open and blocking his ability to open the locker door again, trapping him inside. However, the door came to a gentle stop at a perfect right angle from its frame, which left plenty of space for the locker door to open.

Then he heard footsteps and it sounded like there were two people there. Leaning slightly to one side to look past the open blast door he saw two people come into view and walk away from him through the central section to the T-junction where the two narrow tunnels led off to the launch control centre and the missile silo respectively. They were both Caucasian males and one was tall and well-groomed with black slicked back hair, while the other was shorter and walking half a step behind. They were both wearing what looked like military uniforms with insignia on their shoulders. The tall man's uniform was black and the short man's was white, and both of the men were wearing shiny black shoes. Even though Aaron could only see them from behind, there was something about their uniforms that seemed familiar. The slim-fit jackets with their small tight-fitting collars rang a bell somehow, and then he realised what they reminded him of. Nazi uniforms.

The two men came to a stop around ten metres away from him at the other end of the central section of the complex, just in front of the wall that was directly opposite the inner blast door.

'I will take it from here,' said the tall man in the black uniform. 'The Imperator has asked for a detailed update on the defense suite and the air filtration systems, so this should take about an hour. Return to the office and wait for me there.'

'Yes, Centurion,' replied the man in the white uniform, turning around and beginning to walk back towards Aaron and the blast door in a manner that looked very much like what one would expect from military personnel.

As quietly as he could, Aaron fished his phone out of his pocket and held it up to the slit in the cupboard door. It accidentally knocked lightly against the door as he did so, but the man in the white uniform did not appear to notice as he marched briskly along on the wooden floor. Aaron switched to camera mode and began recording at the highest possible resolution. At the other end of the room, the tall man in the black uniform stood immovable and still facing the wall, clearly waiting for the other man to leave.

As the blast door moved back to its closed position, shutting with a thud and a brief increase in the pitch of the noise from the hydraulics system, Aaron's eyes were locked on the statue-like figure at the other end of the corridor. Holding the phone as steady as he could with one hand, he used the fingers on his other hand to zoom in so that the black-clad man took up the whole screen on his phone.

The man reached out with his right hand towards what looked like a small brass plaque, pressed it in firmly and then removed his hand as the plaque unlocked from its housing and swung open on one side to reveal what appeared to be a standard numerical keypad. Aaron zoomed in even more on the keypad, letting his hand rest gently against the inside of the locker door and holding his breath in an effort to keep his phone as steady as possible. As he did so, he could feel his heart pounding in his chest as if he had just been rushing up the stairs to his apartment back home in Brooklyn Heights.

Looking out through the slit in the cupboard door, he watched as the tall man pulled back his hand from the keypad. After a couple of seconds, there was the sound of another hydraulics system, this time sounding significantly less loud. Another couple of seconds later Aaron heard a brief hiss of air as the entire section of wall directly in front of the man slid back, retracted further in and then swung open to reveal a long lit-up corridor beyond.

Once the door was open, the man stepped resolutely inside, quickly pressing a button on the left as he entered. Immediately, the door began to close again and Aaron watched him proceed about halfway down the corridor before the closing door blocked his view. After a few seconds, the door had closed completely, again giving the appearance of being an innocuous section of wall.

What the hell is this place? thought Aaron. *Secret passages and military uniforms? This was supposed to be a luxury house for some Hollywood eccentric.*

Hesitating momentarily Aaron then tapped the screen on his phone to stop recording. Remaining inside the cupboard he opened the video file and replayed it a couple of times at quarter speed. As he watched the man in the white uniform walk towards him in slow motion, he noticed that the uniform appeared to have a small gold laurel wreath stitched onto the left side above the chest pocket. When he paused the video he was able to see it clearly. It was identical to that on the boilersuit the man in the make-shift office had been wearing, but it did not look like any military insignia he had ever seen.

Unpausing the video, he skipped to the part where the black-uniformed 'Centurion' had flipped open the housing to the keypad. Looking closely at the screen and replaying the video several times, he tried to work out what the right combination for the door had been. It was either 1-9-9-3 or 1-9-6-3. Aaron smiled to himself. The launch complex for Silo No. 570-2 opened in 1963.

Pushing the cupboard door open, he quickly made his way to the wall with the secret door, briefly glancing to his left towards the launch control room which would be his only means of escape if he was caught. Was he in over his head? His gut told him that the answer was most definitely 'yes', but he shook his head and flipped the brass plaque open, resolutely punching in the code. There was no turning back now.

As the door opened, he shifted slightly to be able to see inside. A wide corridor stretched away to another elevator at the other end around twenty metres away, but the corridor was otherwise empty. Wherever the man in the black uniform had gone he must have taken the elevator, and since Aaron guessed that he was currently about 30 metres underground, this meant that there were even lower levels in this complex. And none of what he was looking at had ever been part of the original missile complex.

The corridor was at least three metres wide, and unlike the cylindrical tunnels in the old Titan II complex, this one had a cuboid shape with polished metal panels on the sides and a lattice metal ceiling with lots of small downlights, and it had obviously been completed very recently.

Arriving at the other end of the metal-clad corridor Aaron saw that there was only one button next to the elevator, and he was about to press it when he realised that if there were people down there then he would stick out like a sore thumb. He raced back to the utility cupboard and managed to find a white boilersuit like the one worn by the man in the office up at ground level. It was slightly too big and a bit baggy for him, but he put it on anyway. Then he grabbed the hardhat that hung next to it and put it on his head.

Back at the elevator once more he pressed the button, and after about a minute a small chime sounded and the two large sliding doors opened. The elevator was surprisingly big, more akin to a cargo elevator than one designed for people, but since there was no access to the silo complex other than the main access stairwell, this meant that it must have been designed to carry a large number of people, probably around thirty. Above a similar set of sliding double doors at the other end of the elevator was a digital display reading '0'.

Aaron stepped inside and walked to the far end, where he pressed the button with a down-arrow. The elevator began descending, but the digital display above him just kept showing an animated arrow moving downwards. After about half a minute, the elevator slowed down slightly, and the display changed to read '-5'. Five storeys below the level of the central section of the silo complex.

That's gotta be at least 50 metres below the surface, thought Aaron. *What the hell is down here?*

As the elevator doors slid open, nothing could have prepared him for what he saw. He was first greeted by a muffled cacophony of noises that sounded like they were coming from building works, as well as the voices of workmen. He stepped out into a wide slightly curving corridor, and on the other side of it from the elevator was a window. He stepped over to it and looked through, but it took him a moment to grasp what he was looking at.

It was a huge circular space, similar in feel to an upmarket hotel atrium but much larger than anything he had ever seen. In fact, it was gigantic. The floor was about ten metres below him, and he guessed that it was at least one hundred metres in diameter. The ceiling was a huge dome with a grid of spotlights bathing the interior in white light, and the roughly three-meter-high walls around the circumference of the circular floor had a number of large double doors set into them that were spaced around ten metres apart. Some of the doors were open and revealed what looked like living quarters of some kind. In the middle of the atrium was a circular area where several tall trees grew, apparently able to survive with the artificial sunlight from the many dome-mounted lights overhead. The complex was quite simply vast.

However, what really took Aaron by surprise was the fact that the whole place was teeming with activity. There were workmen everywhere, welding, plastering, painting, assembling scaffolding and hammering and cutting. All of the workmen were wearing dark orange boilersuits with the laurel wreath logo on their backs along with a number. No two numbers seemed to be the same. The whole place was a hive of activity, and as he stood there looking out over it in awe, he spotted the tall man in the black uniform down below talking to someone wearing a red boilersuit who looked like he might perhaps be a foreman.

Aaron watched as the 'Centurion' and the foreman began walking together straight towards a doorway about thirty metres away to their left. When they reached it the foreman looked like he punched in a code on a keypad, and then he opened the door and seemed to leave it open as the two men walked through. Perhaps he thought they would be coming back out shortly.

Aaron decided to follow and picked up a plastic crate full of tools from a pallet, and then walked down a long curving ramp from the corridor with the elevator towards the giant atrium below. Here he walked purposefully along and headed straight for the door that the foreman had held open with a latch on the wall behind it. As he walked, he tried not to ogle too much at all the workmen, but at one point he had to scurry aside when a small electric vehicle carrying a crew of four crossed the atrium floor and disappeared down a long corridor. As he watched the vehicle speed away from him, Aaron was stunned by how large the underground structure was. It made the luxury house inside the silo complex look like a small cave. Catching brief glimpses of the interior behind some of the open doors around the atrium, he could see what appeared to be large comfortable-looking living quarters, not at all looking like military barracks but more akin to normal living rooms or common rooms in a modern house.

He entered through the door that had been left on a latch and found himself in yet another corridor. This one was short and ended in a set of stairs going down. He walked casually down to the bottom and found himself in a large industrial-looking room with lots of bulky-looking machinery whirring away. At the far end was a raised platform with a glass-walled office inside which the 'Centurion' and the foreman were leaning over a computer monitor, the foreman seemingly showing the man in the black uniform something.

Aaron hurried down an aisle between two rows of humming machines and pretended to busy himself with a control panel on one of them. After a few minutes, the 'Centurion' and the foreman left the glass-walled office and walked the length of the room back to the door. Aaron kept his head down whilst watching them out of the corner of his eye. As soon as they had left he hurried to the office, walked up the steps and entered. Inside were several tables with monitors, and along the back wall were server racks with computers that were most likely monitoring and controlling all of the machinery in the room on the other side of the glass wall.

He walked over to the monitor where the foreman and the man in the black uniform had stood. The monitor was still showing a schematic of a machine that Aaron could not identify. He glanced briefly out to the machinery floor to make sure no one else was there and dug into his backpack. Then he pulled out a small USB memory stick and slotted it into the PC. He quickly found the location of the files being displayed on the monitor and copied the entire contents of the folder onto the stick. There were hundreds of files. Sensing that he might be pushing his luck, he yanked the memory stick out and put it back inside his backpack. Then he hurried out of the office and back towards the corridor leading back to the dome.

Back out in the atrium, he walked briskly towards the ramp leading back up to the elevator, having to exercise immense self-restraint to stop himself from running to get out of there as quickly as humanly possible. Beads of sweat were forming on his brow and he could feel his heart pounding in his chest.

'Hey, you!' shouted an authoritative-sounding voice behind him.

Aaron immediately began walking faster, heading up the ramp and risking a quick glance behind him. What he saw made him break into a run because coming up behind him around twenty metres away was a group of four men in black uniforms similar to that of the 'Centurion'. They were carrying pistols in holsters on their hips and walking briskly towards him.

Aaron sprinted up the final stretch of the ramp and back to the elevator. As soon as he had started running, the group of uniformed men had set off after him, the sound of their feet echoing along the corridor to the elevator. Aaron mashed the call button, and thankfully no one had used it since he came down because a couple of seconds later the elevator doors opened and he rushed inside and hit the button with the up-arrow.

'Stop!' shouted one of the four uniformed men and aimed his gun, but Aaron had just slipped inside and the elevator doors were already closing.

By the time the man was banging uselessly on the outer doors, the elevator was already moving upwards, although painfully slowly now that Aaron really needed to get out of there fast. It finally stopped back up at the central section of the silo complex and Aaron bolted out, stopping for a moment and not sure what to do. He looked briefly towards the blast door ahead of him at the other end of the central section but decided it would be too dangerous and probably take too long to try to exit that way. There was also the risk that the exit to the ground level above was locked, in which case he would be stuck and caught.

Before he realised what was happening, the elevator doors closed behind him, and now the elevator was on its way back down to where the group of uniformed men were no doubt waiting for it. This meant that he had just over a minute before they would emerge right where he stood.

He sprinted back through the launch control centre, bounded down the stairs to the engineering level and virtually launched himself through the emergency escape hatch where he grabbed the first rung inside the shaft and began climbing as fast as he could. After about half a minute the muscles in his arms were screaming at him to stop as the lactic acid kept building up, but he forced himself to keep going.

When he finally reached the top, he pushed himself up over the edge and rolled onto the dusty ground amongst the bushes, panting and wincing from the pain in his arms, legs and lungs. But with no time to waste and crouched down low to avoid being spotted, he soon began making his way back towards the hole in the fence. Just as he reached it, he heard the sound of a metal door flying open and voices shouting. This must have been the group of four men finally making it through the blast doors and up through the main access stairwell to the large concrete ramp at ground level.

Aaron was now already through the fence and ran crouched through the bushes back to his car. He opened the door, tossed his backpack onto the front passenger seat and got in behind the wheel. Here he started the engine but did not turn on the light. Instead, he began following his own tracks through the bushes back to Highway 86. Once there he swung across it and into the east-bound lane, where he switched his lights on and headed back towards Tucson. Only then did it occur to him that the group of uniformed men had no means of pursuing him since there were no vehicles at the site. Everyone there clearly lived, worked and slept down in the giant underground complex. The question was - what on earth was it all for?

Five

The Foreign Secretary of the United Kingdom, Malcolm Squire, was in the lobby of the Foreign Office building on King Charles Street, a stone's throw from the Houses of Parliament and Big Ben. The 5-storey off-white mid-19th century building was constructed in the imposing so-called Italianata style, with extremely high ceilings, prominent exterior cornices and large arched windows. It had been finished in 1868 when the British Empire was approaching its zenith, and the offices inside it had served as venues for some of the most momentous decisions ever made by small groups of people wielding power over millions of others around the entire world.

Many of the suspiciously straight lines that today constitute borders between dozens of countries in the Middle East, Africa and other places were drawn on maps put down on tables in this very building, often by government officials who had little or no knowledge of the people who actually lived in those places. As a consequence, those lines had resulted in countless wars over the past several centuries.

Malcolm Squire understood this as well as anyone of course, but he nonetheless never failed to be impressed with the building and its sense of grandeur and stateliness. The former journalist turned politician felt his heart swell with pride in his country whenever he walked through the building, and he was often irritated by the insistence of some parts of the press to keep pushing what he felt were unpatriotic agendas, including so-called 'empire-bashing.'

Leading off from the lobby was the famous and controversial Grand Staircase, which had served to impress foreign dignitaries ever since its creation by the artist Sigismund Goetze in 1914. On large panes of wall surrounding the staircase were painted enormous murals depicting the helmeted figure of the mythical Britannia, the national personification of Britain. In one of Goetze's murals along the colonnaded hallway, she can be seen sending her sons out to rule the empire. In another, she is training them in the arts of war. And in yet another, she is depicted as bringing together the countries of the world, among them America, France, Japan, Italy and several others in a bid to ensure world peace. The cause of the controversy surrounding the murals was perhaps self-evident and unavoidable in modern Britain, but Squire had decided to ignore it during his tenure as Foreign Secretary, and he had been quoted in the news as expressing disdain for the 'lefties' who were ashamed of their country's history.

Standing next to him was the UK's ambassador to Russia, Sir Charles Drake, who happened to be in London on one of his regular visits for meetings with officials from both the Foreign Office and the intelligence services. As they watched the main doors to the exterior open and a small delegation being escorted inside, Drake leaned over towards Squire.

'Here they are,' he said. 'Let's see if we can get to the bottom of this.'

'Sure,' said Squire, fidgeting with his Union Jack cufflinks. 'But let's just not ruffle any feathers unnecessarily. As you'll recall, the government is working on a new natural gas supply contract with the energy firm Rosneft. If we can secure that deal, the British public will be able to enjoy much lower heating bills.'

'By which you mean, the British electorate,' said Drake probingly.

Squire ignored the comment and began walking towards the three people who had just entered the building and were now walking towards them. As they met, Squire extended his hand in greeting.

'Ambassador Nikolayev,' he smiled. 'Thank you very much for coming.'

The Russian ambassador to the UK, Konstantin Nikolayev, was a short and slightly rotund man wearing a pale-blue suit and a dark blue tie with small white dots. He was about fifty years old and had been in his post for almost a decade serving as the Kremlin's loyal mouthpiece in London. He wore small round thin-rimmed glasses that gave the impression of him peering intently at anyone he looked at, and his mouth seemed to be permanently locked in an expression that was somewhere between a reluctant smile and a disdainful smirk, making it virtually impossible to work out what the man was thinking.

'Foreign Secretary,' said Nikolayev and gave a small but insincere bow.

'Please,' said Squire warmly and gesturing to the staircase behind him. 'Please follow me. We have a meeting room set up for us upstairs.'

As they proceeded up the staircase Squire turned to the ambassador.

'You've been here a few times before, have you not?' he asked casually.

'I have,' replied Nikolayev in a heavy Russian accent, looking up at the murals. 'I see you have kept the décor as it was. Images of the great British empire.'

'We have,' smiled Squire affably, detecting a hint of sarcasm in the ambassador's voice. 'This is very much a historic building so we have no plans to change it.'

'Yes,' mused Nikolayev. 'I understand the English like to cling on to their supposed great colonial past. But I am reminded of a quote by Vladimir Lenin. *'Can a nation be free if it oppresses other nations? It cannot.'* That is as true today as it was when he said it.'

Squire was about to retort but decided not to be drawn. The last thing he needed right now was a spat with the Russians about which nation had behaved most appallingly during their respective heydays.

★ ★ ★

In the sumptuous and colonial-looking meeting room down a long wide corridor on the second floor of the Foreign Office building, Andrew and Captain Lynch were waiting. Standing by the window overlooking the Horse Guards Parade and a statue of Earl Mountbatten, they had been asked to wait for the arrival of the foreign secretary and the two ambassadors. Their presence in the meeting had not exactly been welcomed by the Foreign Secretary, but Colonel Strickland had successfully pressured his superiors to ensure that they could attend.

'What's the word from the Atlantic Fleet?' asked Andrew, looking across the parade grounds towards the Old Admiralty Building where a pack of tourists were taking pictures.

'The Norwegian team will arrive at the scene during the next couple of hours,' replied Lynch. 'Once they are in place, they'll launch the ROV and send it down and have a look. It's about 500 metres down to the seabed, so if the Tennessee broke up after the explosion, then she could have ended up a long way from where it happened. This means that the search area could be pretty big and the search itself could take a while.'

'What about sonar?' asked Andrew.

'Hasn't picked up anything,' replied Lynch. 'But the seabed is pretty rough in places down there. The Anton Dohrn Seamount is basically the remnants of an extinct underwater volcano, so there are a lot of jagged ridges and rock formations that mean that the boat could be down there but not visible on sonar.'

'I see,' said Andrew. 'Well, I guess we will see what the Russians have to say. I suppose it is possible that they might have picked up something on their underwater listening network.'

'Oh, I guarantee it,' smiled Lynch. 'That doesn't mean they'll be willing to share it with us, though. But there is no doubt in my mind that they heard exactly what we heard.'

'Well,' said Andrew. 'I have been pondering two possible scenarios in which the Russians could conceivably have been involved.'

'Alright,' said Lynch. 'Let's hear them.'

'One is an act of reckless sabotage either of the submarine, the torpedo or of the submarine's ability to safely launch torpedoes.'

'Yup,' said Lynch. 'I have considered those too.'

'The other scenario,' continued Andrew, 'is a possible forcible boarding of the submarine using special forces and an underwater delivery vehicle.'

'This is what Commodore Spencer mentioned, right?' asked Lynch.

'Yes,' replied Andrew. 'More or less. I am no expert on submarine warfare, but I know a thing or two about special forces operations, and I also know that the Russian Navy have a small special-purpose submersible designated Project 210 and nicknamed *Losharik*.'

Lynch nodded. 'I think I am familiar with that. That's the mini-sub that can be carried by an attack submarine, right?'

'That's correct,' replied Andrew. 'It is small. Only 60 metres long and the Russians have modified the nuclear-powered submarine K-329 Belgorod so that Losharik can attach itself to it and transfer personnel via a specially designed airlock. This allows the

Belgorod to carry the Losharik more or less anywhere in the world and deploy it for covert operations. We know for a fact that it can dive to at least 2,500 metres, so it could easily operate anywhere the USS Tennessee could go. We also know that it has been used by Russian special forces on covert missions in the past to tamper with undersea communications cables and listening stations.'

'So, what are you thinking?' asked Lynch, leaning against the wall by the huge window.

'We don't have the exact specs for the vehicle, but it is conceivable that a special airlock could have been fitted to it, allowing it to latch on to an Ohio-class submarine after which Russian special forces could have boarded it. Now, I am sure that the crew of the Tennessee would put up a fight, but speaking from experience, once inside a submarine like that, a special forces team would have no problems taking over the vessel.'

'So, you think what Spencer suggested might be true?' asked Lynch, looking sceptical. 'But like he said, they'd need someone on the inside. And what about the explosion? If the Russians had boarded the sub, why was a torpedo fired and how do you explain it exploding?'

'We have to consider if the explosion was staged as some sort of smoke-screen,' said Andrew. 'If that was the case then the Russians would understand that we would discover that fact eventually, but it just might buy them enough time to take over the boat and navigate it away from the area, possibly even take it back to one of those underground submarine hangars that we know they have built in Murmansk.'

Lynch nodded. 'I suppose it is feasible,' he said. 'But it would be one hell of a risk. In fact, it would be absolutely nuts. Can you imagine the shit-storm if it was ever confirmed that the Russians had hijacked a U.S. Navy nuclear submarine?'

'I know it sounds a bit far-fetched,' said Andrew. 'I am just trying to be open-minded here. It's not like the Russian have never tried to pull off something crazy like this in the past.'

'I know,' said Lynch ruefully. 'Alright. Let's just drop this on the ambassador and see what happens. They can't really blame us for being a bit paranoid about this whole thing.'

At that moment the tall oak double doors to the meeting room opened and Ambassador Drake entered, followed by Malcolm Squire, Ambassador Nikolayev and his two aides, at least one of which Andrew assumed was from Russia's military intelligence agency the GRU, working under cover of being a diplomat stationed in London.

'Gentlemen,' said Squire, barely acknowledging the presence of Andrew and Lynch. 'Please sit down. Coffee and tea will be with us shortly.'

The three Russians filed onto one side of the long table and sat down with Nikolayev in the middle and the two aides on either side of him. One of them looked like a bookkeeper and the other could have been mistaken for a concierge at a hotel. Andrew was unsure which one was the intelligence agent, and which one was the ambassador's personal aide.

'These are Mr Sterling and Mr Lynch,' said Squire, gesturing to the two men and sounding almost apologetic. 'Intelligence people. They have asked to sit in on this meeting. I am sure you don't mind.'

Nikolayev shrugged indifferently, and took out a pen from his suit jacket pocket, placing it carefully on the table in front of himself.

As Andrew and Captain Lynch sat down next to Squire and Drake they nodded their acknowledgement towards the Russian delegation, but all three men ignored them and focused their attention on the Foreign Secretary.

'Thank you again for coming,' said Squire. 'We only really have one thing on the agenda so let's get straight to it.'

Nikolayev nodded whilst his two companions sat immobile and simply observed proceedings.

'As I am sure you are aware,' continued Squire, 'The U.S. Navy appears to have lost an Ohio-class submarine in the North Atlantic.'

Nikolayev nodded again, but Andrew was unable to tell if he nodded to acknowledge the information or if he indicated his agreement that Russia already knew of the incident.

'The reason we have asked you to come today,' said Squire, 'is to allow the Russian Federation an opportunity to confirm that it had no hand in the disappearance of the USS Tennessee inside UK territorial waters.'

There was a short pause of a few seconds during which time Nikolayev's eyebrows slowly but steadily raised themselves as if he was either waiting for further details or expecting a direct question. When that did not materialise, he took a long deep breath and exhaled slowly whilst reaching for his pen and adjusting its position on the table slightly.

'Secretary Squire,' he finally sighed. 'The Russian people and the Russian government have got used to being painted as - how do you say – a bad actor, for many years now. But in anticipation of your reasons for requesting this meeting, my government has made it very clear to me that we were not in any way involved in this incident, and to imply that we were is deeply insulting to the Russian nation.'

Squire shifted uncomfortably in his seat at the sudden change in the atmosphere inside the meeting room.

'Ambassador Nikolayev,' he said, almost timidly. 'As I am sure you understand, this incident is in the process of being investigated and we are merely attempting to rule out as many theoretically possible scenarios as we can. We are not accusing Russia of involvement but simply providing your government with an opportunity to unequivocally deny that it was involved. I am quite sure that no one in NATO seriously believes that the Russian Federation would do anything so foolhardy.'

Ambassador Nikolayev produced a tired and somewhat caustic smile before beginning what seemed like a carefully rehearsed monologue.

'NATO talks about peace, but it is simply hypocritical,' he said, as if stating a widely accepted fact. 'For half a century there was stability and balance in Europe. NATO was comprised of western Europe, and the Warsaw-pact included Russia and her dependants in Eastern Europe. There was peace and there was stability, even if we did not always see eye to eye on everything. Then came the end of the cold war, and immediately NATO began to offer membership to former Warsaw-pact countries, which had the effect of NATO's border creeping closer and closer to Russia. Now suddenly we are surrounded by NATO countries, and at no point have the western countries acknowledged the Russian Federation's legitimate security concerns in that context. This is a grave insult to the Russian people, and it demonstrates the arrogance of the West and of NATO. And as for the notion that NATO is a defensive alliance, everyone knows that is not true. It was NATO that was used to coordinate western meddling in Libya when Colonel Gaddafi lost his grip on power. It was NATO that was the structure used to organise the bombing campaign against Syrian government facilities and military units during the civil war in that country. It was NATO countries who invaded Iraq and Afghanistan, and who occupied those countries for many years. NATO is quite clearly not a defensive alliance, and every time people like you pretend that it is, you insult people's intelligence. With all due respect.'

Squire sat dumbfounded for a few seconds not knowing precisely how to defuse the situation, so Andrew decided to step in and make sure that the Russian position was crystal clear. He and Captain Lynch had been asked to participate as silent observers only, but Andrew could sense the foreign secretary losing control of the meeting and so he decided to speak.

'Mr ambassador,' he began. 'As I am sure you are aware, there was an explosion in the vicinity of the

USS Tennessee immediately before contact was lost. Can you guarantee to us right now that the Russian Federation had nothing to do with that?'

Squire turned his head and looked at Andrew, daggers shooting out of his eyes.

'Absolutely,' replied Nikolayev matter-of-factly, looking at Andrew with an emotionless expression.

'And can you guarantee that there were no submarines from the Russian Navy in the area at the time of the incident?'

'Absolutely,' repeated Nikolayev.

'Just to be clear,' said Andrew, raising his right hand slightly off the table. 'Does this include the special purpose vehicle Losharik? We know this vehicle has special operations capabilities and we need to be able to rule out that this vehicle was involved in any way.'

Hesitating for a moment, possibly taken aback by the directness of the question, Nikolayev leaned to the side and whispered something in the ear of the man who must have been his aide. The man immediately rose and exited the room whilst pulling out his phone and holding it to his ear. As he exited out into the corridor and the door closed behind him, Andrew could hear his voice already speaking to someone on the other end of the line. Less than a minute later he returned and sat down, whispering a short sentence in ambassador Nikolayev's ear.

'Please be patient for a couple of minutes,' said Nikolayev wearily. 'We are waiting for proof.'

'Proof?' asked Squire, clearly irritated with the sudden turn in the direction the meeting had taken. 'Proof of what?'

'Losharik's location,' said the ambassador.

Squire nodded and glanced sideways at Andrew who leaned back in his chair, calmly awaiting whatever the Russian ambassador had in store for them. There then followed an awkward silence where the attendees busied themselves with their phones, except for the man who Andrew had now concluded was the GRU operative. He simply sat still and expressionless in his chair looking across at his counterparts and barely blinking the whole time, as if he was a robot busily and silently recording the entire meeting.

Eventually, there was a loud electronic ping, and immediately Nikolayev's aide reached for his phone. After a couple of swipes, he put it away and reached inside his bag for a tablet. A few seconds later he showed it to Nikolayev who nodded silently, after which the aide slid the tablet towards the four men on the other side of the table.

They all leaned in as far as they could, craning their necks to get a better look.

'What are we looking at here?' asked Ambassador Drake.

'This is a satellite image from last night taken just before sunset,' replied Nikolayev. 'It shows the Losharik in a dry-dock in Severomorsk, some 2,750 kilometres from the location of the supposed incident with the USS Tennessee. I am sure you will accept that the Losharik could not possibly have been involved.'

Andrew nodded whilst taking another look at the image on the tablet.

'He's right,' he said. 'There is no way the Losharik could have made it from the Anton Dohrn Seamount to Murmansk in that time. And it is sitting in drydock, so it is clearly undergoing some sort of maintenance.'

'You may verify this with your own satellite imagery,' said Nikolayev dryly. 'It should not take you too long. We know you are monitoring our naval bases every day of the week.'

'Well, that's all pretty clear then,' said Squire, glancing angrily at Andrew.

'Foreign Secretary,' said Nikolayev and paused briefly, his eyes locked on Squire's. 'Let me offer you another quote, which I hope you will reflect on. *'We do not covet anything from any nation, except their respect.'*

'Lenin again?' asked Squire uncertainly.

'No,' replied Nikolayev. 'Churchill.'

The bamboozled Malcolm Squire's mouth opened slowly as if pre-empting his brain producing some intelligent come-back or retort, but none ever came.

Then Nikolayev rose.

'I believe we are done here for today,' he said, looking at Squire as he rose and ignoring the other people in the room. 'It was a pleasure to see you again Foreign Secretary.'

Then he began walking towards the double doors, and his aide hurried ahead to open them while the GRU agent casually got up and followed the two others. Before Squire could react, the Russian trio had left the room. He turned to look at Andrew and Lynch, then turned the other way to look at Drake who merely shrugged.

'Welcome to Russia,' said Drake lethargically, as if this sort of meeting was entirely normal for him.

Squire leapt up and headed for the door. When he reached the doorway, he stopped and quickly spun around raising his right index finger in front of himself and pointing vaguely in Andrew's direction as if he was about to say something. But after a couple of seconds, he merely pressed his lips together with an irate look on his face, and then he dashed off after the Russian ambassador.

Andrew and Captain Lynch looked at each other.

'Glad to see that the UK Foreign Secretary is the one in charge here in the UK Foreign Office,' said Andrew sarcastically.

'Yup,' replied Lynch with a sigh. 'Good to know the politicians have our backs. Nikolayev's right about the sub, though. The Russians couldn't have been involved in what happened to the USS Tennessee.'

'I know,' said Andrew looking troubled. 'At least not using the Losharik. We still can't completely rule out their involvement, but this whole thing is beginning to look a lot like some form of sabotage or maybe even terrorism.'

★   ★   ★

The nondescript white van drove through the small town of Belmullet on the Mullet Peninsula in north-eastern Ireland. It was a small town of only about one thousand people, and it was a somewhat dreary and windswept place. The houses were all one-storey buildings that seemed to be desperately attempting to appear cheerful with their various pastel-coloured exteriors. The town centre, if it was possible to call it that, consisted of a roundabout surrounded by a range of local shops such as a bistro, a bank, a pub, a hardware store and a small supermarket. What struck the driver most about the whole area was an almost complete lack of trees. The slightly undulating countryside was dotted with small patches of wild bushes between the many grazing fields that were separated by fences and low stone walls, but there was not a single tree to be seen once he had left town.

What the hell do people even do for a living here, he thought to himself as he looked out at the drab surroundings.

Exiting out the other side of Belmullet in a northerly direction, the van turned off the main road and continued along a single-lane country road across the flat terrain towards the rocky coastline about five kilometres away.

It had been raining most of the day, but now the sun was peeking out between the grey clouds, and it made the black tarmac roads glisten and shine to the point where the driver had to put his sunglasses on.

From the outside, the van might not look like much. In fact, it had been deliberately painted to make it look as ordinary as possible. But inside it sat the result of several years of hacking and spying, as well as a small feat of telecommunications engineering carried out by one of the organisation's many skilled scientists. The device was bolted onto the centre of the floor inside the back of the van and it was about the size of a suitcase, including the transmitter and the batteries. If the driver was to be unlucky enough to be stopped by the police for any reason, he had been instructed to present himself as a geologist working on a survey project to measure earthquake tremors on the island of Ireland. He even had a fake ID naming him as Dr Brian O'Neill from University College Dublin.

The driver continued along the road until he could see the Atlantic Ocean in the distance, just past the point where the grass-covered grazing fields suddenly stopped and the steep drop down to the frothing sea happened. It was a drop of around fifty metres and in many places, the rockface was almost vertical.

As the road curved around to follow the precipice at a distance of around a hundred metres, the driver noticed that there were no houses out here at all, probably because it was simply too windy for anyone to want to build a permanent residence here. Even inside the van, he could hear the roar from the surf far below past the edge of the drop as the huge Atlantic waves crashed into the jagged rock formations, sending plumes of water and white spray shooting high up into the air where the gales then swept it away. Several times the powerful gusts of wind shook the van, and he had to grab the steering wheel firmly to correct its path along the narrow road.

Out to sea in the distance, he could see the Eagle Island Lighthouse which sat on the completely barren and windswept eponymous island. Looking at it from inside the van, he was sure that it had to be in the running for the least hospitable residence in the world. The rocky Eagle Island was only 1,5 kilometres out into the Atlantic Ocean, but because of the almost constant wind and rough swells, and due to the fact that it sat elevated some fifty metres above the sea, it might as well have been 150 kilometres away. The only way to get to and from the lighthouse was by helicopter, and that access was dictated entirely by the weather.

Eventually, he arrived at the designated spot and pulled over as much as the road would allow him. Then he pulled the handbrake and climbed into the back of the van to activate the device. It had been built at considerable expense and a test had never been possible, but he had faith in the organisation's engineers and scientists. Operating it had been made extremely simple. All he had to do was power it on, wait for it to initialise and run self-diagnostics, and then he would use a specially designed app to activate the transmission sequence.

He powered the device on and waited until the display read 'Ready.' Then he opened the app on his phone and tapped in the required passcode. Finally, he selected the only program that had been loaded into the device and tapped the button on his screen that read 'Begin cycle.'

Far outside the human ear's ability to detect it, the device began emitting powerful VLF, or Very-Low-Frequency radio waves on a particular frequency, using a particular signal identifier and encryption, both of which had required significant effort and resources to obtain. After just twenty seconds it was all over and the display on the device indicated that the communications cycle had completed.

The driver waited a couple of minutes until a message pinged in on his phone from another operative who was hundreds of miles away. It simply confirmed that the device appeared to have worked as intended and that the VLF signal was transmitted. Now all they could do was hope that it had also found its intended recipient. If it had, then this transmission would initiate the final stage of a plan that had taken many years to develop, and on which the fate of the world would depend.

SIX

The underwater remotely operated vehicle or ROV named Benthic Surveyor arrived on board a Norwegian navy vessel fourteen hours after the DRAPES network had picked up the sound of the explosion. The audio recording had been analysed by naval intelligence units in both the US and the UK, and both had concurred that it was indicative of an explosion of the standard warhead carried by a Spearfish torpedo.

Before the launch of the torpedo, the USS Tennessee's exact location had not been known. She had been assigned a large area around the surface target, inside which the crew had been ordered to test-fire the adapted Spearfish. But precisely where inside that area the launch would happen, had been up to the captain of the submarine. However, after the explosion, using differences in timing and simple triangulation between the large number of hydrophones that picked up the sound, it had been possible to pin down the exact spot where the torpedo had detonated with an accuracy of less than twenty metres. The assumption was that if the USS Tennessee had been disabled or sunk, then it would have come to rest on the seabed within a few hundred meters of that location, and this was where the ROV was about to be launched.

Weighing just over 200 kilos, the compact and sturdy-looking Benthic Surveyor was nicknamed 'Benny' by the operator team. It was hoisted off the deck of the Norwegian ship at the end of a steel wire that was connected to a purpose-built crane on the ship's deck. Made from carbon fibre components that were mounted on a sturdy aluminium frame and brimming with cameras, sensors, underwater thrusters and a small manipulator arm, the vehicle was a marvel of engineering. It was rated as having a maximum depth of one thousand metres or 3,300 feet, and its components and sensor suite were specially designed for the immense pressures at those depths. Since underwater pressure increases by 1 atmosphere for every 10 metres of depth, the pressure 1 kilometre down is around 100 times higher than at the surface. This means that if someone was to take a basketball-sized balloon down to that depth, its volume would be compressed to about the size of a grape.

As the crane slowly lifted the small yellow ROV out over the side of the ship, the large swells of the North Atlantic made the unmanned submarine move up and down above the surface, until it was finally lowered into the cold water. It was just a couple of degrees above freezing, and there was a strong breeze coming down from the northeast.

As soon as the clamp at the top of the vehicle was released, Benny began bobbing happily in the swells, and a few moments later the ROV engaged three of its eight small but powerful thrusters submerging itself a few meters below the surface. A couple of seconds later the two floodlights mounted at its front came on, lighting up a large volume of water directly ahead and below it.

Inside the warm and comfortable control room on board the mothership, the operator team ran through the last diagnostics checks before giving the ROV the all-clear to descend autonomously. At this location directly above where the explosion had occurred, the ship's sonar indicated a depth of 506 metres and the ROV had been programmed to descend to 450 metres and then hover.

The mothership's sonar had not picked up any signs of the 171-metre-long USS Tennessee, but the seabed was quite uneven on this part of the volcanic Anton Dohrn Seamount, so the only way to be sure was to go down to the bottom. Once at the seabed, the intention was for the ROV to begin scouring the area from the central location and then work its way outward in an increasingly larger circular pattern covering several square kilometres. If the USS Tennessee was located, the ROV would then attempt to establish if the vessel had maintained sufficient pressure hull integrity to allow for there to be survivors. If this was then deemed to be a possibility the NATO Submarine Rescue System or NSRS was already on standby to fly to the location aboard a Lockheed C5 Galaxy transport aircraft. The NSRS is a deep-sea rescue vehicle developed by NATO countries and designed to be able to latch on to the hatches of several different types of military submarines to facilitate evacuation in case of emergency. With a maximum capacity of 12 people, it would mean that it would be necessary for it to perform a significant number of dives in order to extract the entire crew.

Due to the urgency of the operation, both because of the 165 lives at stake and because the USS Tennessee carried a full complement of Trident II missiles, the plan was for a new delivery method to be employed for the NSRS. Instead of the conventional approach where a rescue vehicle is delivered to the location of a sunken submarine onboard a mothership, it would be dropped out of the back of a C5 transport aircraft at 2,000 feet after which it would parachute down to the surface of the ocean. Here, clamps would then release the parachutes and the vehicle would fall the final few metres and then be able to immediately transition into its search and rescue mode. Depending on the location, this delivery method could shave as much as 24 to 36 hours off the time it would normally take to reach a distressed submarine, and this could easily translate into dozens of lives saved.

It took 'Benny' just over half an hour to descend the 450 metres to its holding position. Its onboard gyroscopes allowed it to use its thrusters to nudge itself into position and stay there even with the slow but powerful deep ocean currents attempting to drag it along. At this point, the operator team on board the mothership took their seats behind the monitors, and the lead operator toggled the controls to manual.

Grabbing the joystick with his right hand, allowing him full 360-by-360 rotation, and the throttle with his left hand, he performed a quick pirouette in the water to re-familiarise himself with the ROV's response to his inputs. He then pushed the joystick gently forward to pitch the nose downward and pushed the throttle forward slightly to engage the lateral movement thrusters. 450 metres below him in the darkness, the ROV began gliding gracefully forward and down through the water. A couple of minutes later the grey silt-covered seabed came into view on the monitors inside the mothership's ROV control room.

The lead operator performed a quick 360-degree turn allowing the powerful floodlights to fan over the seabed and the immediate surroundings. Visibility was around 30 metres, which was more than the team had expected, and this particular part of the Anton Dohrn Seamount was relatively flat and showed no sign of any debris from an explosion. The operator pushed the throttle forward some more and the ROV sped up and began making its way through the water at about 10 kilometres per hour towards the point where it would begin its expanding circular sweep of the seabed.

After about a minute it was where it needed to be, and the operator tilted the joystick to one side to allow the ROV to line up with its intended path which was overlaid on the bathymetric map on his monitor. Soon it was underway, and it made quick progress as it navigated through the water in an ever-expanding spiral, continually scanning the seabed in front of it and recording what it saw with a camera. It was also pinging away with a small onboard sonar, generating a detailed 3D map of its immediate environment which grew in size and fidelity every time the ROV completed a full circuit.

As it worked its way further away from the starting point, it began passing over tall rock formations and deep ravines, and every crevice of the seabed was displayed on the monitors in the control room. However, after an hour there was still no sign of the USS Tennessee. There was no debris, which there should have been if the explosion had disabled the submarine, but there was also no sign of the submarine itself. The operator crew were becoming frustrated and perplexed by this turn of events, when suddenly one of them spotted something in a shallow indent in the seabed off to the left.

'There!' he said and pointed at the screen. 'Go left. There's debris.'

The team huddled together around the lead operator as he swung the ROV around to the left and approached the location. When the vehicle was about ten metres away, he engaged the auto-hover which allowed the ROV to autonomously compensate for currents to hold steady in exactly the same position.

The operator zoomed in slightly with the camera, revealing a large cylindrical metal object which seemed to have been ripped open at one end. At the other end was a clearly visible propeller with one blade missing and the surrounding control fins bent severely out of shape.

What they were looking at should not be possible. The high-explosive warhead on a Spearfish torpedo weighs 300 kilos, and when it detonates it has enough power to rip through both the outer hull and the several inches thick inner hull of a submarine. The casing around the torpedo is relatively thin and the explosion leaves no recognisable trace of the torpedo itself. Most of it is vapourised in an instant as the warhead explodes, and what small metal fragments remain are scattered over a wide area and are almost impossible to locate. However, although it was badly damaged and bent out of shape, this was very clearly the rear end of the Spearfish torpedo.

The Royal Navy officer on board the mothership had stood at the back of the control room until now, not wanting to interfere with the ROV operator crew, but he now stepped forward and the crew made space for him to stand next to the monitor and lean in for a closer look.

'Bloody hell,' he whispered slowly, his face betraying the incredulity he was experiencing as he studied the image on the monitor. 'What on earth happened here?'

* * *

The next day at around 10 am, Andrew arrived at HMNB Clyde in Faslane, Scotland. He had been flown from RAF Northolt in London to Glasgow Airport by the small Honda HA-420 jet. It was a light business jet that was used to transport military VIPs, and at just 13 metres in length with a wingspan of 12 metres, it could carry four passengers. Today, however, only Andrew and the two pilots had been onboard. The jet had a sleek design, with two powerful engines mounted at the rear of the fuselage and swept-up winglets at the tips of the wings. With a range of just under 3000 kilometres, Andrew and Fiona had used it once before in their search for the tomb of Alexander the Great.

Today was a very different type of mission. Colonel Strickland had arranged for Andrew to meet with the commander of HMNB Clyde, Commodore Harrington. Andrew wanted a first-hand account of what had happened during the few hours where the USS Tennessee had been at HMNB Clyde, and the commodore had agreed to meet him. He was as keen as anyone to discover whether something might have happened at his base during the submarine's brief visit.

Andrew made his way out through the airport's arrivals terminal and jumped in the backseat of the waiting car which would take him to Faslane. As the driver took him north along the M8 and onto the huge curved bridge over the River Clyde, Andrew reflected on what he had been reading on the plane during the 50 minutes it had taken to fly the roughly 550 kilometres from London to Glasgow.

He had put together a file on historical peace-time submarine losses in order to better familiarise himself with submarine operations and the different possible scenarios that he and Captain Lynch might need to consider during their investigation.

The last time the Royal Navy had lost a submarine was in April 1951 when the HMS Affray went down in the English Channel about ten kilometres off the French coast. All 75 crew members on board perished. Disturbingly, the exact cause of the accident has never been conclusively determined, but it is thought that perhaps the snort mast, through which a submarine takes in fresh air whilst submerged just below the surface, either broke off or that its so-called float valve got stuck in the open position as the vessel dived. This would have caused water to rush in, and because the crew was comprised of relatively inexperienced sailors, one theory posits that they were unable to resolve the issue quickly enough to avoid the submarine taking on so much water that even blowing the ballast tanks was not enough to bring it to the surface.

Another well-known accident was that of the USS Thresher which was a U.S. Navy nuclear-powered attack submarine that sank in April 1963. Having been built with the sole purpose of hunting down and destroying Soviet submarines, the USS Thresher was the first of that class of submarines and was performing a deep-dive test to 400 metres some 350 kilometres or 220 miles east of Cape Cod, Massachusetts. It is thought that either a leak causing a short-circuit or a fault in the electronic reactor control system led to a reactor shut-down, which in turn caused the submarine to lose propulsion. There was then an attempt to blow the ballast tanks, but the high pressure in the pipes between the compressed air tanks and the ballast tanks at that depth caused the pipes to freeze and end up blocked after just a few seconds thus preventing the ballast tanks from being filled with air and stopping the submarine from surfacing. Several audio signatures of these individual events were picked up by the SOSUS network.

At that point, the USS Thresher began sliding backwards deeper and deeper into the ocean for several minutes, until the sound of the vessel's implosion was recorded by SOSUS at a depth of around 730 metres, which was roughly 120 metres deeper than its predicted hull crush depth of 610 metres. It is estimated that because of the extreme pressures at that depth, the implosion took only 0.1 seconds, which meant that the 129 crew and shipyard personnel on board at the time would not have time to register the event happening. The USS Thresher was found on the seabed at a depth of around 2,600 metres, more than four times deeper than its expected hull crush depth. It had broken into five major pieces which were spread out over a large area of more than thirty acres.

Just five years later in 1968, the U.S. Navy lost another nuclear-powered attack submarine, this time the USS Scorpion. The vessel had experienced a run of maintenance issues and chronic problems with its hydraulics systems when it was ordered to observe a group of Soviet warships near the Canary Islands off the north-eastern coast of Africa. It never returned to its base in Norfolk, Virginia, and the U.S. Navy's official report lists the cause of its sinking as inconclusive.

However, there are several theories based on the audio evidence provided by SOSUS, including a so-called *hot-running torpedo*, which means that a torpedo already sitting inside a launch tube suddenly began running its motor or arming itself or both. This would lead to the captain firing the torpedo to prevent an internal explosion. One theory holds that the hot-running torpedo, after it had been launched, curved around and that its targeting system then somehow acquired the Scorpion itself, closed in on the cavitation noises from the submarine's propeller and detonated when it reached it.

Another theory states that a torpedo accidentally detonated while still inside its launch tube, dooming the boat to a watery grave. The Scorpion used Mk-46 torpedoes whose batteries at the time had a tendency to overheat, which in turn risked the warhead detonating.

Another theory suggests that the vessel could have suffered a build-up of hydrogen near the boat's batteries, which was something that occurred regularly. A spark could have caused a hydrogen gas explosion that could have led to the batteries themselves exploding. Some researchers have pointed to SOSUS recordings indicating the presence of two smaller explosions half a second apart followed sometime later by the sound of the hull imploding as evidence of this. The stricken submarine sank to its final resting place at a depth of about 3,000 metres, 740 kilometres southeast of the Azores and taking all of its 99 crew with it.

The last accident Andrew had looked into was a more recent and very well-publicised incident involving the Russian Navy's cruise missile-carrying submarine the Kursk, which was lost in August 2000. The Oscar II-class nuclear-powered submarine that was designed to attack U.S. Navy aircraft carriers, was taking part in a large exercise in the Barents Sea when an explosion ripped through the submarine, causing it to sink to the seabed roughly 100 metres below the surface. Just over two minutes later, a second and much larger explosion happened inside the vessel. The explosion was so powerful that it was picked up by seismographs as far away as Alaska on the other side of the Arctic Circle where it registered as an earthquake measuring 4.2 on the Richter scale.

Incredibly, even though the explosions were felt by other naval vessels in the area, the Russian Navy apparently did not realise that an accident had occurred for another six hours when the Kursk was supposed to have returned to port. It was sixteen hours before the sunken vessel was located.

For four days the Russian Navy tried and failed to attach rescue submarines to the damaged Kursk, during which time the Russian government refused repeated offers of international help from the United States, the UK and Norway. Finally, on day five they relented, and seven days after the explosions had occurred a team of Norwegian divers managed to open the hatch to the Kursk's so-called escape trunk, which is a small emergency compartment for the crew which functions similarly to an airlock. However, at that point, there were no survivors. The entire 118 crew had died in the incident.

As for the reasons for the explosions, it was eventually concluded that a faulty torpedo inside a launch tube had exploded, causing a fire that burned at around 2,700 degrees Celsius. This in turn caused the explosion of an estimated five to seven additional torpedoes.

Later that year it was revealed that 23 of the Kursk's crew had survived the two explosions and had been huddled up in a small compartment that had an escape hatch. Captain-lieutenant Dmitri Kolesnikov who was the head of a turbine unit wrote two notes while there. The first was written almost two hours after the second explosion and read:

"It's 13:15. All personnel from section six, seven, and eight have moved to section nine, 23 people are here. We feel bad, weakened by carbon dioxide. Pressure is increasing in the compartment. If we head for the surface, we won't survive the compression. We won't last more than a day."

Two hours later he wrote the second note:

"It's dark here to write, but I'll try by feel. It seems like there are no chances, 10–20%. Let's hope that at least someone will read this. Here's the list of personnel from the other sections, who are now in the ninth and will attempt to get out. Regards to everybody, no need to despair. Kolesnikov."

When the Norwegian divers reached the escape hatch, they found no survivors. It has been speculated that some of the crew could have been alive for as long as four days after the explosions.

The Kursk was eventually raised from the seabed by a Dutch marine salvage company and brought to a drydock where it was dissected and the remains of much of the deceased crew were found. The nuclear reactor was intact, but only seven of the Kursk's twenty-four torpedoes were recovered.

Andrew had found several other non-combat-related submarine losses recorded across the world over the past half-century or so, but none of them had involved the premature detonation of a torpedo immediately after launch. Once a torpedo is launched it usually takes a number of seconds, determined by the captain, before the torpedo arms itself. This is precisely to avoid a torpedo detonating near the launching submarine. Through all of his reading, Andrew had found no precedent for what seemed to have happened to the USS Tennessee.

Blowing his cheeks out, Andrew sat back in his seat as the car made its way through the checkpoint at the entrance to HMNB Clyde. He shook his head ruefully. Going over past submarine accidents had been harrowing reading, and driving into the naval base and being able to look down to Gare Loch and the submarine piers in Faslane Bay, he felt a new appreciation for his military colleagues who put their lives at risk as a matter of routine, even during peacetime, just simply by working onboard vessels in the submarine fleet. He knew that he would never be cut out for that sort of duty and that he was much more comfortable being able to feel *terra firma* under his feet at all times, but he had immense respect for the sailors who crewed the Royal Navy submarines.

The car came to a stop outside the main administration building, and Andrew walked up the steps to the front door and entered the lobby. Here a receptionist escorted him upstairs to a large corner office overlooking Gare Loch.

'Welcome Mr Sterling,' said Harrington as Andrew entered his office. The commodore was professional and courteous, but Andrew sensed the weight of the incident bearing down on him, and he looked like he had had very little sleep for several days.

'Thank you for coming,' he continued. 'I had a brief chat with Colonel Strickland earlier. He tells me you're one of his best people.'

'Thank you,' smiled Andrew. 'That's very nice of him. I just hope I can be of some help here. I am in the process of liaising with a U.S. Navy counterpart who is looking at this incident from the American perspective, so between the two of us we might be able to help discover what happened.'

'Very good,' said the commodore and gestured towards the sofa in his office. 'Let's sit. There's tea and coffee on the table there. Please help yourself.'

'So,' said Andrew as he sat down, pouring a cup of coffee. 'What can you tell me about the USS Tennessee's visit here. Was there anything unusual about the visit?'

'Not at all,' replied Harrington. 'Well. Nothing beyond the fact that this was the first time an SSBN docked here at Clyde to take a Spearfish onboard. But the visit itself was perfectly uneventful. I met the captain and his XO. We sat here in this room for about an hour chatting. Mainly small-talk. And then they departed for the NATO exercise.'

'What did you make of the two officers?' asked Andrew.

'Both perfectly nice,' said Harrington. 'Seemed very professional. Captain Vandenberg is your typical no-nonsense southern type, and the XO seemed straight as an arrow as well. Both good men, from what I saw.'

'Can I see the paperwork for the torpedo?' asked Andrew.

'Certainly,' replied Harrington. 'I thought you might want to see it, so I have it right here.'

He got up and fetched a folder from his desk, handing it to Andrew who then placed it on his lap and opened it.

After studying the documents, Andrew looked up.

'I presume you have gone over this again after the incident?'

'Yes,' replied Harrington. 'I don't see anything unusual about those documents. The only thing I would mention is a small irregularity during the transport of the Spearfish from the BAE Systems assembly plant in Portsmouth to Clyde.'

'Irregularity?' asked Andrew, looking at Harrington with an apprehensive expression. 'That doesn't sound good.'

'Well,' said Harrington. 'Ordinarily, I would not have thought anything of it, but because of the events of the past two days, I wanted to make sure I mention it to you. Apparently, the police escort vehicle developed some sort of engine trouble on the way here which meant that they had to make an unscheduled stop along the way. Because the transport itself was not allowed to stop at any point during the trip this resulted in the escort losing visual contact with the transport for about fifteen minutes. But they quickly caught up and continued as normal, and the driver of the transport did not report anything unusual in his debrief report. None of the two officers in the escort vehicle had reason to think that something untoward had happened either.'

'Alright,' said Andrew with a furrowed brow. 'I am going to have to look into this. We need to make sure we follow every possible lead.'

'I understand that there was a meeting with the Russian ambassador in London yesterday,' said Harrington.

'That is correct,' said Andrew. 'I was asked to attend it myself.'

'Oh,' said Harrington, looking curious. 'What did he say? Did you get the sense that they might have been involved?'

'I can't say I did,' replied Andrew. 'In fact, quite the opposite. There is no doubt that they could feasibly have pulled something like this off, but the potential fallout both politically and possibly also militarily would be enormous for Russia. As much as they would love to get their hands on an Ohio-class missile submarine, the economic consequences would be very severe and the risk of rapid escalation would be extremely high. The Russians may behave like cowboys from time to time, but they are not stupid. Anyway, Ambassador Nikolayev produced satellite images right there and then which he said proved that the only submarine in their fleet which could have pulled off a boarding operation like that was sitting in a dry-dock in Severomorsk in Murmansk Oblast. We're still working with the Americans to confirm this.'

'Well, that was my own sense of it as well,' said Harrington, seemingly relieved. 'I have spent most of my career with the Royal Navy's nuclear deterrent, so I know better than anyone what utter devastation our weapons and those of the Russian Federation can cause. So, you will have to excuse me if I seem pleased with the absence of Russian involvement in this. As terrible as it sounds, we have to hope that the loss of the USS Tennessee was caused by some sort of accident or malfunction. That would be the least bad outcome by far.'

At that moment the commodore's phone rang and he picked it up. After a brief exchange with the person at the other end, he glanced toward his desk with a concerned look on his face. Then he said goodbye and put the phone down.

'Please excuse me,' he said. 'I have just been told that there is a preliminary report from the team operating the Norwegian ROV in the North Atlantic near the location of the explosion. I need to look at an email briefly.'

While Andrew waited, Harrington walked to his office chair, sat down behind his desk and logged into his email application. He opened an attachment and read through it. As he did so, Andrew studied his face discreetly and it was obvious that the commodore was unsettled by what he read. After a couple of minutes, he leaned back in his chair, still staring at the screen.

'Everything alright?' asked Andrew.

Harrington hesitated, but then sat up again looking at Andrew.

'Since you have full security clearance on all of this,' he said, 'I guess I can tell you what this is about. I have just read the synopsis of the preliminary report, and it seems that they have found remnants of the Spearfish torpedo.'

'Remnants?' frowned Andrew. 'Forgive me if I sound naïve, but there shouldn't be remnants of an exploded torpedo, should there?'

'That's exactly right,' said Harrington, looking concerned. 'The Spearfish carries a warhead that is more than powerful enough to practically vaporise the torpedo itself. There should be virtually no trace of it. But they have found almost the entire tail section.'

'Could the warhead have malfunctioned?' asked Andrew perplexed.

'It is possible,' replied Harrington, 'But if that had been the case, then it would have been unlikely to detonate at all. The explosion is inherently a chain reaction, so if the detonation happened then the entire warhead would have exploded. There is no such thing as a partial torpedo warhead detonation.'

'That does sound odd,' said Andrew. 'Any idea what this could mean?'

Harrington took a deep breath and sighed. 'I hate to say this, but I am concerned that perhaps the torpedo may have been tampered with. I don't know how that could have happened but that would explain what the ROV found.'

'I am going to ask BAE Systems to provide us with any tracking data they have from the transport,' said Andrew. 'That might throw some light on this whole thing. If the torpedo was out of sight of the escort vehicle for ten or fifteen minutes, then that might have been enough time for someone to sabotage it, although I am not entirely sure how that might have happened if it was being driven along the motorway at 60 miles per hour at the time.'

'You'll have to excuse me,' said Harrington hurriedly. 'I need to read this entire report without delay, and then I suspect I will be in meetings for the rest of the day. Can I forward it to you? You might want to read it on the way back to London.'

'That would be great,' nodded Andrew. 'Please do.'

Ten minutes later Andrew was back in the car taking him towards Glasgow Airport. Another hour later he was in the comfortable passenger seat looking out over the Firth of Clyde with its large central island called the Isle of Arran. It was a beautiful sight. The scenery was picturesque and impressive but it also had a rough and slightly barren quality to it, and he struggled to see many villages anywhere. This part of the country was clearly not for most people, perhaps also because of the generally cold, wet and windy weather.

An hour later the Honda HA-420 landed back at RAF Northolt, and Andrew went straight from there to the SAS building at Sheldrake Place where he walked into his office, sat down behind his desk and immediately picked up the phone.

Seven

Fiona was in a taxi in central Rome, known since ancient times as the Eternal City. She had arrived in Italy just a couple of hours earlier and had briefly swung by her pre-booked hotel to drop her luggage and then have a quick shower and a change of clothes.

She had visited Rome twice before, but she had forgotten how busy and noisy it was here. There were cars and mopeds everywhere, and the streets were full of throngs of people, most of them seemingly tourists out to see the sights or locals parading along the busy shopping streets to show off their latest fashion purchases.

Now that she was here, she still had trouble believing that she had accepted Peter Dietrich's offer to work for him. But by the time he had sent her his proposal, including the generous weekly retainer and the prospective bonus should she be able to find Caesar's Corona Civica, however unlikely, she had decided to take the plunge. She had a lot of holidays saved up at the British Museum, and she eventually decided that she had nothing to lose and actually quite a lot to gain. Just as long as she did not tell anyone what she was doing. If she was going to get involved in this effort, she wasn't going to shout it from the rooftops. Firstly, doing a private job for the British Museum's largest donor was just inherently controversial, although not strictly against the terms of her employment. Secondly, the notion of actually attempting to find something as monumental as Julius Caesar's crown might make people think that she had lost her marbles. But she had proven herself an extremely capable researcher and archaeologist in the past albeit as part of a team with Andrew, but she felt confident that maybe, just maybe, she might actually be able to pull this off. And as the saying goes. Nothing ventured, nothing gained.

At one point her taxi had seemed to become permanently stuck in traffic along a narrow street, so she decided to get out and walk the rest of the way to her destination. She had paid the driver, who looked quite annoyed and grumbled something unintelligible, and then she had got out of the car and begun walking.

As she did so, she once again thought about her encounter with Dietrich who she had to admit she had been quite impressed with. Not only because of his charm and affable nature but also because of the way in which he had elected to use some of his immense wealth to support cultural treasures such as the British Museum and other museums like it.

However, the night before, she had suddenly realised how little she really knew about him. She had of course seen his name often in the news since he was a very high-profile tech entrepreneur whose input was often sought from various news outlets. But as far as who he really was as a man, Fiona had no idea beyond her brief meeting with him in London. She had then spent the next several hours finding out as much as she could about him, and it had turned out to be a complex picture of a man whose character was difficult to pin down.

He had been born in Austria to parents who had both worked in middle-management positions in the government bureaucracy. A bright but shy boy, he had been sent to boarding school first in Switzerland and then in the UK. He earned a degree in mathematics and economics from Cambridge University where his peers seemed to remember him only for how unremarkable he was. What was not widely known or publicised amongst the fawning fintech journalists and the general public, was that during this time, Dietrich also took a history degree focusing on the Roman empire. He wrote his thesis on Julius Caesar and the way he, deliberately or not, created the foundation for the concentration of power that eventually resulted in the transformation of an at least moderately democratic republic into an empire ruled by an omnipotent emperor. Fiona had also been unaware of this, but it did make sense in the context of Dietrich's generous donations to museums around the world.

Dietrich then took a job in a large accountancy firm in London and worked there for almost ten years, before quitting to strike out and work full-time on his fledgling new financial services start-up called Blaze. The business eventually launched its first and only product, which was a payment app for international money transfers between retail customers. With its transfer system built around an AI-enabled blockchain as well as its unrivalled low costs, it had been a roaring success, and within a couple of years, the business had floated on the New York stock exchange catapulting Dietrich to being among the twenty richest individuals in the world. From then on, the business had continued its meteoric rise, making it one of the most valuable companies in the world.

Having amassed almost unimaginable personal wealth, Dietrich had seemingly thrown himself into things that most billionaires would never dream of doing. He became a prolific and high-profile philanthropist, and he had set up several investment vehicles whose sole purpose was to generate returns that could then be ploughed into various charities around the world. He funded a well-known New York-based think tank called ARK Research, and an affiliated venture capital firm called the Dietrich Foundation. Both of these two entities had as their mission statement something which probably sounded quite lofty and even arrogant to most people. They were established in order to help ensure the long-term survival of the human species, in a way that would be sustainable for Earth's highly complex ecosystem.

This effort rested on three pillars. One was centred around conventional research efforts and funding related to climate change, sustainable energy production and general resource depletion as well as food and water security in the face of likely wars being fought over those scarce resources.

The second was focused on ensuring the existence of stable future governments across the world, especially in regions where the rule of law was precarious and natural resources were abundant since this combination of factors was inherently destabilising. This work invariably meant that Dietrich had cultivated close relations with the leaders of many countries, and several of them had supposedly become his personal friends.

The third pillar, which sat at the heart of ARK Research's work, was the one that Fiona found most intriguing, if nothing else then just because of the sheer scope and scale of the thinking behind it. It essentially revolved around the creation of a range of diverse insurance policies against complete societal break-down in the face of truly catastrophic, so-called 'extinction level events', such as meteor strikes of the magnitude which wiped out the dinosaurs 65 million years ago, which ultimately created the conditions for the rise of Homo Sapiens. A recent component of this effort was a program to establish a type of missile shield against large incoming meteorites, using nuclear missiles that would otherwise be decommissioned.

In addition, the venture capital arm of Dietrich's empire, the Dietrich Foundation, had invested heavily in technologies that could enable the seeds of humanity to be transferred to other planets, primarily Mars. In this way, if something cataclysmic happened to Earth, humanity would at least still have a chance somewhere else. The foundation had also poured vast resources into research and practical measures to ensure the survival of humanity on Earth, should such a catastrophic event happen before the ability to transfer life to other worlds had been fully developed.

In practical terms, this effort involved amongst many other things investment in technologies that would allow small isolated and self-sustained pockets of humanity to survive for extended periods of time whilst waiting for conditions on the planet to return to survivable conditions after an event such as a gamma-ray burst, a catastrophic meteor impact or even a full-scale nuclear war.

It also involved the creation of multiple so-called seed banks, which were secure locations deep underground in secret locations around the world. Here, huge stores of seeds from every known plant could be kept as a sort of backup plan for humanity. These efforts were similar to already existing government-run efforts such as a well-known complex located inside a mountain on the Norwegian island of Svalbard in the Arctic Ocean.

Dietrich's efforts, however, were much larger in scope since they were comprised of multiple such seed banks spread out across the planet, and rumour had it that they also contained extensive gene banks set up in order to guard against a scenario where the Earth suddenly found itself in the path of a so-called gamma-ray burst, which at least in theory, had the potential to seriously damage the genome in every living organism on Earth. The so-called *Ordovician–Silurian* extinction event around 450 million years ago is thought to have been caused by one such colossal burst of electromagnetic waves tearing into Earth's atmosphere and profoundly affecting its ecology.

The third pillar also included a significant program to protect and preserve human culture in its many forms. It was from this Dietrich-funded program that the donations to the British Museum had come.

The Dietrich Foundation did not release particularly granular details of its finances, but it was clear to Fiona that over the past five years it had spent several billion dollars on a huge range of programs across the world, and as a result, Dietrich had built up an almost cult-like status amongst parts of the chattering classes on the internet and in the general media.

In public, Dietrich had been cagey about his personal political or religious views, except to say that his sympathies tended to lie with libertarian positions and that he believed that governments should play as small a role in society as feasibly possible. Every few years various politically motivated writers, using sources close to him, would attempt to demonstrate his alignment with either far-left or far-right agendas, but they were never particularly successful, and in response, Dietrich would often sue them into bankruptcy. So with regards to politics and most other things, Dietrich was his own man and somewhat of an enigma.

Along with attempting to understand her new benefactor, Fiona had spent the past day and a half pondering Dietrich's proposal and also researching the life of Julius Caesar. She had contemplated precisely how she would approach this task, and eventually she had settled on the simplest approach she could think of. Whereas most historians and scholars focused almost entirely on Caesar's military campaigns, politics and eventual assassination, she would follow any trail she could find relating to Caesar's descendants. However, she had first begun with a deep dive into Caesar's life.

Gaius Julius Caesar was born in the year 100 BCE, into a family of moderate political influence. His father, also called Gaius Julius Caesar, was the governor of the Roman province of Asia, which was comprised of present-day eastern Turkey, and which included the entire coastline facing west towards Greece. His mother Aurelia was from an influential Roman lineage and the family resided in Rome. Caesar's father died in 85 BCE when Caesar was 16, and this coincided with the civil war between his uncle Gaius Marius and Lucius Cornelius Sulla. Both men were army generals that began carrying out brutal purges of perceived opponents, and when Sulla won the civil war, Caesar and his young wife Cornelia decided to leave Rome and flee to Asia where he joined the army and served with distinction.

When Sulla died from illness in 78 BCE, Caesar decided that it was safe for him to return to Rome. Since his wealth had been confiscated by Sulla, he settled in a modest house in Rome and took up legal advocacy and prosecution of corruption and extortion. This was the beginning of his determined and carefully planned rise to prominence in Rome. He was elected to the position of *quaestor* in 69 BCE, which was a type of public investigator and prosecutor, and he served as such in the province of Hispania. It was during this time that Caesar saw a statue of Alexander the Great, who at 32 years of age had conquered the entire known world. Caesar himself was also 32 at that time, and it apparently served as an unpleasant shock to him, and cast into stark relief his own perceived lack of achievements.

Then in 65 BCE, he was elected *curule aedile* of Rome, which left him in charge of public buildings and festivals. In this role, he further cultivated his standing and prestige amongst the Romans by staging lavish games that won him even more attention and popular support. He was elected chief priest of the Roman state religion or *pontifex maximus* in 63 BCE, amidst an election campaign apparently riddled with bribery. In 60 BCE he was named *praetor* or army commander and magistrate of Hispania Ulterior, which is the western Iberian Peninsula. Here he won several military victories, earning him the title of *imperator*.

However, Caesar was deeply in debt, and so he decided to take the four legions under his command into Gaul to conquer those lands. He was hugely successful in this endeavour and even crossed over into Britain in 55 BCE. In 52 BCE Vercingetorix, who was a local king and chieftain, attempted to unite the tribes of Gaul against Caesar but was eventually vanquished, effectively leaving all of Gaul defeated and conquered.

Now in charge of a powerful army, Caesar marched on Rome and crossed the Rubicon River in January 49 BCE with his 13th Legion. This is where the expression 'crossing the Rubicon', taken to mean making an irrevocable decision, comes from. At that time, it was not permitted for any Roman military commander to do so, and so it was effectively an act of war against the Roman republic. This event ultimately triggered a seven-year-long destructive civil war between Caesar on one side and his political archrival from Rome, Pompey the Great, who had now fled Rome to gather his forces. During this civil war, Caesar left Italy under the control of his right-hand-man Marcus Antonius, also known as Mark Antony, who had been made a so-called Master of Horse, effectively making him second in command just below Caesar.

As the years went on and countless battles were fought between various legions of the two armies in locations spread out across almost the entire republic which now included territories around the whole of the Mediterranean, the Roman Senate began bestowing ever more titles and accolades on Caesar in tandem with his military victories and ultimate defeat of Pompey. When he returned to Rome in triumph in September 45 BCE, he filed his will naming his grandnephew and adopted son Octavian as his heir, and leaving to the 19-year-old his vast estate, all his property and his name.

Caesar then began a huge reform program which included establishing a new constitution. Its purpose was to suppress all armed resistance and to create a strong central government for the Roman Republic under his control. To achieve this, he held exorbitantly expensive games and reduced taxes to woo the masses, and he also instituted several measures to weaken the other Roman political institutions. Coins were minted with his image, his statue was placed next to those of former kings, he was granted a special golden chair in the Senate, was given leave to wear triumphal dress whenever he pleased, and a special cult was established around his person with Mark Antony as the high-priest. He also diluted the power of the Roman senate by significantly increasing the number of members, and it, in turn, bestowed on him the title, *pater patriae*, or Father of the Fatherland. In early 44 BCE, the Senate had also decided that Caesar would receive an official *apotheosis*, or elevation to divine status to become the state god of Rome and given the name *Divus Iulius*. During the same senate session, a new priestly office was also established, and Mark Antony was designated as the first *flamen Divi Iulii*, or high-priest of the cult of Caesar. It was also proclaimed that Caesar should be dictator for the next ten years.

Less than a year later, Julius Caesar had been assassinated on the floor of the Senate by 23 dagger-wielding senators who had conspired against him. Those politicians, mistakenly believing that they had saved Rome and the republic from a would-be dictator inadvertently ended up creating such chaos in the wake of Caesar's assassination that another civil war ensued. This in turn eventually resulted in the creation of the First Roman Empire and its first true emperor and dictator, Caesar's adopted son Octavian who eventually took on the name *Augustus* Caesar, the *revered one*.

Through the arc of his 66 years of life Julius Caesar had been a ruthless and opportunist politician, a master manipulator and unscrupulous populist, but also a brilliant general. Ultimately though, he had succumbed to his own worst impulses, seeking for himself absolute power in Rome whilst still attempting to maintain an air of enjoying wide public support. And in a very direct way, this had led to his assassination in 44 BCE.

Fiona had found the study of Caesar's life utterly fascinating, but that was not strictly why she had spent time researching him, and it was not the reason she had travelled to Rome. Her real aim had been to uncover what had happened to the possessions of the first Roman Emperor, Julius Caesar's adopted son Augustus Caesar, previously known as Octavian.

Being Julius Caesar's adopted son and the grandson of Caesar's sister Julia, Octavian had inherited all of Julius Caesar's possessions, and Fiona was speculating that this would almost certainly have included the golden Corona Civica which by then had become a symbol of Julius Caesar and his perceived omnipotence. This was especially the case inside the cult of Caesar which Octavian, now calling himself Augustus, had taken over after the defeat and death of Mark Antony alongside Cleopatra in Egypt during the year 30 BCE. Octavian cultivated the cult of Caesar and his own relation to the great man purely for political purposes, and he would have used the Corona Civica as a way of cementing that relation in the same way that the Macedonian general Ptolemy I had used possession of Alexander the Great's tomb as a way of legitimising his own rule in Egypt a couple of centuries earlier.

The simple but logical approach that Fiona had decided to take was to assume that exceptional artefacts such as the Corona Civica would have been kept safe in the possession of Augustus Caesar's descendants ever since his death in the year 14 CE, and that it would have remained in their keeping all the way up to the modern era. Made of gold it would not have degraded at all, and so if Fiona's theory was correct and it had indeed survived the two millennia since Augustus Caesar's death, then it was likely to still be in pristine condition. The question was - who possessed it and where could it be?

It was obvious that if it still existed, it would almost certainly be held by a private individual claiming lineage from Augustus Caesar since there is no record of it since Caesar's death and no museum has ever claimed to own it. Fiona had therefore spent time researching the genealogy of the Roman emperors, specifically the Julio-Claudian family tree, which began with Sextus Julius Caesar who was Julius Caesar's great-great-grandfather and a *praetor* in 208 BCE. The family tree was complicated, not least because there were several instances of adopted children inheriting the family name, as was the case with Augustus Caesar himself. The same was true for the adopted son of Augustus himself, Tiberius, who became emperor after his step-father. Tiberius's step-grandson Caligula then became emperor after him, after which it was the turn of Claudius who was a descendant of one of Augustus's sister's children. Claudius then had a son with Caligula's sister by the name Nero, and he was to become the last Roman emperor from the Julio-Claudian dynasty since he only had one child, a daughter who died four months after her birth.

The complexity of the Roman dynastic family trees had been enough to make Fiona's head spin, and she had eventually concluded that even if a particular Italian family had claimed to be directly descended from Julius Caesar, it would be next to impossible to prove it. And since Julius Caesar was burned on a funeral pyre in Rome immediately after his death, there was no hope of recovering any of his DNA for analysis. In other words, Fiona's initial approach to the problem had proven to be a dead-end.

This outcome had vexed Fiona, particularly because the fact that Rome's last emperor Nero had no obvious heir did not necessarily mean that he did not possess and pass on the Corona Civica. But there were no records of it being the case and so the trail had effectively gone cold at that point.

Fiona then had to pursue a different avenue, which she had to admit to having slightly less faith in. However, she decided that by far the most likely person to definitely have possessed the Corona Civica would have to be Augustus. As the sole heir to Julius Caesar himself, it was almost inconceivable that Augustus would not have been in possession of the relic immediately after Julius Caesar's death.

She then combined this assumption with a fact that most people did not realise about the first and probably most powerful Roman emperor. As powerful as emperor Augustus Caesar ended up becoming, he was actually quite a physically frail individual, and several times during his reign he was forced to remain in his main residence in Rome for weeks before recovering from bouts of illness. When in August 14 CE he became ill again whilst in the city of Nola some 200 kilometres south-east of Rome at the foot of Mount Vesuvius, it was assumed that he would recover once more. However, within days he was dead. Fiona, therefore, theorised that regardless of what had been written in his official will, Augustus might not have had the opportunity to hand over the Corona Civica to his adopted son Tiberius, since he would almost certainly have kept such an important cult relic somewhere secret and safe. Tiberius, who at the time was hundreds of miles away to the north in Germania might not even have known that the crown was in the possession of Augustus since the latter would most likely have been planning to hand this unique and potent artefact to him personally upon his return to Rome.

What this meant was that the Corona Civica would have remained in Augustus's residence in Rome while he was away on his trip to Nola from which he did not return alive. When he was eventually brought back to Rome, he was buried inside the massive raised Mausoleum of Augustus located on *Piazza Augusto Imperatore* just next to the Tiber River in central Rome.

His private residence *Domus Augusti* however, was located on Palatine Hill. This is the centremost of the seven hills on which the ancient city of Rome was supposedly founded in 753 BCE. This residence is still there today more than two thousand years later, and it can be viewed in the large and sprawling Palatino area of Rome which is now an open-air museum containing numerous excavated Roman buildings, temples and squares. Next to it on its eastern side is the Colosseum.

The Domus Augusti sits at the northwest corner of the Palatino, and this was where Fiona had gone. She was not expecting to simply walk in there and find the crown, but she hoped that it might inspire her as to where to look next, and what possible avenues to pursue.

The Domus Augusti is surprisingly modest for the residence of one of the most powerful men in human history, and much less grand than the palaces of many of Augustus's contemporaries. As Fiona entered the hallway of the ancient residence, she and the other tourists were guided around to the left to file through the building's different rooms. The rooms themselves were empty, but the floors were covered by intricate mosaics, and the walls were full of remarkably well-preserved frescos. Some were of Roman landmarks, another showed the twins Romulus and Remus, the former of which is regarded in mythology as the founder of the ancient city.

One of the frescos in particular caught Fiona's eye. It showed a gathering of what looked like senators with long white togas worn over the *angusticlavia*, which was a tunic with two purple stripes. At the centre of the gathering stood a young man with a confident look on his face. He was wearing the easily recognisable *lorica segmentate*, which was a cuirass with movable metal segments worn by the Roman Legion's soldiers. On his head was a laurel wreath made of bay leaves, but in his right hand, which was held low by his side, was a similar-looking but gilded wreath. The Corona Civica.

The young man at the centre of the gathering was clearly Octavian before he changed his name to Augustus Caesar, and the gathering of senators indicated that this was meant to depict the time of Augustus's ascension to the throne with the backing of the senate. One of the senators, standing behind and to the right of Octavian, rested his hand on the young emperor's shoulder.

The symbolism of the fresco was clear. The young Octavian was about to replace his laurel wreath with the golden Corona Civica, thereby becoming Emperor Augustus Caesar, but the senators were depicted as being instrumental to his rise. One senator in particular, seemed to have asserted his power over the young man, having placed his hand on the youth's shoulder.

On the plaque mounted on a stand in front of the wall, Fiona could read the names of the senators. The most senior of them, whose hand was resting on the new emperor's shoulder, was called Marcus Cornelius Sertorius. Fiona had come across his name before since he was one of the founding members of a Roman banking clan who over the next many centuries eventually evolved into the Medici family, famous for being one of the first and most powerful banking families in Europe.

Whereas almost everyone else who had looked at that fresco saw money and political influence manifesting themselves in a generally corrupt ancient Rome, Fiona saw something else. Her suspicions were further aroused when upon researching the residence later in the day, she learned that the Domus Augustus had been extensively excavated, restored and then opened to the general public just a handful of years earlier and that the descendants of the Medici dynasty had funded almost the entire effort, supposedly for the benefit of the Italian people, and asking nothing in return.

Although none of this was by any means conclusive, all of it taken together was too suspicious to ignore, so she had reported back to Dietrich about her findings. He, in turn, had come back to her just a few hours later with what he said was hard evidence that there had been so-called 'irregularities' in the handling of artefacts uncovered from the Domus Augustus excavation. These related to various missing objects, but the authorities had now supposedly recovered them all. Dietrich had laughed at this notion and had been entirely dismissive of this claim, citing extensive corruption in Italian society as a whole. He had insisted that he could have the entire metropolitan police force in Rome, the *Carabinieri*, on his payroll by the next day, should he wish it so. He had then told Fiona to hang tight until he could come up with a plan for what to do.

Deciding to enjoy her time in Rome, Fiona had checked into a hotel on the other side of the Colosseum and had then taken the opportunity to spend the rest of the afternoon and evening sightseeing, people-watching and having dinner at a cosy local restaurant whilst awaiting Dietrich's plan. She could not have imagined how swiftly things were about to progress from there.

EIGHT

When Aaron finally got the keys to his motel room and closed the door behind him, he dropped his bag on the floor and sat down on the end of the bed. Lying back and looking up at the grimy ceiling that looked like it had absorbed several decades of cigarette smoke from thousands of guests, he began to regret having come to Arizona at all. This had not gone the way he had expected. By now, he should have been in a café putting the finishing touches to a colourful article about the interviews he had done with an eccentric and paranoid prepper community who had dug out a long-abandoned missile silo, rigged up make-shift sleeping quarters and piled a few hundred kilos of food and survival supplies into the former missile silo. And the centre-piece was meant to have been the revelation of some Hollywood actor who had bought into the deranged fever-dream.

But that was most certainly not what he had found. The luxury residence in the old silo complex was one thing, but the giant underground facility, which looked like it could house at least one hundred people, maybe more, had blown him away. If it had not been for the secret entrance and the strange Nazi-like military uniforms, he might just have been able to write this whole place off as some sort of commercial venture catering to the more well-heeled part of the prepper fringe, but the sheer scale of the facility, which dwarfed the original Titan II launch complex, made it seem anything but benign. There was something really 'off' about the whole thing, and despite a creeping sense of anxiety, Aaron was also feeling himself becoming determined to find out what was really going on.

He flipped open his laptop and inserted the memory stick he had used to copy over files from the PC in the underground facility. Within a couple of seconds, he was looking at a list of what appeared to be building plans. They were highly detailed and seemed to cover the entire facility showing every section and every room. As he had been able to glean from his brief and hurried visit there, the facility was centred around a large circular atrium with powerful artificial lighting, that was clearly meant to simulate daylight. The atrium in turn connected to a large number of living quarters which appeared to be of identical design, and able to accommodate as many as 150 people combined. There were also recreational facilities, offices, what appeared to be a market area, and at the back of the facility behind the engineering and utility space where he stole the files, were what appeared to be five large elongated spaces for growing produce. All in all, the facility seemed to contain significant amounts of space dedicated to self-sufficiency. But what was it all for? Was this prepper community really going to be living down there? Was it part of an experiment to see if a self-sustained community like that could survive for extended periods of time, similar to the now long-dead and discredited Biosphere 2 project which had also been in Arizona?

All of those things were possibilities, yet Aaron could not bring himself to believe that it was that simple. The resources that had been poured into this facility were enormous, and he struggled to understand how a project of this size could have been set in motion without some sort of publicity. Most importantly though, the presence of people in military uniforms including the squad that had chased him off the property was enough for him to dismiss out of hand that this was simply a commercial venture or some sort of benign scientific experiment.

Nine hours later, having been completely absorbed by what he had found and where it had led him, Aaron discovered that it was now morning and the sun had come up outside, but he did not feel sleepy at all. In fact, he felt anything but tired and so he went for a quick pancake and maple syrup breakfast at a diner across the street. By the time he got back to his motel room, he had received a reply to an email he has sent in the middle of the night.

Aaron had contacted a colleague who in turn had been in touch with an anonymous source inside the Delaware Department of State's Division of Corporations. The source, who had apparently provided what was meant to be secret information about Delaware registered companies in a guerrilla effort to try to combat the massive levels of illegality that the state facilitated, had assisted Bad Apples in the past by helping to expose a huge tax-evasion scheme a couple of years earlier. The exposé had brought down several prominent Delaware registered real estate companies and put three of their executives behind bars.

This source had now dug up the non-public files on Three Points Realty Holdings LLC and had established that it was a wholly-owned subsidiary of something called ARK Development Holdings, which was registered in New York. From there it had been relatively straightforward to discover that ARK Development Holdings itself was a subsidiary of something called the Dietrich Foundation, which Aaron had never heard about.

He spent the next few hours researching the foundation and found himself perplexed by what he had discovered. By most accounts, the foundation along with its founder and CEO Peter Dietrich was a force for good with numerous charities dedicated to good causes in the US and elsewhere. As always, however, there were the odd negative reports from what appeared to be disgruntled former employees who made Dietrich out to be a power-hungry fraud with far-right tendencies, but the sources rarely seemed reliable and several of them had been sued into bankruptcy by civil defamation lawsuits mounted by Peter Dietrich personally.

However, what really made Aaron sit up and pay attention was the pattern that emerged when looking at all the different activities that the Dietrich

Foundation was involved in. Individually they appeared to be a diverse set of initiatives to help mankind in a multitude of different ways, but taken together they were clearly all concerned either directly or indirectly with one single thing. The possible end of humanity.

Granted, everything that the Dietrich Foundation did appeared to focus on the prevention of such an end, and on the continuation of the human race in the face of catastrophic events. But when Aaron considered all of those efforts in the context of what he had witnessed out in the Sonoran Desert, he simply could not shake the feeling that this was somehow much more sinister than it appeared.

Slumping back onto the bed in his motel room and realising that he had reached the end of the road as far as possible investigative efforts were concerned, he decided that there was only one thing left for him to do which was to try to find a way to confront Peter Dietrich personally, preferably in a public setting where he would not be able to simply ignore what Aaron had found. After searching for future events where Dietrich was meant to speak, Aaron decided on a fintech conference in Seattle which was just two days away.

He quickly packed up his things, went to the motel reception to pay the bill and then began making his way towards the airport where he would catch a flight back to New York. On the way he wrote a brief email to an assistant in the Bad Apples office, asking her to book him a flight from New York to Seattle and to also book him a slot at the fintech conference.

All or nothing, thought Aaron to himself as he walked briskly towards his assigned gate inside Tucson International Airport. *I will either win a Pulitzer Prize for this, or I will end up living under the Brooklyn Bridge in a couple of weeks.*

★   ★   ★

Captain Lynch was in his office at the American embassy on Nine Elms Lane in London. The twelve-storey cube-shaped structure was surrounded by tall buildings on three sides, all of them set back by at least fifty metres. Lynch's office was on the sixth floor facing north, and it had a clear view out across the Thames River which flows east less than a hundred metres from the embassy.

He had just come off a call with the Pentagon who were keen to be briefed on the joint investigation into the disappearance of the USS Tennessee, not least because their officials would need to then brief the president and the Joint Chiefs later that afternoon.

Earlier in the day, Lynch had spent a couple of hours listening to several different underwater recordings from DRAPES around the time of the explosion, and he was about to pick up the phone to update Andrew when it rang.

'Captain Lynch,' he said

'Jack, it's Andrew.'

'Hello Andy,' said Lynch. 'I was just about to give you a call. What's up?'

'I just got back from Scotland,' replied Andrew. 'I went to our submarine base Clyde in Faslane and had a chat with the base commander, Commodore Harrington.'

'Alright,' said Lynch. 'What did he say about the torp?'

'I will get to that in a minute,' replied Andrew. 'First, let me tell you about something he showed me. It is footage from the ROV. I am forwarding it to you right now and I think I can safely say that this changes everything.'

'Well, what is it?' asked Lynch, sitting up in his chair. 'Oh. Wait. It just came into my inbox. Let me open it.'

Lynch clicked on it and the recording from Benthic Surveyor began playing on his computer monitor.

'Skip ahead to 1 hour and 12 minutes,' said Andrew.

Lynch did as he asked and watched as the monitor showed him the view from the ROV as it glided slowly over the grey silty seabed on the Anton Dohrn Seamount.

'Alright,' said Lynch. 'I am watching it now. What am I looking for?'

'Give it a few seconds,' said Andrew, who was simultaneously playing the same video file on his own PC in his office at Sheldrake Place.

'What the f...' said Lynch suddenly and gawped at the monitor. 'Is this for real? Has this footage been authenticated?'

'Absolutely,' said Andrew. 'The Norwegians gave it to our observer on the mothership immediately, and he has forwarded it to us on a secure channel. I am sure our naval intelligence service is sending it to your colleagues in the ONI as we speak.'

Andrew was referring to the Office of Naval Intelligence which is the U.S. Navy's intelligence agency headquartered in Suitland, Maryland.

Lynch leaned in towards his monitor to get a better look. As the footage showed the ROV panning slowly over the wreckage site and zooming in slightly, he paused the video.

'That's the damn torp!' he whispered, not quite able to believe what he was seeing.

'That's exactly right,' said Andrew.

'How the hell is that possible?' said Lynch, tilting his head slightly.

'That is what we have been asking ourselves as well,' replied Andrew. 'Harrington was adamant that if a Spearfish torpedo explodes then there is virtually nothing left of it. The only thing we can think of at the moment is that the torpedo was tampered with and set to explode immediately after being launched from the USS Tennessee. The question is whether that tampering could have somehow affected the effective yield of the warhead. Harrington seemed convinced that something like that was not possible, but I think we have to keep an open mind.'

'If that is true, then you guys have a serious security breach somewhere,' said Lynch.

'We realise that,' said Andrew, sounding pained. 'I am in the middle of chasing down a lead Harrington gave me.'

'Really?' said Lynch. 'What about?'

'It involves what he called a small irregularity with regards to the modified Spearfish torpedo,' replied Andrew. 'At first, I didn't think too much of it, but now that I have seen this footage I am becoming convinced that something happened to the torpedo before it was loaded onto the Tennessee. Anyway, here's what he told me.'

Andrew then proceeded to relay what Harrington had mentioned about the 'irregularity' during the transport of the Spearfish torpedo from Portsmouth to Faslane.

'We are going to get in touch with BAE Systems and discuss this with them,' continued Andrew. 'If they have a security breach inside their torpedo transport operation then they are putting this nation's security at risk, so they should be more than willing to assist.'

'Well, I've got a couple of things from my end too,' said Lynch. 'Remember the satellite images Nikolayev's aide showed on his tablet?'

'Of course,' replied Andrew. 'Have you been able to corroborate them?'

'Yes, we have,' replied Lynch. 'The ONI has its own satellites in orbit and they pass over Murmansk on a very regular basis as you can imagine. The Losharik is definitely sitting in a drydock in Severomorsk just as Nikolayev said. And going back over the footage we can see that it has been there for at least a week. There is no way that sub could have been involved in whatever happened to the Tennessee. And frankly, that makes me doubt whether the Russians had anything to do with this at all.'

'I see,' replied Andrew, sounding pensive. 'I am inclined to agree with you. Unless the Russians were somehow involved in tampering with the Spearfish, which would be a reckless thing to do, then I think we can dismiss the idea of their involvement completely. I guess that leaves us with only two options. Either the torpedo malfunctioned or it was sabotaged, possibly as part of a terrorist plot.'

'Well, given this supposed irregularity during transport,' said Lynch. 'I am leaning towards the latter of the two. Anyway, Andy, there was something else that I wanted to talk to you about.'

'Sure,' said Andrew. 'What is it?'

'It is the audio recordings from the DRAPES network. I have been listening to them for the past couple of hours. There are obviously a lot of different recordings from different locations, but they all convey the same sequence of events. But something about it really bothered me, and I have finally worked out what it was.'

'Well, I have listened to it too,' said Andrew, 'and while I am no expert, I could clearly hear the torpedo tube opening, the launch of the torpedo and then the explosion. Did you hear something else or something more?'

'Actually,' replied Lynch. 'It's not so much about what I heard as it is about what I *didn't* hear.'

'What do you mean?' asked Andrew.

'The tube opens,' said Lynch, 'Then the torp launches. Then there is an explosion, and then there is just silence.'

'So?' asked Andrew.

'So, if the torpedo had damaged the Tennessee so severely that she sank or was disabled, then where is the audio of that? If somehow the torp malfunctioned, exploded and sank the boat, then why are there no sounds of the submarine breaking up or bulkheads buckling or air venting? If hull integrity was compromised then we should have heard tell-tale sounds of water rushing in and air escaping from the inner hull. But there is nothing there. It is as if someone just snapped their fingers and then the sub disappeared.'

'That's a good point,' said Andrew, having to admit that he had not thought of this before now. 'So, what does that mean then?'

'I don't know yet,' replied Lynch. 'I don't want to jump to conclusions, but I don't think the USS Tennessee took any damage. Don't ask me how that happened, but there would have been audio to indicate if it had happened, and there would have been lots of debris on the seabed. Anyway, just to make sure I wasn't going crazy over here, I had two acoustics specialists from the ONI examine the audio independently of each other, and they both came back with the same conclusion. It is as if the Tennessee was nowhere near the explosion when it happened. But that just can't be true. So, I am frankly at a bit of a loss here.'

'Well, thank you for updating me on that,' said Andrew. 'I will have a chat with my people and see if I can get a different perspective. But, you're right about this. The absence of noise after the explosion is highly suspicious. Anyway, I've got to run. I am meeting with Colonel Strickland shortly.'

'Alright, 'said Lynch. 'I think I need to make another call to the Pentagon, but let's keep in touch. I will let you know if anything else crops up on my end.'

'Great,' said Andrew. 'And thanks again for the heads-up on the audio analysis. Talk to you soon.'

★   ★   ★

When she woke up, Fiona took a few moments to remember where she was. She lifted her head sleepily off the soft white pillow and looked around, and then she remembered that the night before she had checked into the elegant five-star Palazzo Manfredi hotel on Via Labicana. It was just under two hundred metres from the Colosseum, and it had an unobscured view of the almost two-thousand-year-old amphitheatre in the heart of the eternal city. It was possibly one of the most expensive hotels in this part of the city, but since Dietrich was covering all of her expenses she was not about to scrimp on things like accommodation.

White sheer curtains wafted gently in the breeze that was coming in through a window she had left partly open during the night, and outside she could hear the sounds of the busy city coming to life. It looked like it was going to be another clear and sunny day, and Fiona felt a thrill as she thought about how close she was to all of those historic sites. They were all within walking distance of the hotel, and she already knew that she would have to spend more time exploring the city now that she was here.

She got out of bed and walked to the elegant white marble bathroom where she took a long warm shower whilst pondering where to go first and which route through the city to take. Then she went to the restaurant to have her breakfast. She asked for a table by the large windows overlooking the Colosseum itself and was about to plot a route through the city on her phone when it rang. It was Dietrich.

'Hello Peter,' she said.

'Fiona,' responded Dietrich affably. 'How are you?'

'Very well. Just about to have my breakfast,' said Fiona and brought the teacup up to her mouth.

'Very good,' said Dietrich. 'Anyway, you'll be glad to know that I have recovered the Corona Civica.'

Fiona almost choked on her tea.

'What!?' exclaimed Fiona, incredulously. 'Really?'

'You sound surprised?' said Dietrich.

'Well,' stammered Fiona. 'I guess I had just expected this to be significantly more difficult than it seems to have turned out to be.'

'Oh,' said Dietrich, and Fiona could hear that he was smiling as he said it. 'I am used to getting what I want.'

'Well. Yes. But how on earth did you do it?' asked Fiona. 'And are you sure it really is the genuine article?'

'Quite sure,' replied Dietrich. 'And as for how, then I suppose you could call it being creative.'

'That doesn't really explain a great deal,' replied Fiona. 'Are you going to tell me or not?'

'Alright,' said Dietrich. 'If you insist, I used a team of private investigators whose expertise and ingenuity I have benefitted from in the past. It turned out that the irregularities in the handling of the archaeological finds from Domus Augusti boiled down to simple commerce. You see, the lead archaeologist Pietro Rosa who uncovered the site in 1865, was a dedicated and talented man. But he was less adept at hiring suitable people for his excavations. One of his assistants who was secretly working for the Medici family, apparently discovered and spirited away several items from the site during 1866 and handed them to the wealthy banking clan. We didn't know any of this for a fact of course, but having investigated Rosa's assistants and observing what was at the time a marked change in the lifestyle of one of them, we simply speculated that this had happened. We then took our speculation to the Medici family and presented it as fact and promising to publicise the proof to back it up, even though of course we didn't have any. And through a prominent Italian legal firm we reminded them that such a revelation would do immense damage to their reputation and probably severely damage their business.'

'But…' attempted Fiona, but she was so taken aback by what Dietrich was saying that she couldn't think of a way to finish her sentence.

'Anyway,' continued Dietrich. 'I instructed our lawyers to deliver a proposal to the Medici family, remaining anonymous of course, essentially conveying to them that unless they allowed us to buy the Corona Civica at a reasonable price then we would go public with our findings. Unsurprisingly, the plan worked and they caved in immediately. And here we are!'

Dietrich had sounded almost proud of his little game of deception and did not seem at all bothered by the moral implications of what he had done.

'But that is blackmail,' said Fiona, sounding both surprised and horrified. 'How can you involve yourself in that sort of thing? I mean, first of all, it is just wrong. And secondly, what if it ever came to light that you had done this?'

'Was it wrong?' asked Dietrich casually. 'What I did was simply to recover a stolen item. And don't worry. A thief is unlikely to run to the police if something is stolen from him, and my investigative team and my lawyers would never reveal a link to me personally. All of this is arm's-length, if you take my meaning.'

'Still,' said Fiona, sounding somewhat dejected and disappointed. 'There are morals to consider, aren't there?'

'Fiona,' said Dietrich, sounding reasonable but ever so slightly condescending. 'If you think you can get to where I am without rubbing a few people up the wrong way, then I am afraid you're just a bit naïve. I really respect your honesty and decency of course, but this is just how the world works. If you want something then sometimes you have to bend the rules a bit.'

Fiona didn't know what to say, so she remained silent for a few moments staring out of the window towards the Colosseum.

'At any rate,' Dietrich finally said. 'It is all done now. Thanks to your insights I have the Corona Civica now, so all I need to do now is pay you the bonus I promised you. I am a man of my words.'

Fiona's facial expression hardened as she listened to Dietrich, and after a few moments of silence, she finally replied.

'No thanks,' she said frostily. 'I don't want your money. My decency is not for sale, and I don't think I want to be connected with this whole thing, even if you did take the crown from a thief. It's just not right.'

Clearly taken aback by her sudden change of tone, Dietrich attempted to push ahead.

'Fiona. Listen,' he said, sounding as if he was about to explain a few simple facts which would then make all the pieces fall into place and allow Fiona to see things the way he did. 'I don't want this to make things awkward between us. I had a very good feeling about you and I was planning something quite spectacular which I really wanted you to be a part of. Please come to New York and let's talk about it.'

'I thought you were still in London?' said Fiona frigidly.

'I am,' said Dietrich emphatically, 'But I will be heading back to my penthouse in the Big Apple shortly, and I would be thrilled if you would join me there. Or you could come with me in a couple of days when I am planning to attend a fintech conference in Seattle. It would be fun. Together we could examine the Corona Civica and perhaps make plans for how best to ensure that it finds its way into the British Museum. That is what you wanted, right?'

'No,' said Fiona evenly. 'Not like this.'

Dietrich did not respond, clearly not used to being surrounded by anything other than yes-men and sycophants, and also expecting Fiona to elaborate further. When she didn't, he sighed heavily.

'Alright,' he said, almost petulantly. 'Your loss. I guess I misread the situation. I don't think you are the type of person I am really looking to hire after all. Maybe you are just not cut out for the great things I have planned.'

'I can honestly say that I hope I am not,' replied Fiona steadfastly. 'I guess I was wrong about you too. Thanks for the trip to Rome. I would have liked to have been able to say that it was worth it, but I can't honestly do that now. Goodbye Peter.'

Fiona ended the call and tossed her phone onto the bed and sat down on the end of it with her head in her hands. This was not how she had hoped things would go. Within minutes Dietrich had gone from affable and friendly to almost child-like in his reaction to Fiona presenting what she firmly believed were perfectly reasonable objections to his methods. He really was nothing like how he had seemed when they first met in London.

She flopped back onto the bed and looked up at the detailed cornice on the ceiling, her eyes tracing the smooth curves and the intricate floral patterns.

I might be in over my head here. she thought. *I need to speak to Andrew. Maybe he can help me make sense of this whole thing.*

NINE

Once again, the Centurion had arrived in the Sanctum at the top of the high-rise building in downtown New York. Making his way up in the elevator to the 58th floor, he had been feeling the weight of the responsibility on his shoulders. What the Order was about to set in motion was going to be a watershed in human history, but he trusted in the Imperator to firmly grasp the wheel and steer them through the coming storm. Once it was all over there would be a chance to reshape the world and start anew. Something humanity sorely needed.

As he walked through the double doors to the throne room, the Centurion suddenly realised that this was likely to be the last time he would see this place. Walking towards the Imperator sitting on his elevated throne on the platform at the other end of the room, he allowed himself to glance at the marble columns, the richly decorated vaulted ceiling and the huge red banner behind the Imperator. As he did so he was filled with a renewed sense of pride and purpose, despite what they were about to do. Arriving at a designated spot just shy of the platform, the Centurion knelt in front of his master and bowed his head in deference.

'Imperator,' he said. 'I have finished my report on the members of the joint investigation team.'

'Sterling and Lynch,' said the Imperator.

'Yes,' replied Centurion. 'They are proceeding as we expected. There is a possibility they might be able to uncover what happened, but we should be able to throw a few spanners in the works and slow them down.'

'Good' said the Imperator. 'Let them continue for now. We have options if needed. Either way, they are not a serious threat. By the time they work out what is really going on, our plans will have come to fruition. But I am also preparing a unique pressure point on Sterling. One that is sure to make him back off if required.'

'I understand,' said the Centurion. 'Miss Keane.'

'Correct,' replied the Imperator. 'I will let you know if action needs to be taken.

The Centurion nodded.

'And the bomb?' asked the Imperator. 'Is it ready?'

'It has already been installed, Imperator. It has been placed at the rear, and it is more than powerful enough to ensure complete destruction. We have set it to detonate after three hours and ten minutes. There will be no survivors.'

'Very well,' said the Imperator leaning back slowly on his imposing throne. 'The crew of the jet will be remembered as heroes. Sometimes there is a price to be paid for great leaps forward.'

'Imperator,' said the Centurion reverently. 'May I ask about the weapon? Is the *Sword* secure?'

'It is,' replied the hooded figure looming over him, a hint of surprise at such a direct question in his voice. 'You need not worry. The Sword is on its way to its destination and readying itself to be unsheathed. Just a few more days now.'

'Praised be,' said the Centurion.

'And as for the final preparations?' asked the hooded figure. 'I am assuming you have had confirmation from all of the senior members of The Order?'

'Yes, Imperator,' replied the Centurion. 'The chosen senators are all making arrangements to depart for the Great Convergence.'

'And the citizens?'

'Almost all of the citizens are already there and busy finalising the facility and preparing for the arrival of the senators. The remaining ones are on their way as we speak.'

'Very well,' said the Imperator. 'Thank you for your service. Go now. Glory awaits.'

★ ★ ★

'Good afternoon, Andrew,' said Colonel Strickland.

He was standing at the window in his office wearing his immaculate uniform and looking south towards Hyde Park, unlit pipe in one hand and the other hand in his trouser pocket. He had given up smoking years ago but firmly maintained that clasping the pipe in his right hand and standing in that exact spot helped him to think.

'Good afternoon, sir,' said Andrew, closing the door behind him.

The two men sat down in Strickland's seating area which included two small brown leather chesterfield sofas and a mahogany coffee table.

'Right,' said Strickland, placing his pipe on the coffee table. 'First things first. I gather you had an interesting meeting with the Russian ambassador yesterday?'

'You could call it that, sir,' said Andrew. 'Not a particularly likeable chap, I must say. Still, I'd prefer his company to that of our foreign secretary.'

'Yes,' said Strickland somewhat ruefully. 'I have had Malcolm Squire on the phone. Apparently, he saw fit to use his valuable time calling me personally to complain about you.'

'Really?' said Andrew calmly. 'I would have hoped that he had better things to do.'

'So would I,' said Strickland. 'He was quite upset about the way you interrogated the ambassador. Actually, I think the word 'irate' is more accurate. He felt you had crossed the line.'

'I asked the ambassador some vital questions that needed answers,' said Andrew evenly. 'I gave him the opportunity to deny their involvement, which he then did. That was an important step in this investigation as long as we are prepared to take the Russians at their word.'

'I agree,' said Strickland. 'Don't worry about him, Andrew. I will fend off any incoming fire from that flank. You just continue doing what you are doing. In all likelihood, Squire will be gone in a couple of years anyway and you and I will still be here.'

'Thank you, sir. Have we had any news from the ROV team?' asked Andrew.

'The Norwegians are recovering what is left of the Spearfish as we speak,' replied Strickland, 'so we should have our people examining it within just a few hours. Hopefully, that will provide us with some answers. Still no sign of the USS Tennessee. The teams have widened the search area, but still no luck. DRAPES is picking up nothing. It's a damn mystery.'

'Well, perhaps not,' said Andrew, placing himself on the edge of the sofa and folding his hands in front of himself, Colonel Strickland now looking at him inquisitively.

'I spoke to Captain Lynch on the phone,' Andrew continued. 'And I also forwarded him the footage from the ROV. I think it is fair to say that he was taken aback by what he saw, as was I when I first watched it.'

'Yes, I had a brief look myself,' said Strickland. 'What do you make of it?'

'Well, this is the thing,' said Andrew. 'I've slept on it, and I think it is now virtually a certainty that the torpedo was sabotaged or somehow tampered with.'

'Yes, that much is obvious at this point,' said Strickland. 'But how and for what purpose? Whatever was done to it did not seem terribly effective, since it didn't seem to have damaged the USS Tennessee, at least not to such an extent as to create debris.'

'I know,' said Andrew. 'But there is more. Lynch mentioned something else. He and two experts from the American Office of Naval Intelligence have been analysing the audio from the DRAPES network, and they point out that there is nothing to suggest any damage having been inflicted on the Tennessee. No sounds of it breaking up, nothing indicating a compromised pressure hull and no sound of air escaping. Literally nothing.'

'That's an excellent point,' said Strickland. 'So, what do you make of this?'

'There can only be one explanation,' said Andrew. 'Commodore Harrington told me that it is inconceivable for a torpedo warhead to partially detonate, so since we heard it explode then the entire warhead would have detonated. However, the apparent lack of damage to the USS Tennessee must mean that the warhead must have been swapped out for a different one.'

'I am not sure I follow,' said Strickland.

'I don't have any evidence of this yet,' said Andrew, 'but I believe that the standard 300kg aluminised PBX high-explosive warhead that would have ripped open the Tennessee, was somehow replaced with something else, probably a shaped charge.'

'A shaped charge?' said Strickland perplexed.

'Yes,' replied Andrew. 'An explosive charge that directs almost all of the energy from the explosion in a certain direction, and in this case forward.'

'Yes, I know what it is. But what on earth for?' asked Strickland, looking utterly confused by the idea.

'To specifically ensure that the explosion did *not* damage the USS Tennessee,' said Andrew, pausing to let the idea sink in.

'You've lost me, old chap,' said Strickland, leaning back in his sofa. 'Who would tamper with a torpedo and perform an act of sabotage in a way that didn't actually damage the target?'

'Someone trying to take over the submarine, and then make it look like it had sunk due to a malfunctioning torpedo.'

Strickland looked at him for a couple of seconds whilst considering the idea.

'Are you talking about the Russians again?' he finally asked.

'Perhaps. Perhaps not,' said Andrew, arching his eyebrows and spreading out his hands. 'It is too early to say. But if I am right and the torpedo explosion was just a smokescreen, then it is perfectly conceivable that a mini-sub was able to latch on to the SDV-hatch used by the Seal teams. All it would then take would be for just one member of the 155-man crew to open the hatch from the inside, and from there it would be child's play for a well-trained special forces squad to take over the entire boat within minutes. U.S. submarines do carry small arms but they are stored in an arms locker, and I can guarantee you that if I was going to board a submarine like that, then my men would have secured that locker as the very first thing they did. And after that, it would have been all over.'

'Bloody hell,' sighed Strickland. 'Have you shared this theory with the Americans yet?'

'No sir,' said Andrew. 'I thought I would run it past you first. I will bring it up with Lynch later.'

Strickland was rubbing his chin and staring straight ahead.

'And here I was thinking I was the one with the shocking news,' he then said.

'What do you mean sir?' asked Andrew.

Strickland hesitated briefly and pressed his lips together for a moment whilst.

'Early this morning I received word that the driver of the transport vehicle that took the Spearfish to Faslane, had died.'

'What?' said Andrew, with a look of surprise and concern on his face. 'How?'

'Apparently, he fell down the stairs in his home,' said Strickland. 'The coroner says there was no indication of foul play.'

'I don't buy that for a second,' said Andrew resolutely. 'There is no way that was an accident. The timing of it is just too suspicious. Someone is tying up loose ends here. And I guess that means that somehow the driver was a part of whatever happened between Southampton and Faslane.'

'I fear you may be correct,' said Strickland. 'In light of the incident in the North Atlantic, BAE Systems has already carried out an extensive internal investigation, and there is no indication that anything untoward happened to the Spearfish before it left the assembly plant. In other words, if something was done to it, it happened at some point along the way.'

'The irregularity that Harrington mentioned,' said Andrew.

'Precisely,' said Strickland. 'Which is why I had BAE Systems hand over the truck's tracking data and it shows an unsanctioned ten-minute stop in an industrial area on the outskirts of the town of Banbury, which is right next to the M40 where the truck was heading north. This happened during the brief time period when the escort vehicle developed engine trouble.'

'That's definitely it,' said Andrew. 'Whatever happened to the Spearfish would have happened there. And clearly, the driver was in on the whole thing. Has he been investigated?'

'The police and GCHQ are doing that as we speak,' said Strickland. 'He had supposedly been a loyal employee for many years, but you just never know about these things. He may have had his reasons.'

'In the end, everyone does,' said Andrew pensively.

'Anyway,' said Strickland. 'A forensics team was sent to the warehouse where the truck was thought to have stopped, but the whole place had burned to the ground during the night just a few hours after the truck made its unscheduled stop there. There was nothing left to analyse.'

'Damn,' said Andrew. 'Someone is clearly busy covering their tracks.'

'Yes, something is very wrong about this whole thing,' said Strickland. 'I will let you know as soon as I hear anything more about the investigation into the driver. Hopefully, that will turn up a lead.'

'Very well, sir,' said Andrew and rose. 'I will be in my office if you need me.'

★ ★ ★

The next day just before noon, Aaron Purnell exited Seattle-Tacoma International Airport and made his way to the SeaTac light railway station which would take him north on Line 1 of the Sound Transit system to downtown Seattle. It took less than five minutes to walk to the station and almost immediately one of the trains arrived. He took a seat by the window on the left side of the carriage and waited for the train to depart. There were only a couple of other passengers there, and Aaron found himself inspecting them whilst trying to look like he was just glancing around the carriage. His experience of being chased out of an underground complex by a group of uniformed Nazi lookalikes in Tucson had made him feel strangely paranoid.

Ridiculous, he thought to himself. *No one knows who I am, or why I am here.*

Eventually, the train departed the station and began snaking its way north, then east and then north again through the suburbs of Seattle. The train stopped several times along the way, mainly taking on more passengers making their way to the city centre. On long stretches of the trip, the light railway was elevated to allow it to seamlessly make its way across the road network, and it afforded the passengers a nice view of the city as they approached the downtown area to the north where the high-rise buildings could be seen sitting in front of the 184-metre-tall Space Needle in Uptown.

Aaron had booked a room at the four-star Fairmont Olympic Hotel on University Street which was a lot more expensive than what he would usually go for, but since this is where the fintech conference was taking place he had decided to pony up. He had also bought a ticket for the conference itself, even though he suspected that most of what was to be discussed there would go over his head. Mainly, he just wanted to be able to loiter around the conference rooms without arousing suspicion, and the best way to do that would be to take on the role of a conference attendee staying in the hotel where the conference was going to take place.

As the train carriage came to a stop at the underground University Street light rail station on 3rd Avenue, Aaron got up from his seat and looked behind him to make sure he had not left anything behind. The man who had been sitting next to him up looked up from his phone but then re-focused his attention on his small screen.

Aaron took the south exit from the station and walked the short distance north along 3rd Avenue to the corner of University Street where he stopped. Glancing to his left and down the hill towards the downtown Seattle waterfront area with its many busy eateries and boat piers, he could see the ferry to the city of Bremerton slowly pull away and head out west across Elliott Bay. Then he walked the last block along University Street to the hotel which was surrounded by high-rise buildings, and as he stood there, he realised that the combination of glass and steel skyscrapers and water nearby made the area feel a lot like New York City, except that here, most of the downtown area was on a large hill overlooking the bay.

Not for the first time during the past week or so, Aaron was beginning to miss his apartment back in Brooklyn Heights. He had tried not to think too much about what he was up against and had reminded himself that his dogged efforts had borne fruit several times in the past. All he had to do was to keep going and forget that the man he was about to accost was one of the wealthiest people on the planet.

Checking in at the front desk, Aaron felt decidedly out of place in the swanky hotel with its polished marble floors, Greek columns and gold-trimmed cornicing. He declined the offer to have a porter carry his luggage to his room and walked to the elevators which would take him to the 7th floor. As he approached the elevator he spotted two men in dark suits standing by the main entrance. Even though they wore clothes similar to most other people in the hotel lobby, the way they carried themselves indicated that they were almost certainly part of some sort of security detail. Perhaps they were waiting for a high-profile conference attendee to arrive. Perhaps it was Dietrich himself.

As he waited for the elevator to arrive, Aaron glanced in their direction and he could have sworn that they were both looking at him. The elevator eventually arrived and he allowed a woman in a grey business suit to exit before stepping inside and then pressing the button to the 7th floor. Half expecting the two suited men to rush over and follow him inside the elevator, Aaron shook his head and looked at himself in the floor-to-ceiling mirror that covered the entire back wall of the elevator.

'Calm the fuck down!' he said sternly to himself. 'No one here cares about you. At least not yet.'

Then he turned back to face the doors, and a few seconds later there was a gentle chime as they slid open. Once inside the plush hotel room, he threw his bag on the bed and went straight for the minibar for a cold drink. He was tempted by the Jack Daniel's

Tennessee Honey & Lemonade but decided against having any alcohol. He needed to stay sharp.

After a quick shower and a change of clothes, he went back downstairs where the conference was about to start in the largest of the hotel's conference venues, which was a huge room about fifty metres long and twenty metres wide. On one side were large windows, and on the other above a long colonnade running from one end of the room to the other was a mezzanine level overlooking the room. More white marble and gold-trimmed Greek columns lined the circumference of the room, and from the ceiling hung three huge crystal chandeliers which looked like they weighed several hundred kilos each.

There were twelve rows of tables and seating on either side of a central aisle leading up to the stage where the panellists would be sitting, and each of them had room for six people. If the event was fully booked, there were going to be close to 150 people in there.

Aaron was early, and only a few dozen attendees were milling around the room fetching cups of coffee and engaging in small talk. He loitered near the cake stands whilst listening in on a few conversations, but they all revolved around financial terms and technologies that he had never heard about and had no interest in.

Against his own instinct, he decided to sit at a table next to the centre aisle near the front of the room. Ordinarily, he would have preferred to sit much further back and be a passive observer, but that was just not going to be possible today. Sitting down in the comfortable light mahogany French chair with its plush upholstery and its partially gilded wood frame, Aaron opened his laptop and created a new document that he intended to use for taking notes.

Over the next ten minutes, the conference room suddenly began to fill up and a grey-haired man in a dark grey suit walked swiftly up to the stage and began adjusting the chairs intended for the panel members. He then made sure the microphone mounted on the small podium that was standing off to one side of the platform was working. Then he disappeared again.

'Is this seat taken?' said a female voice next to him.

Aaron looked up and saw a young woman in a dark blue dress holding a laptop and a handbag. She was pointing at the seat next to him and further in from the aisle.

'Uh, no,' replied Aaron. 'I don't think so.'

'Great,' smiled the woman. 'I like to be near the front. Pretty exciting, huh?'

'Uhm, yeah,' said Aaron uncomfortably. 'I'm Paul. I am a journalist. Here to cover the event. Some high-profile people here today.'

'Oh cool,' said the woman. 'I'm Cindy. I am sitting in for my boss who couldn't make it today. Some sort of unscheduled trip to New Zealand for some reason. Anyway, I work at a venture capital firm here in Seattle, and we wanted to have someone here to listen to what Dietrich has to say.'

'So, is he the only reason you are here?' asked Aaron.

'Pretty much,' laughed the woman. 'The other panellists here today are lightweights, to be honest. But whenever Dietrich delivers a keynote speech you just never know what sort of insights he might be able to drop on his audience. He's just amazing. A true visionary.'

'Yeah, I guess he is,' replied Aaron.

At that moment two men in suits walked up the aisle and sat down on two of the three chairs placed there. Then the conference room, which was now almost full, spontaneously slipped into an expectant hush. The two men on the stage did not move but they simply sat there, clearly waiting for the proceedings to be kicked off by something or someone.

After less than a minute, one of the two dark-suited men Aaron had spotted in the hotel lobby earlier walked past him and placed himself next to the podium by one of the tall Greek columns. A few seconds later there was a quiet murmur behind him, and he noticed Cindy turning around to look.

'He's here,' she said excitedly.

Aaron calmly turned around to look down along the aisle, and there was the impeccably dressed Peter Dietrich striding briskly and confidently towards the stage with two more security guards in tow close behind him.

Without pausing, Dietrich mounted the stage, walked over behind the podium and grabbed the small microphone that was mounted on the podium and pulled it slightly towards himself.

'Ladies and gentlemen,' smiled Dietrich. 'Sorry to keep you waiting. I have asked that we dispense with the introductory note today. Most of you probably know who I am anyway.'

A wave of quiet knowing laughter rippled through the gathering as Dietrich smiled affably.

'Anyway,' continued Dietrich. 'I have been asked to give a keynote speech about blockchain technology in the context of fintech, and how we see it evolving in the future. This will involve a quick history of our international payment app Blaze, and then I will go on to talk about how we believe the international monetary system will develop over the next several decades as central banks reluctantly come to grips with blockchains. I will also briefly touch on what we think this will mean for the global currency trade.'

As Dietrich spoke, Aaron noticed Cindy typing away furiously on her laptop, and all around him, he could see other conference attendees doing the same thing, clearly keen not to miss a word of what this supposed oracle of the financial industry had to say.

Don't they know this whole thing is being recorded and will be online in an hour? thought Aaron to himself.

As he sat there listening to the great man espouse the benefits of his firm's technologies and how it would enable both wealth creation and democratisation of the money supply, Aaron found himself gradually being pulled in as the likeable Dietrich delivered one quotable phrase after another. Aaron didn't know what half the terms Dietrich was using actually meant, but he somehow still managed to make them sound attractive. *The consummate salesman,* thought Aaron.

After twenty minutes, the keynote address was over and the muffled sound of keys clacking on laptops gradually died out as Dietrich stood by the podium, took a sip of water and then turned to the two yet-to-be-named co-panellists on the stage.

'I hope I didn't exceed my allotted time,' smiled Dietrich, and turned back to the audience. 'I'll be happy to take a few questions now. Yes, you in the pink shirt.'

Dietrich picked out a young man in a light grey suit with a pink shirt and a silver tie, and as he stood up, one of the venue's staff hurried over to give him a handheld microphone so that people at the back would be able to hear both his question and Dietrich's answer.

'Mr. Dietrich,' beamed the young man. 'I'm a huge fan. Thank you for taking my question.'

Dietrich did not reply but simply nodded and smiled magnanimously. He was clearly used to this type of fawning by random people he had never met before.

'Can I ask?' continued the young man. 'If the central banks are losing control of the monetary system in the face of these new blockchain-based systems, who will be in charge of the money supply?'

'Me!' exclaimed Dietrich sarcastically, eliciting a wave of laughter in the audience. 'No, I am only joking, of course. The beauty about these systems is that they are self-regulating, so they don't need an overarching control mechanism like a government or a central bank in order to operate. This is one of the benefits of a system like this. Autonomy and a fintech ecosystem where survival of the fittest ensures an optimised payment system which in turn leads to a more efficient economy.'

The young man nodded his gratitude as the venue staffer took the microphone back and curried off to the side again. And so it continued for another fifteen minutes with various people in the audience asking a host of different questions relating to Dietrich's keynote address.

Eventually, having checked the time again and realising that it was rapidly running out, Aaron took a deep breath and steadied himself. Then he raised his hand and craned his neck to try to make eye contact with the microphone-wielding venue staffer.

'Yes,' said Dietrich, pointing at Aaron. 'You. The gentleman in the blue shirt.'

Aaron rose and waited a few seconds for the microphone to arrive. He then gripped it and cleared his throat nervously, accidentally doing too close to the microphone that it resulted in a throaty noise being bellowed out by the PA system.

'Sorry,' he said apologetically.

'That's alright, son,' smiled Dietrich. 'No need to apologise. What's your question?'

'Well, Mr. Dietrich,' began Aaron. 'As everyone here knows, you are a hugely successful entrepreneur. And I am guessing that most people know of your think tanks, which I believe inform much of what your investment vehicles do. And I think some people here are also aware of your prolific philanthropy, particularly with regards to efforts to ensure nothing less than the survival of humanity in the event of some known or unknown catastrophe.'

Dietrich nodded graciously at what he clearly took to be yet another obsequious round of shameless sycophancy.

'However,' continued Aaron. 'What I doubt anyone here knows, is that as we speak a real estate development company registered in Delaware but operating out of Dietrich Tower in New York, is in the process of constructing a huge underground facility at the site of a former missile silo complex in the Sonoran Desert in Arizona.'

The entire conference room instantly fell silent, and for the briefest of moments, a look of surprise and irritation seemed to flash across Dietrich's face as he stood at the podium listening to Aaron speak.

'This underground facility includes living quarters for several hundred people, supplies that could last them weeks if not months, and very extensive service facilities like self-contained water supplies and air scrubbers with filters to remove chemical, biological and nuclear material. Clearly, this facility has been built to deal with some sort of catastrophic event. Don't you think it is a bit strange that someone like you is financing a facility that appears to be preparing for the end of the world?'

Dietrich smiled as an uneasy murmur rippled through the conference room. He was looking straight at Aaron who could feel his knees trembling, and glancing briefly down to his side he could see a horrified Cindy looking up at him as if she thought he had both lost his mind and then proceeded to personally insult a god.

'Son,' said Dietrich calmly, his mouth smiling but his eyes cold as ice. 'I don't know where you are getting this information from, but I can assure you that it has nothing to do with me. There are plenty of these… What do you call them? Preppers, out there getting ready for the apocalypse or the coming of Christ or the end of the Mayan calendar, or whatever it is they believe in these days. But I can tell you that I am not involved in any of that stuff.'

The venue staffer, sensing the mounting awkwardness of the exchange, slowly approached Aaron from the side whilst clearly hoping that his presence would induce Aaron to stop asking questions and hand the microphone back. But Aaron ignored the staffer and pressed on.

'So, how do you explain that the Delaware registered company funding the facility is wholly owned by a subsidiary of the Dietrich Foundation?'

Dietrich shook his head ruefully as if showing sympathy with a poor soul who had completely misunderstood a set of complex information and was now making a fool of himself in front of a large audience.

'Again,' he said, sounding slightly weary this time. 'I really don't know anything about this. You must have been misinformed. I know everything that happens inside the Dietrich Foundation, and I have never heard about any of this.'

The staffer was now standing in front of Aaron reaching tentatively for the microphone, but Aaron gripped it tighter and took half a step back.

'Mr. Dietrich, my team and I have done extensive research on this,' said Aaron, hoping his mention of a non-existent team would buy him another few seconds of time. 'And we have found absolute proof that the money is coming from your foundation. Why are you denying that this has anything to do with you? What is the facility for?'

At that moment, Aaron sensed someone standing immediately behind and next to him in the aisle. He quickly glanced over his shoulder to see one of the dark-suited men he had noticed in the hotel lobby earlier that day.

'Alright,' sighed Dietrich, sounding as if he had run out of patience. 'I think that's enough. This young man is clearly not well. Could we move on now, please? We can't waste all day on this.'

Dietrich looked toward the grey-haired man standing off to his side who had been passed over for delivering an introduction. The man instantly began walking toward Aaron followed by another venue staffer, and at that moment the staffer in front of Aaron reached out and snatched the microphone from his hand. At the same time, Aaron felt a large hand firmly gripping his arm and another reaching over to place itself on his shoulder. The musclebound security guard then began pulling Aaron forcefully out from behind the table he had been sitting at. Cindy was looking up at him in disgust as if he had just vomited all over himself.

Aaron instinctively reached out to grab his laptop, and just managed to snatch it before he was manhandled down the aisle towards the exit.

'Hey! Why won't you answer my questions?' shouted Aaron as he was frog-marched along the aisle with shocked conference attendees looking on. 'What are you hiding?'

'I do apologise,' said Dietrich benignly as Aaron was finally hauled off towards the lobby. 'This sort of thing happens sometimes. I guess it is part of being a well-known figure the way I am. There seems to be an epidemic of mental illness in this country at the moment, especially things like paranoid schizophrenia. It is clearly something we all need to reflect on and try to help solve. I wish him all the best. Hopefully, he will get the help he needs.'

Aaron was hauled through the double doors and back out towards the lobby where he was shunted towards the doors to University Street by what was clearly one of Dietrich's personal security guards.

'Stop!' yelled Aaron. 'I am a guest at this hotel.'

That made the security guard back off, and as a concierge approached looking horrified, the security guard turned to walk back towards the conference centre.

'Are you alright sir?' asked the concierge hesitantly.

'Sure,' said Aaron, as he re-adjusted his clothes which had been ruffled up. 'Small disagreement with a multi-billionaire.'

The concierge said nothing but just stared at him as if he had been a robot whose computer code did not cover this type of incident.

Aaron tucked the laptop under his arm and headed towards the elevator. Several people in the lobby who had watched the scuffle play out returned to whatever they were doing, and soon the lobby was back to being a normal busy hotel lobby.

Aaron spent the next ten minutes pacing in his hotel room trying to decide what to do, but the reality was that there was nothing more he actually could do here. He had got his time with Dietrich, and even though the billionaire had denied knowledge of the facility in Arizona, Aaron still felt that he would have enough for a scoop to deliver to Bad Apples.

He stuffed his few possessions into his bag and went downstairs to check out. He had already paid for the room for one night, but after the altercation with the goons in the conference room, he had no desire to spend any more time in the hotel.

Half an hour later he was on the light rail service back towards the SeaTac station and Tacoma International Airport. More than ever now, he wanted to be back in his apartment in New York.

Ten

'Hey, Andy. It's me,' said Fiona. 'I have been trying to reach you a couple of times today, but I guess you've been busy.'

'Remember the guy I told you about? Peter Dietrich? Well, I decided to do the job he asked me to do, and boy was that a mistake. I'll tell you about it later, but that guy is not nearly as nice as he likes to pretend. Bit of a manipulator to be honest.'

'Anyway, right now I am sitting in the roof terrace restaurant of a five-star hotel in Rome overlooking the Colosseum just a couple of hundred metres away, and it is just gorgeous here. I don't want to sound cliché, but I really do wish you were here. It is *really* nice. Anyway, I hope you get this message soon. Call me when you can. Love you. Bye.'

★   ★   ★

'Excuse me. We're doing WHAT?' asked the shocked foreman.

He and a group of other foremen who were also dressed in red boilersuits with laurel wreath logos on the left side of their chests had gathered around a tall Centurion wearing a crisp white uniform.

'We're clearing everything out and collapsing the facility,' said the Centurion in the white uniform who was at least a foot taller than the foreman and his colleagues. 'Orders from the Imperator himself.'

The foremen looked at each other for a few moments, but eventually they all seemed to accept the idea of undoing what they had spent months living and working underground to achieve.

'I will deal with anything digital. You guys have been ordered to dismantle as much of the structure itself as you can within the next eight hours.

'Eight hours?' said another foreman incredulously.

'That is the time we have been given so make the most of it. After eight hours everyone evacuates and we blow the access tunnel. Then we set up charges to cave in the main access stairway to the old silo complex, and once that has happened, we bring in a team of bulldozers to fill in the silo complex. There will be transports for the workers. Just ensure that they wear their blinded helmets as they exit as usual, alright? This location is still meant to be kept secret for as long as possible. I want all of the men out of here in seven hours, is that clear?'

'Yes sir,' said the foreman, looking nervously at the Centurion. 'What has happened, if I can ask?'

'You cannot,' said the Centurion curtly. 'Just get moving. This is urgent. We can't leave any trace of the access tunnel. That's the most important thing. Go!'

★   ★   ★

'Jack,' said Andrew and got up from behind his desk. 'Good to see you again. Thank you for coming over.'

'No problem,' said Captain Lynch. 'What's going on?'

'Please sit down,' said Andrew. 'I need to show you something.'

The two men sat down on the sofa in Andrew's office and Andrew placed a tablet on the coffee table in front of them and fired it up.

'Remember that theory of mine about a shaped charge?' asked Andrew.

'Sure,' said Lynch.

'Well, unfortunately, it turns out I was right,' said Andrew and flicked through a set of images on the tablet. 'Look at this.'

Lynch leaned in and studied the image in front of him. It had been taken aboard a Royal Navy vessel a few hours earlier and showed the remnants of the Spearfish torpedo. Having been recovered from a depth of around 500 metres, it had been placed on a sturdy metal support frame which seemed to have been welded together for this specific purpose. Only half of the torpedo was there since the entire front half of it was missing. Andrew flicked through several more images.

'This ain't right,' said Lynch. 'If I didn't know any better, I would have said that this looks like the result of a malfunctioning warhead.'

'And now watch this,' said Andrew, and tapped on a video file which began playing.

The person who had recorded the video was holding the camera steady about two metres from the torpedo's mangled propeller. It was still possible to see that it was a Spearfish from this angle, but as he began panning the camera further along the torpedo towards its middle, the damage to it became rapidly more apparent. Around the point where the middle of the torpedo should have been, its metal sides had been ripped to shreds and peeled back towards the rear of the torpedo. The camera operator held that angle for a few seconds and then began walking slowly along the mangled torpedo towards where the front of it should have been and where the fateful explosion had occurred. It was easy to forget just how big a Spearfish is, but as the camera operator walked the roughly six metres or 20 feet to stand where the warhead had been, its true size quickly became apparent.

The camera was then turned back to point directly at the shredded middle of the torpedo, and then it was lowered slightly after which the operator slowly zoomed in on the mangled stump.

'Holy shit,' breathed Lynch. 'You *were* right. That's a half-sphere of some kind.'

'Metal half sphere. Probably lead. Or what's left of it,' said Andrew. 'And it has been rammed back deep into the engine housing of the torpedo due to the force of the blast. But the entire back section of the torpedo is still in one piece.'

'So, the Tennessee didn't suffer any damage from the blast,' observed Lynch.

'That's right,' said Andrew. 'The front of the torpedo was vapourised by the warhead, but because it was a shaped charge, almost all of the explosive energy was directed forward and the lead was there to absorb as much of the force as possible and further protect the submarine.'

'Holy crap,' said Lynch. 'This is bad.'

'Yes,' said Andrew. 'Especially because it can only mean that the Spearfish torpedo wasn't actually tampered with. It was swapped for a replica with a shaped charge where the warhead should have been.'

Lynch shook his head in disbelief.

'The sophistication it took to build a replica like that and then successfully get it on board a United States nuclear submarine is mind-blowing,' he said. 'But that is clearly what happened.'

'I am convinced of that too,' said Andrew, and looked at Lynch. 'But this leaves the real question.'

'Where the hell is the Tennessee?' said Lynch rhetorically. 'And what if you're not just right about this but also about the boat being hijacked by a special forces team after the explosion? If the crew thought that the torp had malfunctioned, the captain would then have ordered a full stop to carry out a damage assessment, and the perpetrators of the torpedo sabotage would almost certainly have understood this to be proper procedure. This could then have given a minisub a time window that could have been long enough to allow it to dock at the

DSV-hatch. After that, all it would have taken was for someone on the inside to unlock and open the hatch, and then the special forces team would have been able to make their way inside and take over the boat. If this is really what happened to the Tennessee, then we would have an unprecedented national security emergency on our hands.'

'Not just an American emergency,' said Andrew ruefully. 'This could spell all kinds of trouble for the entire world. Which leads me to another topic I would like your input on. How difficult would it be for a group of hijackers to launch its nuclear missiles, assuming they had taken full control of the entire submarine?'

Lynch sighed deeply, wringing his hands and looking decidedly uncomfortable.

'Well,' he said. 'The launch procedure is inherently complicated and has lots of built-in checkpoints precisely to prevent an inadvertent or unauthorised launch as well as a launch by a single individual. There is a rigorous authentication procedure in place whereby the captain and the executive officer both have to agree that the launch order is real and coming from the president of the United States. This authentication can only happen if the incoming launch codes match with launch codes already stored in separate safes aboard the sub, and each of the two senior officers have their individual keys to a safe with those codes. Without the keys, and without both officers agreeing that the order is authentic, the missiles simply cannot be launched.'

'I hear a *but* coming,' said Andrew, looking concerned.

'Well,' said Lynch with a pained expression on his face. 'What I have just told you is true, but there is an important caveat here. Most people don't realise this, but nuclear weapons operate with a concept called 'Permissive Action Link' or PAL. Essentially, the US nuclear command and control structure focuses on the prevention of unauthorised use of nuclear weapons prior to presidential authorisation. One of the first barriers to an unauthorised launch is the permissive action link, which is a code that has to be correctly entered into the control systems of a weapon before the warhead can arm itself. If it isn't armed it can't detonate.'

'Well, that sounds reasonable enough,' said Andrew. 'Clearly, a nuclear warhead should only be armed immediately before a missile is launched.'

'Yes,' nodded Lynch. 'It also ensures that warheads are kept safe during transit and storage, and it is also an effective way of preventing detonation by someone unauthorised who might manage to get their hands on one.'

'So far, so sensible,' said Andrew. 'So, what's the catch?'

'The catch is that for submarine-launched ballistic missiles like those on Ohio-class vessels like the USS Tennessee, permissive action links are unlocked *before* warheads are fitted into their launch tubes.'

Lynch paused to let what he had just said sink in.

'Wait,' said Andrew. 'You're saying that the missiles on the USS Tennessee are already armed?'

'Yes,' replied Lynch. 'That happened before the boat left Naval Submarine Base Kings Bay in Georgia three weeks ago. The reason for this is simple. The submarine-based nuclear arsenal only serves as a deterrent if it can still be launched after a first strike on America's command and control structure, possibly including the president who theoretically has the ultimate launch authority. In other words, if the president or even his entire administration has been killed in a first strike by a hostile nation, then there still has to be a credible option for launch and retaliation, otherwise, our nuclear deterrent is completely crippled.'

'Essentially you are saying that an Ohio-class submarine can, at least theoretically, operate and launch its missiles entirely without presidential authorisation?'

'In theory, yes,' replied Lynch. 'But there are obviously safeguards in place to prevent that from ever happening. Mainly, the submarine has to receive the order from the president containing a specific launch code, and as I said before, this then has to be authenticated using physical plastic cards that are already present on the submarine when it leaves port. Only if the launch codes coming from the president match the codes held in the safes can launch be authorised. And again, both the captain and his XO have to agree that the order is authentic.'

'But if both the captain and the XO were somehow forced to open the safes, then the missiles could be fired?'

'It wouldn't even be that complicated,' said Lynch. 'In that type of scenario, since the warheads are already armed, the launch codes and their authentication would be a pointless formality. If under duress the captain and the XO were forced to initiate the launch sequence, then there would be nothing anyone outside of the submarine could do to stop it. It is ultimately in the hands of those two people. The whole point of the submarine as a launch platform for nuclear weapons is that it can operate independently, and without the need for authorisation from either central command or the president.'

'All it takes is those two men,' said Andrew, deep furrows spreading across his forehead. 'That's extremely worrying.'

'Well, the system has worked for more than half a century,' said Lynch, 'but then we have never had to deal with a situation like this before. As far as I know, there is no standard operating procedure for dealing with an attempted hijacking of a submerged nuclear submarine.'

Andrew was rubbing his chin slowly and staring into space. The prospect of an Ohio-class submarine being hijacked with a full complement of nuclear ballistic missiles was terrifying.

'How many missiles does the USS Tennessee carry?' he asked, almost not wanting to hear the answer.

'An Ohio-class submarine has 24 missile launch tubes, each holding one UGM-133 Trident II D5 ballistic missile,' replied Lynch. 'But as I am sure you are aware, it is not quite as simple as that. Each missile carries a MIRV with several warheads.'

'Multiple Independent Re-entry Vehicles,' nodded Andrew.

'That's right,' said Lynch. 'The MIRV allows for several independently targeted warheads to be carried on the missile. Once the missile reaches apogee, its highest point in space at an altitude of around 1,200 kilometres or 750 miles, it is travelling at Mach 24 which is around 29,000 kilometres per hour. The MIRV then opens up and releases several separate warheads which are independently guided towards several separate targets on the ground. And those targets can be many hundreds of miles apart.'

'Remind me of the specs of the D5 missile again please?' asked Andrew. 'How many warheads does one Trident II missile carry?'

'In its current configuration,' replied Lynch, 'each of the missiles on the USS Tennessee carries 12 MIRVed W88 warheads.'

'And the yield of those warheads?'

'The warheads are dialled in to deliver a yield of 475 kilotons,' replied Lynch, with a solemn expression on his face.

'475 kilotons each,' repeated Andrew slowly, quickly doing some maths in his head. 'That is more than 30 times more powerful than the bomb dropped on Hiroshima in 1945. And that's just one warhead.'

'That is correct,' said Lynch. 'There have been huge advances in nuclear weapons technology since those early days, so it is possible to cram significantly more firepower into much smaller delivery vehicles these days.'

'I see,' said Andrew. 'And if each of the 24 missiles carries 12 warheads then that is a total of 288 warheads, each with enough power to completely wipe out a major city the size of New York.'

'That's right,' nodded Lynch. 'These subs carry almost unimaginable destructive power.'

Andrew was silent for a few moments as he tried to take in the magnitude of those numbers.

'Crikey,' he finally said. 'Once you start doing the math on these things, it suddenly becomes a lot less abstract and a lot more real.'

'I know,' said Lynch. 'It is an obscene amount of firepower. And there are 18 Ohio-class submarines in active service.'

'What is the range of a Trident II D5 missile?' asked Andrew.

'The exact number is classified above my pay grade,' said Lynch, 'but it is definitely in excess of 12,000 kilometres, or around 7,500 miles.'

'In other words, if the sub was positioned in an optimal spot it could launch without warning and hit almost any land-based target in the world.'

'Yes,' said Lynch. 'Since most of the world's landmass is in the northern hemisphere, there are several locations in the Atlantic and the Mediterranean from where a submerged Ohio-class sub could strike virtually any target, except for a few in the middle of the Pacific Ocean and parts of eastern Australia and also New Zealand. But all of Europe, North America, South America, Africa, Russia, China, India and the entirety of South-East Asia would be well within strike range. And of course, since the submarine can travel submerged at around 1,100 kilometres per day, it could conceivably relocate relatively quickly to a new firing location and hit any remaining targets from there.'

At this point, Andrew was glad to be sitting down. The enormity and sheer horror of what Lynch had just said was enough to make his head spin and the hairs at the back of his neck stand on end.

'This is an absolutely terrifying prospect,' he said. 'Is there no way to remotely disable the vessel's ability to fire its missiles?'

'No,' replied Lynch. 'That would defeat the whole purpose of being able to operate cut off from central command after a Russian first strike.'

'Bloody hell,' sighed Andrew, closing his eyes and rubbing his temples with the tips of his fingers. 'So, worst-case scenario, we are now having to contemplate at least the possibility of nuclear Armageddon unleashed by a small group of special forces people with unknown motives.'

'Possibly,' said Lynch. 'Although, there is one more aspect of this we need to discuss.'

Andrew opened his eyes and glanced towards Lynch. 'I am almost afraid to ask.'

'If we are correct,' began Lynch, 'and if the USS Tennessee really was boarded by a hostile force, then they would absolutely have needed help from a crewmember. There is just no way they could have opened the DSV-hatch from the outside.'

'A rogue crewmember,' said Andrew. 'That's not exactly what you want to have on a nuclear submarine.'

'You can say that again,' replied Lynch, running his fingers through his hair as he contemplated the idea. 'The question is, who?'

'I assume every member of an SSBN crew is vetted from here to the moon and back,' said Andrew. 'I know that to be the case on Royal Navy Vanguard submarines.'

'Oh, absolutely,' said Lynch. 'Each crewmember has to undergo regular psychological evaluations to be able to serve on a U.S. Navy submarine.'

'But that doesn't necessarily catch people who are not mentally unstable, but who might have some kind of nefarious agenda,' interjected Andrew.

'Yeah, that's true,' said Lynch. 'Out of 165 crewmembers, there could well be someone who has either been paid off or blackmailed or otherwise been compromised somehow.'

'I guess we need to look at all of those personnel files then,' said Andrew. 'Would you be able to retrieve those from Navy Intelligence?'

'I need to go through the proper channels first,' replied Lynch, 'but I should be able to get those pretty fast. I will put in a request as soon as I get back to my office. I am sure there are people already looking at them back at Naval Intelligence in Suitland, but I guess it wouldn't hurt for us to have a look as well.'

'Exactly,' said Andrew. 'I am not sure what we're looking for, but something might stand out once we have a closer look. If there is just one person on board that boat who for whatever reason would be prepared to collaborate with a special-forces boarding party, then the world could be facing unimaginable consequences.'

'Yeah,' sighed Lynch, the magnitude of the situation clearly weighing on him. 'I am going to have to bump our concerns up the chain of command. Man, this whole thing just keeps getting better and better.'

*   *   *

Fiona had spent most of the day exploring the ancient ruins of the Palatino site in central Rome and had taken a quick guided tour through the Colosseum on the way back to the hotel. Along the way she had realised that the name *Palatino* was the ancient root of the modern word *palace*, or *palazzo* in Italian and *palais* in French.

As interesting as the day had been, she had still had trouble enjoying it the way she normally would have. She found her thoughts invariably drifting back towards the Corona Civica and Peter Dietrich. What unsettled her the most, apart from the realisation that Dietrich seemed prepared to do pretty much anything to get what he wanted, was the way in which his personality seemed to have changed in an instant as soon as he realised that she was not on his side anymore.

She reluctantly came to the conclusion that she had been duped and swept up by his charisma and the aura of success and influence that he carried around him. Like most people, she had unthinkingly allowed herself to buy into the idea created by the fawning and unthinking masses that somehow Dietrich was some sort of oracle, and that if he wanted something then by definition it had to be a positive thing. It was exactly the type of uncritical group-think that she had resented all of her life, and yet here she was having fallen for it herself. She had simply failed to realise who the man really was before it was too late and she had begun working for him. The only saving grace of the situation was that she had turned down his money and walked away, so in that sense at least she had done the right thing.

As for the whereabouts of the Corona Civica for whose recovery she would probably never be able to receive credit, she had to assume that Dietrich already had it in his possession and that it would never become part of the exhibition at the British Museum in London. Unless she could get it back somehow.

Fiona shook her head and forced herself to abandon the idea. She had been swimming with this particular shark once already and had just about managed to get away unscathed, but she was sure that attempting to do so again would end badly.

On her way back to the hotel, she swung past a small restaurant and café called La Biga, which is situated on the corner of an old building on Via Nicola Salvi just north of and overlooking the Colosseum. The staff had carried large parasols outside to provide shade for their patrons, and Fiona placed herself at one of the empty tables facing west and enjoying the afternoon sun and the view of the ancient amphitheatre.

The Colosseum was thought to have been named after the 30-metre-tall bronze statue of Emperor Nero erected near the entrance to the Palatino Hill in 68 CE. This statue was itself modelled on the equally tall Colossus of Rhodes, which was a giant statue of the sun-god Helios that stood at the entrance to the harbour on the island of Rhodes in the 3rd century BCE. The huge amphitheatre which was finished in 80 CE had taken almost a decade to build, and its construction had been overseen first by Emperor Vespasian and then later by his son Emperor Titus.

Looking at the ruin now, even in its much-reduced state, Fiona could well imagine what it had looked like during the heyday of the Roman Empire around 1,900 years ago. In those days, the four-tiered structure had capacity for as many as 80,000 spectators who would come to watch gladiatorial contests, re-enactments of famous battles by conquering Roman generals, mock sea battles, dramas based on Roman mythology, animal hunts and even executions.

Fiona ordered herself a small coffee, and since the waiter recommended the pear and chocolate tart, or *Torta Pere e Cioccolato*, she decided to also order one of those. After a couple of minutes, her coffee arrived, and as she was waiting for the waiter to return with the tart, Fiona picked up the copy of the newspaper La Repubblica which someone else had left on the table. Sipping her coffee and flicking idly through the pages she read as much of it as she could, but she was far from fluent in Italian. Just as the waiter returned and placed the tart in front of her she spotted a picture in the business section that made her sit up. It was a picture of Peter Dietrich in what looked like a large conference room. He was standing behind a podium with a concerned expression on his face, and in front of him a young man who looked like he was being forcibly led away by a large man in a suit. Under the picture was a caption with the words *una baruffa in pubblico*, which Fiona knew roughly meant 'a public scuffle'. In the article itself, the words *disturbo mentale* were used in the context of the name Purnell, and *la rivista di New York 'Bad Apples'*.

She surmised that the man being led away was someone called Purnell, from a New York magazine called Bad Apples.

Fiona sat up and inspected the photo. It was definitely Dietrich, and the man being led away clutching a laptop looked decidedly upset and shocked. She stared at the photo for about a minute trying to read the situation. The other people in the picture, who all looked like businessmen and women, looked equally shocked at the spectacle, especially the young woman next to Purnell so it must have been quite a violent affair.

As she studied the picture a knot began to form in Fiona's stomach. A few days ago she would have concluded that the reporter from the New York magazine had somehow been abusive or disruptive during a talk by Dietrich, but not now.

She plucked her phone out of her handbag and did a quick search for 'Dietrich news', and immediately a couple of articles popped up. Clearly, the mass media had jumped at the opportunity to generate revenue by creating clickbait headlines.

She opened one of the articles that looked like it included video footage of the incident and began watching. After having listened to the entire exchange between Dietrich and Purnell, and then watched as the reporter was manhandled out of the conference room, Fiona sat back in her chair with a troubled expression on her face and placed the phone on the table in front of her.

What the hell was that all about? she thought.

During her own research into Dietrich and his many companies and initiatives, she had come across all of the philanthropic endeavours Purnell had mentioned, but at no point had she seen any hint of his involvement with the loopy prepper community. And Purnell seemed to be talking about something on an entirely different scale from the average gun-toting, paranoid anti-government vigilante prepper hiding in a hole in the ground. But what exactly was Purnell referring to? And where had he got his information from?

Part of her wanted to drop it and assume that Purnell really was mentally disturbed as the Italian newspaper had indicated, but there was something about the young man that made what he said sound credible, and her own experience with Dietrich told her that nothing should be ruled out when dealing with him. His affable and sympathetic demeanour during the scuffle did not fool Fiona, even if it might have fooled everyone in the conference room.

After another ten minutes of researching online, she had discovered that Aaron Purnell, a staff writer for the magazine Bad Apples, was an extremely eloquent and thoughtful writer who had several major investigative scoops to his name. Granted, Bad Apples had a tendency to run with sensationalist and even salacious stories most of the time, but Aaron's pieces were always well-sourced, well-written and thoroughly researched. His work had even led to several criminal convictions by the Manhattan District Attorney's office.

Fiona looked at her watch. It was 4:52 in the afternoon, which meant that it would be just before noon in New York. Within less than a minute she had found the section of the Bad Apples website which contained the magazine's contact details, so she tapped the number and copied it into the contacts on her phone. Then she hit the 'dial' button.

The phone rang three times before a woman with a thick New York accent picked up.

'Mjello!' she said, sounding like she was in the middle of her lunch break. 'Bad Apples, Martha speaking.'

'Oh. Hello, my name is Fiona Keane. I would like to speak to Aaron Purnell, please?'

Martha produced a snorting laugh.

'Yeah, you and everybody else, honey,' she said. 'A real shitstorm he's created. Sorry, he's not in the office, and to be honest I don't think he'll be picking up his phone today.'

'I really need to speak to him,' said Fiona. 'I have some information about Peter Dietrich that he needs to hear.'

There was a short pause at the other end of the line. Then the sound of slurping.

'Damn, that's good coffee!' said Martha. 'Alright, listen, Sweetie. I'm not supposed to do this, ok? But since you ask so nicely, and because I know Aaron and I know he'll wanna find out what you've got, I'm gonna go ahead and give you his private phone number. So, this better be for real, alright?'

'Thank you so much,' said Fiona, clearly relieved. 'That is very kind of you. I promise, he will want to hear what I have to say.'

'Fine, fine,' said Martha. 'Here's the number.'

Martha read out the number from a page on the Bad Apples intranet.

'Thank you again,' said Fiona.

'Alright. You're welcome,' replied Martha. 'You take care now.'

Then abruptly, the line went dead.

Fiona spent a couple of seconds entering the number and Purnell's name into her phone's contacts. Then she tapped the 'dial' button again.

The phone rang several times before eventually going to voicemail.

'Hello Mr Purnell. My name is Fiona Keane. I got your number from Martha at Bad Apples. I really need to speak to you. I saw your run-in with Peter Dietrich yesterday in Seattle, and so I decided to get in touch. I was hoping you could tell me more about what you have found out about that site in Arizona and the things you have discovered about Dietrich himself. Also, I have personally had some dealings with Mr Dietrich over the past few weeks which I think you might want to hear about. It seems to me that he isn't anything like the public persona that he likes to show to the world, and I have first-hand knowledge of certain illegal activities he has been involved in recently. I hope you get this message soon and that you will call me back. Thanks. Bye.'

As she put the phone back down onto the table and reached for her coffee cup, Fiona suddenly had an uncomfortable feeling in her stomach, as if she was beginning to swim out to where she could no longer feel the sand under her feet. It was clear from her last conversation with Dietrich that he was probably not a man anyone would want to cross if they could avoid it, but that thought ended up making Fiona even more determined to press on. She refused to be cowed by him. People needed to know the truth.

About ten minutes later her phone rang. It was Purnell.

'Hello?' said a man's voice.

'Mr. Purnell?' asked Fiona.

'Who's asking?' came the reply.

'Fiona Keane.'

'Yeah, I know that's who you say you are, but how do I know if that's true?'

Fiona thought for a couple of seconds. 'Go to the website of the British Museum in London and look me up on the 'Permanent staff' page. There is a picture of me there. Then go to the bottom of the page and click 'Research Projects'. There you'll find a section about an archaeological excavation in Egypt. It has a short video with me explaining what we are doing there. You should be able to see my face and listen to my voice.'

'Give me a second,' said Aaron, doing as Fiona had asked.

After about half a minute, Fiona could hear the sound of her own voice in her phone's speaker explaining which artefacts the dig site in Luxor had yielded so far.

'Alright,' said Aaron reluctantly. 'I guess you're for real. So, why would a British archaeologist be calling me?'

'As I said in my voicemail to you, I have something about Peter Dietrich that you might want to hear about. And I would also appreciate it if you could tell me what you have found out about him.'

'But why are you doing this?' asked Aaron. 'What's your beef with Dietrich, and what's in it for you?'

Fiona hesitated for a moment before replying.

'I just want people to know the truth,' she said determinedly, with a hint of frustration in her voice.

After a brief pause and the sound of a sigh on the other end, Aaron spoke again.

'Alright, Lady. You got me. We can talk but I want to meet in person. To be honest, I feel like I have stirred up a huge hornet's nest here and I wouldn't be surprised if someone is listening to this conversation right now.'

Suddenly feeling self-conscious, Fiona wondered if her calls and messages were also being monitored.

'Ok,' she said reluctantly. 'Where do you want to meet then?'

'In New York,' said Aaron. 'Send me a message when you get there, and I will tell you where to go. I am still in Seattle but I should be back in about ten hours.'

'Uhm. Ok,' replied Fiona, trying to get her head around suddenly having to fly off to New York. 'I don't know how soon I can be there, but I will do my best.'

'Alright,' said Aaron. 'See you then. Bye.'

Then he hung up.

Looking at the other patrons of the restaurant who were seemingly relaxed and enjoying the scenery and the nice weather, her own predicament suddenly felt quite surreal. Once again, she felt the urge to drop the whole thing and just enjoy her time in Rome, but she knew that she would be unable to do so. It was clear to her what she had to do, so she immediately opened a browser and began searching for a flight that would get her from Rome to New York as fast as possible.

Eleven

'Hello Fiona, it's Andy here. I tried to call you just now, but you were on another call. Everything is a bit mad around here. I can't tell you exactly what is going on, but let's just say that something really bad might be about to happen. I know that it's part of my job to look for really bad things and make sure they don't happen, but this is kind of in a league of its own. Anyway, I was wondering when you might be back from Italy. You left with pretty short notice so I assume it was important. Hopefully, your issue with this Dietrich character has been resolved. I want to hear about it when we see each other again. Anyway, let me know when you're back in London. With any luck, this thing that I am working on will be all over by then. Take care. Bye.'

★ ★ ★

It took a few seconds to establish the heavily encrypted video connection from the site in New Zealand to the plush apartment overlooking the bay.

On the Centurion's screen, there was a progress bar with a red velvet effect slowly moving from left to right as the various connections in the chain of virtual private networks were established. The privately-owned dedicated VPNs were only a small part of the effort that had been put in place to make sure that all internal communications remained outside of the reach of the authorities, whether those were federal, state or international.

The entire operation had been planned out in great detail almost a decade ago, and the necessary infrastructure had been built and enhanced in several steps along the way since then. After that, the primary individuals, led by the Imperator himself, had gone to great lengths to recruit like-minded people who were prepared to leave their old lives behind and start anew with a clean slate. This had initially been a relatively straightforward process since the group was small and easily manageable, but as The Order grew into an ever-larger organisation over the next several years, it had then become necessary to impose a structure that would allow effective governance both before and after The Dawn.

The logistics of the operation could have rivalled almost any other private endeavour in recent decades both in terms of scale and cost, so it had been essential to only bring on board carefully selected individuals and their families. When the day came, and even more so in the lead-up to The Dawn, the organisation could not afford more than a few wayward members suddenly having a change of heart and going to the authorities or the news media. A couple could be written off as just a few lunatics, but a large number might endanger the whole project.

Along the way since the inception of the endeavour, the leadership of The Order had felt it necessary to eliminate a few such potential leaks before they had a chance to go public, but that had been taken care of by a small squad of specialists who had been travelling the world for that precise purpose. And although it was regrettable that those people had lost their faith in the project, their elimination had been a small price to pay for ensuring that it remained a tightly guarded secret.

Overwhelmingly though, the secret organisation's members had been committed to the cause for reasons of pure self-interest, and so they had not represented a security risk at any point. They had all understood that after the fundamental schism that The Dawn represented, there were going to be two groups of people in the world, and it did not take a rocket scientist to work out which one it would be better to belong to, although the organisation did, in fact, include several rocket scientists as well as highly skilled and able scientists from a myriad of other fields.

Beginning with a slow trickle of a few handfuls per week coming to the site of the ARK, the rate of arrivals had been growing steadily over the past month or so, and during the past few weeks it had transformed into a surge. The total population was now several thousand strong, but the facility was virtually complete and had been ready to accommodate all of the new arrivals and allow them to settle into their new temporary residences. Having visited the complex in the Arizona desert several times himself, the Centurion knew just how valuable that prototype had been. It had allowed the work in New Zealand to proceed much faster and much more efficiently than if they had started from scratch after completing the initial phase of tunnelling into the mountain and excavating the facility's internal spaces.

The Centurion, sitting in his brightly lit and airy office inside the mountain in New Zealand patiently awaited the connection to the Imperator. He absentmindedly looked at the wall screen that was showing a live view of the lake which was at the foot of the mountain inside which the complex had been built.

The wall opposite the screen was made of glass and had Venetian blinds hanging open in front of them, allowing him to watch as groups of people made their way along the corridor busily preparing the facility for what was to come. Most of them wore smart tailored and slim-fitted charcoal-grey suits similar in style to the latest fashion but made from more functional materials. Others wore different colours corresponding with their function inside what was not dissimilar to a busy beehive. Occasionally, a person wearing a crisp white uniform would walk past, most often accompanied by one or two people in black uniforms.

Suddenly his screen came alive and a picture of the throne room in New York appeared. The throne itself was empty, and it took the Centurion a couple of seconds to realise that what he was looking at was a still image. He would not get to see the Imperator this time, but he concluded that the great leader must have had his reasons for arranging things in this way.

'Centurion,' said a deep authoritative voice, instantly recognisable as that of the Imperator.

'Imperator,' replied the Centurion reverentially.

'Do you have a progress report?' asked the Imperator, sounding calm and business-like.

'Yes, replied the Centurion. 'The facility is essentially ready. We have been applying finishing touches to the interior of the common spaces, but everything in the ARK is functional and ready. May I ask when you will arrive?'

'My flight has been readied, so I will be on my way within a matter of hours.'

'Praised be,' said the Centurion. 'Your presence here will be a huge boost to morale. Everyone is looking forward immensely to your arrival.'

'Very good,' said the Imperator. 'As you know, I was held up slightly by an unmissable opportunity to acquire the historical artefact but that has all been settled now.'

'And Miss Keane?' asked the Centurion.

'Don't worry about her. She is no longer a concern. She will only become important if Sterling and Lynch get too close, but they are obviously running out of time, so I don't imagine they will become a real problem.'

'Praised be,' said the Centurion.

'What is the final status on storage rooms and supplies?' asked the Imperator.

'The last shipment is scheduled to arrive tomorrow,' replied the Centurion. 'That should bolster our essential supplies to last us at least eighteen months. But as you know, with rationing it would be a lot longer than that.'

'It will not come to that,' said the Imperator. 'Don't worry. I am sure we will be able to conduct the great resettling much sooner than that. What about accommodation?'

'Your office and that of the Magister Equitum were completed to your specifications yesterday,' said the Centurion. 'As you requested, they both have direct access to your respective living quarters. All other accommodation sections were completed three days ago. Facility and critical systems testing are ongoing, but everything appears to be working perfectly so far. I am confident that we will be ready for The Dawn.'

'Excellent,' said the Imperator. 'Not long now. The Dawn will bring the light.'

★   ★   ★

It was just before 9 pm when Aaron emerged from Clark Street Subway Station on the corner of Clark Street and Henry Street in Brooklyn Heights to begin the short walk back to his apartment.

It was unusually cold and a fine mist of rain was falling over New York, but there was no wind so the rain seemed to almost hang in the air before slowly falling to the glistening streets below. The streetlights were on but most of the shops had closed several hours ago. Only the restaurants and bars were open, and every so often a group of people would spill out onto the sidewalks and head off to the next watering hole.

Aaron had enjoyed the much warmer and dryer climate in Arizona, and he had his coat wrapped around him and buttoned up tight to keep him warm as he walked.

As he turned the corner of Clark Street and headed south along Willow Street towards his apartment, he glanced back over his left shoulder. The street was empty except for another man in a long coat walking along carrying a briefcase about twenty metres behind him. Aaron swapped to the sidewalk on the other side of the road, and as he did so he saw the man continue west along Clark Street towards the East River between Brooklyn and Lower Manhattan.

Aaron continued walking, suspiciously eyeing a car that was making its way very slowly towards him along Willow Street from the opposite direction. Its headlights were on, fanning their bright lights out into the misty rain, so he was unable to see inside the car. He pulled the collar of his coat up to hide his face as much as he could, and as he and the car passed each other he glanced sideways through the driver's side window to see a couple having what looked like an argument, the man gesticulating out of the windscreen to the road ahead as if to say that he was exactly where she had told him to go, and that she must have given him the wrong directions.

Aaron shook his head as he scaled the eight steps up to the front door of his building in a couple of long strides.

Caution is good. Paranoia is bad, he thought to himself. *Just gotta calm down.*

He emptied his mailbox in the small checker-tiled lobby and walked up the stairs to the first floor where he inserted the key in the lock and turned the handle. The east-facing apartment was small but cosy, and it was like a small cupboard compared with some of the eye-wateringly expensive townhouses on Willow Street. But it was all his. He had paid down the mortgage on it last year using all of his savings and a rare bonus from Bad Apples at the end of what had been a good year for revenue and ad sales in particular.

He dropped his bag on the floor, flung his coat onto a coat stand and walked over to one of the two windows in the small living room that faced out to the street. Using two fingers he pulled down one of the plastic slats in the Venetian blinds and peered out onto the street below. The misty rain made the cones of light being created by the streetlights stand out in the darkness, and as he looked down the street first in one direction and then the other, he saw no cars or pedestrians. About thirty metres from his building on the other side of the street was a nondescript van with its lights off, but he could see the faint glow from a phone being held by someone sitting in the driver's seat.

Aaron stepped away from the window and went into the kitchen where he grabbed a beer from the fridge. He unscrewed the lid and tossed it in the bin, and then he slumped down on his sofa which was facing the far wall of the living room from the entrance to the apartment.

He was about to take a swig from the bottle when his phone rang, and it made him jump and spill beer on his shirt.

'God damn it,' he said irritably, wiping his shirt uselessly with his hand.

He then looked at his phone and saw that it was Fiona Keane.

'Hello?' he said, sounding surprised.

'Aaron, it's Fiona. I just landed at JFK.'

'That was fast,' replied Aaron, sounding surprised. 'You got your own jet or something?'

'No,' laughed Fiona. 'I do know someone who does, but I doubt he would lend it to me now, if you know what I mean.'

Aaron smiled. 'I'll be interested to hear what you have to say about that. Anyway, are you ok to meet for lunch tomorrow? I can give you the name of a café that I like. Where are you staying?'

'Somewhere called the Hugo Hotel on Greenwich Street,' replied Fiona. 'Should be Lower Manhattan, but I am not sure exactly.'

'I know where Greenwich Street is,' said Aaron. 'It's not far.'

'How do I get to you?' asked Fiona.

'You can take the subway from Canal Street to Clark Street in Brooklyn,' replied Aaron. 'From there it's a five-minute walk to a place called the Vineapple Café on Pineapple Street. Can you meet me there at 2 pm tomorrow?'

'Sure,' said Fiona. 'I will be there.'

'Great,' said Aaron. 'See you there.'

After he had ended the call, Aaron just stood there for a few seconds looking down at his phone. Then he turned his head to look at a shelf on the wall. He walked over to it and grabbed a small flexible phone holder, wrapped two of its arms around his phone, and shaped the others into a small stand. Then he placed the makeshift tripod with the phone on the large wooden dining table next to his open kitchen and sat down facing it.

He hesitated for a few moments gathering his thoughts, and then he reached over to the phone to start the recording.

★   ★   ★

The Vineapple Café was just one block away from Clark Street Subway Station, and it was a small but cosy place on the narrow tree-lined Pineapple Street. Its interior had a rustic feel to it due to its dark wood flooring, exposed brickwork, large potted plants in the corners and warm lighting from the table lamps fitted with cream-coloured silk lampshades. Fiona was about ten minutes early so she bought herself a Caffe Latte and a chocolate muffin and went up the wooden staircase to find herself an empty table for two towards the rear of the building. Then she sent a quick message to Aaron.

Am here.
Upstairs, at the back.

She did not have to wait long because Aaron arrived right on time, and as soon as she spotted him she waved discreetly. He was wearing jeans and a dark brown bomber jacket, and he looked geekier than Fiona had imagined from the sound of his voice. As he came over to her table she stood up and smiled.

'Hello,' she said and gave him her hand. 'I'm Fiona.'

'Aaron,' he replied with a cautious smile, looking around the first floor of the half-empty café. 'You're by yourself?'

'Yes. Of course,' said Fiona, sounding slightly surprised.

'Ok,' replied Aaron and sat down. 'So, tell me about yourself and your experience with Peter Dietrich, and then I will do the same after. Fair?'

'Alright,' smiled Fiona, and then she proceeded to relay everything that had happened over the past week or so, right up to the point where she had watched Aaron being ejected from the conference centre in Seattle.

'So, I guess you feel like you got duped,' said Aaron, more as an observation than a question whilst waving a waiter over to order a coffee.

'That's not a bad way of putting it,' said Fiona. 'I just have this really uncomfortable feeling that there is a lot more to this story than meets the eye, and after seeing you in Seattle I became convinced that Dietrich is up to something that he doesn't want anyone else to know about. I want to find out what it is. And now I don't trust that guy to be interested in anyone but himself.'

'Well,' said Aaron. 'Let me tell you about my very *hands-on* experience in Seattle, and then I am going to let you know what I found in Arizona. I will warn you now. It's some weird shit. But it could have Pulitzer Prize written all over it.'

Having relayed the details of the altercation in Seattle and then gone over the unsettling discovery he had made in the Sonoran Desert in Arizona, Aaron leaned back in his chair and sipped his coffee whilst watching Fiona for a reaction.

She shook her head slightly, produced a small smile whilst looking up at the ceiling, and after a brief moment, she shifted her gaze back to Aaron again.

'It sounds pretty crazy, I'll give you that,' she said. 'But I have no doubt that you saw what you say you saw. The question is, what the hell is Dietrich doing? What is it all for?'

'Why does anyone buy an umbrella,' said Aaron rhetorically, before answering his own question. 'Because they think it is gonna rain.'

'So, do you think Dietrich believes some sort of catastrophic event is coming?' asked Fiona.

'It's the only thing that makes sense,' he replied.

'Do you have any proof of what you saw in Arizona?' asked Fiona. 'I mean, I absolutely believe you but if you had to show someone some evidence, do you have any?'

'Sure,' said Aaron. 'I have a couple of photos of the complex and some of the people in uniform, but as I told you I stole a memory stick from the computer in what I think is the engineering section, and that contained a bunch of files which show exactly what they are building. I might let you have a copy of those files at some point. Let's just see how this goes first. Anyway, I have also spent hours researching the ownership structure of these different companies and it all points back to Dietrich and the foundation. Granted, the way I obtained the data from Delaware is technically illegal, but I believe a judge would agree that there is an undeniable public interest aspect to this. So, that should mitigate or remove any criminal liability for myself or my source in the Delaware Department of State.'

'What do you make of the whole uniform thing?' asked Fiona. 'You said that you thought they looked a lot like Nazi uniforms.'

'No, I didn't say they actually were Nazi uniforms,' said Aaron. 'But they had that same sharp cut to them. As if they had been designed to invoke the same authoritarian vibe that the Nazis cultivated, you know? The top-down order and structure of everything and the unquestioning submission to the great leader. That type of thing.'

Fiona finished her chocolate muffin and wiped her mouth with a napkin.

'So, what do we do about this?' she asked.

'There is only one thing we *can* do,' replied Aaron and shrugged. 'I have to publish my piece and include your experience as a first-hand account of what Dietrich's character is really like beneath his phoney respectable-looking veneer, and then we have to hope that we can shake some whistleblowers out of a tree somewhere. There must be a lot of other people who know or have seen things that they have concerns about, but who didn't do anything with it because they thought they were on their own. I have seen that before. As soon as individual victims of a crime see other people come forward with a similar experience, a slow trickle of victims can suddenly turn into a flood.'

'Right,' said Fiona. 'I guess you would need some sort of written input from me that you could use and quote if you needed to.'

'That would probably be the best option,' said Aaron and nodded. 'If I could have what you just told me in writing, then we can also hand that to the authorities. For starters, I bet the Italian police will want to look into this, and I would be surprised if the Arizona state authorities didn't at least go to investigate the site I visited. I would also hope that the FBI would feel compelled to do that same.'

'Good,' smiled Fiona. 'We have a plan then.'

'Just one more thing though,' said Aaron, looking intently at Fiona just as she was about to grab her coat and get ready to leave. 'I have been involved in these sorts of investigations a few times in the past, and I should warn you that there will be a lot of attention coming your way, so if you can't handle that then you might want to try to stay out of sight.'

Fiona nodded pensively.

'I guess you're right,' she said. 'But I am prepared for that. I am not going to let myself be intimidated by any of this. Dietrich can't be allowed to prance around like this, behaving like a king and making everyone shy away from ever criticising him.'

'That's a good attitude,' smiled Aaron warmly. 'I really respect that. Thank you for coming all this way. I am glad you did.'

'Me too,' said Fiona, returning his smile.

The two of them put on their coats, left the Vineapple Café and exited out onto the street where the rain had finally stopped. The street was glistening under the street lights, and steam was rising from a couple of manhole covers.

'Let me walk you back to the subway,' offered Aaron. 'It's on the way to my apartment. I am over on Willow Street just a couple of blocks away.'

'Sure,' smiled Fiona. 'That's very gentlemanly of you.'

'Well,' laughed Aaron as they began walking the short distance along Henry Street towards Clark Street Station, Aaron on the outside next to the road. 'New Yorkers have a reputation for being rude and obnoxious, so call it an attempt to show that nice people live here too.'

Fiona smiled at his sentiment and nodded her approval, just as a motorcycle came around the corner of Clark Street and began accelerating north towards them along Henry Street. Absentmindedly, Fiona noticed that there were two people on the motorcycle, and they were both wearing black leather jackets and black helmets.

Before she knew it the motorcycle had slowed down and stopped just ahead of them, and the passenger had jumped off and begun walking the last few paces towards them. Aaron evidently spotted the gun in the passenger's hands before Fiona had a chance to do so, because he suddenly reached over and pushed Fiona forcefully away from himself, and then he lunged for the gun-wielding man. But it was too late. The gunman had already brought up the small and compact Beretta PX4 semi-automatic pistol, flicked the safety off and aimed the gun at Aaron.

Aaron just had time to whip his head around towards Fiona and yell to her. 'Run! Get out of here!'

Then three shots rang out loudly across the cold and wet street. First two in quick succession, and then another about two seconds later. Fiona was already scrambling to her feet as soon as Aaron had shouted to her, and as the third shot was fired she had thrown herself through the air and into the lobby of the Hotel St. George which is just next to Clark Street Subway Station. As she landed on the ground, two more shots rang out and two bullets smacked into the glass doors of the hotel, shattering the panes and sending glass shards crashing onto the floor of the hotel lobby. Without looking back, Fiona threw herself behind a giant solid-looking pot containing an enormous fig tree that stood inside the lobby.

From her crouched position she then heard the loud noise of a motorcycle engine being revved aggressively, and then after a couple of seconds the noise from its screaming engine as the driver and the gunman raced off towards the south along Henry Street.

Without hesitating, Fiona leapt up and turned around to shout to the person at the hotel's reception desk to call for an ambulance. Then she raced outside to find Aaron lying on the sidewalk. As she hurried over and knelt down next to him, she saw a crimson pool of blood on the pavement that was slowly spreading out from his chest. His face was smeared with red and his breathing was laboured and heavy. Blood was coming out of his mouth.

Fiona put one hand under his head to try to lift him up to a sitting position, and he then grabbed her jacket with both hands looking up into her eyes with a desperate pleading look on his face.

'My apartment,' he whispered, barely able to produce a sound as blood slowly trickled from his mouth. '126 Willow Street. Sunset.'

Fiona looked down at him in horror, shaking her head in disbelief.

'What?' said Fiona, desperation in her voice. 'What do you mean? Aaron, stay with me!'

Aaron spluttered, pink blood from his lungs bubbling up past his lips. He gripped her jacket tighter compelling her to look him in the eyes. It seemed to require a huge effort for him to take another breath.

'Keys in my pocket. Wait for the rainbow,' he said weakly.

'No!' shouted Fiona. 'Aaron! The ambulance is coming. Hang in there!'

Aaron's eyes seemed to gradually lose focus and after a few seconds, they had a vacant thousand-yard-stare. Then his hands loosened their grip on Fiona's jacket and fell onto his chest. Finally, he exhaled one last time and then Fiona could feel the full weight of his head in her hand as his body relaxed. Aaron was dead.

Twelve

A shocked Fiona had stayed with Aaron until the ambulance arrived, but she had then stepped back and observed as the paramedics attempted CPR and defibrillation. Fiona had never thought that she would be witnessing first-hand the call of "Clear!", and then the body of a lifeless person jolt as the electric charge surged through them in an attempt to restart their heart. After several torturous minutes, Fiona had watched them place Aaron's body on a gurney, drape a white cloth over him and put him inside the back of the ambulance before driving off without the sirens on.

Initially, Fiona had decided to stay until the police arrived but she had then suddenly thought better of it. This brazen and utterly reckless assassination on the streets of New York could only have been carried out by the people Aaron had discovered constructing the complex in Arizona. This in turn meant that there was a very high chance of it having been sanctioned by Peter Dietrich himself.

That thought sent a chill through Fiona, and it made her think that if they were prepared to do something as extreme as this, they could easily have paid off the NYPD which was infamous for being corrupt. As the minutes passed, she could feel herself slipping into the grip of panic. After all, the gunman had also attempted to kill her. She was suddenly so far out of her comfort zone that she felt like running away and hiding somewhere.

And yet, Aaron's cryptic last words had to mean something. He had to have been referring to something specific in his apartment that he wanted Fiona to see.

She tried calling Andrew but once again he did not pick up. This was a time when she really could have used his ability to stay calm and think clearly under pressure. After a couple of tries, she left a message explaining what had happened and what she was about to do.

She then put the phone back in her pocket and steeled herself for what was about to happen, and then she extracted herself unnoticed from the back of the small crowd and left the scene of the murder. Ten minutes later she was standing outside the 19th-century redbrick building where Aaron's apartment was located, wondering how she had got herself into this surreal situation. But she decided to press on, and so she walked up to the front door where she used the keys she had taken from Aaron's trouser pocket and let herself in.

★   ★   ★

The cortege of black vehicles with tinted windows swept into the Seattle Tacoma International Airport complex and sped past the main terminals, proceeding instead to a smaller VIP terminal towards the south of the airport. Here it stopped and then the passengers got out and walked briskly towards the entrance. From the middle vehicle exited a tall man in a dark suit, and as soon as he began walking, a group of four bodyguards formed up around him to escort him inside the building.

The large group continued through the small security station where their documents were given a cursory look by the duty officer who then waved them through towards the gates. Within minutes the group had been reduced to just five people. One VIP, his assistant and three bodyguards.

Striding across the tarmac from the terminal to the Gulfstream G500, the tall man in the suit checked his wristwatch and reached inside his suit jacket for a phone. He dialled a number and pressed the phone to his ear as he walked up the five steps to board the aircraft.

The G500 was a sleek 50-million-dollar swept-wing private jet that had been tailored to the specific requirements of its owner. It measured around 27 metres in both length and wingspan, and it had a characteristic pointed nose section that curved down slightly just in front of the two pilots and hinted at its ability to fly significantly faster than most similar private aircraft. Its livery was white with a blue stripe down each side, and the entire tailfin was dark blue with the words BLAZE-ONE written in large white capital letters across it. Powered by two powerful Pratt & Whitney PW800 engines it had a cruising speed of around 950 kilometres per hour or Mach 0.9, and a range of upwards of 9,500 kilometres. This meant that its expected flight time from Seattle to Newark Airport southwest of New York City was just under five hours. From there it would be a relatively quick twenty-minute drive past Jersey City and through the Holland Tunnel under the Hudson River to Lower Manhattan.

Once the last passengers had entered and strapped themselves into the plush white leather seats, the steps were folded back inside the aircraft and the door was flipped up to close and lock. Then the aircraft began to taxi to the end of its assigned runway where it skipped the queue of two small private jets waiting to take off. Within minutes it was racing down the runway almost due north, and soon after that, it lifted off effortlessly and immediately began banking right to head east.

Twenty-five minutes later it had reached its cruising altitude of 43,000 feet. The aircraft was approaching the city of Spokane and about to cross from Washington State into Montana when the two pilots engaged the autopilot. They then sat back in their seats to monitor the aircraft over the next several hours as it streaked across the sky, leaving a thin contrail behind it and rapidly making its way east across the breadth of the United States.

When the bomb exploded, the aircraft had passed over the city of Sturgeon Bay in northern Wisconsin about ten minutes earlier and was headed out over

Lake Michigan in the direction of the city of Frankfort on the eastern shore of the enormous lake.

About 11 kilometres north of Frankfort along the sandy beaches and dunes is the Point Betsie Lighthouse, which sits on a concrete-reinforced promontory overlooking Lake Michigan. Here, two men had braved the windy weather and come to fish. The sun had gone down a few minutes earlier and they were just packing up their equipment when one of them spotted the flash in the sky to the west out over the lake. Grabbing his partner and pointing, the two men then watched as a ball of fire briefly bloomed out due to the aircraft's fuel igniting immediately after the explosion. The flaming wreckage then began curving down slowly towards the lake and only then did the sound of the powerful explosion roll past them with the sound of distant thunder.

It took several minutes for the wreckage of the aircraft and its occupants to fall the 13 kilometres down and hit the water, and both men were able to record most of the event on their phones. Later that evening they sold their recordings to a national news network, as did many other people on both sides of Lake Michigan. Soon there were extensive reels of the incident all over the news media with several of the recordings randomly having caught the moment of the explosion. Authorities had announced that a search effort was underway, but that it would not be able to kick into full swing until daylight and that sadly the chance of finding any survivors was extremely slim.

* * *

'Andy! Thanks for coming over,' said Lynch and got up from behind his desk in the U.S. Embassy in London, grabbing a single sheet of paper from his desk as he did so.

'No problem,' said Andrew and closed the door to Lynch's office behind him. 'What's going on? You said it was urgent.'

'I needed to show you something,' said Lynch, looking as if something was weighing heavily on him. 'But it is highly classified so I am not allowed to take it outside this building. Come and grab a seat.'

Andrew sat down on the sofa, unbuttoning his suit jacket to make himself more comfortable.

'This is going to sound nuts,' said Lynch holding the sheet of paper with both hands and looking straight at Andrew who was sitting across from him, 'but we have received a transmission from the USS Tennessee.'

'Excuse me?' said Andrew, looking flabbergasted. 'A message? How? When?'

'It was picked up by one of the communications satellites the U.S. Navy currently has in orbit.'

'So, where is it?' asked Andrew.

'Well, we don't know exactly,' said Lynch, 'because the signal came from a so-called SLOT buoy, which is short for Submarine-Launched One-Way Transmitter Buoy. It is essentially a buoy that can be launched while the submarine is submerged down to around 150 metres if I remember correctly. But as I said, it is a one-way communication device designed to allow the submarine to get a message to the surface without itself having to surface. Before launch, it is loaded with a message and then it is released from the vessel after which it makes its way to the surface where it begins transmitting for a maximum of one hundred hours.'

'And this signal is definitely from USS Tennessee?' asked Andrew.

'Absolutely,' nodded Lynch. 'One hundred percent. The message has been authenticated by Naval Intelligence as having been sent by the USS Tennessee. It contains a unique encrypted code which only the Tennessee uses, so short of the Russians or the Chinese having got their hands on those highly classified codes and engaged in some elaborate hoax, we can safely assume that this is from the Tennessee.'

'I assume the buoy sends out precise location data?' asked Andrew.

'Yes,' replied Lynch. 'Along with its highly encrypted main message it obviously also transmits its location.'

'Where did it appear?'

'The buoy started transmitting its signal over something called the Azores-Biscay Rise, which is an underwater mountain range in the Atlantic roughly 700 kilometres due west of the north-western tip of Spain, and about 900 kilometres north-east of the Azores.'

'In other words, hundreds of kilometres from where the submarine vanished.'

'Actually, a lot more,' said Lynch. 'It is about 1,600 kilometres from there to the Anton Dohrn Seamount, so it has covered some serious distance since it disappeared.'

'From which we can assume that it suffered no damage in the explosion,' said Andrew.

'That much is clear,' replied Lynch.

'And now it suddenly decided to let us know where it is,' said Andrew, looking perplexed.

'That's the thing,' said Lynch. 'We're not just talking about a location beacon here. The buoy sent an encrypted message which does not appear to have been authorised by the captain or the XO.'

Andrew furrowed his brow and looked at Lynch.

'Well, who then?'

'We are not sure,' replied Lynch. 'Whoever sent it didn't include an identifier, but we have to assume it is one of the vessel's communications crew. No one else could have loaded the message into the buoy and then launched it.'

'Alright,' said Andrew. 'So, what did the message say?'

'Nothing good. Let me read it to you,' said Lynch, looking down on the sheet of paper and beginning to read it out loud.

> USS TENNESSEE HAS LEFT EXERCISE AREA.
> EXPERIMENTAL TORPEDO SABOTAGED.
> RUNNING SILENT. DESTINATION UNKNOWN.
> CAPTAIN INDICATES DEFCON 2.
> AWAITING VLF CONFIRMATION.
> CAPTAIN HAS RELIEVED THE COB OF DUTY.
> SLBM LAUNCH DRILL PERFORMED.
> URGENT: NEED DEFCON STATUS CONFIRMATION.

'Bloody hell,' said Andrew, looking both concerned and confused. 'What the hell is going on here?'

'Something has obviously gone badly awry on this boat,' said Lynch, 'and whoever sent this message has clearly become so concerned about the lack of confirmation of DEFCON status via the VLF-system that they have decided to take matters into their own hands, and then attempted to get word to central command using the only means available which is the SLOT-buoy.'

'It mentions DEFCON 2,' said Andrew. 'That's one of the nuclear alert states, right?'

'Correct,' replied Lynch. 'It's short for *Defence Readiness Condition* and it was designed to indicate the overall state of alert and readiness of the military, specifically the nuclear arsenal. DEFCON 5 is the lowest level and simply indicates normal readiness. DEFCON 1 officially indicates maximum readiness with a view to imminent action, but in reality, it means the outbreak of nuclear war.'

'And DEFCON 2?' asked Andrew.

'As the name implies it is one step away from the release of nuclear weapons,' said Lynch, 'and in practice, it indicates that nuclear weapons are ready to deploy in less than six hours if required.'

'So, in other words, Captain Vandenberg has readied the submarine for the launch of its Trident II missiles,' said Andrew. 'And he seems to have convinced the crew that they are now at DEFCON 2.'

'It would appear that way,' said Lynch. 'There is no way for us to verify this message or otherwise contact the Tennessee, but we have to assume that everything it says is true. Doing anything else would be too risky.

I know that this is how the White House and the Pentagon are treating it. They are scrambling for a plan as we speak. But none of this can obviously be released to the public at this point.'

'I understand,' said Andrew, looking uneasy. 'The message also indicated that the Chief of the Boat has been relieved of his duty, which I guess ought to be a huge alarm bell. And what was that thing about SLBM?'

'That is simply the acronym for Submarine-Launched Ballistic Missile,' said Lynch. 'According to this message they appear to have been running drills on launching the Trident II missiles.'

'Shit,' said Andrew, shaking his head. 'This has to mean that Vandenberg and maybe even his XO have gone rogue.'

'I know,' said Lynch bitterly. 'That is the only thing that explains everything that has happened. And it fits with the explosion of the swapped-out torpedo.'

'An elaborate ruse to convince the outside world that the Tennessee had sunk, and also dupe the crew into believing that they had been sabotaged and that war was about to break out.'

'Man,' breathed Lynch. 'It was never the Russians or a bunch of terrorists. It is our own damn guy. This is pretty much our worst nightmare, except for full-scale nuclear war.'

'We might end up with both scenarios if we don't manage to locate and recover the submarine,' said Andrew. 'If the Tennessee manages to launch just one of those missiles there is every chance that it could trigger a nuclear exchange between the U.S. and Russia, possibly even other nuclear powers.'

'If that is their plan,' said Lynch, looking ashen, 'then we should assume that they are planning to launch all 24 of those missiles, probably at cities around the world.'

'That's 288 cities,' said Andrew, looking horrified. 'That has to be around a third of the world's population. Jesus…'

'It is insane, I know,' said Lynch, 'but the fact that they have deliberately made the boat disappear and then evaded NATO naval forces to now be close to 2,000 kilometres away, should tell us that they have not done this because they have some agenda or outcome that they are trying to extort from the U.S. government. They don't want to talk, they don't want to try to force some political arrangement, and they don't want to be found, which can only mean that they intend to launch those missiles.'

Andrew nodded his head ruefully.

'I don't want to believe it,' he said, 'but I can't think of anything else that seems credible. Can't you track it down? You know where the buoy was launched, right? How many hours ago was this?'

'About 7 hours,' said Lynch. 'But it is not that simple. The Tennessee could have covered almost 400 kilometres since the buoy was launched, so that already leaves us a possible circular search area of just over half a million square kilometres. And that area grows with every minute that passes. Add to that the fact that this submarine was literally designed and built to avoid detection at all cost, and even if we could pick up its audio signature we would struggle to get the assets in place fast enough to deal with it.'

'What about the crew?' said Andrew. 'If whoever sent this message is correct, then this whole thing is orchestrated by Vandenberg and Chisholm, right? But that leaves 163 other crewmembers onboard that submarine who are essentially just following orders.'

'That's right,' said Lynch.

'How would a crew know if the orders their commanding officer gives them are authentic?' asked Andrew. 'I mean, apart from the message authentication procedure you told me about which only involves officers, the rest of the crew have no way of knowing or verifying if the orders are actually genuine.'

'Correct,' said Lynch. 'As you know, that is simply a function of the chain of command. You just don't question orders, but on a nuclear submarine that approach carries with it certain unique risks.'

'That a diplomatic way of putting it,' scoffed Andrew. 'These two people could literally start a nuclear war. I need to inform my superiors right away.'

'I know,' said Lynch. 'I wanted to let you know first since you and I are the main points of contact for the joint task force, but all of this will obviously come through to the UK's military and intelligence leadership very soon. We will have to wait and see what they decide to do. And they will obviously also need to involve the UK government.'

Andrew shook his head.

'Shit. Any luck on the personnel files of the Tennessee's crew yet?' he asked and stood up.

'No,' replied Lynch. 'I was about to go through them myself when this happened, so I haven't had time. But I will get right on it now. Do you want me to send the files over to you?'

'Yes,' replied Andrew. 'Please do. The situation has obviously changed now, but if there is anything useful in those files at all, we need to find it ASAP.'

'Roger,' said Lynch and rose as well. 'I will do that right now.'

'Ok,' said Andrew, looking weighed down by what he had been told. 'I will be in my office back at the Firm if you need me. Let's keep in touch and share whatever we find.'

'Sure thing,' replied Lynch. 'Talk to you later.'

★   ★   ★

Walking along the dark and narrow low-ceilinged corridor and approaching the door to Aaron Purnell's apartment on Willow Street, Fiona suddenly felt extremely vulnerable. The truth was that she had no idea what she might find there, and she had no way of protecting herself if Aaron's killers had come here as well.

Somewhere down the other end of the corridor she could hear the muffled sound of music coming from one of the other apartments, and from the outside through the window at the end of the corridor came the noise from what sounded like a van moving along the street, but she still felt like the sound of her own heels on the hard polished wood floor could be heard a mile away.

The door to Aaron's apartment was the last one down on the left, and as she neared it she discovered to her surprise that it was partly open. She stopped for a moment, trying to listen out for movement inside but she could hear none.

Peering through the gap, she saw the small hallway and a doorframe that looked like it might lead off into a bathroom. Outside the building she suddenly heard the sound of a police siren approaching, its insistent warble growing louder and louder and making her think for a moment that the NYPD was about to arrive at the home of the murder victim who at this point would probably have been identified, but then the sound began receding again. However, it was enough to jolt Fiona into action as she suddenly realised that she would not have unlimited time to search the apartment.

She placed the tip of her right shoe on the door and gently pushed it open to reveal what until today appeared to have been a neat and tidy hallway, but which now had clothes strewn all across the floor. It was obvious that Aaron's flat had been ransacked, almost certainly by the men who had murdered him. It must have happened while he and Fiona were getting to know each other in the café less than an hour earlier.

The thought made Fiona sick to her stomach, and she had to make an effort to remind herself that none of this was because of her. The ransacking of Aaron's flat and his murder would almost certainly have happened anyway. All she could do now was try to find out who Aaron's killers were, and then attempt to discover what his last cryptic words had meant.

Further along the hallway where it opened up into the living room, she could see the contents of drawers and shelves having been thrown onto the floor, and a tall lamp stand having been knocked over to lie across the back of a sofa. She quickly glanced over her shoulder to make sure there was no one else in the corridor, and then she slipped inside and pushed the door to, without closing it fully.

She glanced into the small neat white-tiled bathroom and then proceeded along the corridor to the living room. The sun was spilling in through the windows bathing the apartment in its warm golden light and giving it a warm and friendly ambience.

Fiona walked into the bedroom at the back to find another mess of clothes and possessions spread out in chaotic fashion everywhere, and she noticed that all the pictures on the walls had been torn off, possibly because the two killers would have been looking for a safe.

Walking back into the living room, she noticed a small desk in the corner with a table lamp, two small speakers and a mouse on a mouse pad. There was no laptop though. Aaron might have had it in the small backpack he was wearing when they met. Fiona suddenly realised that when she had run over to him lying there in a pool of blood on Henry Street, he had not been wearing the backpack anymore and she did not remember it being anywhere on the sidewalk. The man with the gun must have snatched it. Was that why they killed him? Were they after the laptop, or were they out to silence him, or perhaps both?

Fiona stepped closer to examine the small desk. This must have been where Aaron would sit and write his articles. It was a nice sunny spot overlooking the street, and with a tall tree outside she could see how that must have been a pleasant and relaxing place to work. As she walked closer, she could see that a small drawer in the desk had been pulled out and rummaged through, but there was no other sign of the assailants.

'Rainbow,' she muttered quietly to herself with a puzzled look on her face as she turned around to look at the living room and the kitchen at the other end of it. 'Wait for the sunset.'

She shook her head. She had no idea what she was meant to be looking for, but she walked over to the window to see the sun now much lower in the sky than when she and Aaron had met. In fact, it looked like it would be disappearing below the roof of the buildings on the other side of Willow Street soon.

She turned around to find that her shadow was being cast onto the opposite wall, where a picture had hung before being thrown onto the floor by Aaron's killers. She walked over to the wall and examined the spot where the shadow of her head had been a few seconds earlier but could find nothing unusual. She briefly considered if there was a hidden cavity inside the wall and if she might need to smash her way through the plasterboards. However, she decided that it would create too much noise, and trashing a murder victim's apartment immediately after his death was going to be next to impossible to explain or justify to the police if they suddenly showed up.

She went to look out of the window again to see if she could spot any approaching police cars, but the street was empty apart from a glamorously dressed woman walking two poodles that were both wearing tartan dog coats and what looked like crystal-studded collars.

Shaking her head, Fiona turned around and sat down on the window sill with her head slumped in front of herself. What was she meant to find here? And how? She was no Sherlock Holmes or Inspector Poirot. She was good at discovering well-hidden archaeological secrets, not investigating murders and performing forensic examinations of apartments.

She sighed and lifted her head again, and that is when she spotted it. Coming in through the window behind her, the sunlight was hitting a small mirror sitting on a shelf. The mirror had bevelled edges, which caused it to refract the sunlight and shine the full spectrum of all the colours of the rainbow onto a small patch on the floor near the far corner of the room.

Fiona sat up and stared at it. Then she looked behind her to see the sun just about to dip down below the rooftop on the other side of the street. Turning again to look at the tiny rainbow on the floor, she then got up and walked over to kneel down next to it. It was moving at a glacial, barely perceptible pace across the floorboards as the sun gradually sank lower in the sky, and as the last rays came in through the window, it began to disappear on the penultimate floorboard running the length of the room just where it met the skirting board.

That particular section of floorboard was unusually short, and it appeared that the carpenter who laid these boards down decades ago had simply cut and fixed a small piece there to make up for the previous floorboard being about a hand's breadth too short.

Fiona reached for the small section of floorboard as the sun finally disappeared behind the rooftop and the tiny rainbow departed with it. Gripping the edges of the small board, she was amazed to find that it came up and out easily, exposing a dark cavity. She leaned over it and looked down. Inside was a small clear re-sealable plastic bag with a USB stick inside it.

'Bingo,' whispered Fiona and reached inside the cavity. 'Aaron, you clever fox.'

Pulling out the bag, she held it up in front of herself and peered at it. It looked like any other USB stick she had ever seen, but she guessed that this one might contain copies of all the documents Aaron has stolen from the underground complex in Arizona.

Fiona quickly tucked the stick into a jacket pocket and then she rose to leave. Just then she heard the sound of a motorcycle accelerating up the street. She froze as the noise became louder, but then let out a sigh of relief when it passed the building and continued on.

Deciding she had stayed for much longer than was sensible, she got up and walked back out into the corridor where she gripped the door handle through the sleeve of her jacket. Then she positioned the door so that it looked the way it did when she had arrived. She walked back to the stairs, down to the raised ground floor and then she hurried back down the steps to the sidewalk.

As she walked along, an NYPD patrol vehicle came round the corner at the far end of the street. She continued walking but forced herself to slow down and look casual. As the patrol vehicle passed her, she buried her face in her phone and pretended to be rubbing the side of her forehead so that the police officers would not be able to see her face. For all she knew, the police already had CCTV footage from the Pineapple Café and the Hotel St. George.

Glancing casually over her shoulder at the patrol car, Fiona then sped up and walked briskly along the sidewalk and away from Aaron's apartment. When she got to the end of Willow Street, she risked another look back towards the building, and a tight knot instantly formed in her stomach when she saw the two officers get out of their parked patrol car and look up towards the first floor of the building. One of them was talking on his radio, probably letting the NYPD dispatch centre know that they had arrived and were about to enter the apartment.

As soon as Fiona had cleared the corner of Willow Street and Clark Street, she began jogging. She crossed the road and took the next left down Hick's Street and soon found herself in front of Joe's Coffee which was a small coffee shop on a corner. She went inside and ordered a cup of black coffee, and then she walked to the back of the shop and found a table for one in the corner of the room where she sat down with her back to the wall so she could see the entrance to the shop.

Above the coffee bar, where two of the staff were busy preparing drinks for their patrons and serving up pastries on small plates, was a wall-mounted TV showing NBC4 New York. The sound had been switched off, but she suddenly recognised the street that was being shown. It was outside Hotel St. George on Henry Street where Aaron had been killed.

For a terrifying moment, she thought she was going to sit there and watch herself at the scene of the murder, but then she realised that the camera crew would have arrived a good while after she had left.

The reporter was holding a big microphone with an oversized NBC4 logo on it and interviewing someone who might have been a witness, or perhaps just someone who lived nearby that had stopped to see what was happening.

Fiona quickly but discreetly scanned the coffee shop to see if anyone was watching her, but the other handful of people in there were either talking to each other or reading books or newspapers, and she seemed to be the only one looking at the TV.

At that moment the waiter arrived and placed the coffee in front of her. She smiled, and as the waiter left she reached into her bag and pulled out her laptop, flipping it open and powering it up. As soon as it was ready she plugged in the USB stick, and immediately an overview of its files popped up on the screen. There was a whole range of files in many different formats, all of them with names that made no sense to her. They seemed to be construction plans, technical drawings and schematics, as well as the odd document detailing what might have been employee rosters.

However, what immediately got her attention was a folder at the top of the overview which had been named, *Fiona – Read Me!*

Fiona stared at the folder for a few seconds, glanced around the coffee shop, and then opened the folder. Inside was a single video file.

She quickly got out her wireless headphones and put them into her ears. Then she clicked on the video file and waited as the playback began. After a couple of seconds, Aaron appeared on the screen. He looked slightly tense but otherwise ok, and he was wearing the same clothes that he had been wearing when he met her, so this must have been recorded only a few hours ago.

'Fiona,' said Aaron's digital ghost. 'If you are watching this, it must mean that something bad has happened to me.'

Fiona swallowed, struggling to keep her composure as she felt her eyes welling up.

'This is a bit weird since I haven't even met you yet,' continued Aaron, 'but I figured I would make myself a backup plan, and you sound like someone I can trust. I really hope I turn out to be overly paranoid about this, but better safe than sorry.'

Fiona blinked a couple of times and produced a small sniff. Hearing Aaron's voice again was surreal, and it made her feel desperately sad.

'Anyway, the files on this memory stick contain a ton of information about the complex I snuck into in Arizona,' continued Aaron, 'but they also contain something else. Something a lot more strange and worrying. There are plans here for a much bigger complex somewhere in New Zealand as far as I can see. It is on a whole different scale from the one in Arizona. There are also long lists of people from all over the world, mainly politicians, finance leaders and industrial types, and they are all listed with what looks like their families. I have not had a lot of time to go through them, but they seem like people that are a lot like Dietrich in terms of their politics and the things they have said publicly. There are also hundreds of other people who each have an extensive personnel file listing their various skills and qualifications.'

Fiona's forehead was now deeply creased as she tried to take in what Aaron was saying, even though it sounded utterly mad.

'So,' said Aaron, 'since I figured no one goes through that much effort and expense for nothing, I think Dietrich either knows something bad is coming or worse still, he might be trying to create some catastrophic event which he and a huge bunch of other like-minded people can then ride out somewhere in a bunker in New Zealand. I still don't know what he might be planning, but maybe you can find a clue somewhere in these files. And listen, I know it all sounds nuts. Like something out of a movie, but look at the files for yourself. It's all there. One last thing before I head off to meet you. This is gonna sound paranoid, but don't trust anyone. There are thousands of people on those lists, so assume that anyone you speak to is in on this crazy plan. I'm gonna stop here. I hope I will be back soon to delete this video, and I really hope I will never need it, but these people mean business so just be really cautious from now on. Take care.'

Fiona watched as Aaron then reached toward the camera with a worried look on his face, and then the recording ended.

'Shit,' whispered Fiona, feeling as if a huge weight was suddenly bearing down on her. 'Shit. Shit. Shit.'

What the hell am I going to do?

About an hour later, Fiona had gone through a large number of the files on the USB stick. Everything Aaron had said on the video turned out to be true. Hundreds of high-profile political and business leaders, mainly on the fringes of mainstream politics and often vocal supporters of libertarian agendas, were on those lists along with their families. But the majority of the people on the lists were highly qualified scientists in almost any field imaginable, as well as scores of different types of craftsmen, engineers, medical professionals and teachers. In short, it was a broad spectrum of skillsets. Everything a community might need for starting over from scratch. It left Fiona numb. The scale of it was as impressive as it was terrifying, and the only conceivable purpose was exactly what Aaron had said. An effort to ride out a coming cataclysmic event, either natural or man-made.

Fiona also discovered information about a handful of secret underground locations spread out across the world where huge amounts of hardware were supposedly stored. Much of it was of an industrial nature, but a large part of it was also military, seemingly designed to equip a small army with the latest and most lethal high-tech weapons and equipment.

Deep inside a separate file structure that seemed to revolve around other military hardware, Fiona found a reference to something called The Sword. Along with it was the designation, SSBN-734. She had no idea what that meant but it only took her a couple of minutes to find out, and when she did, her face turned ashen as the room began spinning and she started to feel slightly nauseous.

Composing herself again, Fiona now knew what she needed to do. She was going to go back to her hotel room and try to reach Andrew, and then she was going to go back to London as soon as possible. She was way out of her depth here, and it would be a question of time before something bad happened to her too.

Five minutes later, as Fiona left Joe's Coffee, a man who had come in a few minutes after her and had sat down by the window got up, placed a twenty-dollar bill on his table and then exited the shop to follow her.

Thirteen

Sixteen Hours Earlier – The Atlantic Ocean

Operations specialist Antonio Martinez was sitting on the floor of the makeshift brig that had been set up inside a small storage locker on Deck 2 of the USS Tennessee just next to the auxiliary machinery room and immediately above the crew's mess hall. The cramped floorspace was too small to lie down on unless he curled up, which he had resorted to doing just to try to get some sleep. He was of small stature, but even he had struggled to fit onto the floor without being so uncomfortable that he was unable to fall asleep. He could hear all the familiar noises of the submarine, both man-made and those emanating from the hundreds of different mechanical, hydraulic and ventilation systems that are required to make something as complex as a nuclear submarine work as one single integrated machine. Formerly known as a Radio Operator, his role and that of his team involved the operation of all communications equipment on the submarine, as well as radar and navigation equipment. The radio room on the Ohio-class submarine is immediately in front of the command & control centre commonly known as the bridge, and it is an integral part of how the submarine is controlled by the captain and his executive officer.

Growing up in the working-class suburb of Bayside West in Tampa Bay, Florida, Martinez had always had a knack for electronics. Not just computers and phones and iPads like many of his friends, but actual electronics built at home from components that he bought off the internet. He had built several shortwave radios during his time in high school, and he had spent hours scanning the airwaves and striking up conversations with random people from all over the country.

Eventually, though, he had ended up discouraged by his discovery that there were really very few jobs available for a tinkerer like him. At one point a friend of one of his cousins had offered to pay him to modify a set of police scanners so that one of the local drug gangs could better monitor police chatter, but Martinez had refused. This had earned him a bloody nose and a reputation for being a straight arrow, but that still did not do much for his career opportunities.

Then one day, one of his friends had suggested that he join the navy, and after initially being reticent since he had never even considered it, and because none of his family had ever served, he had decided to talk to a recruiter. A week later he had signed up and he had never looked back. He loved the U.S. Navy, the job, the lifestyle and the fact that he actually got paid to do something he would have done for free.

This was his second year of service, and he was considering taking officer training and making a real career of it.

Sitting there on the floor inside the storage locker, all of those dreams suddenly seemed a million miles away. Until two days ago, Martinez had been part of a tight-knit, highly qualified and efficient team providing the captain with the information he needed in order to assess the situation outside of the submarine, particularly when it was submerged.

Not once during his time serving on the USS Tennessee had Martinez had reason to question or doubt Captain Vandenberg, but that had changed when the vessel had been rocked by an explosion during the NATO exercise in the North Atlantic, supposedly from a malfunctioning torpedo. After the initial damage assessment, the captain had ordered the ship to proceed southwest instead of immediately surfacing and evacuating the crew, or at least as much of it as could be spared without compromising the ability of the submarine to operate and navigate at a basic level. Not only that, but the captain had then ordered the submarine to descend to 400 metres which was far below normal operating depth, and he had then ordered silent running which meant that he clearly thought the vessel was under threat from enemy submarines or surface vessels.

All of this had happened without there being any indication of hostile vessels on any of the scopes, and the sonar team had reported no contacts anywhere nearby.

Over the following hours, the submarine had made its way quietly south-east along the Rockall Trough, which is a deep-water feature between Ireland to the south-east and the 500-kilometre-wide underwater mountain range called the Rockall Plateau to the north-west. The crew had carried out their orders as usual, but there had been an unusual atmosphere on the boat. At one point, Tom Payne who was the mild-mannered Chief of the Boat and who was only ever referred to as the 'COB', had openly questioned Captain Vandenberg about what his intentions were.

Payne, as the highest-ranking enlisted sailor on the vessel, had graduated top of his class from the Navy's Senior Enlisted Academy and had then been picked by Naval Military Personnel Command for good reason. He was bright, sensible and known to be a thoughtful and fair person, and he was well respected by the enlisted men even on the odd occasion when he was compelled to dole out punishment for minor disciplinary issues.

Without sounding antagonistic, Payne had asked Vandenberg to let the men know why he had decided to suddenly leave the NATO exercise and sail back out into the Atlantic, when navy regulation stipulated that in a situation such as theirs, where a weapon had malfunctioned during peace-time operations, the captain should have immediately attempted to surface and then evacuate the crew if necessary.

Captain Vandenberg had dismissed his concerns but Payne had insisted, clearly sensing that something just wasn't right about the captain's behaviour. He had continued to push for the captain to justify breaking regulation, until suddenly Vandenberg had snapped and ordered him detained, which as far as Martinez knew was something that had never happened on the USS Tennessee before, either during or before Vandenberg's time as captain of the submarine.

After Payne had been marched off the bridge and placed in confinement inside his own small quarters next to the officer's quarters on Deck 2, just below the navigation room near the front of the submarine, Vandenberg had returned to his captain's chair in the middle of the bridge and had stood in front of it for a few moments, visibly tense.

'1 MC,' Vandenberg had then said, indicating his intention to address the entire crew on the main circuit of the boat's PA system.

He had then grabbed the microphone from its overhead holder immediately above the captain's seat and placed it in front of his mouth.

'This is the captain,' he had announced with a hard edge to his voice. 'I have relieved Chief of the Boat Tom Payne of his duty for failing to carry out a direct order, effective immediately. The XO will be taking over the COB's duties until further notice. We are currently in a situation where one of our weapons systems may have been sabotaged, possibly as part of a plan to neutralise this vessel's ability to carry out ballistic missile launch orders from the President. That is as serious as it gets, people. Until we can establish the facts from up top, we are going to assume that open conflict has broken out on the surface. My intention is to get this vessel clear of the likely combat zone and then surface in order to establish two-way communication with CENTCOM and receive new orders.'

Vandenberg had paused as the entire bridge watched him silently, waiting for him to finish his address.

'Now,' he had eventually continued, with a slightly menacing tone of voice. 'If anyone else has any concerns about my ability to command this vessel, now would be a perfect time to keep it to yourself. I will *not* have my authority questioned. We live and die by the integrity of the chain of command. When you question me, you question the United States Navy and by extension the President of the United States. Do *not* forget that. This is the captain.'

Vandenberg had then slammed the microphone back up into its holder with a precision that could only come from having repeated that precise movement of his right arm thousands of times over the past many years.

'Helmsman, adjust heading, One-Eight-Five,' Vandenberg had then ordered.

'Adjust heading, One-Eight-Five,' Chisholm had repeated impassively.

'Ay-Ay, adjusting heading to One-Eight-Five,' the helmsman had called out.

The helmsman had then turned the controls slightly to the left, and about 130 metres behind them the huge rudders on the submarine had pushed out to the left slightly, thereby forcing the submarine to adjust its course slowly and gradually to a heading that was almost due south.

During the entire episode, Martinez had sat frozen in his chair in front of his screens, still carrying out his duties as normal but deeply uncomfortable with the sudden discord and aggression on display on the bridge. This was something he had never seen before, but then nothing like this situation had ever happened before either.

What had initially concerned Martinez the most, apart from the supposedly sabotaged torpedo and the explosion it created, was that this situation had arisen without any confirmation of surface hostilities on the VLF system. If some type of non-nuclear exchange had happened on the surface, the USS Tennessee would almost certainly have received new orders via the VLF system by now, but no such message had arrived. As the boat's on-duty communications operations specialist, Martinez would have been the first to know.

Around three hours after Tom Payne's removal from the bridge, the USS Tennessee had been exiting the Rockall Trough and heading south-southeast over the northern part of the almost four-kilometre-deep West European Basin some 500 kilometres due west of Dursey Point in Ireland. There had been an eerie quietness on the bridge that was unusual, as if everyone knew that things were somehow different but no one wanted to poke their head above the parapet. The captain and the XO had said very little but had talked quietly amongst themselves a couple of times.

At one point, the captain had ordered the helmsman to make his depth just 30 metres. Martinez had been at his station in front of his screens when suddenly the large EAM light mounted near the ceiling had flashed red and a brief but shrill three-pulsed alert noise had sounded from a small speaker next to it. The board indicated receipt of a so-called

'Emergency Action Message', which is a special type of incoming message received via the VLF system. It is typically used to notify nuclear submarines of changes to their required alert level and to relay nuclear launch orders to the commanding officer. The messages are formulated and sent by the National Military Command Center in the Pentagon and relayed by VLF to nuclear submarines using various encryption protocols, and they are formatted in a unique way and are often very brief.

Martinez had only ever seen it flash during exercises which was the way he preferred it. As soon as he saw it, his training had immediately taken over and he had activated his microphone to notify the captain using the old naval term 'Conn', which is short for conning tower, indicating the bridge and the captain's seat.

'Conn - Radio,' he said with a slight urgency in his voice. 'Receiving emergency action message.'

Immediately, the message had begun to appear on his screen, arriving in small sections due to the limited bandwidth of the VLF system. XO John Chisholm had swiftly walked over to stand behind Martinez as the message slowly filled the screen. As soon as it was complete, the built-in printer on the console in front of Martinez began printing out the message. After a couple of seconds, Chisholm had reached in front of Martinez to grab the sheet of paper. As per required procedure, he had then made a show of walking it to the captain whilst holding it up high so that the rest of the crew could see that he was not tampering with it, and that what was handed to the captain was what had come through on the EAM system a few seconds earlier.

'Captain, we have a properly formatted emergency action message from the National Military Command Center,' said Chisholm and handed the sheet the Vandenberg. 'Message indicates this is a drill.'

Vandenberg took the sheet and studied it for a few seconds after which he looked up at the XO.

'Very well. Retrieve the authenticator,' said Vandenberg. 'Secure for battle stations.'

'Ay-ay Captain,' responded Chisholm and grabbed the microphone above him. 'All hands. Secure for battle stations.'

Throughout the huge submarine, the entire crew suddenly broke off what they were doing and then hurriedly began preparing the boat for combat operations.

On the bridge, Chisholm walked swiftly but calmly to a locker immediately behind the centre of the bridge. He opened the locker door to reveal a safe with a dial combination lock. Quickly rotating the wheel three times, he entered the correct combination and opened the safe. Inside were two compartments, one blue and one red. They both held a small clear plastic brick known as 'the biscuits', each of which contained small pieces of paper of the same colour as the inside of their respective compartments in the safe. The blue compartment had a small sign saying *Drill Authentications*, and the red compartment had a sign saying *Launch Authentications*. Next to the red biscuit was a small metal key on a long thin chain.

Chisholm reached for the blue authenticator biscuit and carried it to the captain.

'Request permission to authenticate,' he said.

'Permission granted,' responded Vandenberg calmly. 'Authenticate.'

Chisholm broke open the biscuit and read out the sequence of letters whilst regularly glancing at the EAM print-out to confirm the seven-letter sequence.

'Bravo. Tango. Echo. Alpha. Echo. Delta. Tango'

He looked up at Captain Vandenberg and handed him the message. 'Message is authentic, sir.'

'I concur,' replied Vandenberg, after examining the sheet of paper with the EAM for a few seconds. 'Message is authentic. 1 MC.'

He reached up for the microphone above the captain's seat again and pulled it down to his mouth.

'This is the captain,' he said in his usual steady and authoritative tone of voice. 'Set condition 1 SQ for strategic missile launch. Initiate spin-up sequence for missiles 1 through 24. This is a drill. I repeat. This is a drill.'

Martinez had glanced sideways at one of his colleagues in the radio room, and the two of them looked at each other briefly both knowing that this was not how things were supposed to happen. The chief of the boat, Tom Payne, was also meant to have given his consent that the EAM was authentic, but since he was locked up, Chisholm had taken over his role, thereby effectively removing one of the safeguards against an unauthorised launch.

A few moments later the captain turned to his executive officer.

'XO. Status,' he ordered.

'Target package loaded and confirmed,' said Chisholm. 'All launch systems spun up and nominal. Ready to launch.'

'Very well,' nodded Vandenberg, producing a small satisfied smile.

Then he reached up for the microphone again.

'This is the captain. Set condition 4 SQ. Drill complete. I repeat. Drill complete. Well done, people.'

Vandenberg put the microphone back in its holder. 'XO has the conn,' he announced.

'XO has the conn,' repeated Chisholm.

Vandenberg then got down from his elevated captain's chair and left the bridge.

At the end of his eight-hour shift, Martinez had felt weighed down by what he had witnessed. As he walked down to Deck 1 and back to his bunk, everything on the boat had seemed normal. Everyone was going about their business performing their duties as planned, but Martinez had a gnawing sensation somewhere at the back of his brain telling him that something was not right about what was happening on the boat.

At the bottom of the stairs just as he was about to turn left and head towards the crew's berthing section where his bunk was, he had spotted Chisholm coming from his right towards the stairs. The XO must have been in his cabin for a rest himself, and he was now on his way back to the bridge upstairs.

Martinez had immediately moved over to the right of the narrow corridor with his back to the wall in order to make space for the senior officer to pass. As Chisholm was about to walk past him, Martinez had saluted and Chisholm responded in kind and nodded.

As soon as Chisholm had disappeared up the stairs, Martinez had an idea that he then instantly regretted. But now that it had planted itself inside his head, there was no way he would be able to get rid of it until he had done what he felt compelled to do.

He had made his way away from the crew's berthing section and towards the officer's quarters, and soon he was outside the executive officer's room. Quickly glancing behind him, Martinez had seen just one other person and he was moving away along the narrow corridor towards the back of the boat.

Without hesitating, Martinez had gripped the door handle and turned it. To his surprise, it had been unlocked, but then again someone would have to be out of their mind to enter the XO's private quarters without permission.

Quickly slipping inside, it had only taken him a couple of seconds to spot what he was looking for. The EAM was lying crumpled up inside the waste paper basket next to Chisholm's desk. Martinez had bent down and snatched the sheet of paper, tucking it inside his pocket and then slipping back out into the corridor. The whole thing had taken less than half a minute, and to his relief, Martinez emerged from the room without anyone noticing him. He had then walked back to his bunk, climbed up into it and drawn the small blue curtain that was his only means of achieving some measure of privacy on board the submarine.

His hands were trembling as he extracted the crumpled-up sheet of paper from his pocket. He knew that he could probably be court marshalled and locked up for what he had done, especially if it was ever discovered precisely what he had taken from the XO's room. He had flattened the sheet of paper as best he could and had begun reading it.

* EMERGENCY ACTION MESSAGE *

// DRILL //

NATIONAL MILITARY COMMAND CENTER
USS TENNESSEE (SSBN-734)
AUTHORIZATION FOR NUCLEAR MISSILE LAUNCH

1. SET DEFCON 2
2. LAUNCH TWENTY-FOUR (24) MISSILES
3. TARGET PACKAGE: SLBM 2791/4
4. AUTHENTICATION: BTEAEDT

//DRILL //

On the face of it, the message seemed authentic, but when Martinez looked at it closely, two things did not seem right. The first thing was the character spacing in the bullet points. There seemed to be 1½ character spaces between the bullet point numbers and each individual order. This had never happened on any VLF message he had ever seen. But much more glaring to him was the fact that the target package did not end with '/0' which it should have done if it had been part of a drill using an empty package. Instead, it included '/4' which indicated that it contained a full target package containing a pre-determined target spread of up to 12 targets per missile.

Martinez was by no means one of the most experienced submariners on the boat, but he had been around long enough to know that encrypted U.S. Navy communications had pre-set formats and that they never *ever* deviated from those formats.

The only two possible scenarios that could explain the formatting of this EAM were that either the standard format had been changed without any notice at some point during the past thirty-six hours, or that the message was not authentic.

The first option was completely inconceivable to Martinez since a change to the communications protocol aboard a nuclear submarine would be announced well in advance and implemented with the knowledge of everyone on the bridge, but especially people in charge of the communications equipment itself. People like Martinez.

The second option seemed equally unthinkable, but since the first option could be assigned a probability of zero, option two simply had to be true. The recent unusual behaviour of Vandenberg and Chisholm quickly convinced Martinez that something was very wrong on the USS Tennessee. The only question was - how could he do something about it?

Given that the submarine could remain submerged for many days without having to rise to snorkel depth to get fresh air, attempting to send a message to CENTCOM using standard procedure was out of the question, especially since he needed to make it happen as soon as possible. The only other available option was to attempt to launch a SLOT-buoy with a message to central command, which would then hopefully elicit some sort of response via the VLF system, either to confirm the captain's assertion about open conflict on the surface or to dispel that assertion and then order him to surface the boat and establish two-way communications with CENTCOM.

Martinez had to wait until his next shift to carry out his plan so he had gone to the gym, had his dinner and then tried to get some sleep. He had managed to get perhaps four hours of shut-eye during the next twelve hours, so he had been feeling slightly groggy by the time he returned to his station in the radio room next to the bridge. Captain Vandenberg was not on the bridge at that time, so the XO had the conn.

Waiting until Chisholm was occupied by a conversation with one of the weapons specialists, Martinez had typed a short message on his system and loaded it into one of the SLOT buoys. He had then set it on a timer and made sure to be away from his station for a couple of minutes during the launch, just in case it was noticed. There was no sound as the buoy was released from its pod on the top of the boat, and when Martinez returned to his seat he could see that the buoy had been released and was on its way to the surface. It was likely that the next person in his chair would notice the missing buoy, but hopefully, by then, there would be a response on the VLF system.

As it turned out, it did not take nearly that long. One of his colleagues noticed the missing buoy about ten minutes later, and as soon as he called over the XO who seemed visibly upset by the discovery,

Martinez had known that the game was up. Instead of allowing one of his colleagues to be accused by the XO of the unauthorised launch of a very expensive communications buoy, he had immediately come clean. A few minutes later the captain had arrived on the bridge and come straight to Martinez's station where Chisholm was hovering over him with a face like storm clouds.

A few minutes later, Martinez had found himself locked inside the storage locker and guarded by a tall muscular African-American sailor named Dwayne Jackson. Jackson had been taken off engineering duty to guard Martinez who was now designated a saboteur. Martinez briefly considered talking to Jackson, but he decided it was a lost cause. He was now a pariah on board the Tennessee, and he was sure that rumours were already circulating on the vessel to the effect that he was some sort of spy and that he was working with the enemy, whoever that was now.

Fourteen

When Fiona arrived back in her room at the Hugo Hotel on Greenwich Street in Lower Manhattan, she put the bag with the laptop on the bed and sat down next to it. Pulling it out, flipping it open and pressing the power button, she waited a couple of moments for it to boot up, and then she began copying all the files from Aaron's USB stick to the laptop's hard drive. She then also copied the cache of files to a personal cloud storage account. She could not afford for this information to be lost, stolen or destroyed.

As the files began uploading to the cloud, Fiona rose and got out her phone, hitting the speed-dial for Andrew's number. Once again there was no answer, and Fiona was becoming increasingly frustrated at not being able to reach him. She needed his advice and reassurance more than ever now.

Instead, she spent a few minutes arranging a flight back to London that evening, and then she took a shower and spent about an hour combing through more of the huge files from Aaron's memory stick.

A couple of hours later when Andrew finally called her back, she snatched the phone off the bed, feeling a wave of relief washing over her.

'Andrew, finally,' said Fiona. 'I am so happy you called me back.'

'Are you alright?' asked Andrew, seeming puzzled. 'You sound upset.'

'I am,' sighed Fiona as she sat back down on the end of the bed. 'I think I am in over my head here. Something awful has happened.'

'What do you mean?' asked Andrew.

Fiona told him about the murder, or as she had begun to think of it, the assassination of Aaron Purnell, at which point Andrew had become audibly concerned. She also relayed much of what Aaron had told her at the Pineapple Café, and then she relayed what had happened during her visit to Aaron's flat.

'Are you sure you are alright?' asked Andrew

'I think so,' said Fiona weakly. 'I am not really sure how to feel. The reality is that I didn't know Aaron well at all, but we somehow jelled really quickly and the thought of him just simply being gone is heartbreaking.'

She paused for a moment, before continuing.

'It was as if he already understood that he was a target. When the guy jumped off the motorcycle and began walking toward us, Aaron didn't hesitate. He pushed me away from himself to protect me. As if he knew what was about to happen.'

'That must have been a shocking experience,' said Andrew. 'I am just glad you are unhurt. I'd like to get my hands on the bastard who shot at you.'

'I expect they are long gone by now, said Fiona. 'Anyway, I spent some more time looking through the files on Aaron's memory stick, and I found some really strange stuff about New Zealand. Firstly, there were a couple of documents on the memory stick that Aaron had written himself. They were sort of like his own personal notes on his investigation, and one of them indicated that he had discovered that Dietrich had successfully applied for citizenship in New Zealand.'

'That's odd,' said Andrew.

'Not really,' said Fiona. 'Because it means that he would be able to buy property there, and that is exactly what he has done. It seems that he bought an enormous plot of land on the South Island, using the Dietrich Foundation and a holding company in the Cayman Islands. It is about 80 square miles in size and about an hour's drive into the mountains from the nearest town. Apparently, there wasn't even a road leading to it, so he built one himself.'

'Ok,' said Andrew hesitantly. 'So, what do you suppose that means?'

'Well,' replied Fiona. 'There are construction plans for a huge underground complex inside a mountain there, and the more I look at it the more it becomes clear to me that the Arizona facility was just a small prototype for this much larger complex in New Zealand. The one in Arizona was a circular atrium with lots of apartments leading off from it, probably able to accommodate about 150 people. And of course, it also contained all the support facilities that a small community like that might need to be self-sustained for an extended period of time. The plans for the New Zealand complex show a gigantic central underground area that has tunnels leading off to what looks like ten exact copies of the Arizona facility. If I had to guess, just looking at the size of the facility and its capacity, I would say that it is some sort of underground shelter for hundreds of people, possibly even several thousand. Some type of doomsday bunker.'

'Damn,' said Andrew, now sounding unsettled as he began to get an unpleasant sinking feeling in his stomach. 'Sounds like they are preparing for the end of the world. Have you been able to corroborate any of the information you received from Aaron?'

'No,' replied Fiona. 'I'm not sure how I would do that except to travel to Arizona myself, but after what Aaron told me about his trip there, that is the very last thing I want to do right now.'

'You definitely should not do that,' said Andrew.

'Don't worry,' said Fiona. 'I have just booked a flight back to London. I am leaving tonight. Anyway, I should also just tell you about what happened in Italy.'

She then went on to tell him about her work with Dietrich to recover the Corona Civica, and how he seemed to have become a different person as soon as he realised that she was unwilling to play along with everything he wanted.

'He sounds like a complete megalomaniac,' said Andrew. 'I am glad you decided to stop working with him.'

'Yes, I'd like to be able to look myself in the mirror,' said Fiona.

'This Corona Civica seems like a strange thing to try to find,' said Andrew. 'Did you get any sense of what he wanted it for?'

'Not at the time,' replied Fiona. 'But after everything I have learned since then, it seems clear that Dietrich thinks of himself as some sort of Caesar. There are multiple references to something called *The Order* in those files I got from Aaron. And there are also lists of hundreds of people, almost all of them with some designation or title that harks back to Roman times, like Senator, Praetor, Centurion, Praetorian and so on. It is as if there is already some sort of pre-determined hierarchy in place with Dietrich at the top. And if he really is involved in this end-of-the-world project in New Zealand, then I would put money on him setting himself up as some sort of new emperor, which probably also explains the whole Corona Civica thing. The whole thing sounds completely deranged. I mean, how would he even achieve that outcome?'

Despite his urge to share what he had been dealing with in London over the past several days, Andrew resisted since all of that information was extremely sensitive and highly classified. Telling her would mean risking his career, but *not* telling her just might mean the loss of everything. Or was he getting carried away?

'You seem convinced that Dietrich was behind the murder of Aaron Purnell,' he said.

'It is the only thing that makes sense,' replied Fiona insistently. 'Clearly, Aaron was uncovering some serious aspects to Dietrich and his foundation that no one was supposed to know, and they simply got rid of him. It might even have been Dietrich himself that gave the order.'

'Fiona, I need to ask you if you have watched the news?' asked Andrew. 'I am guessing you haven't.'

'Yes, one of the local news channels over here was covering it,' replied Fiona. 'They must have arrived at the scene soon after I left.'

'No, not that,' said Andrew. 'The news about Dietrich.'

'No,' said Fiona, instinctively turning her head towards the black screen of the TV in the hotel room. 'What about him?'

'His private jet crashed into Lake Michigan yesterday evening,' replied Andrew. 'Apparently, there was a bomb on board which exploded at high altitude.'

'What!?' exclaimed Fiona loudly, now barely able to process what was happening.

'Yes, it is all over the news,' said Andrew. 'They recovered several charred bodies from the lake earlier today, but they haven't yet been able to locate Dietrich who was on the flight manifest.'

'Oh my God,' said Fiona, her voice trembling. 'What the hell is going on?'

'Not sure,' replied Andrew. 'But whatever it is, you should get yourself back here.'

'I guess,' replied Fiona. 'But what about what Aaron found? I can't just ignore it. He was killed for what he knew. I am sure of it.'

'Listen,' said Andrew. 'Both Aaron and Dietrich are dead now. There is nothing more you can do over there.'

Fiona hesitated for a few seconds.

'Is he?' she asked probingly. 'Is Dietrich really dead? I mean, you said they hadn't found his body.'

'Well, that doesn't mean anything,' said Andrew. 'He could have been blown up in the explosion or simply ended up sinking to the bottom of Lake Michigan. They might never find him.'

'I don't think they ever will,' said Fiona, 'because I don't think he is dead.'

'Really?' asked Andrew. 'Do you think he parachuted out or something?'

'I don't know,' said Fiona. 'But I think he just staged his own death. It is exactly the sort of thing someone like him would do.'

'But why would he do that?' asked Andrew, even though he somehow knew what the answer was going to be.

'In order to disappear,' replied Fiona. 'To quietly spirit himself and his nutty associates away to New Zealand to await whatever it is they think is about to happen. There isn't some huge meteor on a close approach to Earth, is there? If there is, then they might think it is actually going to hit us.'

'Not that I am aware of,' said Andrew, momentarily sounding distracted. 'Anyway, I really think you should just come home.'

'I know it is the sensible thing to do,' said Fiona, 'But on the other hand I don't want to just cut and run.'

'Look,' said Andrew. 'I understand why this is upsetting for you, but Dietrich is dead and whatever was in those files might just be some fantasy that has nothing to do with the real world. We don't know if this facility in New Zealand even exists. And the truth is that you don't really know who you are dealing with here, except that they are prepared to kill people. I honestly think you should get back to London as soon as possible.'

He paused for a moment before continuing. 'Not that things are particularly calm here though, I must say.'

'What do you mean?' asked Fiona.

'Oh, there was a major incident here involving the U.S. Navy. Strickland and I are doing our bit, and I am working with someone from U.S. Naval Intelligence to try to work it out. But it is a giant clusterfuck, to be honest with you.'

'The U.S. Navy?' asked Fiona.

'Yes,' replied Andrew. 'I am not actually allowed to tell anyone even a word about this, but I trust you to keep it to yourself.'

Fiona didn't reply but sat immovable on the bed staring into space as Andrew's words whirled around inside her head.

'Hello?' said Andrew. 'Are you still there?'

'Yes,' replied Fiona, sounding like she was in a daze. 'Yes, I am still here.'

'Are you alright?' asked Andrew.

'Andrew,' said Fiona. 'Does what you are working on involve a missing submarine?'

'What?' said Andrew, instantly alert. 'Yes. Why do you ask? I don't…'

'Is it the USS Tennessee?' continued Fiona now more insistently. 'SSBN-734?'

There was a brief pause as she could hear Andrew's brief intake of breath at the other end of the line.

'Andrew, tell me!' said Fiona anxiously, now sounding as if she was now at the end of her tether. 'Is what you are dealing with about a fucking nuclear submarine?'

'How on earth did you know that?' asked Andrew, sounding flabbergasted. 'None of this is supposed to be out in the public domain. It is highly classified on both sides of the Atlantic.'

'Shit,' whispered Fiona bitterly, biting her lip.

'Fiona, talk to me!' said Andrew forcefully. 'How could you possibly know about this? What is going on?'

'There is a section in the files on Aaron's memory stick mentioning SSBN-734,' replied Fiona, trying to remain calm. 'I didn't know what it was when I first saw it, but I do now and the documents reference that submarine as *The Sword*.'

'Oh fuck,' muttered Andrew. 'It's them.'

'Who is?' asked Fiona. 'Andrew, what's going on here?'

Andrew hesitated for a couple of seconds but then decided that the time for secrets was now over.

'Don't breathe a single word of this to anyone else,' he said tensely, 'but the nuclear submarine USS Tennessee disappeared in the North Atlantic several days ago. Initially, it was thought to have sunk after a torpedo malfunction, but we now think the malfunction was staged and that the officer crew may have gone rogue. One of the enlisted men somehow managed to launch a communications buoy, and it is pretty clear from the message that the captain and his second in command have taken control of the vessel and that they are behaving as if they intend to launch their nuclear missiles.'

'Oh Jesus,' said Fiona, standing up and beginning to pace the hotel room. 'What if this is connected to Dietrich's facility in New Zealand?'

'Well, the timing fits,' said Andrew reluctantly. 'I don't want to jump to conclusions, but it seems plausible.'

'Can they even shoot those missiles?' asked Fiona. 'Doesn't that require an order from the president?'

'Technically yes,' replied Andrew, 'but it is a bit more complicated than that.'

He then proceeded to relay what Lynch had told him about the so-called permissive action link and how it is effectively disabled on US nuclear submarines.

'How the hell is that even possible?' Fiona almost yelled. 'Are you saying that these two officers can just fire the missiles if they want to?'

'If everyone on the boat follows procedure then the answer is 'No'. If one of the officers tries to fire the missiles, then it is also a 'No'. But if the officer team work together and if they manage to convince the rest of the crew that they have received an authenticated order from the president to launch, then it is technically feasible for the submarine to launch its missiles even if no such order actually exists.'

'Well, that's just great!' exclaimed Fiona with a sarcastic and almost maniacal laugh. 'Which bright spark came up with that idea!?'

'It's… complicated,' replied Andrew, realising how ridiculous an answer that was, even if it was the truth.

'But you said the submarine was on an exercise,' said Fiona. 'So, was it even carrying live missiles?'

'They always do,' replied Andrew. 'Even on exercises.'

'How many missiles did it have on board then?' asked Fiona.

'24 Trident II ballistic nuclear missiles with a total of 288 warheads,' replied Andrew, the words seemingly taking an effort to say. 'Basically, enough to wipe out a large chunk of humanity in less than an hour and then most of the rest during the aftermath. There would be complete chaos because of the collapse of food and water supplies, energy, communications, you name it. And that is assuming no one else fires more missiles in the confusion.'

Fiona sat down again, feeling numb. 'We are talking about the end of civilisation here,' she said feebly. 'The end of the world. Armageddon.'

Andrew did not respond but remained silent for a moment since he knew that her statement was irrefutable. In the worst-case scenario, a detonation of just one of those warheads could mean the end of everything. A launch of 288 of them was almost guaranteed to virtually wipe the Earth clean of human beings over the course of just a few years, especially if in the confusion it ended up triggering a nuclear war between all the nations currently possessing such weapons.

'I don't know what to say,' said Andrew. 'You are right. There is no question that we are facing a potential catastrophe here, but we can't just sit here like rabbits caught in the headlights. We need to keep doing whatever we can to unravel this before it flies off the rails. Both the US and UK intelligence services are working to find a way to locate the Tennessee and prevent a launch. Dietrich and his crazies can go and hide in a hole in the ground if they want to. What's important is the submarine, and I am afraid there is nothing you can do to help with that whilst you're sitting in a hotel room in New York.'

'You're right,' sighed Fiona, suddenly feeling a strong urge to be at home in her own bed and waking up to find that this had all been a terrible nightmare. 'Ok. I will fly home tonight.'

'Good,' said Andrew, palpable relief in his voice. 'I am sorry, but I have to go now. I need to talk to my U.S. Navy Intelligence contact about this again. They might have a lead on the location of the Tennessee. Call me after you land, ok?'

'Alright,' said Fiona, feeling both dazed and exhausted all at the same time. 'I will. See you soon.'

★ ★ ★

It had only taken Captain Lynch about three hours to request and have delivered to him the complete personnel files of everyone currently on board the USS Tennessee. He had begun going over them himself, looking for anything that might look odd or suspicious, but without any luck. He had forwarded them to Andrew as well and he was also examining them one by one, but having read all of the fifteen files for the officer crew and made his way through the first 30 of the 150 enlisted crew members, the information had begun to blur into one large unmanageable mass of facts and dates and he had to force himself to take a break.

After ten minutes he decided that now that the theory about a Russian boarding party had been completely discredited, looking for possible saboteurs among the enlisted men was probably a waste of time, even if he couldn't entirely rule out involvement from one or more of them. If there was going to be anything to find in the Navy personnel files it would almost certainly relate to the officers. He then went back to open the files on the captain and the XO to see if anything stood out.

Captain Conrad Lewis Vandenberg. Commanding Officer of SSBN-734, USS Tennessee. Raised in Wilson, Virginia just opposite Norfolk Naval Station, he was from a long line of naval servicemen. Graduated from Virginia Tech with a bachelor's degree in Mechanical Engineering and joined the Navy, receiving his commission from the U.S. Navy's Officer Candidate School. He then earned a Master's Degree in Mechanical Engineering also from Virginia Tech.

His first operational assignment was as Navigator on board the USS Michigan, SSGN 727, where he completed three strategic deterrent patrols. He then served on the USS Montpellier, SSN 765, as Executive Officer for four years. He later earned another Masters Degree in National Security and Strategic Studies, before taking up the position of

Commanding Officer on the USS Tennessee which he had held for seven years so far.

He was married with no children. Lost his wife Elizabeth to cancer three years ago, after which he was granted three months' leave. He then returned to active duty, and all of his psychological evaluations since then indicated continued fitness to retain command of the USS Tennessee.

Andrew finished his coffee with a slurp and placed the cup on the table whilst selecting the file for XO.

Lieutenant Commander John Brice Chisholm. Executive Officer of SSBN-734, USS Tennessee. Grew up in Midway, Georgia. Bachelor's degree in Mechanical Engineering from the United States Naval Academy. Served as Navigation and Operations Officer on the USS Texas, SSN-775, and then as Executive Officer on the USS Hawaii, SSN 776. While being forward deployed out of Guam, he conducted multiple exercises with SEAL Delivery Vehicle Team One, as well as several joint exercises in Japan and Korea. Unmarried and living alone in Georgia. Psychological evaluations all suggested no concerns about mental health at any point.

Andrew proceeded to look at the file for the most senior enlisted sailor on the boat, Tom Payne.

Chief of the Boat, Tom Wyatt Payne, USS Tennessee, SSBN-734. A native of Baldwin City, Kansas with a Bachelor of Science degree in Electrical Engineering from the University of Kansas. Served as Machinist Mate Auxiliary on the USS Alabama, SSBN 731 before being reassigned to the USS Tennessee. About to be enrolled in the U.S. Navy's Enlisted to Commissioning Program, with a view to taking a Master of Science degree in Information System Sciences and becoming a commissioned officer.

Andrew leaned back in his chair. So far so ordinary. Nothing about these three men stood out as unusual or otherwise worthy of attention. He got up and walked out of the office to get himself another cup of coffee.

Coming back to his desk with a freshly brewed cup and having thought about Fiona's lucky escape in New York and her insistence that Peter Dietrich was involved in this whole thing, Andrew suddenly had an idea. He sat down at his desk and looked up Peter Dietrich online. There were hundreds of articles about the man, most of them gushing with praise and sycophancy over his brilliant mind and his visionary approach to the future of humanity.

Andrew ignored those articles and instead focused on finding a detailed description of Dietrich's life as far as internet sleuths had been able to establish. Once he had found it, it did not take long for him to suddenly spot something that caught his attention. Dietrich had spent three years at Virginia Tech twenty-six years ago.

Andrew sat motionless a moment, simply staring at the screen. Then he switched to Vandenberg's personnel file from the U.S. Navy and scrolled down. And there it was. According to the file, Vandenberg studied for his Master's Degree in Mechanical Engineering from Virginia Tech during the exact same time that Dietrich was there.

This can't be a coincidence, thought Andrew.

The two would have been young men back then. But what if they had got to know each other and perhaps bonded over something? Andrew looked through Virginia Tech's online database for theses and dissertations and quickly found both the theses of both men. As expected, Dietrich's revolved around financial transaction modelling and Vandenberg's focused on an engineering problem involving crystal oscillators for communications purposes.

Clearly, there could have been no overlap between the work of the two students but they could well have been involved in extracurricular activities together. After some more digging, Andrew found references to an on-campus late-night political debating society of which both men had seemingly been members. There were no further details about the society or any political leanings it might have had, but it seemed to put both Dietrich and Vandenberg in the same place at the same time, in a context that might have fostered some sort of philosophical fraternity between the two of them.

Andrew leaned back in his chair again and put his head back against the headrest, looking up at the ceiling. What he had found wasn't much. It didn't prove anything but it hinted at something. When looked at in isolation it could easily be called spurious. However, when examined in conjunction with everything else that had happened and everything he had learned about Dietrich, it painted a picture of an unsettling possibility. Perhaps Fiona was right. Perhaps the two men really were behind all of this.

He picked up the phone and hit the speed dial for Captain Lynch. An hour later, he and Lynch met up by the Kyoto Garden inside the nearby Holland Park. It was a sunny day and Andrew had sat down on a bench to wait for the American intelligence officer.

'Hey. Jack,' said Andrew, standing up and giving Captain Lynch a firm handshake when he spotted him. 'Thank you for coming up here.'

'No problem,' smiled Lynch. 'I needed to get out of that office anyway. I have spent way too much time there over the past week.'

'How are you holding up?' asked Andrew.

'Not my most enjoyable week in the service, if I'm honest,' replied Lynch dryly. 'I have been thinking a lot about what would happen if we get this wrong. If Vandenberg and Chisholm really have gone rogue and are planning on launching those missiles, then we're all totally screwed. Knocking out all those cities will send the entire world back to the stone age in just a couple of days. Even if the bombs don't destroy everything and everyone, and even if many people survive the blasts and the radiation, then the EMPs created by the detonations will disable the entire global economy.'

Lynch was talking about the electromagnetic pulse that is released in a nuclear explosion. Proportional in power to the yield of the bomb, it has the capacity to damage or permanently destroy electrical equipment, especially small-scale electronics such as computer chips.

'It is easy to forget,' said Lynch, 'but power generation, communications, water supply, food production, logistics, health care, finance. All of it would go down instantly. After a couple of weeks, it would be famine. Total chaos. People would be murdering each other in the street just fighting over food for their children. I know it sounds dramatic, but that is really what we're talking about here. And I haven't even mentioned the possibility of nuclear winter.'

'I know,' said Andrew. 'We need to stay focused and not dwell too much on this stuff.'

'Easier said than done,' said Lynch. 'Anyway, I have also been racking my brain over what the damn point is. Why would they do this? Why trigger the complete collapse of human civilisation? But then I thought about it from a purely military point of view. If such a chaotic scenario were to materialise, then at least in theory it would take only a small but very well-equipped military force to effectively take control of the entire planet. If you're holding a machinegun, and everyone else is standing there with sticks in their hands, it almost doesn't matter how many guys there are holding sticks. Especially if all of those guys are puking their guts out because of radiation poisoning. But Vandenberg has only 165 people on that boat, and I bet the vast majority have no idea what is really going on, and if they did they'd mutiny in a heartbeat. So, what is Vandenberg's play here?'

'I think I might have something on that,' said Andrew.

'Really?' asked Lynch. 'What have you got?'

'Well, it's about Captain Vandenberg,' said Andrew.

'Alright.' said Lynch, waiting for Andrew to elaborate.

'And also, the billionaire Peter Dietrich,' continued Andrew. 'Do you know him?'

'Sure,' replied Lynch, seeming slightly caught off guard. 'Who hasn't? But, what's the connection?'

Andrew stopped walking and Lynch immediately mirrored him and turned towards him with a puzzled look on his face. Andrew then inhaled deeply as if taking a moment to gather his thoughts.

'I think Vandenberg and Peter Dietrich are both behind this whole thing,' Andrew finally said.

Lynch looked at him sceptically.

'Excuse me. What?' he said. 'Peter Dietrich is involved in the disappearance of a U.S. Navy nuclear submarine?'

'Hear me out,' said Andrew, and then he began explaining everything that had happened in Arizona, Rome and New York. How his conversations with Fiona had made him suspect that there was some sort of connection, and how the information from the Virginia Tech website had proven at least the possibility of a connection between the two men.

'Look, Andy,' said Lynch as they began walking along the path next to the fish ponds. 'I trust your judgement on this, and I have no doubt that you believe what Fiona is telling you. Hell, there might even be a chance that she is right. But I simply can't feed that type of information through to Naval Intelligence, the Joint Chiefs and ultimately the President. At least, not without being laughed out of the room and put in a padded cell. There's just not enough here for the top brass to make a decision on. If we want to make progress with this investigation then we need hard evidence.'

'I know,' said Andrew ruefully, 'which means we need to try to find some.'

'What do you mean?' asked Lynch.

'I am assuming that the U.S. Naval Intelligence works closely with the other US intelligence agencies such as Homeland Security, the FBI and those sorts of people, right?'

'Sure,' said Lynch cautiously.

'Well,' said Andrew. 'I was thinking that you might be able to somehow arrange for access to the Dietrich Foundation servers in Dietrich Tower in New York.'

'By *arrange*, do you mean breaking and entering, or hacking?' said Lynch, glancing sideways at Andrew, not quite sure how to react to this unorthodox request.

'Whatever gets results,' replied Andrew. 'But I suppose a hack is probably the best initial step.'

'What are we looking for?' asked Lynch.

'Anything that can corroborate what Fiona told me. Financial data for the Dietrich Foundation and for ARK Research. The records for all the foundation's different subsidiaries and supposed charities. Funding schemes for anything and everything the foundation has poured money into.'

'Alright,' nodded Lynch pensively.

'I am guessing that once a way into their servers has been found,' said Andrew, 'it should be relatively straightforward to essentially copy everything they own to a secure location somewhere on an external server, right?'

'Well, it obviously couldn't be a government-owned served,' replied Lynch, 'but basically the answer is 'Yes'. It is possible. How much cybersecurity we would have to navigate our way through first though, I have no idea at this point. But I am guessing they have state-of-the-art systems in that tower.'

'Most likely,' said Andrew. 'And I should just mention one more thing. I don't want to sound paranoid, but if what Fiona said is true then we can't trust anyone with this. We have to assume that people at the top of the US government might be part of The Order. It just takes one person placed in the president's inner circle, and then we will get shut down immediately or worse.'

'Well, you're definitely right about one thing,' sighed Lynch. 'It *does* sound totally paranoid, but that doesn't mean that it isn't true. I have seen quite a few events in my time in the intelligence community that would have been rejected as too nutty if they had ever been pitched by a screenwriter to a Hollywood studio.'

'That's the thing I keep coming back to,' said Andrew. 'It might be that there is just a small probability that what Fiona and I are proposing is actually about to happen. But the potential consequences of those events are so enormous and catastrophic that we simply cannot afford to ignore them.'

'I understand that logic,' said Lynch and nodded sagely. 'Listen, I will see what I can do. I won't be able to go through the normal channels until we have some more solid evidence to go on, but I think I know someone who might be able to help. I won't tell you her name, but she definitely has the skills to do this. I just need to convince her.'

'Great,' said Andrew, holding out his hand to shake Lynch's. 'Whatever you can do. Will you let me know as soon as you have something?'

'Absolutely,' replied Lynch and gripped Andrew's hand.

'Depending on what you find,' said Andrew as he let go and adjusted his glove, 'I might need to go to New York myself and pay that tower a little visit. But I will cross that bridge when I get to it.'

'Alright,' said Lynch. 'By the way, I need to fly back to the States tomorrow morning. I've got various debriefs lined up.'

'Ok,' said Andrew. 'We'll keep in touch by phone and email. Oh, and that stuff about me paying Dietrich Tower a visit? You didn't hear me say that.'

'Hear you say what?' said Lynch with a wry smile.

Then the two men gave each other a wave and walked away in opposite directions.

Fifteen

When the door to the storage locker opened, it took Martinez's eyes a couple of seconds to get used to the bright lights in the corridor outside. Chisholm then ordered him to stand up, after which the XO and a junior officer had tied his hands and then dragged him off to Captain Vandenberg's private quarters. Chisholm knocked, and after the captain had called for him to enter, Martinez was hauled inside by Chisholm while the junior officer waited outside the door.

Martinez stood just inside the captain's quarters, and Chisholm was demonstratively resting a hand on his shoulder as if to ensure he did not suddenly launch himself at the commanding officer. Martinez, whose entire world had been turned upside down in more ways than one over the past few days, suddenly felt very small and vulnerable. Like a criminal in front of a judge, awaiting his fate.

Vandenberg rose and walked slowly and menacingly towards Martinez who stood with his hands tied behind his back and his head down.

'Quite a mess you've caused,' said Vandenberg in his usual Virginia drawl, looking at Martinez's face. 'Look at me, son.'

Martinez looked up to find the captain's angry face uncomfortably near his as if Vandenberg was studying him like some sort of specimen.

'Anybody put you up to this?' he continued. 'Are you working with the Russians?'

'No, sir,' Martinez replied. 'I am not working with anyone.'

'So, why'd you do it?' asked Vandenberg.

'Sir, I believe the EAM was tampered with,' replied Martinez, beads of sweat forming on his forehead. 'The last message was not authentic, sir.'

Vandenberg's face instantly screwed itself up into a suspicious frown, and his eyes briefly shot over to look at Chisholm who produced a small shake of his head.

'Do you, now?' said Vandenberg with a hint of mockery in his voice. 'And how would you know a thing like that? Write up a lot of EAMs, do you?'

'No, sir,' replied Martinez guardedly, realising that the captain was making fun of him but still attempting to stand his ground. 'I have a sort of eidetic memory, sir.'

'A what now?' asked Vandenberg.

'Total recall, sir,' replied Martinez. 'Photographic memory. They call it different things, sir. I noticed a couple of deviations in the formatting.'

Vandenberg glanced at Chisholm again who did not react.

'I see,' replied the captain. 'So, all by yourself, you decided to launch an expensive buoy without proper authorisation to ask central command for DEFCON status confirmation.'

'Yes, sir,' replied Martinez.

Somehow captain Vandenberg managed to pace back and forth slowly inside the tiny room that was no larger than perhaps two by three metres, but which on a submarine was positively palatial.

'Do you have any idea what sort of risk you have put this submarine at?' said Vandenberg. 'We are at DEFCON 2 because the president ordered it so. There is every possibility that the exchange of fire between US and Russian naval forces in the North Atlantic could escalate into a nuclear exchange. Your little stunt risked the lives of every single sailor on this boat, not to mention the ability of the United States to carry out retaliatory strikes as needed.'

Martinez was now sweating profusely.

'Sir, with all due respect,' he said, voice trembling. 'I do not believe that to be true.'

Vandenberg's eyes flashed and then narrowed as he once again stepped close to the enlisted sailor.

'You're finished,' he hissed menacingly. 'Get him out of my sight.'

Instantly, Chisholm gripped Martinez's shoulder firmly and jerked him backwards towards the door. He then pushed him out into the corridor where the junior officer immediately grabbed his arms and began marching him back towards the storage locker.

Chisholm went back inside the captain's cabin and closed the door behind him.

'Clever little shit,' grimaced Vandenberg. 'He could have brought the whole damn Navy down on us. It could all have been all over already.'

'I know, sir,' said Chisholm. 'But we're well clear of the SLOT-buoy launch position. They won't find us now. Especially not at this depth.'

'What about Payne?'

'Still under guard in his quarters, sir,' replied Chisholm. 'I recommend we keep him there for the duration. He's already shown his colours. He's not going to suddenly change his mind and get with the program.'

'We'll have to find a more permanent solution to that problem at some stage,' said Vandenberg. 'But right now, we have bigger fish to fry.'

'Yes, sir,' replied Chisholm. 'Both Payne and Martinez will have to be dealt with eventually. Should I go to the weapons locker and requisition sidearms for both of us? We might need them.'

'Yes,' nodded Vandenberg. 'I think the time has come for that now.'

'I will do that immediately, sir,' said Chisholm, beginning to turn towards the door when Vandenberg held up his hand.

'One more thing, John,' said Vandenberg. 'What's the status of the EAM system? Has it been disabled?'

'Yes, sir,' replied Chisholm. 'I did it myself. The equipment is still working, but the software has been placed in an infinite self-diagnostics loop. It won't register any more EAM messages from the surface until I re-boot the system. The other radio operators have been ordered to refrain from attempting to restart it.'

'They'd better,' replied Vandenberg icily. 'The next person who decides to pull off something like this will be shoved into a torpedo launch tube and ejected into the Atlantic. And you can tell them that.'

'Yes, sir,' said Chisholm.

★   ★   ★

Back in his make-shift cell, Martinez was sitting on the floor and suddenly finding himself rocking slowly back and forth. The stress of the situation was beginning to really get to him.

The usually calm Captain Vandenberg had been seething with anger and not just about the fact that Martinez had launched one of the SLOT buoys. Martinez sensed that there was a lot more to it than that, and that somehow the launch had interfered with whatever plan Vandenberg and Chisholm were attempting to carry out.

'Yo,' whispered a voice. 'Are you alright man?'

Martinez's head whipped up.

'Hey. Martinez, what the hell's going on dude?'

He suddenly realised that it was Dwayne Jackson.

'Jesus!' said Martinez quietly and got to his feet. 'Dwayne. Something's not right man. The captain and the XO have hijacked the boat.'

'What the hell do you mean?' asked Jackson in a hushed voice. 'They are the captain and the XO. It's *their* damn boat!'

'No, that's not what I mean,' said Martinez. 'They have taken us way outside the exercise area. I'm talking hundreds of miles. And the EAM that triggered the exercise was not authentic. It didn't come in through the proper VLF system. It must have been faked somehow.'

'Dude, I don't know what you're talking about,' said Jackson. 'How do you know all this shit?'

'I saw it with my own eyes,' said Martinez insistently. 'Something is going on man, and it ain't good.'

Outside the locker room in the corridor, Jackson shifted uncomfortably.

'Where is the COB?' asked Martinez.

'In his quarters,' replied Jackson quietly, glancing along the corridor where another sailor was guarding the door to Tom Payne's cabin. 'He's locked in there. I don't even understand why.'

'Listen,' said Martinez. 'I need to get another message to central command. And you need to help me.'

'Dude!' said Jackson, sounding tense. 'You know I can't do that. For all I know, you're a Russian spy.'

'Oh, gimme a fucking break, Dwayne,' said Martinez exasperated. 'I ain't no spy. What's happening here is the captain and the XO have hijacked this boat, and we have a duty to try to stop them. Haven't you noticed how they've been acting all strange?'

'Bro,' said Jackson tensely. 'I've been down in engineering this whole time. I ain't seen shit.'

'But you know we were meant to take part in the NATO exercise for three days,' insisted Martinez, 'and we're nowhere near the exercise area anymore, and the COB and I have been thrown in the brig.'

'I honestly don't know what to think,' said Jackson sounding frustrated. 'But I have to trust the captain.'

'Even if he's gone rogue?' asked Martinez. 'Dwayne, I have an eight-month-old daughter. Alright? You've got kids too, don't you?'

'Yeah, so?' asked Jackson.

'If the captain has gone off the deep end and he and the XO try to launch those missiles, we're not gonna see our children again. Do you understand me, bro?'

'What the hell are you even talking about?' exclaimed Jackson incredulously, whilst trying to keep his voice down to a whisper.

'Listen,' said Martinez. 'This boat has one single purpose and that is to launch nuclear missiles. Why would anyone want to take it over like this unless they were planning to do exactly that?'

'Shit,' whispered Jackson. 'I don't fucking know. How do I know it's not just you who is crazy?'

'Hey, do you think I like being in here?' asked Martinez. 'I am telling you, dude. This shit's serious, and we have to do something about it.'

'I can't help you, man,' said Jackson regretfully after a few seconds. 'Even if you're right, I just can't. I'll just end up locked up too, and then I'll be court marshalled.'

Martinez sighed heavily.

'Alright, listen, Dwayne,' he said, trying to sound reasonable. 'At least just do me a favour. If you hear tapping, please just pretend not to notice, ok?'

'Whatever,' said Jackson indifferently after a couple of seconds. 'As long as you stay in there and stop talking. I don't want anything to do with any of this.'

Inside the locker, Martinez knelt down and felt along the back of the locker where the wall met the floor. As he expected, he found one of the metal pipes that run the length of the boat on each deck carrying electrical cables for the lighting as well as for internal communications systems. He knew that Tom Payne's cabin was just down the corridor on the same side as his storage locker. He took off his belt and gripped the metal buckle. Then he started tapping.

A so-called tap-code uses sets of two numbers as coordinates to identify individual letters which are arranged in a grid. In this way, the number set (1,1) indicates an 'A', and the number set (1,2) indicates a 'B' and so on. Using a simple five-by-five grid where only the letters 'C' and 'K' occupy the same cell, it is possible to communicate simple messages easily. The system is slow but effective, and since Martinez knew that Payne had served as a communications specialist himself before becoming Chief of the Boat, he also knew that Payne would be able to use the system. The only question was if he would be able to hear it through the metal pipe which ran through his cabin.

Martinez tapped once, followed by three more taps in rapid succession, to indicate a 'C'. Then he paused and tapped three times followed by another four taps, to indicate an 'O'. Finally, he tapped first once and then twice, to indicate a 'B'. Then he waited.

Nothing happened. Martinez winced and then he tried again, using the same sequence. C.O.B.

After a couple of seconds, his ears picked up a very faint tapping noise coming through the metal pipe. Five taps, followed by four taps, for the letter 'Y', to indicate a 'Yes.'

Martinez felt a rush of excitement and relief. Tom Payne had answered. He readjusted his position inside the cramped storage locker to try to make himself more comfortable, and then he began tapping gently on the metal pipe again.

★   ★   ★

The cargo ship had arrived at the docks of Aotea Quay in the Port of Wellington near the southern tip of New Zealand's North Island two days earlier. It had been chartered by a local logistics company which was owned by a holding company in New York, and on board had been three large specially built containers. Like the ones before them, the huge charcoal-grey containers had been offloaded and driven to Wellington International Airport where they had been placed inside a large hangar near the edge of the airport's western perimeter.

The next day just before nightfall, three giant helicopters had arrived at the airport from the north and touched down near the hangar. They had made their way from Auckland almost five hundred kilometres due north where they had been shipped in on a cargo ship several months earlier. Shortly thereafter, their Russian crews had arrived and they had been put up in one of the best hotels in the city with strict instructions not to leave. Their exorbitant pay had ensured that they complied.

The three helicopters were all Mi-26 heavy transport helicopters, which had been purchased from the Russian army and put into service in the Wellington-based logistics company. The Mi-26 is the most powerful transport helicopter in the world, capable of lifting up to 50 tons of cargo. It is 40 metres long and 8 metres tall with one large cavernous cargo hold sitting behind the diminutive-looking cockpit. Despite its size and bulky appearance, it is able to cruise at around 250 kilometres per hour, thanks to the two huge turboshaft engines mounted on top of the aircraft. With a service ceiling of up 4,600 metres, it was able to carry cargo across much taller mountains than most of its competitors, and this was one of the reasons why it had been selected for this particular task in New Zealand.

Having made several similar trips over the past few weeks already, the crews now knew what to expect. The trip south was likely to be uneventful as long as the sometimes-unpredictable mountain weather did not suddenly change from what had been forecasted. They watched as the three containers were placed on low twelve-wheeled caterpillar-like vehicles and then driven carefully up the ramps and inside the helicopters. Once that delicate operation was complete, the crews climbed up inside their cockpits, fired up the engines and went through their pre-flight checks.

Fifteen minutes later the three hulking helicopters slowly lifted off from the airport amid a cacophony of noise from their whining engines and the huge rotor blades. They then formed up into a line with a couple of hundred metres between them and proceeded out across Lyall Bay which is just next to the southern edge of the airport. Banking slightly to the right, the convoy of choppers made its way southwest across the Cook Strait towards the South Island. After around twenty minutes, having already covered almost sixty kilometres, they flew over the beach at Cloudy Bay and continued on towards the mountains in the distance.

Another 250 kilometres later, having flown mostly alongside the mountain range running down the centre of the South Island, they were then forced to climb to around 1,500 meters to clear the peaks below them. The weather was still fair but a few clouds were beginning to gather over the mountains. When they crossed over the wide Rakaia River the pilot of the lead aircraft spotted their destination, Mount Taylor, in the distance. He adjusted his course slightly to take the small airborne convoy north of the more than 2,400-metre-high peak.

As the snow-covered peak moved past them on their left, the helicopters gradually descended following the barren and rocky terrain into the valley from where the Swin River springs. Tracking the river with the steep sides of the valley on either side, they finally approached a large flat area close to the mountainside near the northern bank of the river. As they came closer, they could see the three large concrete helipads that had been constructed there, each one with a large 'H' painted on it. Three teams of five people wearing grey outfits were waiting there next to a rail line that over the past many months had been used to transport first construction equipment and then supplies and now people.

It requires at least 50 tons of force to keep a helicopter carrying that same weight aloft, plus the weight of the helicopter itself. Therefore, the downwash from the rotor blades was powerful enough to force the groundcrew to kneel down close to the ground with their backs to the helipads, lest they get blown over. Sitting there next to the helipads, they quickly became enveloped in fast-moving swirling air that was filled with dust.

After the helicopters had touched down and powered off their engines, the ground crew at all three helipads moved up close to the aircraft. Soon the large doors at the back of each helicopter opened and flipped down to allow the caterpillar-like vehicles to carefully transport the huge containers out of their cargo holds and down onto the helipads. From there they drove autonomously to three small rail carts sitting next to concrete ramps. Carrying the containers, the vehicles then drove onto the rail carts and stopped, locking their wheels in place.

As soon as the team leader from each of the three ground crews had signalled that the containers were secure, the three helicopters powered their engines back up again, spun up their rotor blades and then they took off flying back north towards Wellington International Airport. Little did the pilots know that this was the last shipment to the facility and that they would not be coming back to Taylor Mountain again.

Once the helicopters had left and were heading back up the valley, climbing swiftly in order to clear the peaks at the end of it, the three rail carts began trundling slowly along a rail line with the crews walking alongside them. They were approaching a set of enormous reinforced concrete blast doors that had been designed to be able to withstand a direct hit from a nuclear weapon.

When they were sufficiently close, one of the grey-clad people in the lead vehicle remotely engaged the door control mechanism, and amid the muffled sound of a claxon from inside, the huge doors began moving slowly to either side revealing a long and wide two-lane tunnel extending deep into the mountain. One of the lanes doubled as a rail line with the tracks embedded into the concrete and allowing for both wheeled vehicles and the rail carts to move along it.

Once all three carts were safely inside, the giant multi-tonne doors began moving slowly back towards the middle of the tunnel opening, and when they met there was a soft but powerful-sounding thud as they sealed off the facility inside the mountain.

Sixteen

Andrew was in his office poring over the files Aaron had retrieved from Arizona and that Fiona had now forwarded to him. In addition to the various details that Fiona had already mentioned, he had also found an internal report from ARK Research with estimates of supplies needed per person per day for long-term survival in a shelter. These numbers seemed to have been extrapolated out to encompass the requirement for a population of up to three thousand people, most of them adults. Most of them…

Crikey, thought Andrew. *Families with children holed up underground for who knows how long. This whole thing is insane.*

He spent some time looking at the construction plans for the giant bunker facility that was supposedly being constructed in New Zealand, but there was no trace of precisely where it was being built or if the construction work had even begun.

When his phone rang, he picked it up and answered without looking at it, still staring at his screen and the analysis from ARK Research.

'Andrew, it's Jack.'

'Oh hey!' said Andrew, tearing himself away from the screen. 'Afternoon Jack, or I guess it's morning over there.'

'I'm not sure anymore,' sighed Lynch. 'It is all starting to blur into one thing. Anyway, Andrew, you're not going to believe what I have discovered.'

'What?' asked Andrew.

'I hit up an old friend from one of the other intelligence branches,' said Lynch. 'It's better if I don't tell you who she is since this is all off the books.'

'That's fine by me,' said Andrew.

'Get this,' said Lynch. 'I provided her with a burner laptop and a series of VPNs for her to use, and then I asked her to hack into the Dietrich Foundation. When she did, she was able to penetrate their security, which by the way was substantial, and guess what she found.'

'Go on. Tell me,' said Andrew impatiently.

'She found nothing,' said Lynch. 'As in, she literally found absolutely nothing on the foundation's servers. Everything had been wiped to the point where any data that used to be on there had been written over with other random data several times to make any recovery of deleted files impossible. She said it was like accessing a huge network that had just been set up and had never been used.'

'Damn,' said Andrew. 'A kind of scorched earth tactic in cyberspace.'

'You could call it that,' replied Lynch.

'Does the foundation have any cloud storage facilities or backups stored outside of that building?'

'We don't know,' said Lynch. 'If they did, then there is no trace of that either.'

'Shit,' said Andrew, rubbing his forehead and trying to think of a new plan. 'You sounded like you had found something.'

'I have,' said Lynch. 'After discovering that the foundation's servers had been wiped, this old friend of mine suggested that we try the building's mainframe instead.'

'What would that achieve?' asked Andrew.

'That's exactly what I asked her as well,' replied Lynch. 'But within a couple of minutes, she had hacked into the server systems running all the services in Dietrich Tower, including the security systems. The logs in that system show that Peter Dietrich's penthouse apartment at the top of the tower was accessed two days ago.'

Andrew frowned, trying to understand the implication.

'So?' he said. 'The guy died. It would be reasonable to expect that someone would enter the penthouse and begin to make arrangements for the executor of a will or something.'

'Of course,' said Lynch. 'But the thing is. Access to the penthouse requires biometric authentication. Fingerprints, retinal scan and voice identification, and there was only one person listed as having the necessary access credentials.'

'Dietrich,' said Andrew, now sitting bolt upright in his chair.

'Bingo,' said Lynch. 'That security system literally cannot be fooled unless you are carrying the severed right hand of Dietrich, both of his eyeballs as well a high-fidelity recording of him saying a password which only he knows and whose voice-match file is stored in a highly encrypted format on the server. So, it was definitely him.'

'And when did this happen?' asked Andrew.

'Three hours after his jet went down.'

'Holy crap,' said Andrew. *Fiona was right.*

'Yeah,' said Lynch. 'My thoughts exactly. But there is more. We decided to access the CCTV systems which are integrated with the rest of the security software suite, and when we looked at the recording from Dietrich's penthouse, we actually saw him walk there.'

'You saw him yourself?' asked Andrew.

'Clear as day,' replied Lynch.

'What did he do there?' asked Andrew.

'He wasn't in there for long but he went into his office and accessed a safe to retrieve an item. We're not sure what it was. It was in a small box. Then he sat down at his desk and spent about fifteen minutes on a laptop which he then unplugged and took with him. This was probably the point where the server wipe was initiated.'

'So, what happened next?'

'Well, next to the office is a library which he entered. There is no CCTV in there, probably because the only access is through the office and there is a camera in there. Anyway, he never came back out.'

'What is that supposed to mean?' asked Andrew.

'Just that,' said Lynch. 'He went in, and didn't come out again. We fast-forwarded through the entire recording right up until a few hours ago. Dietrich did not exit the library again.'

'So, you're saying you think he is still in there?' said Andrew incredulously. 'Or is he dead? Did he kill himself?'

'Unlikely,' said Lynch. 'But I will get on to that in a second.'

'This keeps getting weirder and weirder,' said Andrew, shaking his head.

'Sure does,' said Lynch. 'But it gets better. The CCTV recordings are stored on the tower's server for two months exactly, so we decided to rewind them and see what happened in the penthouse during the run-up to this entire situation. It was pretty tedious work even though Dietrich doesn't spend a lot of time there. But when we got back to 43 days before Dietrich's final visit to the penthouse, we hit the jackpot. There was a recording of Dietrich receiving two visitors inside his home. They were wearing civilian clothing, but they were none other than Conrad Vandenberg and John Chisholm.'

'You're shitting me,' said Andrew, flabbergasted.

'Nope,' replied Lynch. 'Spent about an hour with Dietrich, sitting at his living room overlooking Central Park and talking about god knows what.'

'I don't suppose there is audio of this?' asked Andrew.

'No,' replied Lynch. 'No such luck. I am trying to find a lipreading expert that I can get on board without having to go through normal channels. It is possible that we might be able to at least get fragments of their conversation. Anyway, just to add to the strangeness of this whole thing, Vandenberg and Chisholm did not enter the penthouse through the front door. They just suddenly turned up from the library. And that's the way they left as well. There is no footage from the lobby of the building which shows them either arriving or leaving.'

'So, there is a secret entrance to the penthouse through the library,' said Andrew.

'There must be,' replied Lynch. 'I figure it can only lead to the underground parking garage, but none of the cameras picked up anything. There might be a number of blind spots down there that they could exploit.'

'Shit,' sighed Andrew. 'I mean, great job on finding all this out, but I can't say I am thrilled with the direction this is going. It seems as if the scenario we feared the most is becoming real. Why else would Vandenberg and Chisholm meet with Dietrich.'

'I agree,' said Lynch. 'So, to sum up. Dietrich was alive after everyone thought he had died. He probably still is. His foundation is like a ghost town at least as far as data is concerned. The offices in Dietrich Tower are all shut, and both the foundation and ARK Research premises seem abandoned. Any data that was ever in that building seems to be gone. And Vandenberg and Chisholm came over for a talk around 45 days ago, which would have been about two weeks before the USS Tennessee left Naval Station Kings Bay in Georgia.

Andrew was silent for a few moments, his thoughts drawn towards Fiona and whether she might be in a lot more danger than he had initially thought.

'So, what's the plan?' asked Lynch. 'What do we do next?'

There was a brief pause before Andrew replied.

'I'm going to New York,' he finally said. 'It's time to pay that penthouse a visit.'

★   ★   ★

The Convergence was moving inexorably towards its final stages. From all over the world they had come. It had begun as a slow trickle a couple of weeks earlier with the arrival of those members of The Order who had administrative responsibilities and those with skills critical to the running of the ARK facility at full capacity. As more and more members had come, so had the requirements for all of the facility's services to be ramped up, which in turn meant more arrivals. Everything was tightly choreographed and had followed a carefully laid plan, so when the senators arrived accompanied by their respective teams of praetorians, it signalled the last stage of the Convergence.

Most of them came in from Wellington International Airport and some of them came from Auckland, but all of them arrived by corporate helicopter at the helipads which became increasingly busy as Day Zero of the New Age approached. Each arrival was greeted by a small ground crew who helped the new arrivals onto the small rail carriages that would take them into the facility. The operation was not dissimilar to that of a small private VIP airport, except that the passengers on the rail carriages being taken through the tunnel and deep into the mountain had accepted that they would not see the sky again for several months. The corporate helicopters that were leased by The Order through the Wellington-based logistics company, were now engaged in a virtually continuous shuttle service between the south-western side of Mount Taylor and the two airports that were several hundred kilometres to the north. Hundreds of people were arriving every day from all over the world, and they were all taken past the two enormous ten-metre-tall reinforced and sloping concrete double doors and into the long wide tunnel leading inside the mountain where the ARK was located.

Suddenly, as one of the rail carriages began to move along the track towards the concrete doors there was a rumbling sound from far up the mountain, like distant thunder echoing off the steep sides of the valley. Turning their heads, the passengers saw the fireball from one of the helicopters having failed to climb fast enough to clear the ridge near the top of the mountain. As the helicopters approached the peak, the air became thinner and thinner, which had a direct impact on the ability of their rotors to generate lift. The pilot of one of them must have underestimated this effect and smashed into the mountainside just before reaching the ridge, even though he would have made the trip several times before.

The driver of the rail carriage stopped the vehicle for a few moments as the burning wreckage tumbled down the partly snow-covered slope. As the distant rumbling sound gradually dissipated, he reached for his walkie-talkie and had a brief exchange with the command centre inside the mountain. Then he placed the walkie-talkie back in its holder and set the rail carriage in motion again.

By one of the other helipads, another ground crew was waiting. They had also been watching the crash up at the far end of the valley, but they soon ignored the pillar of black smoke that was slowly rising from where the wreckage had come to rest on the valley floor. They had another scheduled flight to prepare for.

Five minutes later a white corporate helicopter appeared above the mountain in the distance, and as soon as it had cleared the ridge it dropped down to follow the contours of the valley towards the helipads. As it came nearer, the noise from the turboshaft engines and the thudding sound of the rotor blades fighting the pull of gravity became louder and louder. Finally, with less than one hundred metres to go, the pilot flared out the helicopter pitching the nose up and lowering the throttle to rapidly bleed off speed whilst maintaining his altitude just a few tens of metres above the ground. Then the helicopter touched down and its doors slid open to allow the passengers to disembark.

This time it was a senator with an entourage of assistants and two praetorians. Before today, this particular senator had been the head of a large investment firm in Sydney, Australia. As was the case for most of the arrivals, he had developed a personal relationship with the Imperator over the past several years both through business activities and through seemingly philanthropic and quasi-political endeavours such as think tanks and lobbying firms.

Now, he was about to be catapulted into the absolute elite of the human race.

Throughout the next several hours more helicopters arrived with more passengers, mostly fringe politicians from many different countries, influential nationalists with revolutionary agendas and outspoken global business leaders with what most people would call extreme libertarians views on how society should evolve in the future. All of them had secured for themselves a place inside the ARK.

The two overriding things they all had in common, were firstly a fervent reverence for Peter Dietrich and his vision of a new beginning, and secondly the basic impulse for self-preservation and further acquisition of personal power and wealth. All of them had felt the maddening constraints of the modern world, which through excessive laws and regulations were choking off their ability to fully realise their own power potential. And all this in the name of burnt-out and failing theoretical concepts such as democracy and equality pushed by bleeding-heart liberals who were still clinging on to the naive notion that somehow the human race is a community.

Dietrich's vision was a way for them to finally have those constraints shattered, and to be released into a new world wiped clean of all the old dogma and ready to be reshaped in their own image, free of illusory notions of the common good, society, and human rights, all of which were holding back the human race.

The ARK was the physical manifestation of this vision. It was conceived and built with the sole purpose of keeping a small elite alive, while the rest of the world burned and collapsed into nuclear war, chaos, famine and ultimately depopulation of the Earth to the point where a small but well-resourced force could take ownership of what was left of the planet, and then start anew.

As the sun began to set over the mountains in the west, the groundcrews were preparing for one last arrival. A handful of men in black uniforms had joined them, and the anticipation was palpable on the helipad as the sleek black corporate helicopter appeared in the distance near the peak of Mount Taylor.

A couple of minutes later it flared out and set down dead centre on one of the helipads. The pilot killed the engine and after a few seconds, the door slid open. First to step down onto the helipad was a bodyguard. Then another followed, and the two of them took up positions a few metres away from the helicopter creating a space between them for the VIP to walk through. Then he emerged.

The Imperator was dressed in a dark and slim tailored suit, with a white shirt and a silver tie. Followed by an assistant and two praetorians, he walked briskly towards the small gathering of people by the rail carriage. The most senior of the men in black uniforms moved towards him, offered his hand, and as Peter Dietrich took it the man in the black uniform bowed deeply.

'Imperator,' he said reverentially. 'We are honoured to finally have you join us. Everything is ready.'

'Very good, said Dietrich. 'The New Age is almost upon us. Take us inside.'

'Yes, sir,' said the man in the uniform and stood up straight to gesture at the rail carriage. 'This way, please.'

Dietrich nodded, turned towards the northeast to take one final look at the snow-covered peak of Mount Taylor as it was bathed in the light from the setting sun on the other side of the mountain range. This was the last time he would see it for a long time. He wasn't one for sentimentality, but as he stood there it was hard for him to ignore just how momentous an occasion this was.

Behind them, as the new arrivals mounted the carriage, the groundcrew was already busy removing a set of bolts on the helicopter's rotor blades so that they could be swept back, allowing for the helicopter to be moved along the tunnel and into a huge specially prepared parking area where a large number of vehicles, both civilian and military, as well as four other similar helicopters had already been placed many weeks ago.

These helicopters were intended to eventually ferry crews from the ARK and back up to a separate underground facility about seven kilometres west of Wellington where the three Mi-26 transport helicopters were now safely stored in an underground bunker, along with enough fuel for several thousands of hours of operation. There were similar bunkers about twelve kilometres north-west of Auckland underneath a large industrial estate near the Royal New Zealand Airforce Base Auckland Whenuapai, where several long-range transport planes had been placed several months ago after having been discretely purchased from two former soviet republics.

However, all of those plans were many months away from being activated. For now, the Imperator and his helicopter were to be brought safely inside the mountain, and then the ARK would be sealed one final time. At that point, the only connection to the outside world would be a series of large air intakes placed further up the mountain, through which fresh air would be sucked in and led through a series of long wide pipes to a large filtration system that had been designed to be able to remove potentially harmful particles, including any chemical, biological or nuclear contamination.

As the two giant concrete doors slid into place and sealed off the tunnel from the outside, another set of double doors slid out from recesses in the tunnel walls. As they closed in the middle of the tunnel, there was the sound of a series of metallic-sounding clangs as the heavy locking mechanism was engaged. These doors would remain shut for months. The only way in or out now would be through a small service tunnel sitting behind several reinforced steel airlocks.

The rail carriage sped along the track several hundred metres into the mountain, after which it came to a stop at a small platform where everyone disembarked and made their way towards a heavy blast door similar to the ones that had been installed inside the underground complex in Arizona. The door was open but after everyone had filed through it, it slowly began to close. There was a loud and heavy thud as it came to a stop, and then several thick steel pistons moved slowly from inside the door into the wide steel doorframe, locking it firmly in place. The inner compartments of the ARK were now sealed.

Dietrich, escorted by his praetorians, took the elevator up to level four where he stepped out into a neat and freshly painted corridor with grey laminated floors and a plethora of artificial plants scattered along the walls, giving it a fresh and airy feel.

He then proceeded to his office which was at the end of the corridor and next to the office of the Magister Equitum who was expected to join then in around two weeks. The office was large and bright, and it connected to Dietrich's large private apartment at the back. One of the walls was made of glass and overlooked the gigantic domed interior of the central plaza of the facility. The plaza was three hundred metres across, and the ceiling was studded with light that simulated the day-night cycle outside the mountain.

From there, ten tunnels led off to complexes identical to the prototype that had been constructed in the Sonoran Desert in Arizona. Each complex was designed so that it could remain self-contained for many months, and each tunnel had blast doors so that it was possible to seal each complex off from the main plaza should it become necessary. Now, however, all the doors were open and hundreds of people were in the process of filing through to the enormous plaza.

Dietrich entered his private apartment which had been constructed to look similar to his penthouse in Dietrich Tower in New York. He spent about fifteen minutes freshening up and changing into his uniform. It was similar in design to those of the centurions, except it was made from a golden fabric. As a final touch, he opened a small box and extracted Julius

Caesar's golden Corona Civica and placed it on his head. Then he walked back out into his office.

As soon as he arrived, the two praetorians moved to the glass wall and opened the sliding double doors leading out onto a wide balcony overlooking the plaza. Outside, there was an immediate hush as the assembled gathering below saw the door to the balcony above them open. Then there was complete silence. The inhabitants of each sub-complex stood together expectantly in neat rows, senators wearing red at the front, then centurions wearing white, then the black-clad praetorians and finally the largest section, the grey-clad citizens. All told, there were almost two thousand people there.

When the Imperator stepped out and walked to the balcony's railing, most of his subjects saw him for the very first time. It was an impressive sight as he stood there in his golden uniform wearing the Corona Civica. After a few seconds, the huge gathering spontaneously erupted into rapturous applause, the magnitude of the occasion sweeping through them as they looked up towards their new emperor.

The Imperator raised both hands, not to signal for the crowd to quiet down, but in a subconscious gesture to absorb the reverence directed at him and to emphasize to them the momentous occasion that this was. A new beginning for humanity.

Dietrich had spent months preparing and finessing a long speech which he had learnt by heart, but before he launched into it he took the opportunity to savour this moment. This was his coronation. His ascension to the throne of the new empire. The new world.

Seventeen

The Sikorsky S-76B executive helicopter was not something Jack Lynch was used to travelling in. It was owned by the United States Department of Homeland Security, but Lynch had managed to requisition it for himself. It had been waiting for him at JFK International Airport when he arrived back from London, after which it had swiftly taken him the 355 kilometres south-west over Philadelphia, past Baltimore and Washington DC to land at the Office of Naval Intelligence in Suitland. After a debriefing lasting a couple of hours, he was back on the helicopter to fly across the Potomac River to the Pentagon just under 10 kilometres away, where he had been tasked with liaising between the ONI and the U.S. Department of Defence.

Now, a day after arriving back in the US, he had directed the helicopter to fly back to New York and pick up a single passenger who had been waiting for it at the heliport at JFK International Airport. It was just after 10 pm in the evening when the helicopter landed at its designated pad near the western edge of JFK, and soon thereafter it was airborne again. The pilots had been instructed to fly the roughly 18 kilometres to the southern end of Central Park and then climb to an altitude of 4000 feet. At that point, they were supposed to slow to a stop and hover and then wait for the passenger to open the side door and exit the helicopter. After that, the co-pilot would be allowed to head back into the passenger cabin and close the door, and then the helicopter was to head back to Washington DC.

On the way to its first waypoint above Central Park, the helicopter's lone passenger opened the luggage he had brought from London and had been able to take straight through the airport, using his diplomatic status to allow him to do so without having it inspected. He changed from civilian clothes into all-black tactical clothes, shoved his pistol into his under-arm holster and then strapped on a small and compact parachute. By the time he was ready, the helicopter was slowing down as it came in over the East River, and by the time it made its way over Midtown East he had his hand on the side door's metal handle.

When Andrew flicked the lock and yanked the door to the left, thereby opening up the helicopter and allowing the noise and the downwash from the rotor blades to envelop him, the helicopter was stationary above the glistening and lit-up steel and glass skyscrapers far below him. There were no clouds in the dark sky, and all he could see below him was a sea of lights from the buildings intersected by the white and red grid of light from the slow-moving traffic.

Looking up from street level, all anyone would have been able to see were tiny green and red navigation lights hovering briefly over the city, but corporate helicopters are a common sight, and to have one hover high over Central Park would not seem out of place. This was New York. Anything was possible, and somehow everything seemed normal.

Looking straight down and confirming his exact position and then identifying his target, Andrew stepped out into the void and immediately began to plummet towards the ground, the helicopter rapidly receding above him. Within a few seconds, the air was tearing at his clothes and whipping his short black hair straight back, and if he had not been wearing a pair of skydiving goggles his eyes would have been streaming and he would have had trouble seeing clearly.

After just twelve seconds he had accelerated to close to terminal velocity, which in his so-called 'arch position' with arms and legs spread out and chest facing the ground was just under 200 kilometres per hour. At that point, the helicopter had disappeared in the darkness above him, and he had already fallen almost 450 metres or 1,500 feet, the buildings and streets below seemingly racing up towards him. He used his vertical speed to course-correct slightly towards the north and move himself closer to his target, but he only had a few seconds to do so before he had to deploy the chute.

When he pulled the ripcord, a small pilot chute instantly released dragging the main chute out after it, and as that unfurled in less than a second, he felt as if he was yanked violently upwards when in fact he was simply undergoing rapid deceleration. From one moment to the next, the sensation of hurtling towards the ground with air screaming past his head was replaced with a sense of floating and almost complete silence, except for the faint and muffled cacophony of street noise from below.

Andrew looked up to check his chute. It was made of a light black non-reflective nylon material that would be virtually impossible to see from the ground. This, along with the fact that he was wearing all black clothes, meant that anyone on the ground below or in one of the many high-rise buildings in Manhattan would have to be looking straight at him and know what to look for in order to have a chance of spotting him. He had decreased the risk of this happening even further by deploying the parachute as late as possible. He had pulled the ripcord when he was about 100 metres above the large flat roof of Dietrich Tower, which provided him with just enough time to bleed off sufficient speed and glide down slowly to make a gentle landing.

As soon as his feet hit the roof, he had to take a few running steps forward to compensate for the momentum he was carrying, and as he did so he was already busy pulling in and wrapping up the parachute into a ball. He then unhooked himself from it and discarded it inside the opening of a ventilation shaft that protruded up from the roof and curved around to present a horizontal opening.

Beneath Dietrich Tower on 7th Avenue, Andrew could hear the sound of police sirens, but he barely registered them. This was simply the soundtrack of New York City, and it did not even occur to him that the police might be coming his way.

The roof of the tower was featureless except for two tall communication masts and a large satellite dish that looked to be pointing due south with an elevation of roughly 25 degrees. From this, Andrew concluded that it was probably orientated towards a satellite in geosynchronous orbit just over thirty-five thousand kilometres from Earth. Given everything that he had seen and heard over the past several weeks, he suddenly found himself convinced that this satellite dish was almost certainly facilitating encrypted communications with a commercial satellite launched and operated exclusively by the Dietrich Foundation. This would allow them to bypass other commercial networks and thereby elude any snooping by government agencies.

At the far end of the roof was a low flat-roofed structure roughly the size of a small house with a single metal door leading inside. Andrew ignored it since he knew that while it led down into the tower, it only provided access to an emergency stairwell that bypassed Dietrich's penthouse. The penthouse had been constructed so that it was only accessible through the front door on the sealed-off 58th floor, as well as via the elevator that he and Lynch had discovered connected to the parking garage under the tower.

Andrew unclipped the rucksack that had been attached to his chest and unzipped it. He extracted a thin but high-strength braided carbon-fibre rope and a metal plate roughly thirty by thirty centimetres. He then took out two small spray cans, using one of them to spray the underside of the metal plate, and the other to spray a patch on the concrete roof. After a few seconds, the two adhesives began reacting with the oxygen in the air bubbling up slightly to indicate that they were ready. He then placed the metal plate flat on the sprayed patch of concrete and stepped onto it to press it down. Within a few seconds, the two compounds had reacted forming a glue. Another half a minute later they had been bound together and had hardened into a virtually indestructible mass, ensuring that the metal plate would remain stuck to the concrete roof unless several tons of force was employed to tear it off.

He clipped the rope to the hook-on ring on the metal plate using a steel carabiner, and then he also attached the rope to the harness he was wearing using a clove hitch knot which would allow him to adjust the length of the rope without untying the knot. Even though he knew the metal plate was secure, out of habit he still yanked hard at the rope to make sure it could hold his weight. After all, the 202-metre drop from the top of the tower to the street below would be plenty of time to regret not checking his gear properly before going over the edge.

He checked his gun again making sure it was strapped tightly in its holster, and then he stood up on the raised ledge that ran the circumference of the roof. Turning around and gripping the rope, he looked back over his shoulder and down towards 7th Avenue far below him. Pedestrians, yellow cabs and the odd pizza delivery moped looked like toys down there.

Then he leaned out to an almost horizontal position and began walking backwards down the first few steps. Once he was happy with the grip of his shoes and his gloves, he pushed away from the building and loosened the knot slightly, rappelling down a couple of metres in one smooth movement. He repeated this twice more until he was directly outside Peter Dietrich's penthouse on the 58th floor. Here he locked the rope knot and reached into his belt to pull out a handheld glass cutter that used infrared light set to a wavelength of just over ten thousand nanometres. At this wavelength, the silicon-oxygen bond in most glass absorbs almost all of the laser's energy, which makes it very effective at cutting through even thick panes of glass. The laser itself was connected to a small battery pack that he had strapped to his leg and which provided the laser with enough power to let him operate the laser for roughly two minutes.

He held the small device in his hand and extended his arm up above himself. Then he engaged the laser and immediately began moving his hand slowly in a circular pattern around his position. The laser did not emit any visible light, but he could instantly see the result as it left a neat but very thin cut in both panes of the toughened glass. After just over a minute, he had created an almost perfect circular cut around where he was suspended over the street far below.

He put the cutter back in his belt and loosened the knot, pulling himself upwards and walking back up the large glass pane until he was about two meters above the area where he had made the cut. Then he entered a crouched position on the side of the building and pushed away as forcefully as he could while at the same time loosening the knot slightly. This allowed him to descend just enough to end up directly in front of the circular cut. As the pendulum effect swung him back in towards the building, he then slammed his boots into the circular section of cut glass just as he reached it, and when his heels connected with the glass it shattered into hundreds of tiny crystal-like pieces that flew into the penthouse and were strewn across the wooden floor away from the windows.

Andrew's momentum carried him through the hole in the window and well inside the penthouse at which point he loosened the knot again. At the same time, he twisted his body around and dropped about a metre onto the floor where he landed in a crouched position. He rose quickly, weapon drawn and scanning the room whilst listening out for alarms or movement. He was expecting the penthouse to be empty but he couldn't afford to assume anything.

The large open-plan space was lit only by the faint light from the outside, but it was more than enough for Andrew to orientate himself, and his eyes quickly became accustomed to the relative darkness inside. To his left was a seating area with several sofas and armchairs, and beyond that was a dining area adjoined by a large kitchen section. To his right was an open door to the library and directly in front of him was a long wide marbled foyer leading to the front door.

Through another door opposite the seating area was Dietrich's office, and that is where Andrew decided to go first. He made his way across the floor, gun still gripped with both hands and semi-crouched so as to make as little noise as possible and to make sure that he would be ready to move fast in any direction should someone suddenly enter the penthouse.

The office was about as large as half a tennis court, and unlike most of the rest of the penthouse, it had no windows. All four walls were covered with wood panelling and bookcases, and opposite the door was a large heavy-looking desk.

Andrew made his way around the desk and looked through its various drawers but found nothing of interest. There was no PC or laptop, but there was a disconnected power cable and a mouse pad which indicated that a laptop usually sat on the desk.

Finding nothing, Andrew turned around and examined the wall on which hung a large painting of a snow-covered mountain range. He lifted the painting off the wall expecting to find a hidden safe, but there was nothing but a smooth wall. Then he examined the two smaller bookcases on either side of the painting, and in the bookcase on the right-hand side, he found a section of books that appeared to be fake and stuck to the bookcase. Working his way across them methodically, alternatively pushing and pulling at them, he eventually arrived at one that moved inward about a centimetre when he pushed it. Immediately there was a metallic-sounding click, and then the entire bookcase moved to the right about half a metre along the wall, exposing a small safe behind it.

It had a keypad and a small display at its centre, and Andrew stared at it for a few seconds. He had expected to find something like this and had already spent time pondering what possible combinations

Dietrich might have used. Through a quick exchange of messages with Fiona just a few hours earlier he had received a short list of possible options.

The first one he tried was 1207100, hoping that Dietrich had used the date of Julius Caesar's birth as the passcode. The 12th of July, 100 BCE. The safe produced an angry double-trill, indicating that the passcode was incorrect. He then tried 150344, for the day Caesar was assassinated. This was also not the correct code.

Andrew pressed his lips together feeling slightly tense. For all he knew, the safe was empty, but what if it wasn't? What if it contained valuable information, and what if it went into lockdown mode after a certain number of failed attempts to input the correct code. What if the maximum number of attempts was 3?

On his third try, he entered a code that Fiona had suggested as a possible option. 100149 or the 10th of January in 49 BCE, for the date on which Julius Caesar crossed the Rubicon River with one of his legions, effectively signalling his intention to take over the Roman Republic by force. The safe immediately produced a single high-pitch tone, and then the lock disengaged with a click and the safe's door swung open.

Andrew breathed a sigh of relief. He then turned his head slightly to focus on listening out for sounds of movement in the penthouse. He had been so engrossed in dealing with the safe that he might have let his guard down and missed the noise of someone entering. After a couple of seconds, he decided that he was still by himself, and he returned his attention to the safe. The safe had two compartments, and both of them were empty except for the bottom one which contained a pistol and a small black USB stick at the very back of the safe. Whether it had been left there intentionally or if it had perhaps been missed when the safe was cleared out by Dietrich a few days earlier was impossible to say.

Andrew grabbed the pistol, a Glock 19 with a chrome finish, and also extracted the USB stick from the safe. Since he had no ability to access whatever was on the stick at that moment, he tucked it inside one of the small pockets on the side of his right trouser leg and velcroed the pocket shut.

Turning around and looking at the rest of the office, he decided that he had spent enough time in there and that there was unlikely to be more for him to find. He therefore exited the office and walked past the large kitchen area to the bedrooms at the back of the far end of the penthouse. There were three large bedrooms, none of which appeared to have been slept in. The beds were immaculately made, the small cushions on the armchairs were plumped up to look neat and deliberately placed, the sheer curtains hung perfectly and symmetrically half-drawn across the windows, and going through the cupboards in the expensive-looking marble bathrooms he found them all to be entirely empty as if no one had ever kept as much as a toothbrush or a bottle of shampoo in there.

Making his way back through the main open space in the penthouse past the kitchen area and the sofas, Andrew checked his wristwatch. He had now been inside the penthouse for eight minutes. He looked up and around the large open-plan space to scan for security cameras or heat sensors but saw none, yet he knew that there was at least the one which had captured the footage of Dietrich's meeting with Vandenberg and Chisholm a few weeks earlier. As he approached the other end of the room, he spotted a small white box on the ceiling. It looked like a smoke alarm but it was almost certainly where the camera was located. If there was a silent alarm system still active inside the penthouse, then it would not be long before he would have visitors.

Entering the library which seemed to contain only aged leather-bound books, he stopped for a moment and looked around. Since the room was immediately adjacent to the sofa area where he had made his entry, it also had one of its walls comprised entirely of floor-to-ceiling glass overlooking Central Park. The other walls were covered by bookshelves. On the far wall opposite the door was a three-metre-wide ethanol fireplace, and next to it were two chesterfield armchairs arranged around a small round mahogany coffee table.

As Andrew approached, he spotted a remote control and a set of documents on the coffee table. Picking up the documents, he saw that it was a report produced by ARK Research, the Dietrich Foundation's internal think tank, so he folded it and shoved it into a large side pocket in his combat trousers. There was no time to examine it now.

He then turned around to face the door and recalled the footage from the hidden security camera of Vandenberg and Chisholm. They had clearly entered and exited the penthouse through a secret door somewhere in this room, but where could it be?

Turning back towards the wall with the fireplace, he looked first at the bookcase to its left and then to the case to its right. Given the layout of the penthouse, the secret passage had to be behind one of the two bookcases.

Frowning, he glanced down and to the side towards the small mahogany table. It took him a couple of seconds to fully realise why, but something was off about it. Why was there a remote control lying there, when there was no TV in the room?

He leaned down and picked up the remote control, and then he entered 100149. Immediately there was the sound of a hidden mechanism unlocking somewhere behind the bookcase to the left of the fireplace. Immediately thereafter the right side of the bookcase moved outwards ever so slightly, allowing him to reach out to grab on to the edge of it. He felt it move slightly. It was clearly mounted on hinges on the far side, and when he pulled at it, it began to swing open revealing dark wood panels on its backside.

This was the secret passage and whoever came through here last did not shut it properly, either because they didn't notice the mistake or because they didn't care that it was left partially open. If Dietrich believed he was never coming back to this place, then he probably did not mind whatever was on the other side being discovered.

Andrew stepped through and found himself near the end of a corridor roughly three metres wide and about ten metres long. At the far end of the corridor to his left was what appeared to be the metal doors of an elevator, and to his immediate right was a solid oak door with the words *'Novus Ordo Invictum'* written above it on the architrave.

Spaced equidistantly along the corridor on both sides were red fabric banners with images of various animals as well as names and numbers written in Roman numerals. Andrew was no historian but he was in no doubt that these were replicas of the banners of Roman legions.

Looking once more towards the elevator access, he now understood where he was. This was the elevator leading down through the high-rise building to the parking garage that Vandenberg and Chisholm would have entered and exited through.

Turning back to the solid oak door, he flicked the safety off on his pistol and gripped the door handle. Pressing down slowly, he pushed open the door to discover a large open space with no windows. Along the sides of the room were colonnades, and at the very end was a raised platform with what appeared to be a throne of some kind. There was no movement and no sounds.

Andrew slipped inside still holding his pistol tightly and ready to fire at any threat that might present itself, but as he made his way past the colonnades towards the throne, it became clear that the entire penthouse including this strange ceremonial space was completely abandoned. Andrew took out his phone and snapped several pictures which he intended to share with Fiona as soon as he could.

Stepping up onto the platform he circled the throne once to get a closer look. It was large and imposing, but nothing had been left there which might have provided him with a clue as to its function. However, one thing was for certain. This was part of Dietrich's obsession with the Roman Empire, and the involvement of Vandenberg and Chisholm could only spell bad news for everyone else.

What Andrew had not been able to see as he was walking towards the throne, was that there was a narrow doorway at the back and to the side of the raised platform area that led through to a small room which appeared to be some sort of chapel. Its walls were adorned with Roman imagery and various artefacts and weapons, either genuine or replicas, and one of them stood out in particular because of the fact that it was an empty stand. Examining it closely, Andrew concluded that this stand had been made to hold the Corona Civica that Fiona had helped Dietrich find and retrieve. Whether the crown had ever sat on this stand, he couldn't tell, but what was certain was that wherever Dietrich had gone after his staged death, the crown had no doubt come with him. Andrew took several pictures of the small chapel as well and then exited back out on the raised platform.

Almost immediately after emerging from the chapel, he heard the sound of voices at the other end of the throne room, so he quickly ducked down behind the throne. As soon as he was in cover, the door to the corridor opened and what sounded like two or three men entered. They spoke in hushed tones, and even though he could not hear exactly what they were saying, he could clearly sense the tension in their voices. They were obviously aware of his presence somewhere on the 58th floor, but they did not seem to know exactly where he was.

Andrew pulled out his phone again and switched on the camera. He then nudged the end of the phone out past the edge of the throne to allow the camera to show him what was happening but without revealing his own position.

There were three men there all dressed in NYPD uniforms. This was bad news, not just because they had their guns drawn but because they had not announced their presence as is required by New York City police regulation. This meant that they were almost certainly not acting in their capacity of police officers. Sneaking around with guns drawn inside a private residence without announcing their presence was just not standard operating procedure.

Andrew pressed his lips together. His options were suddenly limited. He could either open fire and risk killing a member of the NYPD who might have simply made the mistake of not following proper procedure, or he could stand up and show himself hoping to be able to diffuse the situation. Escape was not an option, since he would have to make his way past the three officers one way or another.

He decided on the least bad option, tucked his pistol back in the under-arm holster and stood up slowly with his hands raised.

'Don't shoot!' he said loudly as he stood up. 'I am not a threat.'

Immediately the three officers, who were now around fifteen metres away, stopped dead in their tracks and aimed at him with their guns. They all appeared to be carrying Glock 17 9mm pistols.

'NYPD!' shouted one of the officers, sounding both tense and uncertain. 'Who are you?'

'Andrew Sterling. British intelligence services,' responded Andrew. 'I am working with U.S. naval intelligence.'

The officer who had asked the question glanced briefly towards one of the other officers who was standing a few metres away and slightly behind him as if to ask for instructions. The other officer, probably the most senior of the three hesitated for a moment, but then nodded almost imperceptibly.

Something in the way the two men interacted instantly made Andrew's long-honed threat gauge shoot up to maximum. There was nothing standard about the behaviour of these officers, and now his intuition was screaming at him that things were about to turn violent.

He barely had time to duck back down behind the solid throne before all three officers opened fire and their bullets started smacking into the throne and also into the wall behind him.

The sound of the three guns firing filled the throne room, and even though he could no longer see them he sensed that they were now moving around inside the room, most likely seeking cover whilst firing their weapons.

After the first barrage, Andrew pulled out his own gun and risked a quick peek around the left side of the throne. One of the officers was standing half-way behind one of the large columns making up the colonnade on the left side of the room, and either he did not expect Andrew to be armed or he simply did not react fast enough. Either way, Andrew quickly fired two shots which both hit the officer square in the chest. He staggered backwards a couple of steps whilst gripping his chest, and then he fell forwards onto his front, his head smacking into the marble floor with a surprisingly loud thud. Then he lay still.

After a couple of seconds, during which the two remaining officers had probably been watching the body of their colleague fall to the floor, they then opened fire again, shooting uselessly into the heavy wooden throne which again absorbed the bullets.

As soon as Andrew heard one of the pistols click, indicating that its magazine was empty, he stood up again and fired another three shots in the direction of one of the two remaining officers. Two of them missed, but one tore through the officer's lower left arm causing him to drop his weapon which fell clattering to the floor. The officer cried out in pain and fell down behind the column he had been standing next to. As he reached out to recover his gun, Andrew sprinted out of cover towards the nearest column on the same side as the wounded officer whilst firing three barely aimed shots. As he did so, the third officer fired several shots at him. One of the bullets whizzed past terrifyingly close to Andrew's head, but he made it safely into cover behind the column.

Once in cover, Andrew released the magazine and let it fall to the floor, despite the fact that it was still about half full. He had plenty of spare magazines and would rather have a full one in the gun whenever possible. He slammed a fresh magazine into the gun and pulled back the slide to chamber the first round. Then he peeked out behind the column next to the wall towards where the wounded officer was. Immediately he was met with a barrage of bullets which zinged past him and smacked into the wall directly behind him. One bullet hit the column he was hiding behind just above his head, sending small fragments of plaster and dust flying into his face. He had no time to react and was blinded by the dust for a couple of seconds as he tried to use the sleeve of his jacket to wipe his stinging eyes.

'Get him!' shouted the wounded officer. 'He can't see.'

Andrew heard the sound of steps rapidly approaching. Temporarily blinded and having to resist the instinct to panic and flee, Andrew instead dug deep into his training, closed his eyes and directed all of his attention and his ability to perceive the world around him towards his ears. The sound of the steps approaching, the cocking of the gun, the voices, the reverberations inside the large room. Situational awareness and combat intuition honed through years of experience on the battlefield, as well as his heightened senses from the imminent threat of death, all came together to focus his mind like a high-powered laser painting a picture of the room and of the attacker. After a couple of seconds, he had mapped out the room and the location of the approaching assailant in his mind.

Keeping his eyes closed and letting himself be guided purely but the soundscape around him, he waited until the perfect moment arrived. In one fluid movement, still with his eyes closed tight and relying exclusively on his hearing, he knelt down, leaned out past the edge of the column, quickly raised his gun in the direction of the attacker and fired five shots in a narrow spread as fast as he could. Then he swiftly pulled back into cover.

A brief moment later he was rewarded with the sound of a body falling heavily onto the floor, and the sound of the assailant's gun clattering onto the marble and sliding the final couple of metres towards him. He felt it come to a stop right next to his boot, and so he reached down, picked it up, released the magazine, yanked off the top slide and tossed the now useless components aside. They rattled across the floor of the throne room to the other side where they came to a stop against one of the columns in the opposite colonnade.

'Time to make a choice,' shouted Andrew icily as he again wiped his eyes and blinked a couple of times to try to clear his vision. 'Your pals are dead. Either you die here with them, or you turn yourself in. At least then you'll have a chance of seeing daylight again.'

Andrew could hear the officer produce what sounded like a mixture of a scoff and a wince.

'Fuck you,' came the reply in a thick New York accent. 'If I turn myself in, I'll be dead anyway. I'm screwed either way. And so is my family.'

'What are you talking about?' said Andrew exasperated. 'You don't have to die here.'

'You really don't know who the fuck you're dealing with, do you?' said the officer mockingly.

'I think I have a pretty good idea by now,' replied Andrew.

'Nah,' winced the officer, now sounding dejected. 'You really don't, buddy. But none of that matters now anyway. It's all over. You just don't realise it yet.

Just so you know, and whatever they end up saying about me, I didn't have a choice.'

A single shot rang out, and then Andrew heard the sound of the officer's dead body flopping onto the floor. Andrew peeked out and was able to see the officer's head on the floor sticking out from behind the column. A pool of crimson blood was slowly spreading out across the marble. He had shot himself in the head.

'Bloody hell,' whispered Andrew to himself.

Still with his gun out, he advanced towards the body of the officer who lay face down, and when he reached him, he knelt down and turned him over. The bullet had gone in at the right temple and exited near the back of the head. The officer looked perhaps to be in his mid-fifties. If Andrew had met him in a bar, the two of them might well have struck up a friendly conversation. Why would he take his own life? What leverage did Dietrich and his organisation have on him? He had mentioned his family.

What madness is this? thought Andrew.

He searched the officer's pockets but found nothing that might identify him, not even a police badge. He did, however, find a small tattoo of a laurel wreath on the inside of his wrist. A quick search of the other two officers revealed the same tattoo.

Andrew decided that it was time to leave and to find a place to investigate what was on the USB stick from the safe in Dietrich's office, so he got up and headed towards the door that led to the corridor with the elevator. He had decided to take it down to the parking garage and so he headed swiftly along the corridor to press the lone button with a down-arrow.

Suddenly the elevator produced a short two-tone warble, indicating that the doors were about to open.

Immediately realising how exposed he was standing in the middle of the corridor just a couple of metres away, Andrew spun around and sprinted for the passage back into Dietrich's penthouse. He realised that he would be unable to exit through the penthouse's front door, but he also knew that right now he just had to get away from whatever was coming up in that elevator.

He was a couple of metres from the passage when the elevator doors opened, and immediately its three occupants, who were all wearing tactical gear akin to those of a SWAT team, opened fire with what sounded like Uzi submachine guns. The rapid firing submachine guns sprayed bullets along the corridor, but because of their short barrels and stocky shape, the Uzi's are difficult to use effectively beyond just a few metres, especially against a moving target. As Andrew launched himself through the air into the passage to Dietrich's library, a hail of bullets tore into the wood panelling and the oak door leading to the throne room, sending splinters and wood fragments flying everywhere.

By some miracle, Andrew avoided being hit and as he landed on the floor in the library he rolled once, keeping his momentum and was then quickly on his feet again. As he ran for the door to the penthouse's open-plan seating area, he could hear the sound of footsteps and muffled shouting from inside the helmets of his pursuers. From the tense yet disciplined way they communicated, he knew instantly that these guys were professionals, probably either ex-military or an actual SWAT team that had been paid off by Dietrich to eliminate the intruder. As he ran, Andrew released the magazine from his gun and let it drop to the floor, and then he quickly reached down to a side pocket, grabbed a fresh magazine, slammed it up into the gun and pulled back the slide.

Just as he made it to the door, the first of his pursuers reached the passage and immediately opened fire. Once again, a hail of bullets sprayed from the Uzi, but Andrew had just made it out and clear of the doorway so that the bullets whizzed through the door past him, instead peppering the sofa and kitchen area, breaking glass and tearing up the soft furniture.

Andrew stopped for a moment, looking around for somewhere to find solid cover, but there was nothing there that would be able to stop those bullets. In addition, his pistol was no match for three heavily armoured Uzi-wielding soldiers.

Hearing the sound of running feet inside the library, he decided that there was only one thing left to do. He ran as fast as he could directly towards the nearest section of floor-to-ceiling window whilst raising his gun and unloading the entire magazine into it in a spread that was roughly the size of his body. The bullets slammed into the window and tore through the layers of toughened glass, making the huge pane fracture along hundreds of small fissures that spread out from each bullet hole. But the pane still just about managed to stay in one piece.

Just before Andrew reached the window, he leapt into the air and turned sideways, allowing his momentum to carry him forward. As his full weight crashed into the glass pane it exploded into thousands of pieces and sent Andrew shooting out in a long arc, first horizontal and then down towards the street 58 floors below him.

Immediately after crashing through the glass, Andrew had twisted his body around to face the now empty window frame, whilst slamming yet another magazine into the gun. As he fell, he raised his gun back up, and just then one of his pursuers appeared with his gun aimed at him. Andrew fired off a burst of three shots at the rapidly receding target above him, and somehow one of them found its mark in the neck of the pursuer just above his bulletproof vest.

From inside the cloud of shattered glass that was falling towards the street along with him, Andrew could just make out the spurt of blood from his pursuer's neck. Twisting around once again, Andrew spread out his arms and legs to stabilise himself before then reaching up and pulling the cord for his reserve parachute. It was much smaller than the main chute, but it should be enough to allow him to land safely, as long as he had not left it too long before deploying it.

As he was barrelling face first towards the traffic-filled street below, it seemed to take an eternity for the chute to pop out, but when it finally did, he had never been so happy to be yanked up and backwards as the chute caused him to rapidly decelerate. He reckoned that he had fallen as far as the 20th floor by the time it deployed, and he immediately began steering himself across West 59th Street and over Central Park. A couple of seconds later, behind and below him, he suddenly heard a loud crash of metal and glass. His pursuer must have toppled out of the window, fallen the almost two hundred metres to the street below and then slammed onto a car below. Andrew decided not to look. This particular pursuer was definitely no longer a threat.

Andrew was now peering forward to try to find a spot to land. It would not be more than a couple of minutes before police would be on the scene, and he needed to get as far away as possible. Below him, he could see Umpire Rock which is an enormous piece of bedrock sticking up into Central Park near its southwestern corner close to Columbus Circle. He continued north past the Heckscher playing fields and then decided that he would just be able to make it to the large open grass-covered area called Sheep Meadow, which is the size of several football fields.

During the day these places are normally very busy, but at this time of night only a handful of people were on the meadow itself, so he was able to swoop down and land with only a couple of people seeing him. As soon as his feet touched the grass, he unclipped his entire parachute harness as well as his tactical vest, took off his jacket and turned it inside out to make it appear light blue instead of black. Then he tucked his gun back into its underarm holster and began jogging northwest. After a couple of minutes, he had reached the edge of the meadow where he crossed over the roads and footpaths that criss-cross Central Park's southern half, and then made it onto Central Park West which runs the length of the park from Columbus Circle in the south to Frederick Douglass Circle in the north.

He jumped over a low stone barrier onto the pavement and then crossed the four-lane thoroughfare to the corner of West 72nd Street where he could see the sign for the 72nd Street Subway Station. He quickly made his way down the stairs and onto the platform where he slowed down and then walked as casually as he could manage to stand next to one of the grey-painted steel columns that were placed at regular intervals on the platform. Feeling as if he stood out, he looked around casually at the other commuters but none of them seemed to be paying him any attention. He got out his phone and pretended to be absorbed by reading something, while at the same time glancing up from time to time to make sure that he had not been followed. When the train arrived to take him and the other commuters south towards Downtown Manhattan, he again scanned the crowd in as inconspicuous a manner as he could manage, but no one appeared to be interested in him. They all seemed busy reading or messaging on their phones, or absorbed in conversations with each other.

It was only after he had sat down inside the carriage that Andrew discovered that a bullet had torn through his trousers by his left knee. There was a neat little entry and exit hole through the fabric, and he counted himself extremely lucky to have got out of the penthouse in one piece. If that bullet had struck him in the knee, it might well have been him slamming into that car 58 storeys below the penthouse instead.

After around ten minutes, he exited the train onto the platform at Spring Street near Soho intending to find a hotel to spend the night in, when suddenly his phone vibrated. It was Fiona.

'Fiona,' he said surprised. 'Where are you?'

'I'm still in New York,' replied Fiona with a sigh.

'You're what?' blurted Andrew. 'You said you would leave for London.'

'Yes, well,' replied Fiona. 'I changed my mind.'

'Where are you now?' asked Andrew.

'Still at the Hugo Hotel on Greenwich Street,' she replied.

Andrew stopped and walked to the side of the pavement to get out of the way of the other pedestrians.

'I'm only a couple of blocks away,' he said.

'What?' said Fiona incredulously. 'You're in New York too?'

'Yes,' replied Andrew, turning around to look behind him. 'After everything that has happened, and after what you told me about your dealings with Dietrich, Lynch and I decided we needed to get into Dietrich's penthouse. And because it would take too long to get a warrant, and since those efforts would risk being leaked to Dietrich and his goons, we decided that I should go in covertly.'

'So did you?' asked Fiona.

'Well, sort of,' replied Andrew. 'It was covert to begin with, but then I had visitors.'

'Shit. Are you alright?' asked Fiona.

'Yes, I am fine,' replied Andrew. 'Almost ended up with lead poisoning, but I am alright.'

'Listen, Mister,' said Fiona. 'Get yourself over here as quickly as you can. You can tell me more about it then.'

'I'm not sure that is a good idea,' said Andrew. 'Those goons might still be looking for me. I don't want to put you in any danger.'

'I'm already in danger,' said Fiona deadpan. 'And if we don't get to the bottom of this whole thing soon, everything we know will be in peril. We need to talk.'

'I suppose you're right, sighed Andrew. 'Alright, I will try to get a taxi. I should be with you in about ten minutes.'

Eighteen

'That little shit,' said Dietrich, sounding partly surprised and partly irritated as he watched the footage of the intruder inside his penthouse in Dietrich Tower.

He was in his office inside the ARK deep beneath Taylor Mountain scrubbing through the recording of Andrew moving through the penthouse. He watched impassively as Andrew killed the two NYPD officers and as the third took his own life inside the throne room on the 58th floor. He then skipped forward to where Andrew shot out the window and launched himself through it, and then he watched as one of Andrew's bullets hit one of his praetorians sending a spray of blood shooting up and out from the side of his neck, after which the man fell forwards and out of the building.

Dietrich leaned back and turned his gaze to the man in a white uniform standing off to his left on the other side of the large ostentatious wooden desk.

'This is Andrew Sterling. Fiona Keane's other half. I want you to find this vermin and end him. Were we able to track him after his escape?'

'No, Imperator,' replied the soldier, looking uncomfortable. 'But we will be waiting for him when he returns to London. We still have assets there, and there are only a couple of places where he is likely to turn up.'

'I know,' replied Dietrich with a bitter expression on his face. 'Just make it happen as soon as possible. It seems that I underestimated him. At this time he represents the biggest threat to our plans, so make sure this doesn't fail.'

'Yes, Imperator. I will see to it that he is eliminated without delay.'

★   ★   ★

'You've got to be kidding me,' said Andrew.

'I am not,' replied Fiona resolutely. 'I am going to New Zealand.'

'Why?' asked Andrew.

'Because this is too important for me to just sit on my hands,' she said.

They had spent the past hour going through the contents of the USB stick, and it had turned out to contain much of the same information as Aaron had already provided to Fiona, but it also included something else. There were extensive details about the contents of the many different storage facilities dotted around the world that had all been stocked with supplies and equipment, much of it military, over the past several years. However, the precise locations of these storage facilities were not included, so it would not be possible to send teams to try to locate them and determine if they actually existed. But given everything that they had seen and experienced so far, neither Andrew nor Fiona had any doubt that those storage facilities were out there, and that they were ready to be accessed by Dietrich and his crazies once the world had been ground into dust.

They had also had the opportunity to examine a set of internal and unpublished research reports produced by ARK Research, including the one Andrew had grabbed from the table in Dietrich's library, and it had proven to be shocking reading given what they knew. The most disturbing report mapped out detailed hypothetical timelines for what could happen to the global order, both politically, militarily and economically in the event of a series of five different types of nuclear exchanges of increasing severity. Each scenario included a sensitivity analysis designed to establish which additional factors might serve to escalate a conflict, thereby increasing the so-called 'de-population percentage'.

A separate document outlined something called 'The Convergence', which seemed to be a process by which all the hundreds of high-ranking conspirators would gather at a secret location somewhere in New Zealand. Here they would take shelter in a massive underground facility and wait out the collapse of human civilisation. The document listed a large number of individuals from big business, finance, the media, politics and even what appeared to be the intelligence services in a number of western countries. A quick search of around a dozen of them online revealed that almost all of them seemed to have recently announced that they were either stepping down from their positions, had gone on some sort of sabbatical, had mysteriously quit or been fired, or that they had simply disappeared off on some unscheduled holiday somewhere.

It all made for very disturbing reading, and it had left Andrew and Fiona increasingly convinced that this was an extremely well-planned undertaking, and that there was no reason to believe that it was not everything it seemed to be. Convincing other people of this at short notice, however, would not be easy, firstly because the entire endeavour seemed utterly outrageous and implausible on the face of it, and secondly because there was every reason to suspect that Dietrich's organisation had infiltrated a large number of organisations to whom someone might go with an allegation like this. For this reason, the two of them decided to keep their powder dry with regard to alerting the authorities.

'If you go to New Zealand,' said Andrew, looking concerned, 'it is going to be extremely dangerous for you there.'

'I know that,' said Fiona determinedly. 'You risked your own life breaking into Dietrich's penthouse just a couple of hours ago, and you did it because you thought it was sufficiently important and because it was worth the risk. I am not naïve about this. I am going to New Zealand because *I* think that *that* is sufficiently important to take that risk, and there is nothing you can do to stop me.'

Andrew sighed.

'I guess I can't argue with that,' he said. 'Just be bloody careful, alright? These people are no joke. They have no qualms about killing people as you have seen with your own eyes. Always be vigilant, and don't trust anyone.'

'That was exactly what Aaron told me,' sighed Fiona. 'But I *have* to do this.'

Fiona was sitting on the edge of an armchair in the hotel room with her hands folded between her knees and her head down.

'Andrew, you said that one of the police officers had said something about it being too late and that he mentioned his family. If this thing is really about to happen, why wouldn't someone like him go public and try to blow the lid on this whole crazy thing?'

'Think about it,' replied Andrew. 'Can you imagine a single police officer from the NYPD suddenly starting to allege that one of the richest and most influential business people and philanthropists in the world is plotting to destroy the whole planet? Who would take him seriously? No one. He would end up in a mental institution. On top of that, they were clearly holding something over him. Perhaps a threat to his family. Or perhaps he was a crooked cop and they were threatening to expose him. Perhaps Dietrich's people were the ones who corrupted him to begin with, precisely in order to obtain this level of leverage over him. It is not difficult to imagine how something like that could play out. I bet they have done this to hundreds of people all over the world.'

'So, what are you going to do?' asked Fiona.

'I am going to fly back to London as soon as possible and discuss this with Colonel Strickland and the team there,' replied Andrew. 'And then I am going to relay our findings to Jack Lynch and see if he has any bright ideas. At this point, the most important thing that needs to happen is that the USS Tennessee needs to be found and recovered, but I can promise you that all efforts are already being mobilised to do just that.'

'Alright,' said Fiona and rose. 'Good. Now, I need to get online and book a flight to Auckland.'

'Ok,' said Andrew. 'You do that. I am going to write up a quick report to send to Strickland before I arrive back in London. Something tells me he is going to need some time to process all of this.'

★ ★ ★

Martinez and Tom Payne had spent several hours communicating with each other using tap code. It was slow and laborious but it worked, and as their tapping conversation had progressed, they had been able to significantly speed up their exchange as they learnt each other's shorthand, and also by omitting most vowels which had little effect on their ability to understand each other, but which saved a lot of time.

Eventually, Martinez had stood up and walked over to the door where he brought his mouth up close to the ventilation slits to the corridor outside.

'Yo, Jackson,' he whispered.

'Shit,' sighed the large man. 'Now what?'

'The COB and I have a plan,' replied Martinez.

'Dude, I told you not to drag me into this,' said Jackson sounding irritated and having to stop himself from turning around to face the door behind him.

'Yeah, well,' said Martinez matter-of-factly. 'You are in it now whether you like it or not. We all are. You can't afford *not* take sides this time. There is too much at stake. If we are wrong here, then the worst that can happen is that we end up with a dishonourable discharge.'

'Yeah, well I ain't thrilled with that prospect,' said Jackson.

'But,' continued Martinez, 'if we are right and we do nothing about it, then everything you know and love will burn.'

Jackson bowed his head and looked down to the floor.

'Shit,' he sighed after a few moments. 'Are you really sure about this thing, Martinez?'

'As sure as I have ever been about anything. The captain and the XO have gone off the deep end, and the only way it makes sense is if they intend to launch those nukes. And then it's bye-bye world.'

There was silence for a few seconds while Jackson tried to take in what Martinez was saying.

'Shit,' he finally said. 'Alright. I'll help you. What's your plan?'

'You need to create a distraction, and then Payne and I will make our way to the sonar room and attempt to launch another buoy. That will tell the Navy where we are, and then hopefully they can find a way to stop this.'

'A distraction?' said Jackson. 'How? With what?'

'We need you to get to the auxiliary engine room and damage one of the batteries connected to the backup diesel engine. They are old-school lead-acid batteries, so if you can make one of them leak, then the acid will eat away at the floor and produce a lot of fumes.'

'Are you nuts?' said Jackson. 'I could kill us all.'

'Relax Jackson,' said Martinez placatingly. 'It will create a lot of smoke and it will smell like hell, but if it is sealed quickly there is no danger to the boat or its crew. But it might just give Payne and I enough time to get to the sonar room, program another buoy and launch it. And of course, you need to unlock this door and help me get Payne out.'

'How are we going to do that?' asked Jackson. 'Payne is locked inside his cabin and ensign Palmer is guarding the door.'

'Palmer's a douchebag,' said Martinez dismissively. 'And he's about half your size. Just get me out of here and take me past Payne's cabin pretending I need to hit the head. We can take him, no problem.'

'Without getting noticed?' said Jackson. 'Fat chance.'

'There's no other way,' said Martinez. 'Come on. Let's do this.'

'Crap,' said Jackson. 'I'll be strung up for this. They're gonna surface the boat and make me walk the damn plank.'

'Or you'll be celebrated as a hero once this is all over,' said Martinez.

'Alright, enough talk,' said Jackson and turned around whilst fishing the keys to the storage locker out of his pocket. 'Here goes nothing.'

★ ★ ★

When the Honda HA-420 landed back at RAF Northolt in London Andrew felt somewhat groggy. He had only been able to sleep for a few hours on the flight from New York, and he had found himself worrying intensely about Fiona. She was as stubborn as they come and she was incredibly resourceful. But one thing she wasn't, was bulletproof. Even though none of them knew where Dietrich's underground facility might be, she was almost certainly putting herself in harm's way and he felt weighed down by the fact that he had let her go off on her own. But he had his own responsibilities to consider, and thinking about it objectively he also knew that there was a much better chance of him helping to prevent a nuclear Armageddon by being actively engaged in the situation from London, than if he went running around aimlessly somewhere in New Zealand.

Spending another couple of hours combing through the contents of the USB stick he had taken from Dietrich's safe, he had also discovered a chilling document that contained what appeared to be target information for an all-out nuclear strike against 288 locations all over the world. Almost all of them were major cities.

However, the document also contained a handful of precise coordinates for locations that appeared to be in the Atlantic Ocean, the Mediterranean, the Indian Ocean and the Pacific. Andrew guessed that they might be designated launch locations for different target packages, which, depending on the actual targets, would be the ideal locations for reaching all of those intended targets all at once.

The problem he was facing was that the USS Tennessee could be approaching any one of those many locations by now, so sending recognisance planes and submarines to find the Tennessee would require more equipment than could be mobilised on such short notice. In other words, he would have to guess, which was the very last thing he wanted to have to do in this situation.

Andrew walked outside the terminal building and extracted the wireless key for his Aston Martin DB9 and pointed it at the car which was parked around fifty metres from the building's exit. Nothing happened. He frowned and raised his hand again to point at the car. This time it worked, and the car flashed all eight of its orange indicator lights and produced an electronic-sounding trill to indicate that the locks had been disengaged. He opened the door and got in. It felt good to be back in this car. He strapped himself in and pressed the engine ignition button.

The engine instantly sprang to life, revved up and then settled down into a low purr as it idled. He revved it a couple of times, put it into gear and then drove past the security barriers out of the RAF Northolt airport complex and south towards the A40 which would take him towards central London.

After a couple of minutes, he was speeding along and making his way towards Kensington and the SAS headquarters at Sheldrake Place, when a black Audi came up next to him from behind as if to overtake, only to fall back again. As it did so Andrew glanced to his side, sensing that something was off about the way the driver of the car was behaving. Turning his head,

Andrew just caught a glimpse of the driver and the passenger before the car began to slip further back and out of view. Both men looked to be Caucasian and in their mid-thirties, and they were both looking in his direction.

Andrew barely had time to react, when in his wing mirror he saw the Audi pull slightly to one side and then immediately swerve violently back towards his car. The front of the Audi slammed into the rear left corner of his Aston Martin, causing its rear end to step out slightly, almost making the car fishtail as it sped along on the highway.

'Shit,' exclaimed Andrew as he held the wheel firmly and regained control of the car, partly thanks to its wide tyres which provided it with a firm grip on the road. The Aston Martin was also a heavier car than the Audi, so he just about avoided losing control.

'You picked the wrong car for the job, you bastards,' grimaced Andrew as he gripped the wheel tightly and glanced up at the rear-view mirror to see the Audi swerve from side to side behind him.

He changed gears and floored the accelerator, at which point the Aston Martin's V12 540 brake horsepower engine roared and pushed him back into his seat as the car leapt forward, quickly pushing past 100 miles per hour.

Andrew had to swerve and weave his way between the other motorists to try to create some distance between himself and the black Audi, but the driver of the pursuing car was clearly adept and stayed with him.

As Andrew glanced up into the rear-view mirror again and saw that the Audi was stubbornly maintaining a distance of around thirty metres, Andrew decided that he would be unable to outrun it here on this busy road, and the longer the chase went on the more likely it was that innocent motorists would end up injured or even killed.

Racing along the A40 through the London suburb of Acton, he soon reached the slip road to the large dual-lane Westway Roundabout. With the Audi still close behind him, he swerved onto the slip road and shot down the ramp to the roundabout which lay directly underneath the A40. He changed down a gear and turned the wheel hard to follow the roundabout whilst looking in the rear-view mirror to see where the Audi was. It was still right behind him so he decided to try to throw off its driver by doing laps inside the roundabout. He had more grip than the Audi and so he would be able to drive faster than it without slipping off the road and crashing into the barriers.

'You picked the wrong car, and you picked the wrong guy to mess with,' sneered Andrew, having to use all his strength to hold onto the wheel as the Aston Martin shot around the roundabout.

He managed to open up a small gap between himself and the Audi but it was not nearly enough, so after three laps which left the tyres of both cars smoking and screeching loudly, he whipped the wheel to the other side and exited the roundabout south towards Holland Park.

As he raced towards the Holland Park roundabout with the Audi in pursuit, he noticed an uncomfortable sounding noise from his car's rear left tyre. The bodywork must have been damaged when the Audi had slammed into him, and it now sounded like the tyre was grinding against the bodywork. Pretty soon the tyre would blow so he had to find a way to end this fast.

Turning left onto the usually calm tree-lined Holland Park Avenue, the tyres of the Aston Martin screeched and the engine growled as it slid sideways around the corner and accelerated along the avenue. The Audi was now just a couple of metres behind him, and suddenly he heard the distinct sound of shots being fired and bullets slamming into the back of his car.

Glancing quickly up into the rear-view mirror, Andrew decided that enough was enough. He had to put an end to this immediately before someone got hurt. He hit the button to roll down the driver's side window and reached under his left arm to grab the Glock 19 he was carrying. Swerving first right and then left, he then twisted the wheel hard to the right whilst pulling the handbrake which made the car spin around 180 degrees. He then immediately pushed the clutch down to allow the car to continue moving backwards along the road under its own momentum, while he brought his gun outside the window and aimed at the Audi.

Trying to aim whilst driving backwards at high speed along a London thoroughfare was challenging to say the least, but he took his time to aim carefully and fired three times at Audi which was now only ten metres away. All three bullets slammed into the windscreen which shattered, blocking the view of the driver. Andrew then hit the brakes hard, rapidly slowing the car to an almost complete stop and pushing him forcefully back into his seat. A short moment later the Audi smacked into the front of the Aston Martin with a loud crash, causing shards of glass from the mangled headlights to fly everywhere, and the front of both cars to deform and spew out smoke and steam from the ruined engines. As the impact happened, Andrew was thrown forward violently inside his car. However, his seatbelt did its job and a few seconds later both cars came to a screeching halt amid the sound of metal grinding against metal and road.

The force of the collision had made the windscreen of Andrew's car shatter and detach from the chassis, and as the cars stopped in the middle of Holland Park Avenue with pedestrians screaming and running for cover, he was able to see the driver and the passenger both scramble to get out of the Audi.

Wasting no time, Andrew unlocked his own seatbelt, opened the door and threw himself out of the car and onto the road with his gun pointing in the direction of the Audi. Behind the passenger door emerged a man wearing a black leather jacket and what looked like army boots. He was holding a shotgun.

Andrew did not hesitate and immediately fired two shots into the man's chest. He staggered forward with a surprised look on his face, dropped his shotgun and then fell forward onto this front, his head hitting the tarmac with a nasty meaty thud.

Andrew could not see the driver, but he was not about to hang around and wait for him to show himself. Leaping to his feet and scrambling around to the back of the ruined Aston Martin, he caught movement out of the corner of his eye, and immediately several shots from a pistol rang out. Two of them hit the bodywork of the Aston Martin, but behind him, Andrew could hear the sound of a storefront window shattering and crashing to the floor. He had to end this now.

Leaning out quickly past the edge of the back of the Aston Martin, he spotted the driver standing in partial cover behind the open driver's side door of the Audi with his pistol aimed in Andrew's direction. As soon as he showed himself the driver fired four more shots that all slammed into the bodywork and one of the tyres of his car.

Andrew pulled back and threw himself flat onto the road so that he could see underneath the Aston Martin to where the Audi was. Through a gap between the Audi's front tyres, he was able to see the driver's feet so he brought up his gun, aimed carefully and fired twice. Both bullets found their mark and smacked into the driver's ankles, shattering the bones and causing him to fall to the road screaming in agony. Andrew held his aim, and as the driver was writhing in pain on the road ahead of him his head eventually presented itself in the small gap. Andrew fired a single shot, and the driver's head jerked to the side as the bullet impacted and tore through his skull. The sound of screaming stopped instantly as the driver's dead body slumped to the ground and lay still.

Not prepared to risk being complacent, Andrew immediately spun around and proceeded in a low crouch around to the other side of the smoking Aston

Martin and advanced towards the passenger side with his gun out and pointing at the motionless man. A pool of blood was forming around his torso, and as Andrew reached him, he kicked the shotgun away and knelt down next to his head. He was dead too.

Andrew glanced at the man's right arm which was lying extended from the body along the road. He reached over, grabbed the sleeve of the man's leather jacket, pulled it up and twisted his wrist. There on the inside of his wrist was the tattoo of a laurel wreath he had seen before on the NYPD officer in New York less than a day earlier.

'Bloody hell,' whispered Andrew.

This was a conspiracy that was larger and ran much ran deeper than he had feared. Dietrich's men were everywhere, and yet so far Andrew had no solid proof of anything.

He rose and made his way towards the other side of the Audi where the dead driver lay. He quickly examined him, and he turned out to also have the same tattoo. At that moment a police car came racing around the corner of a nearby street, and as it came to a screeching halt some twenty metres away, two officers armed with submachine guns exited the passenger seats. Andrew calmly stepped away from the dead driver, put his gun onto the road, placed his hands on top of his head and knelt down. Now would be a very bad time to get shot by the Metropolitan Police, so he wanted to avoid making them nervous.

He announced to them who he was, but sensibly enough they did not take his word for it. Instead, they placed him in handcuffs and marched him off to the police car just as two more patrol units arrived.

* * *

Just over an hour later, Andrew was back in Colonel Strickland's office at Sheldrake Place having been vouched for by the colonel and released from custody.

'Quite a show you put on there, old boy,' said Strickland. 'Tell me what happened.'

Andrew proceeded to update Strickland on everything that had happened in New York both with himself and his visit to Dietrich's penthouse, and with Fiona and her brush with Dietrich's henchmen. Then he relayed the details of how he had ended up having to kill two hitmen on the streets of London.

'Pretty damn brazen of them to try to murder someone in central London,' said Strickland.

'Yes,' said Andrew. 'I think it just demonstrates how much they believe is at stake here, which has me thinking that everything Aaron told Fiona, and everything we have discovered since then just might be true.'

'Well,' said Strickland. 'Dietrich and his organisation are of secondary importance right now. At the moment, the only thing that matters is finding the USS Tennessee and establishing whether it actually represents a threat to global peace and security, and then possibly taking control of it if need be. If we can locate the submarine and establish what is really going on, then we can deal with Dietrich later. I have to say though, given how everything you and Fiona have discovered seems to fit together with the notion of a hijacked submarine, I worry that there really is nefarious business afoot.'

'Same here,' said Andrew. 'The more I think about it, the more I am convinced that such a plan is underway, but I am also convinced that us being very public about it would be counter-productive. Not only would it induce panic, but it would alert Dietrich and his organisation to the fact that we are on to them and that we know what they are planning.'

'Given what happened today, I think it is fair to say that they already realise that we have them in our sights,' said Strickland. 'But they probably don't fully understand just how much information you, Lynch and Fiona have been able to uncover. And you are right, we need to keep it that way. The last thing we need now is for them to speed up their plans.'

'Yes,' replied Andrew. 'The more time we have to find the Tennessee the better.'

'So, anyway, Fiona has gone to New Zealand by herself then, has she?' asked Strickland. 'Seems like risky business.'

'That's what I told her as well,' said Andrew. 'After today, I am actually very worried about her. Perhaps I should try to convince her to abort. But then, I know her well enough to know that she would never listen to me. Once she's got her mind set on something, she just won't quit.'

'Well, she's got a good head on her shoulders,' said Strickland. 'I am sure she wouldn't do anything stupid or dangerous.'

Andrew pressed his lips together and looked doubtful.

'I would like to believe that too,' he said.

'Anyway,' said Strickland. 'I need to update you on a couple of things the Americans have been doing. Firstly, they have decided to dispatch two Virginia-class fast-attack submarines to the Atlantic Ocean with the explicit purpose of hunting down the USS Tennessee and disabling it if necessary. These are the latest hunter-killer submarines in the United States Navy, and they are equipped with the most advanced target acquisition as well as the fastest and most effective torpedoes. If there is a type of submarine that can find the Tennessee, it is the Virginia-class.'

'They are prepared to sink their own submarine?' said Andrew

'If required, yes,' replied Strickland. 'If they manage to locate it, then they will obviously attempt to establish communications first, but ultimately they are cleared to neutralise it if necessary.'

'Makes sense,' said Andrew. 'Let's hope it doesn't come to that. After all, there are 165 people on board, the vast majority of whom will have no idea what is actually going on. At least, if what that radio operator said turns out to be true.'

'I know,' said Strickland. 'Unfortunately, there is a real risk that this step may need to be taken. Which leads me on to the second point I wanted to tell you about. This is also from our American friends and is to be treated as highly confidential. As you know, the DRAPES network is constantly active in the Atlantic and also in other bodies of water all around the world. All the information coming in from the listening stations is in real-time, but sometimes it takes a bit of time to process the raw data. This is especially true if the audio has to be filtered and run through a so-called subtraction algorithm.'

'I am not sure I follow,' said Andrew. 'What does that do exactly?'

'Well, it is all to do with the known audio profiles of ships and submarines, both civilian and military. You see, American naval intelligence has built an enormous database full of the audio profiles of pretty much every ship and every submarine ever constructed. Every vessel has its own unique audio profile across the entire spectrum of hundreds if not thousands of different measurable audio wavelengths. This means that as soon as even a brief snippet of a vessel is picked up, it can then immediately be matched with the vessels in the database, and from there it is a simple task to retrieve all the information about which ship or submarine it is.'

'Ok,' said Andrew. 'So, what is the relevance here?'

'The way it has been explained to me,' said Strickland, 'and I am no expert on this, quite often there are multiple vessels operating in the same area at any given time, and so the Americans have built an artificial intelligence algorithm that can extract different audio profiles from a recording of a complex underwater soundscape by subtracting known profiles one by one from a whole set of profiles. Whatever is left is then held up against the database to try to identify an unknown vessel. And it just so happens that something interesting was picked up in the Straits of Gibraltar yesterday. As you know, it is quite a busy and narrow strait with the distance from Spain on one side to Morocco on the other being as little as fifteen kilometres at its narrowest point.'

'Yes,' said Andrew. 'I have sailed through there myself a couple of times. There is a lot of traffic coming through there every day.'

'Indeed,' said Strickland. 'Now, what the Americans have picked up with their hydrophones near the entrance to the strait was an ever so slightly unusual audio profile from an oil tanker by the name Zenith, which is registered in Liberia. This oil tanker has passed through there numerous times and its profile is well known, but there was something slightly out of the ordinary about it yesterday. Nothing that could have been picked up by the human ear, but the artificial intelligence identified it as suspicious and ran a subtraction algorithm on it, and what turned out to be left when the profile of the Zenith was removed, was an almost perfect match for the silent running profile of the USS Tennessee.'

'Really?' said Andrew, sounding intrigued. 'So, the Tennessee was using the oil tanker as cover?'

'It appears that way,' replied Strickland. 'In fact, using triangulation between the four hydrophones that were close enough to be able to pick up the sound, it appears that the Zenith and the USS Tennessee were in exactly the same location during the entire time the Zenith was making its way from the Atlantic and into the Mediterranean. In other words, the USS Tennessee had positioned itself directly underneath the oil tanker the whole way.'

'Wow,' said Andrew. 'That is sneaky.'

'Yes, and very clever,' said Strickland. 'Unfortunately, because of the processing time and the need for human eyes and ears to verify the algorithm's results, it was only several hours later that it was confirmed that it was most likely the Tennessee that had passed through there. And by then the signal had disappeared somewhere in the Mediterranean. Most people don't realise this, but the Mediterranean is actually quite deep in places, so it would have been easy for the USS Tennessee to dive deep and disappear again.'

'Do they have any idea why it might be making its way in there?' asked Andrew.

'Yes, apparently there are locations in the eastern part of that ocean that have been designated as possible launch locations for SSBNs, all depending on the intended targets of course.'

'Oh shit,' mumbled Andrew, and then he proceeded to tell Strickland about the different so-called ideal launch coordinates that he had discovered on the USB stick he had taken from Dietrich's safe.

'That is grave news indeed,' said Strickland, looking concerned. 'Every new piece of information we get seems to point in the same direction.'

'I am going to go and call Lynch,' said Andrew and rose. 'He might have some more information from DRAPES or from the attack submarines. Everything is pointing to Vandenberg and Chisholm being close to launching those missiles. It might be matter of days now.'

'Very well,' said Strickland. 'I will keep you updated if I hear anything.

'Thanks,' said Andrew.

'And Andrew,' said Strickland just before Andrew disappeared out into the corridor. 'Do let me know if you hear anything from Fiona. If she's right about any of what she has been suggesting Peter Dietrich is up to, then she might need some assistance.'

Nineteen

When Fiona landed just after 6 am at Auckland Airport, she felt exhausted from the effects of both the jetlag since New Zealand is 18 hours ahead of New York, as well as the lack of sleep. It had been a gruelling twenty-hour journey beginning with a late afternoon United Airlines flight from Newark to San Francisco, and then onwards late that evening to Auckland with Air New Zealand. The crossing of the Pacific Ocean had taken almost exactly 13 hours, and she had only managed two short stints of sleep, each lasting three or four hours.

Walking through the terminal, she decided to stop at a café and buy a cup of coffee and a bagel before heading through to customs. She was only carrying hand luggage, so there was no need to rush to the baggage claim. As she walked along sipping a coffee, she also checked her phone. There was a brief text message from Andrew asking if she had arrived safely and what her plan was.

She smiled as she sent her reply. The truth was that she did not actually have a plan, other than to go to the address that Aaron had uncovered. Dietrich was supposed to have bought a house in Auckland in the upmarket suburb of Chatswood. It was on the other side of Auckland Harbour, also known as Waitemata Harbour, to the west of the Auckland Harbour Bridge.

Fiona finished her coffee and walked through immigration and customs, and then she exited the arrivals hall and got into a taxi. She had booked a room at the Park Hyatt Hotel right on the quayside of the Viaduct Basin, which is on the northern edge of the city centre. As the taxi made its way along the Southwestern Motorway in a long clock-wise arc around the suburbs of Mount Eden and Mount Albert, she was able to see the 328-metre-tall Sky Tower in the distance near the city centre, with its observation decks and its famous Orbit restaurant which slowly rotates a full 360 degrees once every hour. The tower sat in the middle of a group of around a dozen glass and steel high-rise buildings which comprised the central business district.

After a journey lasting around 25 minutes, she arrived on Halsey Street next to the Viaduct Basin, where she paid the driver and got out. It was pleasantly warm and there was a slight breeze of fresh sea air coming in from the harbour. Overhead a few seagulls were circling, making their characteristic squawks.

Walking through the foyer and into the cavernous atrium of the six-storey Park Hyatt Hotel, Fiona was struck by how stylish and calm the interior was. It was minimalist yet had been created to look warm and welcoming with soft lighting and an inviting seating area in the middle of the space, consisting of two long gently curving sofas with soft grey fabric and wood surrounds sitting on an enormous rug with an organic brown and off-white pattern. Adding to the relaxed feel of the atrium was the flat roof six storeys above her, which had several large skylights that allowed natural light to flood into the space.

Fiona's room, which was on the corner of the building on the 5th floor, was equally elegant and soothing, and the floor-to-ceiling windows gave her a spectacular view of the high-rise buildings in the central business district on one side and the harbour on the other. Down below, the Viaduct Basin was full of pleasure boats, large and small, and several people were milling around on them, getting ready for a day out on the water. It was all quite idyllic, and the thought of what Dietrich and his organisation were about to do to this and hundreds of other cities all over the world sent an icy chill down her spine.

She ordered room service, had a shower and then lay down on the bed for a few minutes to try to relax and regain some of her strength. She wanted nothing more than to take a nap and try to catch up on her lost sleep, but she knew that she would be unable to fall asleep with everything that was going on. After about fifteen minutes she got up, grabbed her handbag and her key card and then took the elevator down to the foyer where she exited the building and hailed a taxi.

A few minutes later she was in the back of a taxi crossing the Auckland Harbour Bridge to Stokes

Point. On her left, she could look down towards Little Shoal Bay where dozens of small pleasure boats were anchored. It was a calm and peaceful scene. Because Auckland is built on a large volcanic field, much of the city is sitting on rock formations that protrude many metres above sea level, but that then drop precipitously to the sea at their edges. Chatswood is no exception, and as the taxi finally weaved its way through the hilly and pleasant-looking suburbs of northern Auckland, Fiona could often catch glimpses of the city's natural harbour through trees and between houses, and across the water she could see the city centre including the area on the waterfront where her hotel was.

The vegetation along Onetaunga Road was mainly deciduous, but interspersed between the abundant beech trees were also several Rimu and Kauri trees which can grow as high as fifty metres, as well as different types of palm trees that were dotted around the gardens of the large houses that lined one side of the road. The other side, which was nearer the water, had no houses except for at the very end of the road where a couple of large mansions had been built.

Fiona double-checked the notes on her phone. 'Onetaunga Road 160'. This was the right place, so she paid the driver and got out next to a van that had been parked by the side of the road. Judging by the name and phone number emblazoned on the side of it, it belonged to a local construction firm. Next to it behind a high concrete wall with a metal gate was a large leafy plot with a modernist two-storey house set back around fifty metres from the road. The house looked newly constructed, and next to it on the drive was a mobile site office which Fiona guessed was where the driver of the van was.

She pressed the button on the intercom panel next to the gate and waited, but instead of receiving a reply, a construction worker in overalls and a hardhat came out and looked in her direction. He then ambled casually down the drive to the gate and greeted her with a wave.

'Kia ora,' said the man with a wide smile, using the informal Māori greeting which roughly translates into "*be healthy*". 'Can I help you?'

'Hi,' smiled Fiona. 'My name is Jill Newman. I am a journalist with the Waikato Herald. I am looking for Mr Dietrich?'

'Peter Dietrich,' asked the man looking sceptical. 'He's not here, lady. I'm not sure if he's ever been here.'

'May I ask who you are?' asked Fiona.

'My name is Brian Haines. I'm the site manager here.'

'But this is Mr Dietrich's house, isn't it?' asked Fiona.

'Well, that's what they say,' replied Haines. 'I wouldn't know, to be honest with you. I am just the guy who was in charge of the construction work here, but I have never met Mr Dietrich. In fact, I have never seen anyone here that wasn't part of my crew, and we've spent the past eight months building this house. Except for one guy who was here for a few days last week. Locked himself in the old chapel and didn't leave for hours on end. I have no idea what he was doing in there.'

'Oh,' said Fiona, sounding disappointed. 'Pardon me, but you seem to be speaking in the past tense. Is the work complete?'

'No, not by a long shot,' scoffed Haines. 'But everyone's been sent home. I have no clue why, but the work has been stopped as of yesterday. And the main house is only half finished.'

'That's odd,' said Fiona sympathetically. 'You just mentioned the main house. Are there more buildings here?'

'Sure,' said Haines. 'We've finished the pool complex and the exterior render of the chapel. And the tennis courts are done too. So why they don't want us to finish the house is a bit of a mystery.'

'There's a pool complex and tennis courts?' said Fiona, sounding impressed. 'Oh, how the other half lives, eh?'

Haines suddenly seemed to become self-conscious.

'Sorry, I am not really supposed to tell anyone about what we have been building here. It was all a bit hush-hush for some reason. I guess I am just a bit mystified by the sudden stoppage. I mean, I've got to pay my guys somehow, right?'

'Yes, I see your predicament,' replied Fiona. 'Well, I hope things get sorted out for you somehow. Anyway, if Dietrich is not here then I guess I am wasting my time. But thanks for coming down to talk to me.'

'No worries,' said Haines. 'I was off to lunch anyway.'

Then he pressed a button on the inside of the wall next to the gate, and the gate began to slide to one side amid the sound of whirring electric motors.

'Take care now,' said Haines and headed for the van whilst the gate closed again. 'Nice to meet you.'

'You too,' said Fiona and waved.

A couple of minutes later, she was standing by herself looking at the wall and the gate.

I'll be damned if I am going to let this stop me, she thought to herself.

Looking around, she saw no one else on the street. All the other houses were similarly set back from the road and almost entirely hidden by trees and bushes. Having seen where Haines had reached to in order to open the gate, she walked over to the wall and stuck her arm through a small gap between it and the metal gate. Fumbling around for a couple of seconds, she eventually felt a plastic housing with something circular and rubberised in the middle of it. She pressed it, and immediately the gate began to open again.

She headed up to the mobile site office and entered. Inside it there was a desk and a chair, and on the walls were lots of drawings of the various rooms and features of the house, no doubt so that Haines could reference them easily and show them to the construction workers to make sure they followed the plans exactly.

Taking a moment to look at them all, Fiona quickly gained a good sense of the layout of the main house. She glanced out of the site office window and noticed that all the rooms of the house that were facing out towards her appeared to be completely empty. They had not even been painted, and it did not look as if lighting had been put in yet either.

Turning back to the drawings, she could see the plans for the pool complex and the tennis courts, but what stood out were the drawings for the chapel, and not just because it was well known that Dietrich was famously atheist. Examining the drawings revealed that there seemed to be some sort of sub-level below the chapel with a spiral staircase. However, there were no indications as to what that space might have been designed for.

Fiona left the site office and made her way past the bland-looking empty shell that was the main house, and then proceeded around it to the back garden. It was not what most people would think of when thinking about a back garden. It was more akin to a park with a huge open space covered by a freshly cut lawn, and a two-metre-wide gravelled footpath leading down a slight incline towards the back of the garden some seventy metres away where the chapel stood. Behind it, past the cliffs and the five-metre drop down to the water and across the large natural harbour around which the city had been built, she could see the centre of Auckland with the Sky Tower standing proud right in the middle of it.

She followed the footpath past the tennis courts and the pool complex to the Chapel. It was around six metres high and had been designed in the style of a Roman temple with a colonnade at the front, a low-pitched roof and a set of wooden double doors that were at least four metres tall.

She pushed against the doors and was surprised to find them unlocked, and then she cautiously entered the brightly lit space beyond. The chapel had windows all around the sides set about three metres above the white marble floor, and the entire internal circumference had colonnades identical to the one at the front of the building. What surprised her the most was that the interior space was completely empty, except for a larger-than-life and centrally placed statue towards the back of the chapel. Walking closer, Fiona quickly recognised it as Julius Caesar wearing his legionnaire's armour and the Corona Civica and holding a short sword in his right hand. In his left hand was a scroll.

Fiona slowly walked around the statue, studying it closely as she did so. It was placed on a large square base that was a couple of metres across, and the base itself seemed to be floating just a few millimetres above the marble floor. Kneeling down and examining the floor behind the statue more closely, she could just make out two very faint lines where the sheen of the marble seemed different from the surrounding stone as the light from the outside reflected off it.

Fiona stood and looked first at the floor, then at the statue and then at the floor again. Then she walked around to the front of the statue and looked up at Caesar's face. As far as she could tell from his expression and his armour, this was an exact replica of a statue back in the British Museum in London, except that this one had one small detail that was very different. Unlike the one in London which was made entirely of limestone, the ends of the scroll that Caesar was holding here in this chapel seemed to be made of polished brass. Looking closely at the scroll, Fiona spotted what appeared to be a small white plastic button on the end of the scroll that was facing the floor.

Hello there! she thought and reached up.

As soon as she pressed it, a muffled sound of some hidden mechanism could be heard inside the chapel, and the statue began to slowly slide backwards across the marble floor. As it did so, it revealed a circular spiral stairwell almost two metres across that was leading down under the chapel.

'I knew it,' whispered Fiona and smiled.

After a few seconds, the stairwell was completely exposed and the statue of Caesar came to a gentle stop. Then a set of lights that were set into the stairwell wall came on along the handrail snaking its way down next to the steps. Fiona began descending gingerly. Recalling the drawings that she had seen in the site office, the staircase should be no more than three or four metres deep, and there had appeared to be only one level and one large room at the bottom. This turned out to be correct.

She emerged a few moments later into what could best be described as some sort of command centre. It was around five by five metres in size, painted black and very dimly lit from tiny yellow spotlights in the ceiling. Fiona guessed that this place might have been used to coordinate the transports to Dietrich's underground facility that she and Aaron had speculated had been taking place. There were banks of monitors and keyboards arranged side by side on a long desk, and on one of the walls were server racks with computers that were still switched on and humming quietly. On the far wall was projected a mosaic of twelve squares, each with what looked like security camera feeds. Or rather, this is what seemed to have been the case, because now only one of them actually displayed an image. At first, Fiona struggled to make sense of what she was seeing, partly because she had no sense of scale. However, after a few moments, it appeared to her to be a set of giant concrete doors with a rail track leading to it. It was somehow reminiscent of old photos she had seen from the Second World War of huge Nazi concrete structures on the northern coast of France. Structures that had been built in anticipation of an invasion on those beaches. The other eleven squares showed only static.

Initially, Fiona thought she was looking at a still image, but then a bird landed near the rail track and began pecking at something on the ground. Fiona looked at her watch and then looked closely at the shadow of the bird on the ground next to it. If this feed was from somewhere in New Zealand, then it was almost certainly a live shot.

She walked over to the only computer monitor which was still switched on, sat down and grabbed the mouse. Within a couple of clicks, she had accessed a file directory which contained what appeared to be detailed flight plans and a schedule for a fleet of four transport helicopters flying to a location on the South Island. The dates stretched back months but had become increasingly frequent over the past weeks and days. Some were for equipment and supplies, but the closer to today's date she got, the more of them included passengers until all four helicopters seemed to have been dedicated to ferrying people south.

None of the flight manifests showed anyone returning from wherever the destination was.

After a few more minutes she came across a set of coordinates. 43°29'04.4"S 171°16'10.2"E. She had no idea where that might be, but she knew that it had to be relatively close, since the range of most helicopters is in the hundreds of kilometres as opposed to jet planes which typically have much greater range.

Fiona typed the coordinates into her phone to make sure she could analyse them later and then continued rummaging through the files on the computer. She quickly came across what appeared to be more schematics for the massive underground complex that Dietrich's organisation seemed to be building. After looking at it for a few minutes, she deduced that what she was watching on the live feed on the wall were the massive blast doors that led to the facility. She was unable to see much of the surrounding area, but from what she *was* able to see, it looked barren and lacking in vegetation. It was most likely somewhere in the mountain ranges of the South Island.

According to the schematic, there was a long tunnel behind the blast doors which led to the interior of the facility, but there was also a long service tunnel running parallel to it. The service tunnel had passages leading to the main tunnel at regular intervals, as well as guard posts at each end. This led Fiona to suspect that there might be an alternate way into the facility that could be accessed without opening the giant blast door. Looking up at the image of the live feed again, she was reinforced in that suspicion since there appeared to be a narrow slit into the concrete to the side of the blast door, which she guessed was about the size of a standard door. Perhaps there was a personnel entrance there which did not require the blast doors to open, possibly for maintenance purposes.

Searching the computer further, she discovered that this was indeed the case and that there was a list of passcodes that were meant to be changed every week. The final passcode on the list was 01010001, which she had no doubt was meant to signify day one of month one of whatever new age Dietrich was envisaging. Next to each passcode was written the time window where that particular code would be valid.

She checked the date on her phone. Today was seemingly the last day that the final passcode on the list was still valid. If she was going to get inside the facility, it simply had to happen today.

Shit, she thought. *How the hell am going to do that?*

There was no way for her to copy and bring with her any of the information she had found, and the computer was on a closed network without access to the internet so she had to write up a quick summary of her findings on her phone. This took a lot longer than she would have liked. Suddenly, time was a precious commodity.

Once back up and out of the chapel, she copied the coordinates she had found into a map application as she walked back up the gravelled path towards the main house, and within a few seconds, she was shown a detailed satellite image of a mountain range on the South Island. The precise coordinates indicated a location a couple of kilometres to the southwest of a peak called Mount Taylor. The mountain was almost 900 kilometres from Auckland. How on earth was she going to get there in time?

Then she had an idea. From her hotel room, she had seen helicopters taking off and landing about a kilometre away along the waterfront. After a quick search online, she discovered that there was a commercial sightseeing operator located there, which offered customers a trip around Auckland in one of their helicopters.

Fiona quickly found the number for a local taxi company, and less than ten minutes later she had been picked up and was making her way back towards central Auckland. She instructed the taxi driver to take her back across the bridge, past the container ports along Quay Street to the far end of the Ferguson Container Terminal by the edge of Judges Bay where the helicopter sightseeing company was based.

Hurrying into the office, she walked up to the reception desk and asked if it was possible to hire a helicopter for later that day and if there was one available with a long range. Luckily, the chopper which suited her needs best was an AgustaWestland AW109S Grand, and it had just come back from a brief flight doing the circuit of the whole of Auckland. It was just in the process of being serviced and refuelled, so Fiona was told that she would have to wait a couple of hours. She winced slightly at the long wait, but there was no alternative at this point so she decided to go ahead and book it. Once she told the clerk where she wanted to go, she was met with a dubious look. This was clearly an unusual request, but the clerk eventually shrugged and entered the desired destination into her computer system, which then produced a flight plan, a fuel consumption estimate and finally a price.

Fiona had to steady herself when she was told how much it was going to cost, but she quickly regained her composure and fished out her credit cards from her purse. She had to max out two of them to pay for the helicopter flight, and she couldn't help herself feeling a hint of absurd gallows humour at the notion that the money she was paying with was quite possibly about to become completely worthless if Dietrich and his cult were successful in carrying out their apocalyptic plan.

On the way back to the hotel she swung by a couple of shops in downtown Auckland to buy herself a warm jacket, some hiking boots and a backpack. Then she returned to the Grand Hyatt, retrieved her belongings from her room and went to the front desk to check out. Afterwards, she took ten minutes to sit down with her laptop on one of the sofas in the hotel's lobby to write an email to Andrew back in London, updating him on her findings and letting him know what she was planning to do. As she wrote the email, she suddenly felt horribly out of her depth but she was committed now. There was no turning back given what was at stake.

She then made her way outside to the waiting taxi, and around fifteen minutes later she was walking from the small terminal building at the quay-side heliport towards where the AgustaWestland AW109S Grand was waiting. It was a small but impressive looking corporate helicopter with a pointy nose and a sleek aerodynamic body that was painted in an elegant metallic charcoal-grey livery. It could carry four passengers inside its comfortable lounge-like executive cabin, but today Fiona was the only passenger. As she sat down, strapped herself in and the doors were closed by one of the ground crew, she was keenly aware that this might very well be her last ever taste of luxury like this unless she could do something to foil Dietrich's insane plan. She was also praying that somehow Andrew, Lynch and Strickland had been able to make progress in finding the USS Tennessee. She hoped very much that they would be able to receive assistance from the intelligence services, but based on what she had experienced so far, there was every reason to suspect that even they had been infiltrated by Dietrich's organisation.

As soon as the door to the passenger cabin was closed, the pilot quickly ran through a pre-flight checklist and then the two Pratt & Whitney turboshaft engines fired up with a noise that seemed to continue increasing higher and higher in pitch. Each engine delivers 735 brake horsepower, and by the time the 10-metre rotor blades were spinning at several hundred RPM and the entire body of the helicopter was vibrating slightly, the pilot then increased the collective which caused the blades to tilt slightly and thereby generate enough lift to pull the three-tonne chopper up into the air.

The helicopter quickly gained altitude, and soon thereafter the pilot gently pushed the flight stick forward making the helicopter pitch down and causing it to quickly begin accelerating out over Auckland Harbour. It curved around to the left whilst continuing to rise, and then it settled on a course almost due south towards Wellington just under 500 kilometres away.

During much of the first leg of the journey, Fiona was looking out of the window to the left as the North Island passed underneath the helicopter, and after around 250 kilometres it passed between the two towering volcanoes of Mount Taranaki to the west and Mount Ruapehu to the east, the latter of which is still active.

After just under two hours, the pilot took the helicopter down into the heliport adjacent to Wellington International Airport for refuelling, and half an hour later they took off again for the final and shorter 370-kilometre leg of the trip to Mount Taylor. This leg took an hour and twenty minutes, with the final stretch being at a relatively high altitude in order to clear the snow-covered mountain peaks. The dark grey mountains themselves were almost completely barren and covered in patches of large snow. There was virtually no vegetation at this altitude.

Using the headphones of the helicopter's intercom, Fiona instructed the pilot to head over the peak of Mount Taylor and down through the valley. As soon as she spotted the helipads, she made him swerve slightly south and set down on a relatively flat area of rock some three hundred metres from the pads and the entrance to the complex.

Once the helicopter was on the ground and the pilot had partly spun down the rotor blades, Fiona opened the door and was greeted by the loud whine of the turboshaft engines, as well as the chill of the crisp mountain air washing into the cabin. She then jumped out, pulled out her backpack after her and walked around ten metres away from the helicopter whilst crouching down to shield herself from the downwash of the rotor blades. There she turned around and gave a thumbs-up to the pilot, who then responded in kind before revving up the engines again and lifting off to make his way up over the tall mountain range and back towards Wellington.

Fiona could have sworn that he had a look of bemusement on his face as if he thought she was completely mad to want to be dropped here by herself. Perhaps she was, but she was not about to back out now.

She watched and listened as the helicopter made its way back up through the valley and then up and over the ridge high above her where it finally disappeared from view, leaving the valley virtually silent. This was it. She was committed now.

Twenty

The USS Montana, also known as SSN-794, had been built with a single purpose. To find and sink Russian ballistic missile submarines. Like the other twenty-one Virginia-class hunter-killer submarines on active duty in the U.S. Navy, it was also more than capable of attacking surface vessels such as destroyers or even aircraft carriers, but that was considered shooting fish in a barrel. Prowling the ocean and hunting for enemy submarines using its state-of-the-art stealth capabilities and weapons systems, was what the USS Montana had been designed to do. However, its captain, Commander James Walker, had never in his wildest dreams thought that one day he would be instructing his crew to find and potentially sink another US submarine. But those were the orders that had come through from Central Command.

The almost eight thousand tonnes, 115-metre-long attack submarine with its crew of 135 submariners, was bristling with different types of weapons to perform its various tasks. Its armament included Mark-48 ADCAP torpedoes launched from four torpedo tubes at the front of the boat, twelve vertical launch tubes for Tomahawk BGM-109 cruise missiles that could hit targets at sea or on land more than two thousand kilometres away, and finally, a complement of UGM-84 Harpoon missiles which are short-range sea-skimming anti-ship missiles. The Harpoons can be launched from a submerged submarine through the forward torpedo tubes, after which they surface, unfold their manoeuvring fins and then use their turbojet engines to fly at almost nine hundred kilometres per hour at an altitude of just a few metres towards their targets out to a maximum range of 140 kilometres.

The USS Montana had entered the Mediterranean through the Straits of Gibraltar just a couple of hours earlier. It had been the only Virginia-class vessel to take part in the NATO exercise in the North Atlantic, and so it had been the closest asset available that could be employed to find the USS Tennessee. Walker had received a detailed briefing of what was thought to have transpired during the NATO exercise, and he had been informed that naval intelligence was now of the opinion that the captain of the USS Tennessee, and possibly several other members of the crew, had gone rogue and were intending to launch their nuclear missiles at cities all over the world.

Walker had met Captain Vandenberg once during a Navy gala dinner in Washington, but otherwise had no personal relationship with him. What was on his mind more than anything was the prospect of having to fire his torpedoes at a vessel with a crew of 165 Americans on board. There was just no way to find peace with that, but he knew that the potential repercussions of allowing the USS Tennessee to launch its nuclear missiles would be unthinkable, and so he might end up having no choice. First, however, he and his crew had to find the Tennessee, and that was not going to be easy. It had been designed to be as silent and undetectable as possible, and Vandenberg was a very experienced captain who at this stage no doubt understood full well that he was being hunted.

The dark sleek shape of the USS Montana made its way into the Mediterranean, submerged and gliding almost silently through the water like an orca searching for prey. Captain Walker was on the bridge, sitting in the captain's chair just behind the large horizontal tactical LCD display table that at all times showed a high-resolution 2D representation of the submarine, its surroundings and any surface or submerged vessels that had been detected by its powerful sensor suite. The precise capabilities of its sensors were highly classified, but it was said that at least some of the instruments could pick up the tell-tale signs of vessels out to a range of 1000 miles depending on how much noise they were making. The USS Tennessee, however, was now without a doubt running silent, and the Montana would have to get much closer than that in order to have a chance of detecting her.

Captain Walker had just spent several minutes on the main circuit of the PA system explaining the situation to the crew. It was only right that they should understand what was happening and why they had now been given this unenviable task.

A grim hush had fallen over the bridge, each serviceman remaining professional and intently focused on their individual tasks, but at the same time no doubt considering their potential role in what was to be the first time a United States Navy submarine would potentially end up opening fire on another US vessel.

Captain Walker sat back in his chair and allowed the crew to get on with the task ahead. His XO, Bill Howard, was directing proceedings as the Montana switched to silent running and the crew settled into their routines.

The key to success on the battlefield for a submarine that is trying to locate and defeat another submarine is the ability to detect its opponent before being detected itself, and then to engage that opponent before it has a chance to fire its own weapons. This requires the submarine to excel at two basic tasks. Firstly, using its sensors to detect the enemy submarine outside of that vessel's own detection range, and secondly, to leverage its stealth capabilities in order to avoid detection for as long as possible thus enabling it to get into firing position. Tactics and experience also play a significant role in determining the outcome of a battle between two submarines, and on that score, Walker knew that Vandenberg had the edge. However, Walker had the advantage in terms of stealth and sensors.

For the USS Montana as well as its Virginia-class sisterships, this meant superior stealth characteristics such as acoustic dampening of engines and machinery to reduce internal noise, a new propeller design that largely eliminated cavitation even at higher RPMs, and external so-called anechoic rubber coating, which can absorb much of the energy contained in the sonar pings coming from enemy submarines. These factors would all work in unison and potentially allow Walker to get close enough to the USS Tennessee for a torpedo launch before being detected.

Walker also had the advantage of being assisted by so-called Maritime Patrol Aircraft or MPAs, which are highly sophisticated recognisance aircraft that carry a range of advanced sensor equipment such as radar, sonobuoys that are dropped in the water and work autonomously to ping their surroundings for submerged vessels, as well as infrared cameras that can pick up the faint heat trail left by submerged vessels. They also carry magnetic anomaly detection equipment, that can detect the iron in a submarine's hull if it is sufficiently close to the aircraft and if the submarine is not submerged too deeply. It does this by detecting the anomaly in the Earth's magnetic field that is created by the several thousand tonnes of metal that a submarine is made from. In the case of an Ohio-class nuclear submarine like the USS Tennessee, its total weight is around eighteen thousand tonnes.

However, in addition to these more technology-related factors, certain other elements have a bearing on the outcome of an underwater engagement. While it is true that the intelligence gathering and sensor capabilities of submarines have evolved substantially since the first direct engagements between submarines took place at the beginning of the 20th century, certain other things that are dictated by the ocean have remained the same.

One of the keys to outmanoeuvring an enemy submarine is still the ability to use the natural tendency for seawater to exist and move in layers with different temperatures and salinity. The boundaries between these layers of water, which are often quite abrupt, have the effect of deflecting soundwaves hitting them from a shallow angle such as those from a submarine's active sonar pings, but this phenomenon also occurs with other sound waves such as those generated by engines or propellers.

This means that if one submarine uses its active sonar to try to locate another submarine, even if the two vessels are relatively close to each other then those acoustic signals will often bounce off the boundary between two seawater layers, and the sonar-emitting submarine will then fail to receive the return signal or echo that would otherwise have been detected. As long as the two vessels maintain a certain distance from each other, this effectively makes the submarine that is being hunted invisible to the hunter, at least temporarily and for as long as the two are at different depths and on different sides of such a boundary. On top of that, the submarine being hunted, presuming that it is using only its own passive sensors, can potentially register faint traces of the hunter's active sonar thereby allowing it to either evade and escape or engage on its own terms.

As was customary, Captain Walker had used the main circuit to announce his intentions for precisely how to carry out his orders, so that everyone on the Montana understood what was going on and what the captain was trying to achieve. This would allow for better communication between crew members as well as speedier decision-making.

His intention was to use the deeper operational depth of the Montana to try to sneak up on the USS Tennessee inside a deeper thermal layer. He would then assess the behaviour of the Tennessee and open fire if any hostile act was detected such as the opening of its torpedo tube doors.

This approach was necessary simply because the Montana's detection range is huge, whereas the range of its torpedoes is relatively short at just under 40 kilometres. In addition, with an MK-48 ADCAP torpedo having a top speed of 102 kilometres per hour, it would take up to 25 minutes for it to reach its target at that range, which would give the Tennessee a huge amount of time to launch countermeasures, take evasive action and potentially return fire. Therefore, the Montana would ideally need to get very close inside a different thermal layer before firing.

Over the next several hours and covering just over 350 kilometres, the USS Montana made its way through the Alboran Sea, which is the westernmost part of the Mediterranean Sea situated between Spain and Morocco. From there it proceeded for another almost 700 kilometres out into the much larger and deeper Algerian Basin between Algeria and the Balearic Islands, where it then turned in a westerly direction south of Sardinia towards the Strait of Sicilia, which is the relatively narrow strait between Sicily and Tunisia.

Throughout this journey which took more than twenty-four hours, the crew had been operating in shifts manning the banks of sensor equipment, and analysing the complex soundscape around them using sophisticated audio-analysis algorithms in an attempt to extract the profile of the USS Tennessee from the background noise of the hundreds of other vessels in these busy waters.

Walker had just come back to the bridge and positioned himself at the tactical table in front of his chair when one of the sonar crew members on the bridge raised his voice.

'Conn. Sonar,' the operator called out. 'New submerged contact bearing 128. Estimate range 87 miles, heading 147 at 24 knots.'

'Sonar. Conn,' said Walker and sat up in his chair. 'Designate new contact Omega Charlie 01. Narrow the search band and continue tracking.'

'Ay-ay, sir. Designating target Omega Charlie 01.'

Walker then turned to his XO who was standing next to a bank of terminals that were manned by two signal analysis specialists who were busy overseeing the analysis algorithm and reporting the results to the submarine's officers.

'How is it looking, Bill?' asked Walker.

'Too early to tell, Captain,' replied the XO, 'but the signature looks similar. We'll need to move closer.'

'Any Russian subs in this area at the moment?'

'Not as far as we know, sir,' replied Howard.

'Other NATO subs?'

'Negative, sir. We are the only one operating in the Strait of Sicilia at the moment.'

'Helmsman,' said Walker calmly but in a raised voice. 'Come right to heading 135. Make your depth 100 feet. Maintain speed. Zero bubble.'

'Ay-ay. Heading 135. Making depth 100 feet. Maintaining speed,' repeated the helmsman and began turning the rudder gradually to the right.

The change in heading and depth was virtually imperceptible inside the huge vessel, but it meant that the Montana was now making its way through the Strait of Sicilia in the direction of the island of Malta some 90 kilometres south of Sicily.

Over the next hour or so the USS Montana was silently tracking the faint sonar contact ahead of it whilst managing to gain slightly on it, reducing the range to around 50 kilometres. It was now clear that it was definitely a military submarine, and the more data that came in for analysis through the Montana's extensive sensor suite, the higher a probability the analysis algorithm assigned to it being the USS Tennessee.

The Montana was just passing the Italian island of Pantelleria less than 20 kilometres to the south when the sonar operator engaged his microphone again.

'Conn. Sonar,' he called out. 'Contact Omega Charlie 01 is slowing down.'

'All engines stop,' called Captain Walker. 'Zero bubble. Talk to me, Bill.'

'Contact has slowed to around 8 knots,' replied the XO. 'Seems to be turning slightly towards the south. He may be adjusting his heading before passing south of Malta, sir.'

'Ident?' asked Walker.

'Algorithm now suggests almost 100 percent certainty this is the Tennessee, sir,' replied Howard. 'We have to assume this is her. What's the likelihood of them realising we're here?'

'Hard to say,' replied Walker. 'Vandenberg is shrewd so it's best to assume the worst. Prepare to engage contact with two ADCAP torpedoes. Calculate and upload firing solutions.'

Bill Howard grabbed the microphone from its overhead holder and held it to his mouth.

'Torpedo room. Conn. Load two ADCAP torpedoes into tubes 1 and 4, and prepare to receive firing solutions.'

'Conn. Torpedo room,' came the reply from what sounded like the voice of a young man. 'Loading ADCAP torpedoes into tubes 1 and 4. Ay-ay, sir.'

'Conn. Sonar,' said the sonar operator suddenly, sounding tense. 'Contact Omega Charlie 01 has disappeared.'

'Sonar. Conn,' said Walker. 'Say again?'

'Contact has disappeared off the scoped, sir,' said the operator. 'It was here a few seconds ago, but now there is nothing. Our passive sensors are picking up nothing.'

The XO looked at Captain Walker.

'He might have slipped down into a lower thermal layer, sir,' he said.

'I know,' said Walker. 'Helmsman, make your depth 600 feet. Speed 16 knots.'

'Ay-ay Captain. Making depth 600 feet. Speed 16 knots,' repeated the helmsman.

'We will try to descend through the thermals and see if we can pick him up again,' said Walker. 'He is still out there somewhere.'

As the Montana descended deep into the ocean, it kept listening out for the faint audio signals that might have given away the location of the Tennessee, but it registered nothing. As is did so, the pressure hull of the vessel produced brief metallic sounding creaking noises as it began to come under strain from the pressure generated by the massive amounts of water now bearing down on it. They were unsettling noises even for experienced submariners, but the Montana had been tested to well beyond 800 feet, and the crew had faith that the hull would hold and keep them safe.

Eventually, the submarine levelled out at 600 feet less than 100 feet off the bottom of the Pantelleria Bank.

'Sonar. Conn,' said Walker. 'Anything?'

'Negative, sir,' replied the sonar operator. 'There's no trace of her. It's like she just vanished.'

Twenty-One

Fiona made her way back up the steep incline of the ravine towards where she had spotted the helipads and the entrance to the underground complex. Cresting the ridge, she discovered that the giant reinforced blast doors were even more massive than they had appeared on the live feed that she had watched inside Dietrich's command centre in the sleepy Auckland suburb of Chatswood. They were at least six metres high and easily ten metres wide and looked like they would be able to withstand just about anything any army could throw at them. They were set into a section of the mountainside where a big chunk of rock seemed to have been sliced off to allow for the excavation, and Fiona guessed that the entire construction project had first begun right here, tunnelling machines grinding their way deep into the bedrock under Mount Taylor many months or perhaps even years ago.

To the left of and adjacent to the blast doors, there was a separate section of concrete with what appeared to be a narrow opening to a small tunnel. If there really was a door in there somewhere, then it was hidden from view from where she stood. She decided that this had to be where the service access was located.

Fiona stayed low as she snuck around to the left behind the crest of the incline and just out of view of the doorway. She assumed that there might be a CCTV system somewhere, although she had not been able to spot one from her previous vantage point. Eventually, she made it all the way around the large levelled area with the helipads and the rail track and was able to approach the doorway from the side, creeping along close to a concrete wall just under what she hoped was the field of view of three CCTV cameras mounted above the blast doors.

She quickly slipped in through the doorway and found herself in a narrow tunnel with two ninety-degree turns first to the left and then to the right, clearly designed to absorb some of the energy of a shockwave from a powerful explosion, nuclear or otherwise. At the end of the tunnel was a completely featureless but solid-looking steel door and next to it on the concrete wall was a thick metal handle. Gripping the handle, she realised that it allowed for a small hinged section of the concrete wall to be pulled out and to the side, revealing a shoebox-sized compartment with an electronic keypad. Before pressing any buttons, she reached into her jacket pocket to make sure that her newly acquired self-protection device was still there. She felt its solid and heavy plastic form in her hand and extracted it. It was a jet black close-contact Vipertek stun gun, which she had never used before, but which was supposedly able to incapacitate even a grown man using a powerful electric charge. It was shaped like a heavy-duty flashlight and had a set of powerful LEDs for lighting up the dark, but its main purpose was to release thousands of volts of electricity into an assailant through the two small metal prongs on either side of the LED lights.

Here goes nothing, she thought and typed in the final passcode from the list she had found underneath Dietrich's chapel.

0-1-0-1-0-0-0-1

The keypad produced a gentle two-tone chirp, and then the heavy reinforced steel door swung inwards to reveal a small chamber with smooth concrete walls, a single light mounted on the low ceiling and another steel door at the other end. Once she stepped inside, the door behind her closed and then she could hear the gentle sound of air hissing as it passed through valves. This was clearly a tightly sealed airlock of some kind. Next to the door at the other end of the chamber was a large green plastic button. She walked across the room and pressed it, and then the steel door in front of her began to swing inwards into a room on the other side.

On the other side of the steel door was a small drab-looking guard post ensconced inside what appeared to be thick concrete walls on all sides. There was a desk with a PC displaying CCTV footage from outside the blast doors, a small but thick glass window out to the main tunnel that led into the facility as well as two doors. As soon as the steel door slid aside, the lone occupant of the room leapt to his feet and spun around. It was a heavily built man in his mid-forties with close-cropped hair, who was wearing a dark orange uniform and heavy black boots.

'Who the hell are you?' he asked gruffly, looking agitated and reaching for the gun at his side.

Fiona immediately raised her hands involuntarily, looking surprised and frightened.

'I was… hiking,' she stammered.

The guard frowned

'Hiking?' he said suspiciously, pulling his gun from the holster. 'Nobody hikes out here. I'm calling this in. Turn around and face the wall. Put your hands behind your back.'

As he barked his orders, Fiona noticed that he had not flicked safety switch on his gun. Either that, or the safety switch was already off, but the latter somehow seemed very unlikely. Fiona decided she had to gamble.

'But, sir!' she attempted in a pleading voice as she slowly turned her back towards him. 'I just…'

'Shut up!' said the guard sternly, approaching her cautiously whilst extracting a set of handcuffs from a pouch on his belt. 'I said lower your arms and place your hands behind your back. Do it now!'

'Alright, alright!' exclaimed Fiona with a hint of panic, and began slowly lowering her arms in front of herself to bring them around her hips to her back.

As she did so she adeptly unhooked the Vipertek stun gun from her belt, and as soon as she sensed that the guard was right behind her she flicked the switch to turn it on, spun around grabbing the wrist of the hand with which the guard was holding his gun and then pushed it away from herself. At the same time, she slammed the end of the stun gun into his neck, where it instantly produced a rapid series of pulses of blue lightning and an angry electrical crackling noise. With his eyes wide open and his mouth producing a pained grimace, the surprised guard instantly began to spasm uncontrollably as several thousand volts shot through his entire body. After two or three seconds, Fiona yanked the stun gun away from his neck and he then slumped to the floor in a heap, sending his gun and handcuffs clattering onto the concrete.

Fiona stood over him panting for a couple of seconds, slightly shocked by what she had done, but then knelt down to pick up his gun. She placed her hand on his neck and was relieved to find that he still had a pulse. Despite the prospect of an imminent apocalypse caused by these people, she was not about to add to the body count over the past few weeks if she didn't have to.

Pulling out a knife from her backpack, she cut a long strip from the unconscious guard's trouser leg and used it to gag him. Then she picked up the handcuffs, dragged him inside the airlock and put them on him. She had no idea for how long he might be unconscious, but she had no alternative but to leave him in there and hope for the best.

She stepped back into the guard post and hit the large plastic button to close the steel door, trapping the guard inside the airlock. Then she turned around and walked over to the PC monitor, studying the various CCTV images that were being streamed live to the terminal. Several of them showed the ravine outside of the blast doors including the helipads. Others seemed to be mounted at regular intervals along the wide tunnel leading into the mountain. At the far end of the tunnel there appeared to be another set of huge blast doors, and in front of them on either side were parked two black-painted bulky-looking cars that looked like they might have been Humvees or some other similar type of military vehicle. However, the camera feed that got her attention was the one showing a long narrow tunnel with ceiling lights every three metres or so. She concluded that this had to be the service tunnel that she had seen on the drawings underneath the chapel in Auckland. This might allow her to reach the blast doors at the other end of the main tunnel unseen.

She turned her head away from the monitor to look at the wall at the far end of the guard post. There were two doors there, one of them clearly leading out to the main tunnel. She got up and walked over to the other door, opening it slowly to peek out through the gap. Just as she had suspected, a long narrow tunnel stretched away into the mountain running parallel to the huge main tunnel. If she was to make it inside the facility, she would have to somehow get to the other end of the service tunnel unnoticed and through whatever security measures had been put in place there.

Closing the door again and looking around the room, she spotted two metal lockers built into one of the walls. Inside she found what she was looking for. There were several boilersuits and an orange uniform like the one the guard had been wearing. Deciding to use a disguise and attempt to look as inconspicuous as possible, she decided to put on a boilersuit and then donned a cap which she pulled down as far as possible to conceal her face. Emblazoned across the back of the boilersuit was written '*Maintenance Crew*', and on the left front pocket was a strip designed to have a name tag velcroed onto it. Finding no loose tags inside the locker, she decided that she would have to manage without. Hopefully, she would avoid having to explain herself to anyone.

'No time like the present,' she muttered to herself and then picked up her backpack and reattached the stun gun to her belt.

She slipped into the service tunnel and began walking briskly towards the far end, her footsteps echoing through the dimly lit concrete corridor. Every ten metres or so there were short passages through to the main tunnel, and as she approached the far end of the service tunnel, she could see that there was another guard post there, seemingly identical to the one she had just left. In the distance she could hear voices, so she knew that the guard post was manned by at least one person. She had to make a conscious effort to resist the impulse to turn around and get out. This could get tricky and possibly very dangerous. What she needed now was a diversion.

When she was close to the point along the main tunnel where the cars were parked, she ducked into one of the short passages, knelt down and crept to the edge of the main tunnel, looking towards the second set of blast doors. One of the cars was just a few metres away, and if she stayed low and close to the wall, she might be able to get to it without being spotted by the two guards that she could now see inside the guard post through its small window.

Moving in a low crouch, she slipped out into the main tunnel and quickly made her way quietly to the nearest car. Praying that it was unlocked, she reached up to the driver's side door handle and pulled at it gently. The door opened, and Fiona breathed a sigh of relief. She looked inside the car but found nothing she might be able to use. Then she had an idea.

Still crouched and staying out of sight, she went to the rear corner of the car and opened the flap to the filler. Reaching inside, she unscrewed the filler cap, tore a strip from her scarf and lowered it into the fuel tank. After a few seconds, she could feel it getting heavier as it absorbed the fuel, so she then extracted it and squeezed the fuel onto the driver's seat. It wasn't much, but she was sure it would be enough. Then she repeated the process but left the strip of cloth hanging out of the filler. Unhooking the stun gun from her belt she then pressed it against the fuel sodden seat and fired the stun gun once.

It immediately produced a small blue spark that instantly ignited the fuel on the seat. She hurried back towards the short passage to the service tunnel and waited there. She could already hear the sound of the flames consuming the highly flammable foam inside the car seat, and within a couple of seconds, she heard voices shouting from the direction of the guard post. Then she heard the sound of footsteps and of several pairs of feet running.

This was her chance. She turned the corner back into the service tunnel and walked quickly towards the door at the end. Upon reaching it she pulled it open and to her relief discovered that the guard post was empty. Both of the men that had been inside must have run to the burning car.

Suddenly she heard the sound of a dull explosion coming from the main tunnel, followed by more shouting. The fire must have reached the car's fuel tank and ignited its contents.

The interior of the guard post was almost identical to the one she had just come from, except that there was a steel door opposite the door to the service tunnel. This door also had a keypad next to it, but Fiona had no idea what the passcode might be. It was highly unlikely to be the same as the passcode for the access door to the outside.

Shit, she thought and glanced over her shoulder through the small window to the main tunnel. She was unable to see the burning car from where she stood, but she could tell from the bright orange light that the fire had now taken hold and was in the process of consuming the entire car. She could hear the loud hiss of fire extinguishers being used.

Suddenly the keypad next to the door chirped and the door flew open. A group of men in protective gear stormed through the guard post, completely ignoring her and rushing out through the door to the main tunnel. They were hauling various equipment with them including several fire extinguishers, and she had to step out of the way to avoid being run down.

Seizing the moment, she slipped through the steel door before it shut by itself to find herself in yet another concrete room. This one, however, had large windows out to a large open space on the other side. For a few seconds, Fiona felt slightly disorientated as she looked out of the windows. She knew that she had to be at least a couple of hundred metres underneath a huge mountain, but her eyes were telling her that she was looking through a window to the outside. It was bright as day out there, and somewhere between fifty and a hundred metres away she could see trees and bushes. Stepping closer and peering through the window she spotted what looked like flowing water. Was that a waterfall she could see?

Suddenly another team of firefighters entered the room and hurried through to the guard post on the other side, and as Fiona looked out, she could see what looked like a large electric golf cart carrying another team of people approaching her location. She decided to use the general confusion to exit the room and step out of the door.

Taking a couple of steps away from the door she could barely believe what she was seeing. She was standing near the edge of a giant domed atrium, and she almost felt dizzy as her brain grappled with trying to take in the sheer size of it. With her mouth half open and her eyes blinking a couple of times, Fiona continued walking slowly away from the doorway and further out into the gigantic circular space. Looking first to the left and then to the right and following the gentle curve of the cavernous space all the way around to the far side, she estimated that it was perhaps as much as 300 metres across and easily 50 metres from the top of the dome down to the floor below. There were hundreds of artificial lights mounted on the inside of the dome, each giving off a diffuse white light that seemed to have been calibrated to sunlight during midday, and together they gave the illusion of the huge space beneath it being in daylight. Underneath the centre of the dome was a small park, complete with tall trees, bushes, flower beds, benches, a small stream and a waterfall. It all looked quite idyllic, and yet at the same time utterly bizarre.

The first thing that sprang to mind as she tried to take it all in was the interior of the Millennium Dome in London, which contains the O2 Arena and which has capacity for around twenty thousand people. But this was no entertainment venue, and unlike the O2 Arena there was plenty of space for the relatively few people she could see from where she stood. Around half of the cavernous space was occupied by the small park which itself was surrounded by a wide circular concourse that wrapped around the circumference of the enormous dome. Along the edge of the dome were multiple single-storey buildings, and on closer inspection, Fiona could see that they were shops offering goods and services similar to what one might find in any town centre.

This wasn't just some drab and soulless doomsday bunker where people would sit out Armageddon under gloomy lights, sleeping on the floor and eating freeze-dried meals. This was a functioning city, seemingly complete with all the services that are required to sustain thousands of people for months or perhaps longer.

Fiona did a quick calculation in her head to estimate that the circumference of the dome was close to a kilometre in length, and interspersed between the low buildings at intervals of around fifty or sixty metres were wide gateways to tunnels that stretched away from the atrium to unseen locations. However, recalling the schematics she had seen of the facility, she knew that these tunnels provided access to the twelve separate smaller domes that were likely to be identical to what Aaron had found in the Arizona desert.

Fiona suddenly realised how she was gawping at everything around her, which probably made her stand out like a sore thumb amidst the seemingly highly organised bustle of people that were busily moving around inside the dome. Everyone looked like they were on their way to somewhere, and they all wore different coloured uniforms or other attire suitable for their roles in this immense beehive. While most of them were walking, there were several of the golf carts that were moving across the giant open space as well as coming out of and going into the gateways to the twelve smaller domes deeper inside the mountain.

Fiona got out her phone and surreptitiously took a couple of photos of the dome, and then she began walking purposefully along, despite having no idea where she was going. As she walked, she looked around casually, and suddenly she spotted a row of tall glass windows high above her. Almost halfway up the curved dome, there was a balcony with what appeared to be an office space behind it. From a distance, it looked small inside the giant volume of space under the dome, but judging by the height of the floor-to-ceiling windows behind it, the balcony would have been at least ten metres wide and jutting out three or four metres towards the centre of the dome. Fiona instantly knew that this was where

Dietrich would be. An ostentatious solitary position for the supreme leader located high above his subjects.

She did not have an exact plan for what to do, but all she knew was that she had to get up there and uncover precisely what was going on, and also find a way to show it to the world before Dietrich was able to complete his insane scheme. She simply had to find a way into that office somehow. She scanned the area directly below the balcony and spotted an entrance opposite the small central park area, which was appreciably smaller than the twelve tunnels that led to the sub-domes.

She headed towards the park and decided to walk through it. Inside on the lush soft-looking grass were small groups of people. They mostly appeared to be mothers with small children that were still too young to go to school. As Fiona walked past them on a narrow gravel path, she was barely able to process what she saw.

What's wrong with these people? she thought. *How can they carry on so calmly in the face of what is about to happen? How has Dietrich managed to induce a mass delusion into these people, so that they really believe that the destruction of the world is justified?*

As she walked further along, she studied the faces of some of the people she passed, and she couldn't help feeling that there was something slightly off about the way they behaved. It was their facial expressions. The way they interacted with each other. She couldn't quite put her finger on it, but it somehow seemed as if they were strangely detached and simply going through the motions of enjoying themselves. As if in some way they were operating on autopilot. As if they weren't quite there.

Leaving the park behind, she continued towards the entrance that was underneath the balcony high above and entered. On the way, she saw what looked like a platoon of around twenty soldiers in black uniforms and shiny black boots marching towards the main access tunnel. She pulled her cap down further in front of her face and continued on towards the entrance below the balcony.

Inside the entrance was a room akin to a foyer with a central elevator and two stairwells, one on either side of it. She stepped into the empty elevator and looked at the panel with the controls. She was on Level 0, named 'Atrium', and there seemed to be four levels above her and two below. She had no desire to visit Level 2, which said 'Barracks', and she was about to press the button for Level 4 which said 'Executive', when she decided that she wanted to see what was on the sublevels, so she pressed the button for Level -1 which said 'Agriculture'. The one below that, Level -2, said 'Power Systems & Engineering'.

To her surprise, the trip down to Level -1 took at least half a minute as the elevator descended a significant distance down the elevator shaft. When the doors opened, she guessed that she had travelled at least three regular storeys down into the bedrock from 'Level 0', and what greeted her almost took her breath away. It was a huge high-ceilinged room at least two hundred metres long with steel columns placed at regular intervals throughout, and row upon row of multi-layered grow beds stretching away towards the far end of the cavernous space. Each bed was full of plants and vegetables of different kinds and was lit with what looked like banks of LED lights that were no doubt dialled in to emit the optimal wavelength for photosynthesis. The air down here was humid and warm, and there was a sweet scent of fertile earth wafting around her as she exited the elevator onto a metal concourse which ran the circumference of the enormous underground greenhouse. From the various signs on the different grow beds, it was clear that there was hardly a single type of vegetable that was not grown somewhere inside this space.

There must be enough fresh produce here to feed thousands of people, she thought. *Especially if they also have plenty of dry staples like rice or pasta.*

Spotting two workers wearing dark green uniforms walking toward her about a hundred metres away, Fiona decided she had seen enough. She quickly and discreetly took a couple of pictures and then hurried back inside the elevator where she pressed the button for Level -2.

A few moments later the elevator came to a stop and the doors opened to reveal a large space with giant machinery that she guessed was freshwater pumps that were most likely tapping into the groundwater, air filtration systems, water treatment equipment, heat exchangers and more. It looked like a busy factory floor, but there were only a handful of people milling around as well as two more in a raised office on the right side of the space. A mixture of noises emanated from the many machines, and from somewhere in the distance came the sound of clanging from what sounded like a hammer on metal, mixed in with the noise of what might have been power tools whirring and grinding. Deciding not to risk investigating further, she took a few more pictures on her phone and stepped back inside the elevator.

She now pressed the button for Level 1 which said 'Leisure', and after about half a minute she exited the elevator into what seemed more akin to a shopping centre than anything else, except there were no goods to buy. On both sides of a long and wide underground street that was lined on both sides with tall potted palm trees, were many different types of entertainment venues such as fitness centres, bowling alleys, cinemas, bars and restaurants and even a swimming pool.

Gosh, they have really thought of everything here, thought Fiona.

Walking along this unusual street she could see dozens of people in all of the different venues, especially the fitness centres, and she guessed that people here probably worked in shifts to maintain the smooth running of the facility and that these venues most likely never closed. Halfway down the street, she decided to turn back, suddenly feeling self-conscious wearing an orange uniform in this place. That was probably an unusual sight, so she decided to leave before she was challenged, and instead head further upwards to Level 3, which was called 'Administration'.

As the elevator doors opened to Level 3, a couple of people in grey business-like uniforms were waiting outside, and as Fiona stepped out of the elevator they entered whilst looking first at her face and then at her orange uniform. There was a look of mild surprise on their faces. Her presence on this level clearly drew attention, so she needed a new plan fast.

Immediately across from the elevator was a large open-plan office space behind a glass wall with a single entrance through a door with an electronic keycard reader. Behind the glass wall sat around twenty people in small cubicles roughly two metres apart, and above each cubicle was a sign indicating the function of the person in that cubicle. One of them read 'Security', one read 'Communications', another read 'Air and Water Facility Management' and so on. This was clearly the nerve centre for the operation of the entire facility.

At the back of the office space were a number of smaller offices also with glass walls, most likely for supervisors, but only one of them was occupied by a middle-aged man in a grey uniform. Apart from the slightly militaristic vibe, it was the sort of corporate environment that she would have found if she had walked into any number of large office buildings in central London, New York, Tokyo or Hong Kong. Some of the office workers were walking between cubicles, and a couple of them were standing by a coffee machine having a conversation. Once again, Fiona was struck by how normal it all looked considering what the purpose of this entire facility was.

She spotted a small painted metal panel behind her on the wall next to the elevator and walked over to it, opening it up and doing her best to look busy. To the people inside the offices, she would have looked like a technician inspecting electrical wires in the wall. Or so she hoped. She began to feel like she was pushing her luck and that she needed a new disguise.

As Fiona pretended to busy herself with the electrical systems behind the open wall panel, she glanced over her shoulder and saw a young woman get up from the desk in her cubicle and head towards the glass door to the corridor outside. Like the other women working in this office, she was wearing grey trousers, a white blouse and a grey beret with a small gold insignia on the front, and her hair was almost the same length and colour as Fiona's. When she reached the glass door, she extracted her keycard and swiped it across the reader. The door beeped and swung open, and then the woman walked through it and proceeded down the corridor away from Fiona.

Making a mental note of the location of the woman's cubicle, Fiona closed the wall panel and hurried after her as fast as she could whilst still trying to look inconspicuous. Fiona saw her disappear into the ladies' restroom at the end of the corridor, and so she followed her inside whilst gripping the stun gun inside her jacket pocket. As Fiona entered, the woman was washing her hands at the washbasin and she looked up at Fiona who smiled and nodded. The woman's facial expression revealed that she was surprised to see someone like her in there.

Fiona made her way towards the cubicle at the very back, which meant that she had to walk behind the woman. When she was immediately behind her, she whipped out the stun gun and jammed it into the woman's back. Her whole body began to spasm uncontrollably and then she slumped to the floor unconscious. Fiona quickly grabbed her arms and hauled her along the floor into the nearest cubicle where she began taking off her own uniform. Then she undressed the woman and put on her uniform instead. She pulled the woman over to the back wall and propped her up against it. Hopefully, it would be a while before she came to.

Fiona then snatched the woman's keycard and put it in her pocket. Then she locked the cubicle and climbed over the door so that it would look occupied from the outside. She took a moment to look in the mirror, straighten her clothes and don the beret before she exited the restroom and walked calmly along the corridor towards the glass-walled office.

When she got to the door, she swiped the woman's keycard across the reader and the door opened for her, much to her relief. No one seemed to take any notice of her as she made her way to the woman's cubicle and sat down. Above it was the sign for 'Air and Water Facility Management'.

It had only been a few minutes since the woman had left her cubicle, so her PC had not yet locked itself. This allowed Fiona to start to investigate the systems that this workstation was controlling. After a few moments she had found schematics for the air and water pipes for the entire facility, and she was amazed to find that they ran to tens of kilometres of pipework. In addition to the air and water treatment facility she had seen on Level -2, each of the twelve sub-domes also had their own auxiliary systems. Fresh air was provided by a complex system of air intakes at the surface, each of which fed air through a filtration system which seemed to have been designed to extract or nullify all types of contaminants, including radioactive as well as biological and chemical materials. She also discovered that the entire facility was powered by a nuclear reactor located at the back of level -2, which required several sets of additional credentials to access.

Trawling through the various control systems and hoping to find some way of perhaps sabotaging some of the facility's vital services, she came across something strange. There seemed to be a separate sub-system in the water treatment control application that allowed for various nutritional additives to be mixed with the facility's drinking water. This would have been a sensible idea for keeping people healthy if they were to be cooped up underground for months, but one of the additives stood out like a sore thumb. It was labelled as a Selective Serotonin Reuptake Inhibitor or SSRI. Fiona had read about these in the past, and she knew that they are synthetic chemicals that have the effect of suppressing normal emotional responses in people. In other words, they cause so-called emotional blunting, which, at least in theory, allows people to suffer through trauma more easily or to carry out violent acts without being weighed down by their conscience. Some armies in certain countries had apparently experimented with these types of drugs for soldiers on the battlefield.

Holy crap, thought Fiona. *That explains the vacant look in the eyes of those people in the park. Dietrich is drugging everyone here.*

She decided to try to access the control system for the SSRI dispenser system. If she could disable the system, then that might help some people here snap out of their lunacy and perhaps even challenge

Dietrich to put a stop to it all. Or was that a naïve idea?

She quickly looked over her shoulder in the direction of the ladies' restroom to make sure that the woman had not regained consciousness yet and come out. Then she opened up the dispenser interface on the terminal only to find that it required a four-digit passcode. She decided to roll the dice and try several combinations, beginning with 0-0-0-1 but they all failed, and after the third attempt she was locked out of the system.

She glanced up, half expecting to be surrounded by security guards but there none, and everyone else in the office was still busy with their own tasks on their own terminals.

She got up calmly from the desk and was about to head for the door, having decided that she had now outstayed her welcome. At that moment the elevator doors opened and a group of four men in black uniforms walked out and headed briskly straight for the door to the office.

Shit, thought Fiona. *They're on to me. The computer terminal lockout must have alerted a security team.*

Standing up and expecting to be surrounded, she was surprised to find that the four soldiers entered the office and then proceeded straight to the small glass office at the back where the supervisor sat, without paying attention to anyone else in the room.

As the men walked briskly along, Fiona decided that this was going to be her only chance to get out, so she got up and hurried towards the door. The team of four soldiers were almost at the glass office some twenty metres away, and there were several banks of cubicles between them and her so she jogged the final few metres to the door and made it outside. Here she walked as fast as she could towards the nearest set of stairs next to the elevator, and then she hurried unseen up to Level 4.

This level, the so-called Executive Level, looked nothing like anything she had seen so far. It was more akin to a swanky hotel than anything else, with a wide corridor covered with a soft light brown carpet stretching away from the elevator for about thirty metres, dark wood-panelled walls, soft lighting and groups of large potted plants arranged here and there to give it an organic and inviting ambience. Every ten metres or so there were wooden doors on either side sitting inside gilded metal doorframes, and next to each door was an engraved brass plaque indicating whose residence it was.

The plaque nearest the elevator on the left side said *'Magister Equitum'*, which was the term used in Ancient Rome for the emperor's right-hand man and caretaker when the emperor was away from Rome. The most famous of these had been Julius Caesar's magister Equitum, Marcus Antonius, or Mark Antony as he was also known. Fiona wondered who this suite might belong to.

Opposite the suite on the other side of the five-metre-wide corridor was an identical door. Fiona walked across the corridor and read the text on the brass plaque. It said *'Imperator'*.

She grabbed the door handle and to her surprise found that the door was unlocked.

Strange, she thought and looked back towards the elevator and the stairwells.

It seemed odd that these doors would be left unlocked, but then again, anyone entering these suites without proper authorisation would not exactly be able to leave the facility swiftly since the whole thing was locked down. Or perhaps everyone here was so completely on board with the program that they wouldn't even dream of doing such a thing.

Whatever the reason, it allowed Fiona to slip inside and close the door behind her. What met her was what looked like a huge open plan apartment with hardwood flooring, a comfortable looking seating area, a large open kitchen, and several rooms at the back, possibly bedrooms. To her right was a doorway into what looked like a library.

It all looked very exclusive and luxurious, however, what caught her eye more than anything else was the wall stretching away on one side. It had been constructed to look like floor-to-ceiling windows that one might find in a typical high-rise building, but instead of glass, there were huge LCD displays showing a simulated skyline which she quickly recognised as being that of Manhattan in New York City.

Fiona gawped at the extravagant scene in front of her. After a few moments, it dawned on her that what she was looking at must be a replica of Peter Dietrich's penthouse in Dietrich Tower.

Through the library, she found another door next to a wide ethanol fireplace, which led to the space she had been able to see from the atrium several stories below. It looked like an office, with a large wooden desk at one end, a couple of low sofas in the middle, and access out to the balcony directly opposite the door to the library. This balcony was where Peter Dietrich, the megalomaniac, would be able to stand and soak up the adulation from his crowd of future imperial subjects.

Fiona walked over to the tall floor-to-ceiling windows and looked out across the enormous cavernous space under the dome. It was an incredible feat of engineering, and as she stood there she noticed that the light from the hundreds of fist-sized clusters of LEDs that were arranged all over the dome had now turned slightly more yellow. She checked her wristwatch to discover that it was now late afternoon. Clearly, the lighting system inside the dome was simulating the normal 24-hour day-night cycle that was progressing out on the other side of the sealed blast doors.

'You!' said a deep voice behind her in a tense but commanding tone of voice. 'Put your hands above your head, and don't move a muscle.'

Fiona turned her head to see a small group of black-clad soldiers in the doorway to the library behind her. She briefly considered making a run for it, but then she sighed and did as she had been told, slowly raising her hands.

'Turn around,' said the voice.

She turned slowly to see soldiers carrying submachine guns with red-dot laser pointers attached, and they were all aiming at her making the tiny red points of light dance around on her white blouse.

'Kneel,' continued the soldier, and then he glanced sideways at one of the other men. 'Cuff her.'

The other soldier moved around to her back and grabbed her wrists roughly, pulled them down below her back and snapped on a set of handcuffs. Then he took out a black cloth hood and pulled it over her head.

'Let's go,' said the soldier and yanked her to her feet, and then he pushed her forward and to the side. 'Start walking.'

From inside the stuffy black hood, Fiona was able to sense that she was being taken to the other end of Dietrich's office. Here she was then pushed unceremoniously down into a chair, wincing as the cuffs bit into her wrists.

Breathing nervously inside the hood, she sat there for a few moments waiting for what might happen next. Then she heard the sound of footsteps approaching and stopping just a couple of feet immediately behind her.

'Fiona, my dear,' said a familiar voice calmly. 'How lovely to see you again.'

Twenty-Two

'Take this damn thing off me,' shouted Fiona angrily.

Peter Dietrich walked calmly past her chair and sat down opposite her behind his desk. He then nodded at one of the praetorians, who stepped forward and yanked the black hood off of Fiona's head.

'There,' smiled Dietrich. 'Is that better?'

'What is actually wrong with you,' said Fiona disdainfully. 'Did the other kids in the playground bully you? Did you have really bad acne?'

'Dearest Fiona,' said Dietrich, still smiling calmly. 'What on earth are you talking about?'

'This!' said Fiona heatedly and jerked her head towards the windows to the dome. 'This whole insane operation of yours. How sick does someone have to be to think this fucking bunker is the solution to the world's problems?'

'Ah,' said Dietrich, leaning back in his chair. 'You put your finger on it, right there. The world's problems. There are an increasing number of problems in this world that the current world order has proven itself incapable of solving, and the basic problem is governance.'

'Meaning what, exactly?' asked Fiona, sounding exasperated.

'The problem is democracy,' replied Dietrich gesticulating gently in the air in front of himself. 'As I told you already when we met in London. 'Do you remember when I mentioned a quote to you by the Roman historian Lucius Cassius Dio?'

'Yes,' replied Fiona. 'I believe the quote was *"Monarchy has an unpleasant sound, but is a most practical form of government to live under"*, or some nonsense like that.'

'Very good!' smiled Dietrich, sounding both impressed and slightly condescending. 'Democracy is a fine idea in theory, but in practice, it is a degenerate form of government. It quite evidently does not work, partly because of how we humans have evolved. You see, human beings are nothing but descendants of apes walking upright, and by looking at our evolution it becomes clear that we have changed our own environments dramatically faster than our psychologies and our intellects have been able to adapt.'

'What does that even mean?' said Fiona derisively.

'Our brains,' replied Dietrich, seemingly oblivious to Fiona's disdain, 'as well as both our cognitive and emotional abilities, evolved over millions of years to solve problems in low-tech, small scale, face-to-face societies. The world we have now created for ourselves is the exact opposite of those things. It is suddenly extremely high-tech, which means that the majority of humans have no idea how most things in their lives actually work, including the vital systems that their lives depend on every single day. We have gone from small scale hunter-gatherer groups to villages to global communities of hundreds of millions of supposed kinsmen, with hundreds or even thousands of acquaintances, in person or online. Most people simply are not capable of responsibly and intelligently navigating this modern world the way it has evolved, and the reality is that those people are much better off being governed than they are governing themselves.'

'And how do you arrive at that conclusion?' asked Fiona.

'Well,' replied Dietrich. 'Part of the problem is that we have set up systems of government that rely on all citizens being very knowledgeable and informed about a huge number of highly complex issues, and then to cast their vote based on thorough consideration of all of those issues, but it is just not realistic to expect them to be capable of that. And amongst the small minority of people who are prepared to at least attempt to live up to those responsibilities, only an even smaller minority actually manage to fully do so. And yet, most of those relatively enlightened people fail too, simply because they don't have the time required to become experts on all the different things that a society has to grapple with on an ongoing basis. Modern humans in these supposed democracies have to be experts on economics, international treaties, climate science, military capabilities and spending, foreign policy and so on ad nauseum. The result is a deeply dysfunctional and easily manipulable system of governance that is a democracy in name only. Democracy only works when everything is going well. As soon as there is a serious problem, like a war, a natural disaster, an economic depression, a pandemic or a climate crisis, it suddenly becomes the least effective and least flexible and adaptable way to govern. And that is the case even if elected officials are intelligent, responsible and non-corrupt people, which I think you'll agree is the exception rather than the rule, right?'

Fiona shrugged. She found it difficult to argue with that particular point.

'The fragile systems that humanity has built to sustain our current civilisation simply break down at the slightest hint of a serious problem, and we are left mired in chronic short-term indecision and squabbling over small pathetic details, when we should be focusing on the big long-term goals for our species, such as survival in the face of all manner of threats to our existence. And the entire human race suffers as a result. The basic truth is that democracy in the modern world is quite simply an utterly naïve and dysfunctional concept. It is a short-lived failed experiment in governance that may have worked for groups of hunter-gatherers or even small villages, but it is completely unfit for purpose in a world of billions of people. And many of us are waking up to that fact.'

'And I suppose those people are your fellow occupants here inside this perverted Noah's Ark of yours,' said Fiona, glancing out towards the dome on the other side of the windows.

'The ARK *is* the solution,' nodded Dietrich. 'We have a chance to start again, and reset humanity once and for all, creating a system of governance that can last for millennia.'

'Another Thousand Year Reich,' scoffed Fiona. 'Where have I heard that one before? And we all know how that ended.'

'Everyone currently inside the ARK believes like I do that humanity needs to start over under one leader who can make bold and tough decisions quickly. Someone who can adapt and be decisive when required.'

'And I suppose you think that you are that person?' asked Fiona scornfully.

'Can you think of anyone better to do it?' smiled Dietrich mockingly. 'Yourself perhaps?'

'NO!' said Fiona angrily. 'And that's the whole point. Even if I thought I was the best person to do it, I just might be wrong! It is called humility, and I believe human civilisation depends on that.'

'You are lacking in confidence,' observed Dietrich dispassionately. 'That is part of what sets people like me apart from people like you. Self-confidence trumps humility any day of the week in my book. Do you know the story about how Julius Caesar was kidnapped by pirates?'

'Something about a ransom?' asked Fiona, sounding exasperated and as if she was unsure where this was going.

'Correct,' replied Dietrich. 'Caesar was captured by pirates on the way to Rhodes when he was 25 years old. Realising that they had caught themselves a nobleman, the pirates were planning to ask for a ransom of 20 Talents of silver, which would be around one million dollars in today's money. Caesar was incensed and offended by the low amount, and immediately demanded that the pirates ask for at least 50 Talents. They took his advice, and while waiting for the ransom to be paid, Caesar lived amongst the pirates. He did promise them that one day he would hunt them down and kill them all, which of course he eventually did.'

'Yes, that is a fascinating story,' said Fiona sarcastically. 'But where you see confidence, I see hubris. Just another young man with a wildly inflated sense of self-importance. Not unlike someone else I know.'

Fiona glared at Dietrich pointedly, but he simply looked at her for a few seconds with a mix of disappointment and pity.

'I really had hoped you would have been able to think bigger than this,' he sighed and smiled sardonically. 'Perhaps when the world has changed you will see things differently.'

'You mean when you have committed an act of genocide,' sneered Fiona.

'It is necessary,' said Dietrich matter-of-factly.

'Isn't that what Hitler said?' asked Fiona caustically.

'Hitler was a delusional lightweight,' replied Dietrich dismissively. 'He squandered a great chance for order in this world.'

'And yet, you follow in his footsteps,' retorted Fiona. 'But as a great man once said; *"All bad precedents begin as justifiable measures."'*

'Well done,' smiled Dietrich mockingly. 'Anyway, when someone begins to quote Caesar at me, I think perhaps the conversation should be coming to an end.'

'Tell me,' interjected Fiona angrily. 'How did you become like this? What happened to you to make you this cold? To turn you into such a sick bastard.'

Dietrich smiled overbearingly, tapping his fingertips on his desk.

'I guess you could say I have been on a journey,' replied Dietrich. 'I used to be like you. Small. Closed-minded. Cowed by pathological self-doubt induced in me by so-called 'society'. Afraid of releasing my own potential just in case it might disrupt the lives of others. But that philosophy, if you will, rests on the idea of fairness, which I along with many others have now come to realise is utter nonsense. You see, I eventually came to the conclusion that the only thing that really matters is power. Pure and simple. Agency to do things. And those with agency will end up ruling those without, whether they want to or not. Some have agency, some don't, and there is no such thing as "fairness". So, we should dispense with those sensibilities, and powerful people should embrace that destiny and do as they please. It is more likely to ultimately be for the benefit of the human race than outdated notions of liberalism and broken forms of government like democracy. As a species, we are already fighting a losing battle, simply because of the way procreation has developed.'

'What on earth are you talking about?' asked Fiona.

'Natural selection,' replied Dietrich evenly, sitting up in his chair and folding his hands on the desk in front of himself. 'Natural selection is an evolutionary feature that has now effectively been disabled. It is a well-established fact, although not talked about openly, that less intelligent people have many more children than more intelligent people. Our societies, through publicly funded services and support structures, allow for unsuitable genes to continuously be carried forward through procreation by people who are at the bottom of the IQ distribution, whilst people at the other end of the distribution have much fewer offspring. The net result of that, of course, is that the average IQ for the human race is dropping rapidly, and has been doing so for decades. Where do you think that is going to take us eventually?'

Fiona decided not to reply, and simply looked at him, deadpan.

'In the new world that we are going to build,' continued Dietrich, 'the strong will again dominate the weak, and there is no point in being sentimental about that. It has always been that way, and it is frankly a prerequisite for the continued successful evolution of human civilisation. It is part of the very foundation of human progress. Without that selection mechanism, we are doomed to be mired in mediocracy forever. If we hold back the potential of exceptional individuals in the name of vacuous tropes about fairness and equality, even to the point of prioritising equality of outcomes over equality of opportunities, then human civilisation will enter a terminal decline which will eventually end us as a species. History has shown us time and time again that we need destruction in order for creation to manifest, and this goes for our genetic material as well. Eugenics may look bad at the individual level, but it is absolutely necessary at the collective level in order to keep humanity from degenerating.'

Fiona shook her head.

'I feel like I am listening to Joseph Goebbels,' she said and sighed. 'Anyway, so you are just going to sit here while the whole world burns? Is that really the plan?'

'That would be putting it a bit crudely, but essentially, yes,' replied Dietrich. 'Except, of course, we won't be entirely passive. As soon as our missiles begin launching, that will only be the beginning. We have carried out extensive research on how a nuclear exchange might escalate, and we have studied in great detail the individual military doctrines of all of the world's nuclear powers in order to optimise the timing and sequencing of our launches for maximum effect. I believe that with our strategy we can almost guarantee that all the nuclear weapons that are on alert today will be launched, which will leave the world cleansed of the defective systems that have evolved over the past century. We will then be ready to emerge once the cleansing has happened, and we have a sophisticated plan for how to steer human civilisation back on track after that.'

'Oh really?' asked Fiona sounding both exasperated and dubious. 'And what does that plan look like?'

'Our New Empire will be divided into a number of magistrates, which roughly correspond to the world's major regions, and each one will be governed by praetors who report directly to me. They will also have at their disposal a cadre of apolitical bureaucrats who will oversee the re-seeding of Earth. We also have an extremely well-equipped and highly mobile military force of almost two thousand soldiers ready. This may not sound like much, but with a force of that size equipped with drones, tanks and missiles up against what will be bands of people with sticks and stones, it will be more than enough to subdue any resistance and assert our dominance. But anyway, our researchers deem such pockets of resistance to be quite unlikely to survive.'

'You really are completely sick,' spat Fiona. 'And what about the people down in that park?' she asked, tipping her head slightly towards the windows. 'I saw mothers and children down there. Do you really think that they will be able to grow up happily knowing what their parents did?'

'Well,' said Dietrich, 'It didn't seem to bother anyone in Europe when the people of that continent took over the entire world at the point of a gun during colonial times. Millions were brutally killed during those many decades, and no one batted an eyelid. Deep down everyone understands that sometimes sacrifices have to be made in order to ensure great leaps forward.'

'Great leaps forward?' scoffed Fiona. 'Wasn't that what Chairman Mao called it when he tried to change the world by realising the communist dream? Millions of innocent people died as a result.'

'Communism is a completely flawed idea,' shrugged Dietrich dismissively, 'It's even worse than democracy, so of course it didn't work.'

'And what did you do to those people down there?' asked Fiona. 'You're feeding them SSRIs through the water supply. That doesn't exactly smack of confidence.'

Dietrich pressed his lips together and produced a pained smile.

'Some minds are weaker than others,' he said, 'Even in here. And those minds may need to be fortified in times of stress. We are simply ensuring that there is cohesion and discipline here inside the ARK whilst the world goes through its necessary transformation process.'

'What a lovely euphemism,' said Fiona acerbically. 'Are you taking those drugs yourself too?'

'I don't need to,' replied Dietrich calmly.

'No kidding,' said Fiona with a derisive scowl. 'You're not going to get away with this, you know. We're on to you. They are hunting down the USS Tennessee as we speak.'

'Oh, I am sure they're giving it a good go,' replied Dietrich calmly. 'But it is already much too late. In a few hours, my good friend and future Magister Equitum, Captain Vandenberg, will launch the submarine's entire complement of nuclear weapons, almost certainly setting off World War 3 in the process. And after a year or so, we here in the ARK will emerge and take the reins of what was already a broken and deeply dysfunctional world. And then we will rebuild a better future. I believe that in time, history will thank us for it.'

'You're a lunatic,' said Fiona. 'Pure and simple.'

'Well,' sighed Dietrich evenly. 'I am far from alone in my firmly held convictions, as you have seen with your own eyes.'

He gestured out towards the dome.

'Anyway,' he continued. 'I have allowed you to take up quite enough of my time today. I had genuine hopes that perhaps you might come to see things as clearly as I do and perhaps even join our cause, but I guess I overestimated you.'

'I have never been happier to have someone say those words to me,' replied Fiona scathingly.

'Right,' said Dietrich and rose. 'Take her away, please.'

Immediately two praetorians stepped forward, put the hood back over her head, grabbed her arms forcefully and yanked her to her feet. Then they marched her out of the office and back towards the elevator. Fiona was unable to see anything, but having obtained a sense of the layout of the facility, she realised that she was taken down to the barracks on Level 2 where she was pushed along a corridor and through several doors and rooms until her hood was removed and she was shunted violently into a small cell. Then the heavy cell door slammed shut, and the only thing she could hear inside the featureless concrete-walled cell was the sound of receding footsteps as the two praetorians left.

'Shit,' she breathed, her voice trembling as she closed her eyes, hanging her head. 'What the hell do I do now?'

★　　★　　★

Andrew had just woken up when he discovered that an email had come through from Fiona during the night. He sat up in his bed, rubbed his eyes and tapped on the email.

Hi Andy,
Just a quick note to tell you that I have arrived in Auckland and have been to Dietrich's residence. The house is still being built but work has been terminated. It is a building site and no one has lived here yet. I managed to get into a chapel in the garden and found a command centre that seems to have been used to coordinate lots of flights to a location on the South Island over many months. Lately, it seems that hundreds of people have been taken to it, and I am flying down there in about an hour to investigate. These are the exact coordinates:
43°29'04.4"S 171°16'10.2"E
I will try to stay in touch, but I don't think there will be mobile phone coverage in those mountains. So, if you don't hear from me this evening, then don't worry.
Or perhaps do...
Anyway, I don't know what I am going to find there, but I have to go and see for myself. I owe it to Aaron to do what I can to help stop this thing.
  Love, Fiona.

'Shit,' grumbled Andrew and jumped out of bed.

He quickly had a shower and some breakfast, and then he drove to Sheldrake Place where he parked the loaner car that he had received from the insurance company while the DB9 was being fixed.

Knocking on Colonel Strickland's open door, he did not wait for a reply from the colonel who was sitting at his desk reading a document.

'Sir,' said Andrew. 'I have a bit of a situation to discuss with you. And I believe you wanted to talk to me about something as well?'

'Ah! Good morning, Andrew,' said Strickland. 'Yes, there's been a development of sorts. We've had the coroner's report back on the two men you dispatched on Holland Park Avenue the other day, and he discovered something unusual about both of them. They both had a tiny capsule with a microchip inserted under the skin of their right hand, and they were identical to one that has been found on the man who fell out of the window and ended up crashing onto a car next to Central Park in New York.'

'A chip?' asked Andrew intrigued. 'What sort of chip?'

'They were both so-called RFID chips, which I understand means radio-frequency identification chips. Small radio transmitters that can broadcast a weak electromagnetic signal when prompted by a scanner.'

'You're basically describing the microchips used to keep tabs on dogs,' said Andrew, looking slightly bemused.

'Well, yes,' replied Strickland, 'except these are much smaller and more advanced, and they have much more bandwidth. They also appear to be two-way, which means that they can also receive and store information. They are like mini-computers, and our tech wizards tell me that instead of just being an ID chip they are more akin to a cross between a smartphone and a passport. We're still trying to work out precisely what they might have been designed for.'

'I think I have a pretty good idea,' muttered Andrew.

'Oh?' said Strickland surprised. 'What?'

'I will get on to that in a minute,' replied Andrew. 'First, I need to tell you that I've just received an email from Fiona.'

Andrew explained what she had discovered and that she had become convinced that she had found the location of another underground complex similar to the one Aaron Purnell had discovered in Arizona, but most likely much bigger.

'If there really is a massive underground doomsday facility under a mountain in New Zealand that only a select group of people are allowed access to, then RFID technology would be an obvious way to manage that access efficiently and also avoid ambiguity about those people's identity.'

'That's not a bad theory,' nodded Strickland. 'I think that makes a lot of sense. Only the initiated would be able to enter.'

'Could I have one of those chips?' asked Andrew.

'Of course,' replied Strickland. 'But what for?'

'Well,' said Andrew with a troubled look on his face. 'I realise that there is no hard evidence for any of this yet, which is why I am requesting permission to go there myself.'

Strickland nodded sagely.

'Look,' continued Andrew. 'I fully understand that we can't deploy military assets such as special forces to another country on what I am sure would be called hearsay, but I know Fiona, and I am sure she is right that something very sinister is going on. I simply can't just let her do this on her own.'

Strickland rubbed his chin and looked somewhat dubious.

'Well,' he said. 'From where I am sitting, I think you are right on two counts. One – whatever Fiona believes she has uncovered is unlikely to be acted upon at this stage. Not even I could convince the politicians to sign off on a covert insertion of the SAS into a foreign country based on the speculation of a single person, on the back of information from a single source working for what one might call a sensationalist New York magazine. Two – Fiona is a force to be reckoned with, and I don't doubt for a second that she is onto something here.'

'So, what's your answer?' said Andrew. 'We know what the intention of Vandenberg is, and the Americans are already attempting to hunt down the Tennessee. There is nothing further I can do to assist in that effort sitting here in London.'

'I won't give you formal permission,' said Strickland finally, 'but if you decide to take a few days off and travel to say the southern hemisphere somewhere, then I obviously won't object. You've earned your time off more than anyone else I know.'

'Thank you, sir,' said Andrew and nodded. 'I would like to use the plane as well, if possible.'

'Alright,' said Strickland hesitantly. 'I suppose I could arrange for it to be flown to New Zealand. Call it a field-test of its effective flight range with those new enlarged fuel tanks.'

'Great,' smiled Andrew knowingly. 'How soon can the paperwork for that be completed?'

'Shouldn't be more than a couple of hours,' replied Strickland. 'Get yourself to RAF Northolt for 2 pm, and it will be refuelled and ready to go.'

'And I will need to make a visit to the armoury,' said Andrew. 'I just might need a few things when I get there.'

'Fine by me,' said Strickland. 'Take what you need. I'll sign off on it.'

'Perfect. Thank you again,' said Andrew and rose.

'And try to stay in touch,' said Strickland. 'I will attempt to assist you from here as best I can, whether you end up finding anything or not.'

'Will do, sir,' said Andrew, walking swiftly towards the door. 'See you in a few days. Hopefully…'

Andrew swung by his office to grab his things and then proceeded down to the basement level where the armoury was. Here, the quartermaster allowed him access to a treasure trove of advanced weaponry, tactical equipment, clothing, flashbangs and hand grenades, as well as a few other gadgets that Andrew thought might come in handy.

He then set off for RAF Northolt where the newly modified Honda HA-420 was in the process of refuelling. It had just been fitted with higher capacity fuel tanks both in the wings and in what used to be the small cargo hold. This modification more than tripled the aircraft's effective range, which was exactly what Andrew needed right now. He had a quick word with the two pilots and showed them his intended destination and what he planned to do to get there.

The pilots gave each other a brief look, and then nodded. They then put together a flight plan including refuelling stops, and twenty minutes later the small twin-engine aircraft lifted off RAF Northolt and banked right to head east-northeast. It quickly climbed to its cruising altitude of 38,000 feet and began making its way across the North Sea, over northern Denmark, Sweden, Finland and then into Russia's Arkhangelsk Oblast about a thousand kilometres north of Moscow.

Just over seven hours later, the jet passed the Chinese coastal city of Dalian and headed out over the Yellow Sea where it performed a dog-leg to the left to avoid North-Korean airspace on its way in to land at Incheon International Airport, which is constructed partly on an artificial island around 40 kilometres due west of downtown Seoul in South-Korea. Here the aircraft was refuelled and then it took off again to head south-southeast across the Philippine Sea towards Papua New Guinea, from where it embarked on the final stretch across the Coral Sea and the Tasman Sea to New Zealand's South Island.

The entire journey had covered just over eighteen thousand kilometres and had taken more than twenty hours, so by the time Andrew woke up from his second sleep when the aircraft was over the Tasman Sea, he was beginning to suffer from cabin fever.

During the flight, he had had plenty of time to pore over the schematics of the huge facility that Fiona had sent to him and that she had set out to enter. Andrew was having trouble grasping just how enormous it was, and he kept finding himself looking at details of the underground complex and then checking the scale in the lower right-hand corner to make sure that the dimensions really were that huge.

He had briefly considered attempting to find a way to use the passcode that Fiona had sent him, but he decided against it since it would almost certainly have expired by now, and he also suspected that anywhere where such a passcode could have been used would probably be crawling with many more of the fanatics that had attacked him in New York.

Luckily, he had just discovered something that might provide him with another way into the facility. Sticking up from the main complex deep inside Mount Taylor and extending up through the mountain, there appeared to be a number of ventilation shafts reaching up to the surface several hundred metres above. These shafts were clearly marked on the schematics, but he had to try to make an educated guess as to where on the map they might be since he did not have the exact location and orientation of the interior of the enormous complex. He would simply have to try to locate them after arriving on the mountain.

At around 5 pm local time, the Honda HA-420 zoomed in over the western coastline of the South Island, having just descended to around 20,000 feet. It passed over the town of Hokitika and headed southeast towards the South Island's Southern Alps mountain range, which stretches over 500 kilometres along the spine of the island.

After a quick word with the pilots, Andrew went back to the passenger cabin and closed the door to the cockpit firmly. Then he opened his large holdall and extracted his equipment, clothes, helmet and weapons, as well as his parachute. A couple of minutes later he was suited up and ready.

Looking out of the window he could both see and feel the aircraft continue to descend until it was at around 10,000 feet above sea level, which meant that it was some 2000 feet above the peaks of the snow-covered mountain range directly below. Out of the window to the right and ahead of them in the distance he could see Aoraki or Mount Cook as it is also called, which reaches more than 3,700 metres or 12,000 feet up into the air.

When the aircraft had reached the agreed-upon coordinates above Mount Taylor, the pilots slowed the aircraft down to close to stall speed and did a so-called 'wing-wave', rocking the plane's wings up and down a couple of times to indicate that it was time.

Back in the passenger compartment, Andrew grabbed the large metal door handle and yanked it downwards, thereby unlocking the door. Then he pressed a button on a panel which prompted a hydraulics system to push the door out just enough so that it could be slid sideways along the side of the aircraft. Instantly, the previously calm passenger cabin became a loud maelstrom of icy air, and Andrew could feel the pilot having to adjust the heading of the aircraft as its aerodynamic profile was suddenly altered drastically.

Aware that time was ticking, Andrew performed one last check of his parachute, harness, helmet and other gear, and then he grabbed the sides of the doorway and placed his feet on the edge of the aircraft exit, the tips of his toes just protruding while he looked down at the snow-covered mountains below. Taking another quick moment to orientate himself and locate the valley where he was intending to land, he then took a deep breath, pulled himself hard out through the doorway and launched himself out into the torrent of crisp cold air rushing past the aircraft. He tumbled over in the air a few times before regaining control, and then he spread out his arms and legs to begin to steer himself towards his target.

Within seconds the loud whine of the small jet had receded above him, and as he began accelerating rapidly towards the ground, he could see the aircraft bank to the left and disappear towards the north. The air was now rushing past him and tearing at his clothes and equipment, but his helmet with its large full-face visor allowed him to see clearly and begin to adjust his trajectory down towards the valley where he had decided to touch down.

Waiting until he was about 300 metres above the ground, he finally pulled the cord and the parachute quickly shot out and unfolded above him. Feeling the familiar violent jolt of deceleration, he then checked his altimeter and compass. Looking out towards the horizon to the west the sun was just about to set, and below him, he could see that the sun's rays were no longer reaching down into the valley.

He performed a few S-shapes as he descended in order to bleed off speed, and pulled the parachute's control handles to further reduce speed and perform a landing flare, ending up touching down in a slow jog across the ground. He immediately disconnected the chute which billowed in the steady breeze in the valley and quickly took cover behind a large rocky outcropping where he stuffed the rolled-up chute under some rocks.

Taking a moment to catch his breath, he then pulled out his GPS navigator which showed him a detailed map of the area on a small display. Before leaving from London he had entered Fiona's coordinates into the navigator, and according to the device, he was now around three hundred metres further up the valley from those coordinates. He released the clasps on the parachute harness, switched his backpack from his chest to his back and placed the harness and the helmet under the rock along with the chute. Then he quickly checked his weapons to make sure that they were ready for use.

Making his way carefully over the rough terrain a bit further down the valley, he was constantly scanning the ridges ahead and to his sides. The risk of detection was probably small, but he did not want to find himself suddenly surprised either by a patrol or by CCTV cameras that might have been placed around the facility. The ground was uneven and there were loose rocks and pebbles everywhere which made it a treacherous slope to descend.

Recalling the positions of the air intake shafts as they had appeared on the schematics, Andrew began looking for what he assumed would be relatively large metal ducts sticking up from the ground, but he could see nothing here that looked even remotely man-made. Stopping for a moment next to a huge boulder on a flat bit of terrain to double check his position, he was suddenly aware of a low humming noise coming from somewhere nearby. To his astonishment, he realised that the 'boulder' was in fact not a large rock but was instead made of hard plastic that had been painted a mottled grey to camouflage it perfectly amongst the other rocks and boulders on this part of the mountainside.

He turned to face the 'boulder' and took a few steps back to get a better look at it. It was roughly the size of a van, and it was only when he looked closely that he discovered that a wide section near the top was not solid, but instead made of a painted fine metal netting through which air was drawn in by what he assumed was some unseen fan system located deep below him inside the mountain.

He climbed on top of it and discovered that most of the top of the structure was made from the same camouflaged netting, and as he stood there, he could now feel the air moving around him, down and into what he could now see was a roughly two-metre-wide air duct directly beneath his feet.

Kneeling down, he pulled out his hunting knife and slammed it down and through the netting which shredded easily. Soon he had made a long slit, which allowed him to grab the netting, rip it open and create a hole large enough for him to get through. Down below he could hear the sound of air rushing through the duct, and of what sounded like a large whirring fan. Stopping for a moment, he suddenly had an idea so he jumped back down and made his way up to where he had landed less than ten minutes ago, in order to retrieve the parachute.

Once back on top of the concealed air intake, he squeezed through the hole and dragged the bundled-up parachute after him. Then he attached one of his climbing ropes to a metal support strut inside the structure and clipped a mountaineering carabiner onto it. Finally, he donned a head-mounted LED torch and switched it on. The inside of the duct was dull grey metal, but it looked like it had been built recently as there was no sign of wear or weathering.

As he swung himself out into the middle of the vertical duct, swaying back and forth a few times amid the sound of the creaking rope, he looked down but was unable to see the fan that he could hear down there somewhere. Then he took a deep breath.

'Nothing ventured, nothing gained,' he said to himself, and then he gradually loosened the knot around the carabiner to allow himself to begin the descent into the darkness.

Twenty-Three

As Dwayne Jackson walked Martinez along the narrow corridor towards the toilets, his large left hand resting on Martinez's shoulder, ensign Palmer turned his head and looked at them. Palmer was a short and lightly built man in his mid-twenties with short-cropped blond hair and a permanent scowl on his face. He was known on the boat as someone who liked to suck up to the senior commissioned officers, perhaps himself hoping to one day become one, which did not endear him to the rest of the crew.

'Remember what I said,' whispered Martinez. 'I'll distract him, and you take him out.'

'Alright, alright, dude. I've got it,' said Jackson in a hushed tense tone of voice. 'I will probably end up court marshalled, but I'll do it.'

Martinez kept his head down and walked slowly ahead of Jackson.

'Dude's gotta pee again,' said Jackson, looking ahead towards Palmer who was watching them approach.

Ensign Palmer scoffed but said nothing.

'Buttshark!', coughed Martinez into his hand as he passed him, using a derogatory submariner's slang for a brownnoser.

Palmer's head whipped around to look at Martinez.

'What did you just call me?' he said in a threatening tone of voice. 'You little spic.'

Martinez stopped abruptly a couple of steps past Palmer and turned around slowly, chuckling disparagingly.

'Palmer, you've always been a fucking FLOB,' said Martinez in a mocking tone of voice, using a term to describe someone who is not carrying their share of the load. It is short for 'Freeloading Oxygen Breather'.

'Fuck you, Martinez,' said Palmer angrily and took half a step towards him. 'One more word, and I'll report...'

In a flash, Jackson had grabbed Palmer's head in one hand and smacked it into the door to Tom Payne's quarters. Palmer was knocked out instantly, and Jackson adeptly stepped forward to grab him and prevent him from falling onto the floor. Then Martinez rummaged through the unconscious ensign's pockets, quickly finding the key to the door and unlocking it.

As the door opened and Jackson and Martinez barged in, Jackson still holding up Palmer as if he had been a life-size ragdoll, Payne jumped to his feet, watching the scene in front of him with a startled look on his face. Jackson closed the door behind them and dumped Palmer on Payne's bunk.

'Damn!' said Payne. 'Good job, Martinez. The plan worked. Jackson, thank you for letting Martinez out. We have a serious problem on our hands.'

'Yeah,' sighed the big man. 'Martinez told me already. So, what do we do?'

'You head back aft to try to punch some holes in a couple of the lead-acid batteries. A screwdriver should do the job nicely. We're not trying to damage the boat. Just to cause some confusion. I will make my way to the torpedo room and start a small fire. Nothing crazy of course. Just enough to create some smoke. As you should already know, Navy regulations dictate that in the case of fire on board during peacetime, a sub has to surface as soon as the fire is detected. We might be able to force the evacuation of the boat, in which case the captain will be unable to launch the missiles. The launch mechanism relies on high air pressure to eject the missile up and out of the launch tube, and that simply won't work unless the boat is submerged. Martinez is the backup plan. If we can't force the captain to surface the boat, then Martinez will try to sneak up to the radio room and launch another buoy to give central command our position.'

'But won't they launch missiles at us?' asked Jackson. 'If they know what the captain is trying to do, they won't hesitate to stop us, whatever it takes.'

'You are probably right,' replied Payne. 'But it is a risk we have to take. There is so much more at stake here than just us.'

'Shit,' sighed Jackson, shaking his head and looking down at the floor. 'I knew I should have left you in there, Martinez.'

Martinez smiled and reached up to place a hand on Jackson's bulky shoulder.

'Buddy,' he said, giving Jackson's shoulder a quick shake. 'We know it sucks, ok? But think of it this way. If this works, you get to be a hero.'

'And if it doesn't?' asked Jackson, looking up.

'The you will probably never know,' replied Payne deadpan. 'We simply have to do this. Are you with us?'

Jackson pressed his lips together, looking weighed down by the responsibility that had suddenly been thrust upon him.

'Yeah,' he finally said quietly, nodding a couple of times. 'I'm with you.'

★ ★ ★

On board the USS Montana there was almost complete silence as the vessel pushed slowly through the dark waters near the island of Pantelleria using only its passive sonar to try to locate the audio profile of the USS Tennessee. They were still at a depth of 800 feet and about 100 feet from the seabed, making their way towards the eastern edge of the Pinne Marine Bank which is a large rocky undersea bank south-east of Sicily and due west of Pantelleria. From here the seabed begins to fall away gradually for another 30 kilometres until it meets the Malta Trough, where it drops away almost vertically to a depth of as much as 1,800 metres or 6,000 feet. Had this precipitous underwater feature been on land it would have been significantly taller than the famous Troll Wall in Norway, which is Europe's tallest vertical rock face, or the Half Dome peak in the Yosemite National Park in California.

As the submarine made its way slowly and cautiously through the deep, Captain Walker was pondering the various ways in which a possible underwater torpedo fight with the USS Tennessee might play out. Technically, the Montana ought to have the edge, but with someone like Vandenberg at the helm of the Tennessee, nothing was a given.

Walker suddenly found himself wishing that the Montana could have been fitted with one of the next generation torpedoes that he knew both the US, Russian and European navies had been developing. These were so-called supercavitating torpedoes that travel several times faster than conventional torpedoes at upwards of 370 kilometres per hour. They are fired from torpedo tubes as per normal procedure, but once launched their rocket engine propulsion systems ignite, pushing the torpedo forward through the water with immense power far beyond what a propeller can generate. A small specially designed nosecone mounted at the front of the torpedo then uses the principle of cavitation to create a sleeve of tiny air bubbles which envelop the entire torpedo, This, in turn, drastically reduces drag and allows it to accelerate through the water at previously unheard-of speeds. Since higher speed reduces the reaction time of a target, supercavitating torpedoes have the potential to catch enemies off guard and destroy them before they can take evasive action.

However, Walker did not have those torpedoes yet, since they were still in development, but then neither did Captain Vandenberg.

'Sonar. Conn,' said Walker. 'Are you picking up anything?'

'Negative Captain,' said the sonar operator. 'Just cavitation from merchant vessels and the usual background noise, plus a couple of dolphins.'

'He is still out there somewhere,' said Howard pensively.

'I know, Bill,' said Walker tensely. 'He's hiding.'

'Sonar,' said Walker. 'Give me one ping only.'

'Captain,' said Howard nervously.

Walker raised his hand to cut off his XO.

'Sonar. One ping only, please,' said Walker.

'Ay-ay, Captain. One ping only,' responded the sonar operator, and a couple of seconds later came the characteristic dull and hollow-sounding ping of the submarine's sonar.

Walker waited for the operator to report back and glanced at his XO who met his eyes with a concerned look on his face.

'Nothing,' said the sonar operator. 'No local contacts. Not even a shoal of fish.'

'Could he have pulled out of range and around to the north of Malta?' asked Howard.

'It's possible,' replied Walker evenly. 'Helmsman, make your depth 700 feet and increase speed to 18 knots, heading 095.'

The helmsman repeated back the orders, and the Montana then began to move slightly closer to the surface whilst moving through the water somewhat faster than before. With no return signal coming from the active sonar, it was now clear that the Tennessee had somehow evaded them, possibly after realising it was being tracked.

About an hour later, Walker and Howard were both hunched over the tactical table on the bridge when the helmsman called out.

'Captain, we are now directly above the western part of the Malta Trough.'

'Understood,' said Walker. 'Maintain speed and heading. XO, mark our position. Sonar, have you got anything?'

'Negative, sir. Still nothing,' replied the sonar operator.

★   ★   ★

On the USS Tennessee the entire crew had been completely stationary and silent for over an hour now. No one was allowed to move around on the ship, the engines had been shut down with the nuclear reactor dialled down to its minimum output, and the only thing that was performing a function was the passive sonar and its operator.

The atmosphere on the bridge was tense, not only because Captain Vandenberg had relayed to the crew that they were being hunted by a rogue Virginia-class submarine whose captain and first officer had turned out to be Russian agents, but because Vandenberg had then proceeded to take the Tennessee into the

Malta Trough, diving far beyond its maximum operational depth of 800 feet, causing its hull to creak and groan as it attempted to withstand the immense pressure at this depth. Every few minutes there would be a brief muffled metallic clank traveling through the vessel as the steel plates of its inner hull fought the crushing pressure.

The digital depth gauge mounted above the helmsman's station at the front of the bridge was reading 1262 feet. Now however, the submarine was completely immobile, nestled inside an underwater ravine almost at the bottom of a large rocky shelf that protruded out near the western wall of the Malta Trough. Vandenberg had used nothing but the acoustic signals from the immediate environment to determine the features and characteristics of the area, and he had successfully directed the sub to slowly settle into a stationary position there.

Almost directly above them, they had soon been able to pick up the faint but characteristic signature of a Virginia-class submarine moving through the water, and as the crew of the Tennessee held their breaths, the sonar operator had listened intently as the Montana had continued past them and proceeded further out into the Malta Trough.

Eventually, when the Montana was estimated to have moved five kilometres further out, Vandenberg had given the order to gradually ascend back up to 1000 feet and to then begin to move slowly towards the target.

★ ★ ★

Back on the USS Montana twenty minutes later, Walker and Howard were discussing the situation in hushed voices as they stood over the tactical table when suddenly the sonar operator yelled out.

'Torpedo in the water!' he shouted with a nervous edge to his voice. 'Bearing 248. Estimate distance 3,000 metres and closing.'

Instantly all of the crew on the bridge sat up rigid at their stations, and there was suddenly palpable tension in the air. Captain Walker rushed to the tactical table where a plot of the surrounding seabed as well the positions of all sonar contacts was being displayed. They were now directly above one of the deepest parts of the Malta Trough, and a few kilometres to the west of them was the almost vertical undersea mountain leading into it.

Shit, thought Walker. *He outsmarted me.*

'Torpedo type?' he then shouted.

'Sounds like Mark 48, sir' said the sonar operator, speaking rapidly and with a tense demeanour. 'Must be one of ours.'

To the crew, Walker looked focused and tense but still calm, yet inwardly he felt a chill run down his spine as the realisation of what was happening hit him. They were being fired upon by another U.S. Navy submarine. Captain Vandenberg was trying to sink them.

'Time to target?' asked Walker tensely but evenly.

'Estimate impact in 29 seconds, sir' replied the sonar operator, small beads of sweat now forming on his brow.

'Come hard left to heading 330,' ordered Walker. 'Cavitate!'

'Coming left to heading 330', repeated the helmsman as the submarine's propeller spun up to provide as much forward thrust as possible.

The huge eighteen thousand tonne steel beast began its left turn to attempt to face the Tennessee, but its turning circle is several hundred metres wide, and even with full power to the propeller it would take longer than it would take the torpedo to reach them.

'Prepare countermeasures,' ordered Walker, looking over at his XO.

'Prepare countermeasures,' Howard called out. 'Full spread. Await launch order.'

'Sonar, light him up,' ordered Walker. 'Tell me where he is!'

The sonar operator engaged the active sonar which immediately began pinging away loudly through the water. There was no point in trying to remain silent any longer. Within a couple of seconds, the USS Tennessee had been located to within a few metres.

'New contact, bearing 248,' the sonar operator called out. 'Estimate distance 2,900 metres. It's the Tennessee, sir. Looks like she's below us.'

'Keep coming around,' said Walker, and then he grabbed the microphone from its holder above his head.

'Torpedo room. Conn,' he yelled. 'Load two Mark 48 ADCAP torpedoes into tubes 1 and 4. Await firing solution.'

The loader in the torpedo room repeated the order back to Captain Walker, and instantly a well-rehearsed and coordinated flurry of activity erupted as the three loaders extracted two of the eight-metre long, three-tonne torpedoes and used a specially designed conveyor system to load them into their designated launch tubes. Then the hatches were shut and sealed, as the crew awaited a firing solution to input into the guidance system.

There followed a tense wait for about another ten seconds while Walker waited for the torpedo to close part of the distance to the Montana so that the countermeasures would be launched at exactly the optimal time for a maximum chance of working.

'Launch countermeasures!' Walker ordered, and immediately a whole series of different acoustic countermeasures were launched from a number of dispensers near the back of the vessel.

Some of them simply expelled pressurised air whilst spinning in the water to emulate cavitation noise from a propeller. Others were the more sophisticated stationary jammers that generate a high amount of energy spread over the entire reception band of the acoustic head of the torpedo. By emitting such high-intensity noise, the jammers mask the target echo as well as its noise profile thereby preventing target acquisition by the torpedo. The last type of countermeasure was the so-called Mobile Target Emulator which can produce simulated echoes for any type of vessel. It does this by using a sophisticated transponder that simulates the audio profile of an actual target, in this case the Montana, and then it generates real-time acoustic echoes to spoof the incoming torpedo and draw it away from the targeted submarine.

'Firing solutions ready,' the weapons systems operator called out.

'Load firing solutions,' ordered Walker. 'Open torpedo tube shutters.'

'Loading solutions. Opening torpedo tube shutters,' repeated Howard.

'Sonar, talk to me! Time until impact?'

'Eleven seconds, sir,' replied the sonar operator, his voice trembling.

'Steady, men!'

Then Walker grabbed the microphone to address the whole crew. 'Brace for impact! Brace for impact!'

Less than a second later the entire submarine shuddered as the torpedo reached one of the countermeasures and detonated. The MK-48 was just under a hundred metres away when its onboard guidance and target acquisition software had erroneously determined that it had reached its intended target. This was far enough for it to do no damage to the Montana, except to shake it violently as the shockwaves from the powerful explosion propagated through the water and slammed into its hull.

'Damage report,' shouted Walker as he steadied himself on his feet.

'No damage,' responded Howard after a few seconds of conferring with several junior officers in charge of different systems on the vessel.

'Weapons!' Walker called out. 'Prepare to fire.'

'Target acquired. Ready to fire, sir.'

'Sonar?' said Walker and looked directly at the sonar operator.

'Target now dead ahead, sir,' responded the operator. '1,900 metres. Depth 900 feet.'

'Fire tubes 1 and 4,' ordered Walker.
'Firing!'

★   ★   ★

On board the USS Tennessee, Dwayne Jackson had been walking along a corridor on Deck 2 towards the back of the submarine. He had to squeeze through narrow doorways a few times to get to where he needed to go, but he had got used to that by now. Some people are unable to become fighter pilots because they are too tall, and others are unable to become submariners because they are too wide. Jackson had been right on the limit when he joined the navy in both categories, but he had put on a lot more muscle since then, so navigating the corridors of the Tennessee was a tight fit from time to time.

Just as he arrived in the boat's engine battery compartment where hundreds of small power units were arranged in large banks, the captain had come on the main circuit and ordered everyone to stop what they were doing, power down non-vital systems and remain where they were. Walker had then proceeded to inform them that the officer crew on a rogue US Virginia-class submarine had gone over to the Russians, and that it was now actively hunting them. Supposedly, the Virginia-class had used its active sonar to ping for the Tennessee and so Vandenberg had decided to descend almost to crush depth to try to evade the hostile vessel.

With everything Jackson had heard from Martinez and Payne, he knew that Vandenberg was lying, and this was a very unsettling thing for him to now hear with his own ears. He had always respected and trusted the captain, so this sudden change in behaviour was immensely disturbing.

As the captain's message come on, Jackson stopped in his tracks next to one of the battery banks and then checked to see how close the nearest sailor was. With such a large crew, there were almost always other people nearby regardless of where on the boat he was or what he was doing. Pretty much the only truly private moments anyone ever had was when going to the toilet.

Spotting no one, Jackson extracted a screwdriver from his pocket. He hesitated for a moment and almost reconsidered what he was doing. Sabotaging his own vessel whilst submerged and potentially being in the middle of an engagement with a hostile submarine might be a really terrible idea, but he had given Payne and Martinez his word. And besides, if the Tennessee could be forced to surface, then this whole thing just might be over with quickly without a single shot being fired and without Vandenberg being able to launch the missiles. At least, that is what he hoped.

He punched several holes in the nearest battery bank, and acid immediately began to trickle out and onto the floor where it soon started to give off a faint wispy vapour as it began to eat away at the metal floor. Jackson took a couple of steps to the right and punched some more holes in another battery. Then he walked briskly back past the boat's crew berthing towards the front of the vessel.

'Stop fucking moving around,' someone hissed at him as he passed a row of bunks where some of the crew had been sleeping. 'Captain's orders!'

'Battery leak,' he whispered back at them. 'Gotta tell the bridge, and I can't use the intercom.'

At that moment, there was a faint shudder coming from the front of the vessel, and then the entire submarine suddenly came to life.

'What the fuck?' someone said nearby. 'Was that a torpedo launch?'

Shit, thought Jackson, as he began running forward along the corridor. *Are we too late?*

Up on the bridge, Vandenberg was out of his chair, standing over the weapons systems operator.

'Time to target?' he said calmly.

'31 seconds, sir,' said the operator with noticeable nervousness.

'Come right to heading 110,' said Vandenberg. 'Maintain speed and depth. Ready launch tubes 2, 3 and 4.'

'Readying tubes 2, 3 and 4,' repeated Chisholm and relayed the order to the torpedo room.

'Any second now,' said Vandenberg quietly, almost as if he was speaking to himself.

'She's launched countermeasures, sir,' said the sonar operator.

A couple of seconds later the sound of a distant explosion enveloped the submarine's hull, penetrating inside so that everyone on the boat could hear it.

'Torpedo impact!' the sonar operator called out. 'It went for the countermeasures.'

Vandenberg nodded as if he had been expecting this, and then, in anticipation of the other submarine's actions, he ordered the boat to veer off at an angle.

'Come hard right to heading 190,' he ordered. 'Evasive manoeuvres. All ahead full.'

'Torpedo in the water!' the sonar operator suddenly called out. 'Estimate range 1,900 metres.'

'Prepare countermeasures,' ordered Vandenberg. 'Load torpedo firing solutions.'

After another ten seconds, he looked over at Chisholm and issued another order.

'Launch countermeasures! Two full spreads.'

From the sound of his voice, even he was now beginning to feel the pressure of the situation. Then he turned to the helmsman and barked his next order in his direction.

'Come hard left to bearing 045,' he yelled.

'Torpedo impact in ten seconds!' the sonar operator called out.

The entire bridge was as frozen, with no one moving as the seconds ticked away. Then suddenly the entire vessel shook violently, and both Vandenberg and Chisholm had to steady themselves against the walls and chairs on the bridge. The rest of the crew grabbed onto their desks to stop themselves from being flung out of their chairs. Immediately, several sirens and alarms began blaring, and there was a distant sound of loud hissing coming from somewhere further towards the back of the boat.

'Give me a damage report!' yelled Vandenberg.

'Small leak amidships,' replied Chisholm. 'Looks like a pressure valve. Hull appears intact.'

'Weapons?' called Vandenberg.

'Firing solutions locked, sir.' replied the weapons operator. 'Target acquired and torpedoes ready.'

'Come left to heading 020,' shouted Vandenberg. 'On my mark, launch torpedoes from tubes 2, 3 and 4.'

'Coming left to heading 020, sir' said the helmsman through gritted teeth. 'Just a little further. Ok, we're there.'

'Launch!' yelled Vandenberg.

'All three torpedoes away!' the weapons systems operator called out. 'Time to target, 22 seconds.'

'This had better work,' said Chisholm tensely.

'It will,' said Vandenberg. 'Their autoloaders won't have had time to prep another full spread of countermeasures. They will only have partial cover.'

'Target has launched countermeasures,' said the sonar operator. 'Sounds like a small volley.'

Vandenberg glanced over at Chisholm with a sly knowing smile.

The sound of a distant explosion moved through the vessel.

'Torpedo One. Impact on countermeasure,' said the sonar operator.

Then a few seconds later there were another two explosions in quick succession.

'Good hits!' the sonar operator called out. 'Two good hits. Propeller noise has stopped. Venting noises.'

Vandenberg nodded and then drew himself up slowly to his full height. He knew what was coming next, and as the seconds ticked by, everyone on the bridge turned their heads to look in his direction.

A dull but forceful-sounding crump could then be heard, and then there was silence.

'She imploded, sir' said the sonar operator, suddenly sounding slightly disturbed, as if the full implication of what was happening had just now hit him. 'Hull is breaking up, sir. She's sinking.'

The USS Montana was now a twisted wreck, mangled by the violent implosion that had squashed her like a can of sardines once her pressure hull had failed. With air continuing to billow out and upwards from her interior, and the sound of tearing and bending steel emanating from her gutted form, she was now sinking inexorably deeper and deeper through the dark water, slowly beginning her final journey almost two kilometres straight down to the bottom of the Malta Trough. This would become the final resting place for the vessel, as well as a graveyard for her 135 souls.

Twenty-Four

Jack Lynch was standing in the corridor on the fourth floor of the Office of Naval Intelligence in Suitland, Maryland. He was checking his wristwatch absentmindedly as he waited for the elevator to arrive and take him down to the underground car park. The elevator dinged and the doors opened. There was only one person inside. It was a large man in a tweed suit and an off-white shirt, and he was leaning against the back wall in the lefthand corner of the elevator.

'Hey there Bill,' said Lynch.

'Afternoon, Jack,' replied the man and nodded.

Bill Hurley worked in the SigInt section of the 6th floor, and he was known as a highly intelligent but somewhat awkward character. He had been involved in several significant operational successes where the ONI had provided highly valuable and actionable intel to the special forces community, particularly in conjunction with anti-piracy operations in the Gulf of Aden off the Horn of Africa. Lynch did not know him well, but he had spoken to him briefly a few times over the years.

'Going home to the wife and kids for the weekend?' asked Lynch casually as he stepped inside and pressed the button to close the doors.

Hurley had already pressed the button to go down to the car park. The doors closed and the elevator began to descend as Lynch placed himself in the middle of the floor facing the doors.

'Yup,' replied Hurley in a resigned tone of voice. 'Can't wait to listen to them screaming at each other.'

'I am sure it ain't that bad,' said Lynch and smiled, briefly glancing over his shoulder and secretly thinking to himself that he probably under-appreciated his own freedom as a bachelor.

Suddenly the big man stepped up behind Lynch and wrapped a strong arm around his neck and began to squeeze hard.

Unable to breathe, Lynch grabbed Hurley's arm and tried to pull it away from his throat, but he was incapable of moving it. Hurley had him in a vice and he could hear the sound of him grunting from the exertion as he kept squeezing ever more tightly. Lynch grabbed onto Hurley's shirt and jacket sleeve and pulled as hard as he could, but the fabric merely tore, exposing Hurley's forearm which was still locked around Lynch's neck. It was at that moment Lynch spotted the scorpion tattoo.

As the realisation hit him that the seemingly affable Hurley was trying to kill him right here inside the ONI building, Lynch's training finally kicked into gear. He slammed the heel of his right boot down onto Hurley's toes which produced a crunch and elicited a cross between a grunt and a shriek, but the big man did not yield. Lynch then used his right elbow to repeatedly punch Hurley in the side of his rib cage, but to no avail. Hurley was like a man possessed and somehow capable of feats of strength that Lynch would never have expected of him. He simply squeezed tighter and tighter.

Finally, Lynch grabbed onto Hurley's arm with both of his hands and strained to pull his head as far forward as he could. It compressed his larynx to the point where the pain was almost unbearable, and he could have sworn that parts of it were deforming unnaturally, but it allowed him to then ram the back of his head into Hurley's face where it connected with the bridge of the big man's nose. There was a muffled crunch as Hurley's nose broke, and he immediately and involuntarily let go of Lynch who instantly took a step forward, spun around and reached under his left arm to pull out his pistol from its holster. As the moaning Hurley staggered backwards and slumped down onto the floor with blood gushing out of his broken nose, Lynch disengaged the safety and brought up the pistol to point it at Hurley's forehead.

'You crazy mother*fucker*,' panted Lynch in a croaky voice. 'You're going away for life for this.'

Even behind Hurley's big bloody hands, Lynch could see a defeated yet hateful grin spreading across the big man's face.

★   ★   ★

Andrew continued to lower himself slowly down into the air shaft using his head-mounted torch to light the way. There was a steady flow of air coming down through the shaft, and down below him the fan noise was becoming ever louder as he descended. After a couple of minutes he began to worry that the climbing rope would not be long enough, but then he spotted a ninety-degree turn roughly ten metres below him which appeared to lead horizontally away from the vertical shaft.

A couple of metres above the end of the vertical shaft he ran out of rope, so he had to undo the slip knot and drop the final distance down to a dusty concrete floor. As his boots landed, a small cloud of grey dust rose around him, and the noise from the impact reverberated up through the air shaft above him. Next to him was an opening a little less than two metres wide leading to a horizontal tunnel. It was blocked off by very sturdy-looking metal netting similar to chicken wire but made from metal wires that were around half a centimetre thick, and behind it about five metres further along was a large spinning metal fan. The air flowed freely through the netting but he would have to cut his way through, so he opened his backpack and pulled out a pair of heavy-duty wire-cutters.

He snipped the metal wires in a long circular cut, and then pulled the detached section away and slipped through to the other side. Turning to face the fan which was almost two metres in diameter, he then walked slowly towards it, wary of slipping and being sucked into the spinning blades. The air was rushing past him quickly now that the tunnel had narrowed somewhat, so he crouched down to reduce the drag on his body. He stopped about two metres from the fan and pulled his rolled-up parachute from his backpack, making sure it did not suddenly billow out and drag him into the fan.

Taking care not to be attached to it, he held it out in his outstretched arms and began to unfurl it. Quickly the rushing air began to pull at the large nylon chute. Gradually letting go of it he allowed it to begin to billow out as the air began to fill it. Soon it was pulling away from him with so much force that he had to let go.

As the chute covered the final distance to the fan, it billowed out and filled almost the entire width of the tunnel and then it smacked into the fan and got caught. Parts of it immediately began wrapping itself around the central axis of the fan where the electric motor was sitting. Soon the whole chute had wound itself tightly around the motor and been pulled through small gaps into the motor itself as it wound the chute tighter and tighter around and into the metal sleeve containing the ball bearings of the motor housing.

Within a few seconds, the motor groaned and began to spin down as the chute prevented the fan from rotating, and then there was a loud snap and a burst of blue sparks as the electric motor stalled, locked up and burned out. The parachute caught fire and quickly began to burn with a deep orange flame, producing a small cloud of black smoke. It mainly drifted away from Andrew and deeper into the horizontal shaft, but now that the fan had stopped spinning, some of it was also trying to make its way out of the tunnel and up through the vertical air shaft.

Andrew slipped through a gap between two of the now stationary metal blades and continued swiftly along a tunnel on the other side of the fan. Now that the fan's motor had ground to a halt, he could hear the faint hum of more machinery in the distance coming from further along the tunnel.

As he walked along, the humming grew louder and eventually, he found himself in a square metal chamber roughly four by four metres in size with a series of smaller vents along the sides. Each vent was around half a metre wide and they all drew in air from the chamber, apparently funnelling it further into the facility. The vents were too small for him to fit through, and for a moment he thought he would be stuck in a dead-end, but then he spotted a square hatch in the floor the size of a manhole cover with black and yellow checkered markings painted along the edges.

Kneeling down next to it he could see the words 'Maintenance. Keep shut.' written on it. It was hinged on one side and clearly designed to be opened outward, which meant there had to be some sort of room underneath it. There was no handle, but the locking mechanism was clearly visible near its edge. Grabbing it with both hands he was able to twist the latch to one side so that it came free of the frame, and immediately the hatch dropped down and swung open into a poorly lit space below. Up through the opening came the loud humming of what sounded like a number of different machines.

Lying down and quickly poking his head through, Andrew realised that he was near one corner of a massive high-ceilinged space at least as large as half a football field. At first glance, it looked like an enormous factory floor, and it was crammed with row upon row of different machinery, most of them the size of cars or bigger. There was a cacophony of different humming, whirring and grinding noises, and pulling his head back up into the chamber he realised that he was in the beating metal heart of the facility from where all water, air, power and other services were processed and distributed.

He sat on the edge of the opening, sticking his legs down through it, and then he dropped down onto the floor below where he immediately crouched down and snuck over to the side of what looked like a huge water pump. Looking around, he saw no one else, but there were bound to be teams of workers constantly monitoring and servicing the machinery here. This looked and felt more than anything like a factory floor, and it had to require a lot of manpower to operate continuously.

As he began to move along the back wall of the grimy and noisy space, it became clear that each of the long rows of machinery were dedicated to different services. Some were for water, some were for air, others were for sewage processing. At the end of each row was a high-tech monitoring station, and Andrew snuck over to one of them and had a quick look. It had a large touch-screen display showing telemetry on a whole range of air pumps, filtration systems, charts with duct pressures along various parts of the facility and so on. There was also a separate section that showed a group of machines which appeared to be inactive. Looking closely, it became apparent that they were scrubbers that were responsible for extracting harmful materials such as nuclear, chemical or biological agents from the air intakes, and they could clearly be enabled quickly from this terminal.

Dietrich has clearly planned ahead, thought Andrew.

Briefly tempted to try to mess with the controls, Andrew instead decided to move along one of the aisles towards the far end of the complex where he could see what looked like stairs and a door to an elevator. Perhaps he would be able to use the machinery control panels to create a distraction later. What he needed to do first was try to find Fiona, although that might be a tall order given the sheer size of this place.

As he snuck along, a man in orange coveralls suddenly walked out from between two machines a few metres away whilst holding a tablet in front of himself. He was walking along slowly and looking at the tablet when he suddenly lifted his head and saw Andrew crouched less than two metres away. A look of confusion and then fear flashed across his face, and just as he began to turn around to flee, Andrew shot forward punching him hard in the solar plexus and then pouncing on him and dragging him to the ground in a chokehold. Andrew squeezed tight as the man tried to wriggle free, clawing at the attacker who was now choking him and preventing him from breathing. Andrew pinned him to the floor, and after less than a minute the man's limbs suddenly relaxed and flopped to the floor as he lost consciousness.

Andrew dragged his limp body in between two of the large noisy machines and left him there partially hidden under one of them. He then slipped back out into the aisle and proceeded towards the staircase at the far end, when two black-clad and armed soldiers appeared. They were coming through a small door up high on the wall and out onto a raised walkway that was several metres above the floor. They began walking clockwise around the enormous air and water services complex. This was clearly some sort of patrol, but they seemed to be walking along the walkway calmly, seemingly having done this countless times before. They had not been talking to each other but they seemed relaxed as they strolled along.

Andrew decided to get out of there, and so he quickly made his way back a few metres along the aisle towards where he had entered, and then he cut across to an adjacent room about five metres away. Just as he hurried through the doorway, there was a shout behind him.

Shit, he thought.

Either someone had seen him running, or one of the guards had spotted the unconscious worker on the floor.

The room he had run into looked like some sort of waste disposal room. It was roughly two storeys high and it had a number of square support pillars and a gangway running the length of the room just below the ceiling. Andrew hurried to the back of the room and slipped behind one of the pillars just as the first soldier entered.

'Halt!' shouted the soldier, at the same time as Andrew heard him pull the slide on his submachine gun. 'You are not authorised to be in here. Come out with your hands up.'

Realising that he was now cornered and deciding that he could not afford to give the guard time to call in reinforcement over the radio, Andrew quickly pulled out his silenced pistol and flicked the safety to OFF. He knelt down next to the pillar, took a quick breath and held it, and then he swiftly leaned out raising his pistol and firing two quick shots at the soldier. The bullets smacked into the soldier's chest and he immediately collapsed on the floor, falling onto his submachine gun which was in a strap around his shoulder.

Andrew pulled back into cover and then saw that the pillar he was hiding behind had metal bars set into it at regular intervals all the way up to the gangway above. Still in cover, he immediately began to climb up and quickly made it to the gangway where he then began sneaking quietly back towards the door where the other soldier was now appearing. The soldier took a couple of steps inside the room and then he spotted his colleague lying face down on the floor with a small pool of blood spreading from his torso.

The second guard brought up his submachine gun and entered a combat stance as he slowly and nervously proceeded past his dead colleague into the room. Andrew stopped dead in his tracks and waited for the soldier below to walk past him. Then he moved out to the edge of the gangway to get a clear shot, but as he did so a metal buckle on his backpack scraped ever so slightly against the railing. It was not much of a noise, but it was enough for the soldier to sense movement above him. He instantly threw himself to one side and onto the floor and brought up his submachine gun. He managed to fire a volley of three rapid shots but was unable to aim them properly as he fell, so all three bullets whizzed past Andrew and smacked into the ceiling just above his head, creating a small scattering of dust and bits of concrete that fell towards the concrete floor below.

Andrew held his nerve and aimed carefully even as the bullets tore past him and fired a single shot into the forehead of the soldier. The soldier's head whipped backwards and he instantly went completely limb like a rag doll, his body flopping onto the floor as if he had been a life-sized robot that had suddenly had its power supply cut.

Andrew knelt down and sat completely still for a few moments listening out for approaching footsteps, but none materialised. The three shots from the submachine gun had seemed loud inside the small room, but the ambient noise out on the machinery floor had ensured that no one else out there had heard the shots.

Andrew swung himself over the edge of the gangway and dropped down onto the floor next to the second soldier. He then dragged both of them along to a waste compactor unit, where he stood over them for a few seconds deciding which uniform would fit him the best. Then he quickly undressed one of the soldiers and put on his uniform on top of his own clothes. He then unsheathed his knife and cut out the RFID chip from the soldier's skin on his right hand, and put it inside a pocket. It all felt quite morbid, but as far as Andrew was concerned everyone in this facility had elected to put themselves above all other human beings in the world and had effectively signed up for being part of a deranged genocidal plan, and so they were not deserving of the respect that one might normally afford someone who had just been killed.

Putting the soldier's cap on his head and pulling it down in front of his face, he then lifted the dead bodies up and dumped them unceremoniously inside the waste compactor, closed the door to the unit and hit a large green button to start the machine. He then exited the room and made his way calmly along the wall towards the far end of the noisy space where he had spotted the stairs and the elevator. As he walked along, he could see several workers going about their business seemingly oblivious to what had happened in the waste disposal room.

When he reached the stairs, he saw a sign that said 'Level -2. Power Systems & Engineering', which seemed to be the lowest level in the sprawling underground facility. He walked up one flight of stairs to Level -1 which had a sign that read 'Agriculture'. He stopped for a couple of seconds marvelling at the huge multi-level expanse of growing beds with many different crops all lit up by artificial overhead lights that were no doubt set to generate the maximum amount of photosynthesis in the plants.

Another flight of stairs later and he was on Level 0, and here he was left completely stunned by the enormity of the facility's main dome. The size of its floor area was breathtaking, possibly as much as ten football fields, and the dome itself was studded with small lights all over its inside. However, they had now all been dialled down to a very low level and had a slightly blueish tint, clearly in an attempt to simulate moonlight. He looked at his wristwatch to see that it was now 8:20 pm. The facility was mimicking the lighting cycle outside of the mountain, and there were only a few small groups of people visible under the giant dome. They were all walking along briskly looking as if they were still on duty and on their way to somewhere. As a couple of workers in green uniforms emerged on the stairs from the level above, Andrew casually turned his back on them and let them pass. None of them paid him any attention.

On a schematic attached to the wall, he could see that the next level up was called 'Level 1. Leisure', followed by 'Barracks', 'Administration and finally 'Executive' at Level 4.

He passed Level 1 without paying it any attention, except to note that it looked more like a huge shopping mall than anything else, and then he headed further up towards 'Barracks'. He felt sure that somehow Fiona had got caught after entering the facility, and that this would be where she was being kept. Sure enough, adjacent to the entrance to the barracks where small groups of soldiers in different uniforms were coming and going on a regular basis, was a set of double doors with a sign above them saying 'Holding Cells.' Clearly, the facility was prepared for at least some level of dissent during the expected multi-month self-confinement of the people now inside the ARK.

Andrew walked over to the double doors and pressed against them. They were locked. Glancing to his right, he realised that there was a small panel with an electronic reader mounted on the wall next to the door, so he walked over to it, extracted the RFID chip he had taken from the dead soldier and held it next to the reader. The door lock snapped open audibly, and a small green light began flashing rapidly next to the handles indicating that he had only a few seconds to pass through.

He quickly pushed the doors open, and to his relief, he found that there was no one else immediately on the other side. Straight ahead was a set of stairs which he descended to arrive in a narrow corridor lined with metal doors to a number of holding cells. Next to him on the left was what appeared to be a small office with a single window out to the corridor, and inside it sat two guards in dark uniforms facing away from him. Andrew snuck over to peek in through the window.

In front of the guards was a large bank of displays which showed live footage from inside all of the holding cells. There were twelve displays each with four live feeds for a total of 48 holding cells, but only one of them was occupied. On the bed in what seemed to be Cell 22 was a slightly built female form curled up on the bed.

Fiona, thought Andrew, feeling himself suddenly flush with anger at seeing her locked up like this.

The guards did not appear to be paying any attention to the displays, but were instead busy watching a TV show on a laptop sitting on their desk. Next to them was a packet of potato chips and a couple of soft drinks.

Andrew pulled his gun out and silently pulled the slide back to chamber a round, and then he grabbed the door handle and opened the door. As soon as he did so, both guards turned their heads towards him, and seeing him wearing a black uniform they did not immediately register a threat. However, as soon as they spotted the silenced pistol in his hand, they both jumped up reaching for their own weapons.

Andrew fired once, instantly dropping one of the guards.

'Don't,' said Andrew icily and aimed at the head of the other guard whose hand was hovering over the gun still in its holster on his belt. 'You'll be dead before you know what happened. Do as I say, and you might live.'

'Alright,' said the guard sounding jumpy as he slowly raised his hands. 'Who are you? What do you want?'

'Never mind who I am,' replied Andrew stonily. 'Open the cell door.'

'Which door?' said the guard, clearly trying to play dumb.

'The door to the only fucking cell that is occupied, you little shit,' sneered Andrew, his eyes flashing anger as he took half a step towards the guard. 'Now!'

'Ok!' said the guard nervously, turning slowly towards a control panel next to the bank of displays. 'I'll do it now. Opening Cell 22.'

He quickly entered a passcode and hit a button on the control panel's touch-screen display showing all the cells in the holding cell complex, and immediately the colour of Cell 22 on the display went from red to green.

'It's open,' said the guard, looking over his shoulder. 'Now what?'

'Hands on your head,' ordered Andrew. 'Kneel.'

The guard did as he was asked, and Andrew walked over to him whilst pulling a zip-tie from a pocket in his trousers.

'Lower your hands slowly behind your back,' said Andrew.

Once again, the guard did as he had been told, but as soon as Andrew reached down with one hand to begin to put the zip-tie around his wrists, the guard suddenly grabbed Andrew's wrist and spun around whilst reaching for his gun. Andrew reacted instantly, kicking the guard in the torso to make him slam back into the edge of the desk, and then he brought up his pistol and shot him twice in the left side of the chest.

Wide-eyed and with a look of surprise at Andrew's lightning reaction, the guard slumped down sideways onto the floor and let out a dry wheeze as the air left his lungs for the last time.

'You had to try it, didn't you?' said Andrew bitterly, shaking his head. 'Stupid bastard.'

Then he exited the small office and hurried down the corridor towards Cell 22 whose door had now swung open. He was holstering his pistol as he entered the cell, wondering what he would find. Had Fiona been hurt? Interrogated? Was she drugged? Would she even be conscious?

Andrew only had time to take a couple of steps inside the cell and see that the bed was empty before something rammed into him from the right making him smack into the doorframe and stumble backwards. Immediately, hands grabbed onto the front of his uniform and attempted to drag him into the cell towards the wall.

'Come here, you arsehole!' shrieked Fiona, using all her strength to try to force him to trip and fall onto the floor.

'Fiona!' yelled Andrew. 'It's me, damn it!'

Immediately she let go and staggered backwards a few steps.

'Andrew?' she said incredulously, tears suddenly welling up in her eyes. 'You're here?'

'Well, I couldn't just sit there in London while you ran off and got yourself caught,' said Andrew guardedly, seemingly not quite convinced that Fiona was done trying to manhandle him to the floor.

Fiona flung herself forward, thudding into him and wrapping her arms around him.

'I am so happy to see you,' she whispered and squeezed him tight. 'I thought I was going to be stuck in here for months while the whole world burned.'

Then she pulled away and looked down at his uniform.

'How did you get your hands on that outfit?' she asked.

'I found a willing donor down in engineering,' Andrew shrugged. 'He won't be needing it anymore.'

'Right,' said Fiona, holding up both hands in front of herself. 'I don't need all the details.'

Andrew reached out, grabbed both of her shoulders and took a good look at her

'Are you alright?' he asked. 'Did they hurt you?'

'No,' said Fiona, shaking her head. 'I guess in hindsight, coming here was a mistake. I achieved nothing except for getting thrown in a jail cell.'

'You found out where the ARK is, and you got me in here,' said Andrew with a half-smile.

'Let's just get out of this place,' said Fiona. 'What's your plan?'

'I don't have one yet,' replied Andrew.

'What?' said Fiona. 'What do you mean?'

'Well, I didn't know exactly what I was going to find here,' he said. 'Having the schematics for a facility like this is all well and good, but if you don't know how many men are stationed there, then you can't really plan ahead. We will have to improvise. But I think we should try to make it wherever Dietrich is holed up.'

'Oh, I already know where that is,' said Fiona. 'That's how I ended up in here. Why do you want to go there?'

'Because something occurred to me on the way here from London,' said Andrew. 'I think that somewhere in this facility is a way of contacting the USS Tennessee. Some means of communication that could function as a sort of circuit breaker, should that ever become necessary.'

'Why do you think that?' asked Fiona.

'Because Dietrich is no fool,' said Andrew, 'and when planning this whole operation, he would have understood just how fundamentally fluid and unpredictable a situation he was creating, and so I think he has a contingency plan for a scenario where the launch of the missiles would need to be either scrapped or at least postponed. If some component of the master plan failed to slot into place at the right time, either because of an accident or perhaps even sabotage, then it is conceivable that the entire scheme might not work. So, in that scenario, he would need a way to contact the Tennessee and provide new instructions.'

'And how exactly would he do that?' asked Fiona.

'I believe there is a communications device here in this facility that is connected to a VLF transmitter, which is the only way to communicate with a submerged submarine. Or if the VLF transmitter is located somewhere else, then there would have to be a way for this facility to communicate directly with it, after which it could then relay a message to the Tennessee. If we can get a message to whoever launched that buoy, we might be able to help them scupper Dietrich's plans.'

'How?' asked Fiona.

'I spoke to Strickland on the way here about eight hours ago,' replied Andrew, 'and we may have a solution for how to deal with the Tennessee. We've got the Americans on board with it and we already have a team ready at RAF Akrotiri in Cyprus, but we will need help from someone inside the submarine.'

Andrew then went on to explain the details of the contingency plan that he and Strickland had been putting together over the past 24 hours.

'That sounds extremely difficult to pull off,' said Fiona, 'but it is obviously worth a shot. As for your idea that Dietrich has a VLF system installed here, I think you might be right about that. It is exactly the sort of thing he would do. He never leaves anything to chance.'

'Precisely,' said Andrew. 'And the only place such a system would be accessible is in Dietrich's office or private quarters. So that is where we have to go.'

'It is heavily guarded,' said Fiona. 'We can't just walk in there even if we have the right uniforms. Everyone here had some sort of chip implanted that allows them access to certain areas but bars them from entering others.'

Andrew reached into his pocket and extracted a tiny black plastic capsule. It still had a smudge of dark red blood on it.

'You mean like this?' he asked.

'How did you...?' began Fiona, but then she stopped herself. 'Actually, don't tell me. I don't want to know.'

'Ok, fine,' said Andrew. 'Anyway, here is what I propose we do.'

Twenty-Five

'Helmsman, bring her up to 200 feet,' ordered Vandenberg as he took his seat in the captain's chair. 'Heading 090, speed 25 knots.'

There was palpable relief on the bridge, but also a subdued atmosphere at the realisation that they had just sunk a United States Navy submarine. The crew were manning their various stations and working their terminals and equipment as normal, but once in a while, they would glance sideways at each other, grim looks on their faces. This was what they had trained for, yet confusingly at the same time, this was nothing like what they had trained for.

Chisholm came over and stood next to Vandenberg who looked calmly down at his wristwatch and then leaned towards his XO.

'Good work, John. Expect contact in four minutes,' he whispered, making sure none of the rest of the crew could hear him.

'Yes, sir,' replied Chisholm quietly. 'Just in time.'

Vandenberg reached up to grab the microphone above him.

'1 MC,' he ordered. 'Crew of the USS Tennessee. This is the captain. We have successfully defeated the rogue vessel USS Montana. However, we may have sustained damage so my intention is to sail for the Salamis Naval Base in the Saronic Gulf. It is the home of the Greek submarine fleet and we will be able to perform an inspection of the Tennessee there. It is some five hundred miles due east of our current position so we should be arriving in roughly twelve hours. I understand how this situation might make you feel, but I expect you to continue carrying out your duties as normal. This is the captain.'

Vandenberg put the microphone back in its holder and glanced at Chisholm who gave a small nod.

A couple of minutes later, the EAM light suddenly flashed red and the three-pulsed alert noise sounded.

'Conn. Radio,' said the junior radio operator who had taken over from Martinez. 'Receiving an emergency action message.'

Chisholm walked briskly to the operator and waited a couple of seconds for the EAM to be printed out. He grabbed the printout and quickly read through it.

* EMERGENCY ACTION MESSAGE *

NATIONAL MILITARY COMMAND CENTER
USS TENNESSEE (SSBN-734)
AUTHORIZATION FOR NUCLEAR MISSILE LAUNCH

1. SET DEFCON 1
2. LAUNCH TWENTY-FOUR (24) MISSILES
3. TARGET PACKAGE: SLBM 2791/4
4. AUTHENTOCATION: TTABTDA

Then he held the print-out up for the crew to see and walked it to the captain.

'Captain,' he said. 'We have a properly formatted emergency action message from the National Military Command Center.'

'Very well,' said Vandenberg. 'Retrieve the authenticator.'

'Ay-ay Captain,' said the XO and grabbed the microphone above him. 'All hands. Secure for battle stations.'

Then he hurried to the locker behind the captain's chair, opened it, and extracted the 'biscuit' from the red *Launch Authentications* compartment as well as the small metal launch key. Then he hurried back to Vandenberg.

'Request permission to authenticate,' he said.

'Permission granted,' responded Vandenberg. 'Authenticate.'

Chisholm read out the sequence of letters, checking against the EAM as he went.

'Tango. Tango. Alpha. Bravo. Tango. Delta. Alpha.'

He then gave Vandenberg the message. 'Message is authentic, sir.'

Vandenberg examined the printout himself for a few seconds and nodded.

'I concur,' he said. 'Message is authentic. 1 MC.'

Once again, he reached for the microphone to address the crew.

'This is the captain,' he said, with a taut tone to his voice. 'Set condition 1 SQ for strategic missile launch. Initiate spin-up sequence for missiles 1 through 24. This is not a drill. I repeat. This is NOT a drill. This is the captain.'

Vandenberg replaced the microphone and looked at Chisholm.

'Status,' he ordered.

'Target package loaded and confirmed,' said Chisholm. 'All launch systems spinning up and looking nominal. Ready to launch within ten minutes.'

'Helmsman,' ordered Vandenberg. 'Maintain present course and make your depth 30 feet.'

At the current depth of 200 feet, the USS Tennessee would be unable to launch its intercontinental ballistic missiles since the initial expulsion of the missiles from their vertical launch tubes is done by pressurised air, which catapults the missiles out of the tubes and up above the surface of the water, after which their rocket engines ignite and begin to propel them towards space and their intended targets. If this is attempted at below 50 feet, the missile will not have enough momentum to break the surface, which will in turn result in rocket engine failure. Vandenberg, therefore, wanted the boat at 30 feet which would be sufficient to ensure a successful launch of all of the submarine's twenty-four missiles.

'Conn. Sonar,' the sonar operator suddenly called out. 'I've got multiple active sonar contacts in the water, bearing 235. Estimate range 12 miles. Detecting no surface contacts in that area.'

'Sonar buoys,' said Chisholm and turned to Vandenberg with a concerned look on his face.

The captain nodded and rose from his chair.

'Clearly,' he said calmly. 'Dropped from Russian planes.'

'Sir,' said the sonar operator dubiously. 'They sound more like SSQ-47s. I think they are ours.'

The operator was referring to the AN/SSQ-47 Sonobuoy, manufactured by the Florida-based company Sparton which produces anti-submarine warfare equipment such as sonar buoys used by NATO countries.

Vandenberg ignored the sonar operator and turned instead to the helmsman.

'Helmsman, delay that order,' he said. 'Make your depth 900 feet.'

'Making depth 900 feet,' repeated the helmsman and began pushing the controls forward, which in turn rotated the dive planes on the sail, pushing the submarine deeper as is moved through the water.

'What the fuck's going on?' whispered the sonar operator to the radio operator who was manning the console next to him.

The radio operator shrugged with a confused and worried look on his face whilst silently mouthing, *'I don't know.'*

'XO, initiate silent running,' said Vandenberg. 'We will go deep, evade detection and then proceed east towards a new launch location.'

'Ay-ay, captain,' replied the XO and was about to get on the intercom to relay the order, when at that moment there was a sudden commotion by the door to the stairs leading down to Deck 2.

A large muscular man barged through the doorway, looking agitated. Vandenberg and Chisholm, who knew everyone on board by sight, immediately recognised him at Dwayne Jackson. There was simply no one else on board the vessel who was anywhere near his size.

'Captain,' shouted Jackson. 'Battery leak in the aft power banks. Acid is leaking out and it is eating through the floor. Fumes everywhere.'

'Seaman Jackson,' said Chisholm in a stern voice. 'What the hell are you doing up here. Why aren't you in engineering taking care of the problem? And why didn't you use the intercom?'

'Intercom is down, sir,' replied Jackson, appearing out of breath and seeming panicked. 'The fumes are too much to deal with without protective gear. We need to surface the boat.'

'Seaman Jackson,' interjected Vandenberg angrily. 'I am the captain on this boat. Who the hell do you think you are giving orders around here?'

'Captain,' shouted Jackson agitatedly, taking a couple of steps towards Vandenberg. 'Those are toxic fumes. If we don't surface and vent immediately, people could die down there.'

'Seaman Jackson, you are hereby relieved of duty,' ordered Vandenberg with an irate expression on his face. 'XO, restrain Seaman Jackson. What in the hell is wrong with you, son?'

Immediately, Chisholm and two other sailors leapt to their feet, converged on Jackson and placed their hands on him to restrain him and lead him off the bridge. However, the giant man resisted, and soon a virtual wrestling match was underway to the consternation of the entire crew on the bridge. It looked almost as if the battery fumes had caused the normally affable and even-tempered Dwayne Jackson to suddenly lose his mind.

★ ★ ★

Before leaving the holding cell complex, Andrew and Fiona dragged the two dead guards into Cell 22, disabled its security camera, closed the door and then reset the security code for the cell door's lock from the office. Fiona had almost retched as Andrew pulled the uniform off one of the soldiers to give to her and had needed to wipe a small spatter of blood off his jacket.

'You can't walk around out there in those,' said Andrew, pointing at her clothes. 'Put these on instead and grab a cap from over on that hook on the wall.'

Fiona donned the uniform and cap, and then the two of them left the small office and headed back up the stairs and out of the barracks complex. They passed several soldiers that appeared to be on nightly patrol duty, and they even passed a senior officer wearing a distinctive white uniform who gave them a surly glance before heading into the barracks.

Then they headed back down to Level -2, descending to the huge noisy floor with the many whirring air and water processing machines. They were walking briskly down the central aisle towards the far end when Andrew spotted another officer in a white uniform coming towards them. Andrew immediately grabbed Fiona's sleeve and tugged at it as he made a right turn in between two machines and into the next aisle.

'Follow me,' he whispered.

They had continued down the aisle for another ten metres or so when the officer suddenly appeared again. He had also swapped aisles and was now only about five metres away and coming straight towards them.

'Stop,' he ordered, whilst continuing to walk towards them. 'What's your patrol number?'

Andrew and Fiona both stopped and quickly glanced at each other.

'Your patrol number,' repeated the officer, now sounding and looking suspicious.

'Uh,' said Andrew. 'We are not on patrol. We were sent down here to check on the waste disposal unit. Apparently, it has clogged up.'

The officer looked at him with a dubious expression on his face.

'Alright,' he said. 'I will come with you. Lead the way.'

'Yes, sir,' said Andrew and began walking with Fiona hurrying along beside him as he headed towards the doorway to the waste disposal room off to their right.

As they walked, Andrew could feel the officer's eyes boring into the back of them, and he was convinced that any second now he would spot the bullet holes. The three of them entered through the doorway and Andrew was leading them towards the back where the disposal unit was located, when suddenly the officer stopped dead in his track.

'Stop!' he ordered, and Andrew and Fiona immediately did as he said.

Andrew heard the unmistakable sound of the clasp on a leather holder popping open and a pistol being extracted and cocked. Then he felt the barrel of the gun against the back of his head.

'There is a pool of blood on the floor. I am going to give you one chance,' said the officer. 'Who are you?'

Without even looking at her, Andrew could sense Fiona trembling with fear as he turned his head ever so slightly to one side to allow him to sense the officer's location in his peripheral vision. Then he produced a deep sigh and lowered his head.

'I guess they didn't train you too well,' he said.

'What?' said the officer, sounding irritated. 'Who the hell are you? What are you talking about?'

'What I am saying,' replied Andrew calmly, 'is that you're standing too close to me.'

'What do you…?' began the officer.

Before he could finish his sentence, Andrew had leaned forward slightly and spun around to his left with lightning speed whilst bringing up his left hand and grabbing the wrist of the officer's gun-wielding arm. As he came face to face with the officer, he then gripped the pistol with two hands and yanked it down to his chest whilst twisting it forcefully around to point at the officer's chest. Two shots rang out in quick succession and Fiona yelped loudly. The expression on the officer's face was one of shock and surprise as the two bullets ripped through his torso. He had barely had time to react. Wide-eyed and swallowing, he then produced a small cough which resulted in a small amount of blood coming out of his mouth and dripping off his lower lip. Finally, he exhaled with an unpleasant sounding gurgling noise and then his legs began to give way. Andrew continued to grip his hands as he lowered the officer onto the floor.

'Oh god,' whispered Fiona, sounding terrified.

'Had to be done,' said Andrew evenly. 'Remember why we are doing this.'

'I know,' said Fiona, still shocked and glaring at the officer now lying lifeless on the floor.

Andrew pulled the jacket off the officer and ripped one of the sleeves off it. Then he proceeded to rip smaller pieces of fabric from the sleeve and stuffed them in his own jacket pocket.

'These will come in handy,' he said. 'Let's get out of here.'

He dragged the dead officer off to the waste compactor, and then the two of them left the room and headed for the hatch through which Andrew had entered the ARK. However, their plan was not to leave the facility but to use the air ducts inside the mountain to create a distraction that would allow them to head back up towards Dietrich's penthouse.

Having spotted several jerry cans on his way through the huge engineering area a few hours earlier, he quickly found them again and checked their content, expecting it to be either petrol or some sort of fuel oil.

'Diesel oil,' he said. 'Perfect. It doesn't burn very easily, so it will create lots of smoke.'

They then took one can each and carried them to the very back of the engineering level where the hatch he had come through earlier was still open. Whilst Fiona was keeping a lookout to make sure they weren't surprised by another set of soldiers, Andrew climbed up and through the hatch, after which Fiona handed him the two cans. Walking around inside the large rectangular metal chamber he poured diesel through all of the twelve smaller vents that he speculated distributed air to all of the sub-domes inside the mountain. Then he splashed a good amount of it onto the floor, left the jerry cans, took out a climbing rope and cut off a long piece which he tied to a metal strut inside the chamber. Then he dropped the rest of it down through the hatch where it just reached the floor. He then climbed down and out of the chamber, leaving the hatch open.

Taking out the strips of fabric he had torn from the officer's sleeve, he quickly rolled them up into little balls and placed five of them close together in a neat row.

'Improvised fuse,' he said and glanced up at Fiona. 'I am going to light this one on the end, and then it should take about thirty seconds for the last one to catch fire and then set this rope on fire. By the time the flame has crawled up the rope to the diesel in the chamber, we need to be out of here. Ready?'

'Yes,' replied Fiona. 'Let's do this.'

Andrew got out his Zippo lighter and lit the edge of the ball of fabric that was furthest away from the rope. It created a small flickering flame, but soon it was engulfing the entire ball and beginning to lick against the one next to it.

'Come on,' said Andrew as they walked away briskly towards the stairs some 100 metres away. 'Don't look back.'

The two of them walked as fast as they could without looking like they were in a hurry, and when they were almost at the stairwell they heard a distinct whoosh, as the flame had finally made its way all the way up to the metal chamber with the twelve ducts. The diesel had ignited, fed by the supply of fresh air coming through the air shaft to the surface and the open hatch at the bottom of the chamber. As the temperature rose, the diesel began to burn better, producing lots of black smoke which was instantly sucked into the twelve ducts and through the extensive pipework towards the twelve sub-domes.

Suddenly a loud blaring fire alarm went off, and within seconds several workers emerged from adjacent rooms, and several guards and offices emerged onto the raised walkway above them shouting and gesticulating. By this time, however, Andrew and Fiona had reached the stairwell and hurried up several levels past the atrium, the leisure level and the barracks towards the executive level. As they passed the barracks, several groups of soldiers were rushing out of there, some of them carrying fire extinguishers and all of them carrying submachine guns.

Reaching the executive level they headed straight for Dietrich's penthouse, but then had to veer off and pretend to be walking further along the wide corridor as a couple of men who had the appearance of being senior commanders emerged from their residences and began making their way to the stairs whilst still putting on some of their clothes. As Andrew had correctly suspected, a fire was something that had been identified as an extremely serious risk to the ARK, requiring immediate attention from the facility's senior officers.

As the corridor emptied once more, Andrew and Fiona both noticed that there was already a faint smell of burning petroleum in their air as the smoke from the engineering level began to gradually permeate the entire ventilation system in the ARK. In the wide corridor on the executive level, a relatively subdued electronic dual-tone was alerting the residents to the danger.

At the end of the corridor near the elevator, just a few feet from the front door to Dietrich's penthouse was a tall and narrow window affording a view down into the dome, and through it, they could see that there were already dozens of people coming out from most of the twelve tunnels leading to the sub-domes. The people in those domes were deeper inside the mountain and had probably been instructed to make their way out to the main atrium as fast as they could if there was a major incident such as a fire.

'It's working,' said Andrew. 'Let's get inside. Dietrich has got to be in there.'

He quickly double-checked the corridor to make sure no one else was there, and then he pulled out his silenced pistol.

'Stand clear,' he said, waiting a couple of seconds for Fiona to move behind him, and then he fired twice into the lock which disintegrated with bits of wood and metal flying off and falling to the floor.

Andrew took a quick step towards the door whilst lifting his right leg, and then he kicked as hard as he could, smashing his boot into the broken lock which immediately broke apart as the door flew open.

Inside the hallway on the other side of the door was a black-clad praetorian who was clearly surprised at the sudden violent entry, and he was still grappling for his weapon when the door opened violently and slammed into the wall next to it. Andrew raised his pistol and fired three times, hitting the praetorian in the chest with all three bullets. The soldier staggered backwards a couple of steps and then fell onto his back with a loud noise, his submachine gun clanking onto the hard wooden floor.

'Take cover,' shouted Andrew to Fiona, who threw herself clear of the doorway and moved close to the doorframe on one side whilst Andrew found cover behind the other.

'There will be more,' he whispered to Fiona, as he heard the sound of footsteps coming from inside the penthouse. 'Here. Take this.'

He quickly put a new magazine into his pistol and threw it across to Fiona who caught it with a surprised look on her face, handling the pistol as if it was hot and might burn her hands.

'I can't…' began Fiona.

'Yes, you can!' interrupted Andrew tensely. 'Wait a few seconds, and then follow me inside.'

He reached around to his right side under the stolen dark grey jacket where the silenced and compact Heckler & Kock MP5SD submachine gun was strapped tightly to his tactical vest. He quickly undid the straps, brought the MP5 out in front of himself and pulled back the bolt to load the first round in the magazine into the chamber and then released the safety. Then he quickly peeked around the corner inside the penthouse hallway, and almost immediately a hail of bullets tore past him, some of them slamming into the wooden doorframe.

He instantly pulled his head back and then, seemingly unphased by the torrent of metal having been fired at him, he reached for a flashbang which was attached to his belt. Quickly showing it to Fiona, she immediately knew what to do and pulled back from the doorframe, covered her ears and closed her eyes.

Andrew pulled the pin on the flashbang, waited three seconds and then tossed it inside the hallway where it exploded almost instantly with a searing bright flash and a deafening noise. Unlike like fragmentation grenades that are designed to create destruction by producing a hail of sharp metal fragments, the flashbang is designed to overwhelm the senses of combatants in close quarters combat.

Immediately after the flashbang went off, Andrew was through the door with his MP5 up in front of him and advancing quickly but in a slight crouch which would allow him to either pull back or evade quickly if needed. Inside the penthouse, he found two more praetorians, one kneeling by a corner next to the hallway and the other further back and standing next to a wall. Both appeared to have been aiming in the direction of the door when the flashbang had gone off, but they were now reeling from the ear-splitting explosion of just under 200 decibels as well as the brief but blinding flash that for a split second produced as much light as around one million candles.

Without hesitation, Andrew continued his forward momentum and brought up his MP5 to aim at the nearest target. He had set the fire selector to bursts, and as he approached, the silenced submachine gun spat out three bullets in rapid succession, all of them finding their target in the praetorian's torso. He twisted and fell backwards, but before he had even hit the floor Andrew had shifted his aim to the second soldier and fired another burst. Two bullets struck the man in the upper chest and the third slammed into his forehead, making his head whip back as he crashed to the floor in a heap.

Further inside the penthouse, Andrew heard something fall over. There were clearly more people in there. As he progressed a few metres further, he realised to his amazement that he was inside an exact replica of Dietrich's New York penthouse. Checking the corners carefully he proceeded cautiously further inside, walking silently next to the wall past the open seating area towards what he assumed would be the bedrooms.

Suddenly he heard two quick pops behind him, and then the sound of something heavy falling onto the floor. He instantly spun around and kneeled down close to the floor to discover that a third soldier had emerged behind him from the library where he must have been hiding when the flashbang went off.

Appearing from the hallway, trembling and with the silenced pistol held out in front of her, Fiona came around the corner and glanced in Andrew's direction whilst still keeping the pistol trained on the soldier she had just shot. Once it was apparent that he was dead, she seemed to relax her shoulders and let her arms drop.

A couple of minutes later they had cleared the whole penthouse, assuring themselves that there were no more soldiers in there. However, it would be a matter of minutes before the whole place would be crawling with them.

Heading back to the library, they went through a door set into the wall between two bookcases, which lead into Dietrich's office. The office turned out to be empty, so Andrew walked briskly to the floor-to-ceiling windows that led out onto the balcony overlooking the atrium. Here he craned his neck to look down. There were now what seemed to be hundreds of people congregating around the park in the middle of the huge circular space under the dome.

'If there is a VLF system in this facility, then it has to be in here somewhere,' said Andrew. 'Start looking.'

Fiona sat down at Dietrich's computer but it was locked. She tried a couple of passwords that she thought might work, but none of them did. After three attempts the PC shut down and left her staring at a dark blank screen.

'Fiona,' whispered Andrew, jerking his head to beckon her to come closer. 'There's a secret passage here.'

He was pointing at a bookcase in front of him, which seemed to be hinged on one side and protruding slightly from the case next to it on the other.

At that moment they both heard what sounded like a door being unlocked somewhere on the other side of the bookcase.

'Panic room?' whispered Fiona.

'Possibly,' nodded Andrew. 'Get ready.'

They looked briefly at each other, and then Andrew nodded, bringing up his MP5 and using the barrel to nudge the bookcase to one side and make it swing open on its hinges. On the other side was a short narrow passage and then a set of stairs going up.

Then they heard the sound of running feet on a hard surface, the noise seemingly echoing slightly as if whoever was making that noise was inside a large space. Then they could hear the clunk of a door closing firmly.

'Dietrich,' said Fiona urgently.

Andrew rushed through the doorway and along the passage and then bounded up the steps at the far end. At the top was a small landing and a solid-looking wooden door. He gripped the handle but it was locked.

'Firing,' he said over his shoulder, and then he brought up the MP5, set it to automatic, aimed at the area around the door handle and fired a long volley of shots that tore into the wood and sent splinters flying everywhere as the hail of metal ripped the door and the doorframe apart.

By the time he stopped, he had spent almost an entire magazine, but the formerly solid-looking door was now a ripped-up mess. He released the magazine and let it drop to the floor, instantly slamming a fresh one into the submachine gun and then he took a couple of fast steps forward, ramming his shoulder into the door as hard as he could. It flew open, and what was on the other side left him momentarily disorientated.

He was standing at the end of the sanctum that he had already been inside once, except that the last time he had been inside it, he had also been in New York. This was yet another faithfully reproduced replica of the original on the 58th floor of Dietrich Tower. But his attention was immediately drawn to the far end of the throne room, where a figure was hobbling along around twenty metres away. The figure, who was wearing a dark suit, was making his way up onto the platform and off towards the side. It was Dietrich, and he seemed to have been shot in the leg. One of the bullets from Andrew's MP5 must have hit him when he had shot out the wooden door, and Andrew now noticed a small trail of blood on the floor.

'Stop! Don't move!' shouted Andrew and brought up his MP5.

Dietrich ignored him and continued off towards the righthand side of the platform behind the throne. Andrew had Dietrich in his sights and could easily have taken the shot, but he wanted him alive. As Dietrich disappeared off to the right and around the corner, Andrew took off and sprinted towards the platform. A couple of seconds later he reached it and made for the corner Dietrich had disappeared behind. He here found a short passage to a rectangular room that was about four metres on either side, containing a desk facing the wall on the far side which had several computer terminals on it and a huge bank of large displays above it on the wall. Each display was showing real-time CCTV footage of dozens of locations inside the ARK. Dietrich had his back to Andrew and was hunched over near one of the terminals. Andrew could see different control systems being manipulated on the screen in front of Dietrich.

'Stop!' shouted Andrew again. 'Hands on your head. Back away from the terminal. Now!'

Andrew fired a single shot over Dietrich's head and the bullet slammed into one of the displays directly above and in front of him, sending small pieces of glass flying off and onto the desk below.

Dietrich seemed to freeze, but Andrew noticed another couple of movements of his right hand, and he could hear the faint sound of tapping on the keyboard. He fired once more into the display.

'Last chance!' commanded Andrew sternly. 'The next one goes into the back of your head.'

Dietrich finally straightened himself and put his hands on his head. Then he took a couple of steps backwards and away from the terminal, although he was clearly encumbered and in pain from the bullet that seemed to have hit his right thigh. Dietrich gave Andrew a disdainful glance over his shoulder.

'Well done, little soldier,' he said sarcastically. 'But you haven't won yet.'

Andrew advanced towards Dietrich on his left side, never taking his eyes off his hands and aiming the MP5 at his head the whole time. Fiona had now caught up and was entering the room behind them.

'It's over, Dietrich' said Andrew icily as he came up behind him. 'Your lunatic project has run its course. Time to give up.'

Dietrich chuckled and turned his head slightly towards Andrew. There was a pained but sly smile on his face. He was panting slightly and beads of sweat had formed on his forehead as he staggered momentarily and winced from the pain in his leg.

'Alright,' he said. 'Whatever you say.'

'Nice setup you have here,' said Fiona coldly, coming up on Dietrich's right side whilst pointing her gun at him. 'Is this so you can watch all your little subjects twenty-four hours a day? To make sure that none of them fall out of line? Is your drug program not enough to keep them compliant? This whole thing is sick!'

Dietrich shrugged slightly and bowed his head with a petulant smile.

'So you keep telling me,' he said. 'What I am doing here is part of the solution. All you'll ever be is part of the problem.'

'You have no idea how ridiculous you sound,' retorted Fiona, contempt dripping off every word.

'Enough!' said Andrew sternly. 'Show us your VLF system. We know you have it here.'

Dietrich hesitated and then glanced sideways at Andrew.

'What if I don't?' asked Dietrich condescendingly. 'What will the SAS man do then?'

Andrew stepped up to Dietrich and planted the barrel of the MP5 on the back of his head, intentionally using enough force to tip Dietrich's head forward and make it hurt.

'Then your brain ends up splattered across these screens,' said Andrew menacingly. 'And we both know the only thing you care about is yourself. This project of yours is not really about a new beginning for humanity. It was only ever about you and your pathological thirst for power. Everything else was just a tool to create loyal minions. You're a megalomaniac and psychopath.'

'That's what my therapist told me when I was 12,' sighed Dietrich. 'I never did like her very much. She's dead now, of course.'

'Just fucking show it to us,' said Andrew angrily. 'And then set it to the correct frequency to contact the USS Tennessee.'

'Alright, alright!' said Dietrich, and gestured towards the terminal in front of him. 'Can I?'

'Don't try to be clever,' said Andrew, keeping the MP5 aimed at Dietrich's head. 'You only get one chance to get this right.'

Dietrich leaned over the terminal, entered a couple of commands and brought up a console connected to a large VLF antenna that had been placed inside a building near the top of Mount Taylor which was masquerading as a weather station.

After a few more seconds, a window opened up inside the VLF application with a small cursor blinking on the left side.

'It's ready,' said Dietrich, glancing over his shoulder towards Andrew.

'Now, step back,' ordered Andrew.

'Let me sit down over here,' winced Dietrich and gestured to a plush-looking chesterfield armchair by the wall a couple of metres away. 'I am afraid you've rather messed up my leg.'

'Fine,' said Andrew and waited for him to sit down, after which he turned to Fiona. 'Make sure he stays there. Don't hesitate to shoot him in the other leg.'

Fiona moved over to stand a few metres away from Dietrich, gripping her gun with both hands and pointing it at him.

'It would be my pleasure,' she said icily.

As Andrew stepped up to the terminal, he suddenly spotted activity on the screen displaying live CCTV footage from outside the ARK. Just in front of the enormous external blast doors, two military helicopters were just landing and several teams of what looked like special forces soldiers began fanning out from them.

'Looks like the cavalry is here,' said Andrew, glancing over his shoulder to where Fiona was covering Dietrich.

'You are so screwed,' smiled Fiona disdainfully at Dietrich.

'How do I open the blast doors?' asked Andrew and looked at Dietrich, demonstratively placing his hand on the MP5.

'Left side of the screen,' said Dietrich. 'The purple battlement icon. Main window, second tab along. The controls are in there.'

Andrew followed the instructions and pressed the button to open the blast doors.

'Thank you,' he said coldly, glancing over his shoulder at Dietrich. 'I hope your men are going to lay down their weapons. There's no way out for them now.'

He then returned his attention to the console. He still had to try to get a message to whoever the person on the USS Tennessee was that had attempted to prevent Vandenberg from launching his missiles.

He placed his MP5 on the desk, extracted his phone to access the information he needed to relay, and then he began typing a brief message. Just as he hit the 'Send' button, Fiona suddenly gasped audibly.

'Andrew!' she said, sounding alarmed. 'We have company. Lower right corner.'

Andrew's head whipped up to look at the lower right-hand display. The screen was divided into a number of small tiles, each with CCTV footage from various places on the executive level, and several of them were suddenly showing a lot of activity. At least two teams of black-clad soldiers were now inside Dietrich's penthouse, and one of them was just entering his office. From the way they moved and covered each other, Andrew could see that these were professionals and not just a bunch of hired goons.

'Looks like they are on to you,' grinned Dietrich. 'Not many places to run and hide in here.'

Andrew grabbed his MP5 and bolted for the passage that led back out to the throne room.

'If he tries anything,' said Andrew, glancing over his shoulder on his way out of the room and pointing at Dietrich, 'then shoot him until he stops moving.'

Fiona raised the pistol to point directly at Dietrich's head.

'Don't think I won't,' she said, looking at him frostily.

Dietrich smiled sardonically, tilting his head slightly to one side with an almost regretful expression on his face. 'I do like you, Fiona.'

'Well, the feeling isn't mutual,' she sneered.

Twenty-Six

The USS Tennessee was making its way from the Mediterranean into the Ionian Sea which lies between southern Italy and Greece. Its destination, determined many months ago, was a position roughly 75 kilometres off the coast of Peloponnese, which is the large geographical feature in southern Greece which is often described as having the shape of a hand.

Chief of the Boat Tom Payne had remained inside his quarters during the engagement with the USS Montana and had felt the torpedoes being launched from the torpedo room which was directly below his quarters. Upon hearing the faint sound of the distant explosion that finally sank the Montana, he had felt sick to his stomach. There was no doubt in his mind that the captain had gone off the deep end, and that the rogue boat was the Tennessee, not the Montana. More than a hundred US sailors had just died a horrible death, but if Vandenberg had not managed to sink the Montana, then they themselves would surely all have perished. It was a completely unfathomable situation that he suddenly found himself in, and it was difficult for him to process what was happening. All he knew was that he had to try to help prevent Vandenberg from launching the nuclear missiles.

There was no way for just himself, Martinez and Jackson to do that on their own, and they had no idea who else on the boat they might be able to trust. All they could do was attempt to force the submarine to the surface by sabotaging it.

Jackson's efforts in the boat's battery compartment were designed to cause enough of a commotion to allow Payne to make his way to the torpedo room where he was going to start a fire. Nothing severe enough to cause a risk to the ship, but enough to force Vandenberg's hand. Martinez was then going to try to make his way up the radio room where he would attempt to launch another buoy containing a message telling NATO forces exactly where the Tennessee was and where it was going.

After the loss of the Montana, Central Command would clearly already have a very good idea about the whereabouts of the Tennessee, but if they were given precise coordinates then perhaps some sort of intervention could be mounted. At least that was their hope, and at this point, it was their only realistic chance of stopping Vandenberg. All three of them understood that they might not survive, but deep down they knew that their deaths would be a small price to pay to prevent the cataclysmic events that were about to unfold.

Having watched Jackson run along the corridor from the battery compartment towards the bridge,

Payne knew that this was now his time to act. He made his way forward to the nearest set of stairs, and after assuring himself that no one else was coming up, he descended and quickly entered the torpedo room. There was one sailor in there, Ensign Clark, and he immediately spotted Payne as he entered.

Payne knew Clark well, even though the youngster had only been on the boat for about three months. As the COB it was Payne's job to get to know the crew, build team cohesion among the enlisted men and generally facilitate the smooth running of the boat on behalf of the captain.

'COB,' said Clark, looking surprised. 'I thought you…'

Payne held up his hand to stop Clark mid-sentence.

'The captain has had a change of heart,' grinned Payne and shrugged. 'Realised he couldn't run the boat without me.'

'Oh,' said Clark with a half-smile, still looking somewhat doubtful. 'So, what can I do for you? I heard some shouting just now. Is everything ok?'

'We have a battery leak,' replied Payne. 'It is being dealt with, but the captain asked me to come down here and make sure all the torpedoes are secure in their racks.'

'Right,' said Clark, looking confused. 'But they are always secure.'

'And the XO has asked that you bring the breathing masks from here to the battery compartment immediately,' continued Payne. 'The acid is giving off toxic fumes so we need more masks.'

'Right,' said Clark, snapping into action and quickly making his way to a locker on one of the walls. 'I'm on it.'

A couple of minutes later Clark had disappeared up the stairs to Deck 2 and down the length of the boat towards the battery compartment. Payne wasted no time. He took off his shirt and doused it with thick engine oil he had brought in a small bottle. Then he stuffed it inside a wall-mounted storage compartment and lit it with a lighter. It quickly caught fire, and soon thick black smoke was filling up the space under the ceiling in the torpedo room. A couple of seconds later the fire alarm began shrieking loudly throughout the submarine. Fire is possibly the biggest danger to a submerged submarine and so everyone on the boat knows to drop what they are doing and immediately assist in either putting out the fire or getting out of the way of the people doing it.

Payne hurried out of the torpedo room and ran up the two flights of stairs towards the bridge. As he approached the doorway into the bridge itself, he saw Jackson being manhandled out onto the landing. Amid the noise from the fire alarms and the shouting of orders, he barged past Jackson and the two sailors attempting to restrain him and onto the bridge.

'Fire in the torpedo room!' he shouted as he entered. 'Captain, we need to evacuate the boat.'

'Payne,' yelled Vandenberg. 'What the hell are you doing here? You are to remain confined to your quarters.'

'Captain,' persisted Payne. 'Navy regulations state that we must surface immediately.'

There was a short pause where the only sound was the noise from the fire alarms throughout the vessel.

'He is right, sir' said Chisholm reluctantly. 'Captain, we need to surface and get the men out onto the boat.'

Then the XO took a quick step to stand close to the captain. He leaned in towards him and spoke in a hushed voice that was inaudible to the rest of the crew amid the noise from the fire alarms.

'We can still carry out our mission,' he whispered. 'But we need to deal with the fire first.'

Vandenberg hesitated for a couple of seconds, an angry and suspicious expression spreading across his face, but then he turned to the helmsman, barking his first order.

'Helmsman, engine stop!' he yelled.

'Ay-ay, sir. Engine stop!' repeated the helmsman.

'XO, blow ballast tanks and prepare to surface,' continued Vandenberg. 'And secure the reactor.'

'Ay-ay, Captain,' replied Chisholm and left the captain's side to issue a barrage of orders to the crew on the bridge.

Vandenberg grabbed the microphone and brought it to his mouth with a bitter look on his face.

'Crew of the USS Tennessee. This is the captain. We have a fire in the torpedo room. Firefighting crews are to make their way there immediately. My intention is to surface the boat and evacuate all crew except for officers through the forward and aft escape hatches as well as the sail. As soon as we have surfaced, the crew is to make their way out and onto the boat and remain there until we can assess the situation. This is the captain.'

'XO,' said Vandenberg bitterly. 'Get Payne out of my sight and get someone to escort him and Jackson topside.'

'Yes, sir,' said Chisholm, turning to instruct a junior officer named Reeves to remove Payne and Jackson from the boat.'

'I have a good mind to leave them up there,' mumbled Vandenberg quietly to himself.

Loud gurgling noises filled the submarine as the water inside its multiple ballast tanks was expelled and replaced by high-pressure air, quickly making the vessel much more buoyant and causing it to rise quickly towards the surface. Within a couple of minutes, the sail broke the surface, and shortly thereafter the whole submarine was rocking slowly back and forth in the shallow waves, water running off its dark glistening surface and the escape hatches popping open at both ends. The crew quickly began to spill out onto the top of the huge submarine, and within a couple of minutes, it was packed full of people. As per standard operating procedure, a large number of inflatable lifeboats had also been brought topside in case the order was given to abandon ship.

Down in the torpedo room, the smoke had filled the entire space and begun to spill out into the corridor and up through the rest of the boat. The first firefighting team to make it down there quickly established that the fire was small and not a result of a malfunctioning torpedo battery, which was a well-known problem on submarines. In fact, it was not a result of any kind of mechanical or technical failure. It was clearly caused by an arsonist. Wearing protective gear and breathing apparatuses, they quickly got the flames under control and then radioed the bridge which was now deserted except for the captain and the executive officer.

'Captain,' said the XO. 'Firefighting crew reports that the fire in the torpedo room has been put out. They say it looks like it was started deliberately.'

A grim look of rage began to form on Vandenberg's face as his eyes narrowed and he pressed his lips together.

'Motherfuckers,' he hissed. 'I have a damn mutiny on board my boat.'

'It looks that way, sir,' said Chisholm.

'It has got to be Jackson and Payne,' said Vandenberg angrily. 'Two accidents happening like this is no coincidence. Is Martinez accounted for?'

'I don't know,' replied Chisholm.

'Well, send someone down there to check,' ordered Vandenberg angrily. 'I will not tolerate mutiny or insubordination on my damn boat. And open the weapons lockers. I want all officers to carry firearms from now on.'

'Ay-ay, Captain,' said Chisholm and marched off to the weapons locker near the back of the bridge.

* * *

Just a few metres away, Martinez had been hiding inside a nook just outside the radio room when the evacuation order was given and everyone suddenly leapt up and abandoned their stations to head for the nearest hatch. Turning his back on the groups of people rushing past him and out of the radio and sonar rooms whilst pretending to be busy rummaging around inside a locker, Martinez waited until everyone had left for the forward escape hatch. As soon as the radio room was empty, he rushed to his old seat just out of view of the bridge which was in the next room. He sat down and attempted to log in to the system, and to his relief and surprise, he found that for some reason his credentials had not been revoked.

Sloppy, thought Martinez and shook his head.

Now that the submarine had surfaced, he would not need to launch the buoy but could simply send a message using regular satellite communications. He had just begun typing a distress message that included the Tennessee's exact location when he spotted that another VLF message seemed to have arrived just seconds before he had sat down. It had gone unnoticed amid the noise and general confusion of the fire alarm going off and the order to evacuate having been issued. However, this was not an EAM message.

Checking the frequency that the message had arrived on, he realised that it was neither sent from central command nor from the new transmitter which had sent the initial EAM that arrived just after the exercise in the North Atlantic. This was from a third transmitter that had not been logged in the system until now.

It simply read:

FROM ARK COMMAND
TO USS TENNESSEE
ATTENTION BUOY OPERATOR

SLBM LAUNCH COORDINATES
43°29'04.4"S
171°16'10.2"E

CENTCOM REQUESTS ETA
SDV ACCESS REQUIRED

Martinez stared dumbfounded at the message for a few seconds. He had no idea what 'Ark Command' was or precisely where the indicated coordinates were, but he immediately understood that the message was intended for him, and that it was sent by someone who understood what was about to happen.

Somehow the sender of the VLF message had been able to determine the precise coordinates where Vandenberg and Chisholm intended to launch the Tennessee's nuclear missiles, and they were asking for assistance with the Seal Delivery Vehicle hatch. They were also asking when the Tennessee would arrive at the coordinates.

Martinez blinked a couple of times, trying to work out precisely what this all meant and what he was supposed to do now. He quickly brought up a navigation map and entered the coordinates that had come through on the message. They indicated a position southwest of Greece somewhere on the border between the Ionian Sea and the Mediterranean. The exact plan behind this was unclear to him, but he understood enough to realise that some sort of boarding attempt was being planned. However, the sender clearly could not have known that the Tennessee had been sabotaged in the meantime. This might complicate things. Or perhaps it was an opportunity.

Plotting the most direct course from the Tennessee's current position to the indicated coordinates yielded an estimated time of arrival of just over an hour, assuming the submarine was travelling at full speed. No wonder Vandenberg was irate. He was almost at his destination when Payne's torpedo room fire had forced him to surface.

Martinez quickly composed a short message to Central Command, copying in the coordinates and also including what he guessed would be their ETA. He had just hit the 'Send' button when suddenly Chisholm appeared in the doorway to the bridge.

'What the hell?' he shouted.

Martinez quickly deleted the VLF message that had just come in, and then he bolted for the door at the other end of the small radio room. Behind him, he could hear Chisholm giving chase and shouting for him to stop. He ran to the stairs and used the railing to slide down to the bottom where he immediately began running along the long corridor towards the back of the submarine. The boat was deserted now that everyone had exited through the escape hatches and so he was able to sprint along the corridor, his boots hammering on the metal floor. Behind him he could still hear running footsteps, so he quickly glanced over his shoulder as he ran.

Chisholm was about fifteen metres behind him but losing ground. Unlike Chisholm, Martinez was young and fit, and as he navigated the hatches and narrow corridors of the submarine, the distance between himself and his pursuer only grew.

Suddenly there was a loud dry crack behind him, and instantly a bullet struck a bulkhead above his head. He was now struggling to keep panic at bay. Chisholm was actually shooting at him.

Eventually, he came to the door leading into the middle section of the submarine where the launch tubes occupy two floors inside a roughly forty-metre-long space. The launch tubes are arranged two by two along the spine of the submarine, but there is also a false tube nearest the front of the boat which contains a small chamber and two pressure doors connecting to the Seal Delivery Vehicle hatch on top of the submarine's main hull.

Martinez opened the door to the launch tube compartment and made it through just as another shot was fired. Then he slammed the door to the forward section shut and ran to the false tube where he opened the circular hatch which was roughly half a metre across. Next to the hatch was a control panel which operated the exterior SDV hangar hatch, and he quickly made sure to unlock it. He then climbed through to the inside of the false tube and shut the hatch behind him. A couple of seconds later inside the damp and dark tube, he held his breath as he listened to the noise from the door to the forward section opening and then the sound of feet running past his hiding place.

Martinez breathed a sigh of relief and looked up above him using the light from his phone. Immediately above his head was the hatch to the diver lock-out chamber. This connected to the exterior hatch, which in turn led to the small SDV hangar that was attached to the outer hull. He gripped the wheel on the hatch and began turning it. It squeaked slightly, but he eventually managed to unlock it. He was then able to open it, climb through and then close and lock it behind himself. All he had to do now was wait for the Tennessee to dive and move towards the intended launch position, and then hope that help would arrive in time.

★ ★ ★

Payne and Jackson were being escorted by Lieutenant Reeves towards the sail of the submarine where they were meant to disembark along with the rest of the crew. Reeves was a lanky young man with a bookish demeanour who mostly kept to himself, and right now he seemed nervous. They were the last people about to climb up and out of the sail, and they were almost at the ladder leading up when Payne suddenly stopped and turned to Jackson who was walking next to him.

'Hey, Jackson,' he said calmly.

'What?' said Jackson nonchalantly as he stopped and looked at the COB.

'I think I might have a way to resolve this little predicament we're finding ourselves in right now.'

'COB,' said Reeves in an attempt to sound stern. 'Please move along. The captain wants you two off the boat.'

'Do you, now?' replied Jackson, ignoring Reeves and looking at Payne. 'And what might that solution be?'

'Well,' replied Payne. 'I would like to tell you, but there's a small problem.'

'Damn it, COB,' said Reeves, now sounding increasingly frustrated.

'And what problem is that?' asked Jackson.

'Three is a crowd,' replied Payne and glanced briefly at Lieutenant Reeves.

Jackson did not hesitate, and before the junior officer could react, Jackson's huge clenched fist had connected with his jaw so hard that his head whipped backwards and he immediately lost consciousness.

'Let's get him out,' said Payne, catching and holding the limp officer before he hit the floor.

'Sure thing,' said Jackson and grabbed the officer, hauling him towards the ladder leading up through the sail.

He slung the unconscious officer over his shoulder and began climbing up the ladder. Soon he was at the top where a young ensign was standing, having just exited himself.

'Is that Reeves?' said the ensign. 'What happened?'

'Passed out,' replied Jackson. 'I think the fire freaked him out.'

'Alright,' said the ensign, shaking his head. 'I'll take him from here.'

'Thanks,' said Jackson and disappeared back down through the hatch.

At the bottom of the ladder, Payne grabbed Jackson's shoulders and looked him in the eyes.

'Listen,' he said with a severe look on his face. 'We need weapons, but they are inside the weapons lockers and I don't have a key. So, we need to break into one of them. The nearest one is just outside the XO's quarters.'

'Ok,' said Jackson. 'Whatever you say, COB.'

'Alright,' said Payne. 'Let's go.'

The two of them snuck down a flight of stairs and made their way forward towards the officer's quarters. Jackson was carrying a crowbar that he had grabbed from a toolbox as they were passing the auxiliary machinery room which is on the same deck as the officers' quarters just below the bridge.

They quickly found the weapons locker, and within less than a minute Jackson had rammed the crowbar in behind the lock and wrenched the door open. Inside it were six pistols and two shotguns, which as far as any of them knew had never left the locker before. Firing weapons inside a submarine is generally a terrible idea, and they were only on board in order for them to be available as a last resort against an external threat such as a hostile boarding party.

They grabbed a pistol each as well as a couple of full magazines, and then they headed towards the nearest set of stairs which led up to the radio and sonar rooms just forward from the bridge.

As they snuck quietly up the stairs, they could faintly hear Captain Vandenberg's voice as he was addressing the remaining handful of junior officers on the bridge.

'Men,' he said. 'We are now at war. As you know, we have received an emergency action message ordering us to launch our missiles, and it is my intention to do so as soon as possible. We have also suffered several acts of sabotage from the enlisted men, and it is my determination that several of them could be Russian sleeper agents. For these reasons, we will now prepare the boat to dive immediately and leave the enlisted crew in their lifeboats. We will proceed towards our designated launch coordinates in the Ionian Sea.'

There was a short pause during which Payne and Jackson looked at each other dumbfounded as they realised what the captain was about to do.

'Therefore,' continued Vandenberg, 'my orders are to seal all hatches, dive to 300 feet and make for our launch position. The crew that is topside have lifeboats with communications equipment, and they will be safely picked up by NATO naval forces that are not far from this area. XO, prepare the boat to dive. Officers, man your stations.'

'Ay-ay, Captain,' responded Chisholm without hesitation.

Immediately two of the junior officers hurried out of the bridge and headed for the two escape hatches. A third went to close up the hatch in the sail. Seconds later, there was the sound of water refilling the ballast tanks under high pressure. The USS Tennessee was slipping beneath the waves, leaving almost all of her crew currently standing on its hull suddenly scrambling for the inflatable lifeboats.

Tom Payne could only imagine the shock and confusion that the crew up there would feel, as the giant black steel hull of the submarine began to sink into the sea leaving them adrift in the ocean. He looked at Jackson and leaned towards him.

'We need to move,' he whispered. 'This is our only chance. If we don't stop this now, it's World War Three.'

Jackson looked down and nodded pensively for a few seconds. Then he lifted his head and looked into Payne's eyes with a determined expression.

'Alright, COB,' he said coolly. 'Let's do this.'

Payne led the way as the two armed sailors ascended the stairs, hurried through the sonar and radio rooms and then burst onto the bridge with their weapons drawn.

'Nobody move!' shouted Payne, raising his gun and pointing it at Captain Vandenberg.

At the same time, Jackson appeared next to him aiming first at Chisholm and then at the junior officers, several of whom had leapt to their feet at the sudden intrusion.

'Captain,' said Payne loudly with a steely voice. 'Under the authority of Regulation 731-C of the United States Navy Regulations, I hereby relieve you of your command of the USS Tennessee. I have evidence that the emergency action message authorising the release of nuclear missiles was *not* genuine and that it was *not* issued by Central Command, and that you and the XO are part of a conspiracy to launch nuclear missiles without authorisation from the president.'

At first Vandenberg and Chisholm barely reacted, but then Vandenberg turned slowly towards Payne with his head tilted to one side and a dubious look on his face.

'You are making a big mistake, son,' he said with an irritated and disdainful expression.

'Officers,' continued Payne in a commanding voice. 'The evidence in my possession is unequivocal. Captain Vandenberg and the XO are attempting to illegally launch this vessel's nuclear missiles. Arrest the captain and the XO and escort them to their quarters. *Now!*'

Payne's natural authority and the respect he had always enjoyed amongst the crew left the junior officers stunned and confused by what they had just heard. Several of them seemed to waver, their eyes flitting back and forth between Payne and Vandenberg.

Chisholm was moving ever so slowly back towards the captain's chair, his hand creeping up towards the holster on his belt that contained his sidearm.

'Ignore that order!' shouted Vandenberg angrily. 'Mr Payne has already been relieved of his duty, and had been confined to his quarters for blatant insubordination and refusing to respect the U.S. Navy chain of command.'

There was a short pause where Vandenberg and Payne were staring each other down.

'Put down your weapon, Mr Payne,' said Vandenberg icily. 'Put it down if you want to walk off this boat alive. You too Mr Jackson.'

'I can't do that, sir,' replied Payne with steely determination in his voice. 'I can't let you launch those missiles.'

Vandenberg sighed and gave a small shake of the head. He glanced at Chisholm, who was now to his right and slightly behind him, and then he nodded almost imperceptibly. Chisholm immediately brought up his pistol and fired several rounds at Payne and Jackson whilst Vandenberg leapt behind a console and drew his own gun. As Chisholm scurried into cover behind the captain's chair still firing his gun, three of the junior officers threw themselves down onto the floor but two others pulled out their guns and opened fire on Payne and Jackson who were now scrambling to retreat into the sonar room.

The bridge had suddenly erupted into chaos as the bullets tore through the air and slammed into walls and equipment everywhere, sending electrical sparks flying and causing several of the computer terminals to blink out.

Payne yelled out as he threw himself on the floor of the sonar room and rolled away from the doorway. Jackson had taken cover behind a section of wall next to the door to the corridor at the other end of the room.

'I'm hit!' shouted Payne as he kept shooting. His shirt was soaked with blood near his abdomen and it was spreading fast.

Jackson was emptying his magazine, shooting haphazardly into the bridge where the officers were taking cover and returning fire. He had only ever fired a weapon a few times on a shooting range and had never in his wildest dreams imagined that he would end up firing at the officer crew inside a submarine. Eventually, his gun clicked several times as he ran out of ammo.

'Get out of here,' hissed Payne. 'I will hold them off.'

'I'm not leaving you,' replied Jackson resolutely.

'Go now, damn it, or I will shoot you myself,' winced Payne.

Jackson knew that there was no point in arguing, so he turned around to leave, but just then a bullet struck Payne in the head and his lifeless body slumped onto the floor.

Jackson's head whipped around to see the COB lying dead inside the sonar room, and a tortured expression formed on his face. Then he bolted for the stairs down to the level below where he began running as fast as he could towards the back of the boat. His body was moving but his mind was frozen in near panic. He had no idea where to go or how to escape. The boat was already submerged and there was no way he would be able to open a hatch and escape. Even inside one of the small airlocks by the escape hatches, the water would gush in and prevent him from getting out. And even if by some miracle he managed to exit, he would never make it to the surface now since the boat was already at least 100 feet below the surface.

Smashing into obstacles and ramming through open pressure doors he eventually came to the door to the missile launch tube compartment. He yanked it open, and now that he had stopped running he could hear voices shouting somewhere behind him. He turned around to look along the corridor but could not see anyone yet. However, he was clearly being hunted down by the armed junior officers, and he had to find a way to fight back or hide.

Slipping through the pressure door to the missile tube compartment he quickly slammed it shut and began making his way past the missile tubes towards the other end of the room, when suddenly he heard a metallic-sounding clunk and then a familiar voice from behind him.

'Yo! Jackson,' said Martinez.

Jackson spun around to see Martinez' head poking out of the hatch to the SDV tube.

'Payne is dead,' blurted Jackson, out of breath. 'We were shooting. Trying to stop the captain. It's all fucked up, bro. They're coming for me. And they're gonna launch the missiles.'

'Damn it,' said Martinez with a pained expression on his face. 'Payne was a good guy. Get in here, Jackson. I think the cavalry is on its way.'

'Shit, I can't fit through that hole,' protested Jackson.

'You either fit or you die,' said Martinez evenly. 'Now, come on. Get inside!'

Twenty-Seven

Andrew burst out into the throne room just as the sound of running feet began to emerge from the other end of it where he had shot out the oak door about ten minutes earlier. He continued across the platform past the throne and took cover behind the corner of a wall, giving him a better view of the door where he was expecting soldiers to come through any second now.

Instead of a soldier, the first thing that came through was a flashbang that someone must have lobbed from halfway down the steps to Dietrich's penthouse replica. Andrew just had time to close his eyes and turn away, but then the flashbang exploded with an ear-splitting crack which reverberated around the long throne room. He winced at the pain in his ears and momentarily felt unsteady on his feet as the deafening sound waves caused havoc with his inner ear and his sense of balance. However, because he was more than twenty metres away he quickly recovered, and as the first two soldiers entered the throne room he brought up his MP5 and let loose a volley that instantly dropped one of them to the floor and made the other scramble behind one of the pillars whilst returning fire.

Andrew pulled back behind the corner just as a couple of bullets slammed into the wall behind him, and by the time he had changed the magazine and peeked out again there were already several more soldiers inside the throne room taking cover behind pillars, and there were even more of them coming up the stairs.

Deciding that he was almost out of options, he reached down to his belt and detached one of his small black spherical M67 hand grenades. Containing a 180-gram high explosive mix of materials including TNT, and a fuse with a four-second delay, it packs a serious punch. At the moment of detonation, the shockwave from within the grenade travels outwards at more than eight kilometres per second, giving it immense destructive power over its immediate surroundings, especially considering it is only about the size of a small apple.

He pulled the pin, waited two seconds and then hurled the grenade towards the other end of the throne room. As soon as the soldiers spotted him emerging from behind the corner they opened fire, but upon seeing him throwing the small black sphere in their direction they instantly scrambled for cover. It took roughly two seconds for the grenade to travel to the other end of the room, so it exploded almost as soon as it hit the marble floor. The explosion was not as loud as that of the flashbang but the effects were devastating. Two soldiers instantly slumped onto the floor, having been thrown against the walls by the force of the explosion right next to them. Another was behind a pillar yelping and grabbing his leg which had pieces of shrapnel in it.

As Andrew peeked out again, two more soldiers emerged in the doorway and Andrew instantly opened fire with several three-round bursts, dropping one of them and making the other retreat down the stairs. He was about to hurl another grenade toward them when he heard Fiona's voice calling his name and sounding panicked.

Andrew fired off the remaining bullets in his magazine as he ran back across the platform and behind the throne towards Dietrich's command and control room where Fiona and Dietrich were. As he was just about to slip behind the corner of the wall, he tossed another grenade along the floor without waiting for the fuse to partially burn out. The grenade rolled rapidly along the marble floor towards the far end of the room, and he could hear agitated voices as the remaining soldiers attempted to take cover.

The grenade detonated just as Andrew sprinted through the passage and into the control room, but his attention was suddenly no longer on the soldiers but instead on the fact that Fiona was alone in there.

'He escaped!' she shouted, wide-eyed and with a distressed look on her face.

'What the hell do you mean?' shouted Andrew, releasing the empty magazine from the submachine gun and loading another.

'He was in the chair when the first explosion went off,' blurted Fiona, 'He must have pressed a hidden button or something because the wall behind him opened up and the whole chair shot inside with him in it. Then the chair came back out and the wall closed up again. I didn't have time to react.'

'Shit,' said Andrew, quickly turning back towards the passage where his pursuers would be coming through any second now. 'Find the button!'

Fiona tucked her pistol into her belt and frantically began examining the chesterfield armchair whilst Andrew ripped the marble slab from a coffee table and picked up the metal frame it had been resting on.

'I think I've got it,' Fiona called out, pointing at the armrest. 'The leather button inside this hole on the armrest is different from the others. That's got to be it.'

'Alright, get ready to press it,' said Andrew, carrying the metal frame over to the armchair. 'Stand clear of it.'

'Ready?' said Fiona tensely, glancing towards the passage.

'Ready,' nodded Andrew.

Fiona pressed the button and in less than two seconds the wall behind the chair had split open and folded back inside the wall. The chair then slid along on two small rails embedded into the floor behind it, and as it came to a stop, it spun around to face the opposite direction. Just as it came to a stop and began rotating, Andrew leapt forward and jammed the metal coffee table frame in between the two false sections of the wall, thereby preventing the mechanism from resetting itself and keeping Dietrich's ingenious escape route open.

At that moment they heard the sound of shouting and running inside the throne room.

'Get in,' shouted Andrew. 'Quick!'

Fiona clambered past the chesterfield chair and further into the cavity, whilst Andrew lobbed his last grenade out through the passage and onto the throne platform. It detonated just as he slipped through on the other side of the chair, and then he turned around and yanked the wedged coffee table frame free. The chair instantly slid back out into the room and then the two doors closed behind it leaving Andrew and Fiona in darkness.

Andrew switched on the built-in flashlight on the MP5 and in the gloom he brought a finger up to his lips to indicate to Fiona to be quiet. He was betting that none of the soldiers now rushing through the passage and into the control room would know of the secret escape route, and soon they could hear them shouting angrily, no doubt flummoxed by Andrew's sudden disappearance and the fact that Dietrich was nowhere to be seen either.

Andrew pointed along what turned out to be a long concrete-lined corridor which seemed to run for around ten metres before it ended at two sliding metal doors with a button next to them. The two of them walked carefully and quietly without speaking toward the sliding doors, and by the time they reached them, it was clear that they were looking at an elevator. But to where?

Deciding they had no choice but to enter, Andrew pressed the lone unmarked button on the panel, and after a few seconds of whirring and clicking, the doors opened to reveal a small space just large enough for two or perhaps three people at a push.

They entered and then Fiona pressed the only button on the panel inside it. The doors closed and then they felt the elevator begin to accelerate upwards. They both looked at each other.

'Where the hell does this go?' said Fiona. 'To the surface?'

'Possibly,' said Andrew, checking his weapon and handing Fiona another magazine for her silenced Glock. 'I guess Dietrich always has an escape plan just for himself, being a great defender of the future of humanity and all that.'

'He's such an arsehole,' scoffed Fiona, but then her face changed to take on a troubled look. 'What if he's got more strings to his bow?'

'What do you mean?' asked Andrew.

'What if he doesn't just have a plan B but also a plan C and D?' she asked, looking at him uneasily. 'He has been working towards this for over a decade and spent billions on this facility and all the other assets that are spread out around the world. And all of it to achieve this one single destructive goal. I somehow suspect that he might have a few aces up his sleeve, just in case his master plan was threatened.'

'You might be right,' replied Andrew, wincing slightly at the thought. 'We need to stop him, whatever it takes. And as far as trying to detain him, I think that train has left the station now.'

'You want to kill him,' said Fiona with a grim but determined look on her face as she realised what they needed to do.

'Yes,' said Andrew resolutely. 'He a dangerous psychopath. We simply can't risk letting him get away.'

★ ★ ★

Having been on standby for several hours at RAF Akrotiri in Cyprus in the eastern Mediterranean, Colin McGregor and his small SAS team of five others were eager to suit up and board the waiting RAF C-130K Hercules transport plane that had arrived just half an hour earlier. It had kept all four of its engines running at idle while its special cargo had been loaded through the lowered ramp at the rear.

The SEAL Delivery Vehicle Mark XI was just under 7 metres long and weighed 15 tonnes, and it looked like an oversized torpedo with a rounded nose and a screw propeller at the back. However, it had a slightly more cuboid shape with rounded corners. It also sported side accesses both at the front and the rear for the special forces teams that ride inside it, making it a so-called 'flooded' design. It is equipped with navigation, communication, and life-support equipment, and because it is powered by an electric motor and silver-zinc batteries it is extremely difficult to detect using passive sonar, and its small profile, especially when moving directly towards a target, makes it challenging even for active sonar to pick it up. With a top speed of 11 kilometres per hour or roughly jogging speed and a range of about 30 kilometres, it offers special forces teams significant flexibility in terms of their ability to infiltrate enemy coastal positions from the sea or covertly attack enemy naval assets.

The vehicle had been designed so that it could be airdropped but this was a rare occurrence, and it had never been attempted with a special forces team already inside the vehicle. Having been told that it was theoretically possible for this to happen and that they would be the first to attempt it, McGregor and his team had shrugged, exchanged looks and continued cleaning their weapons and packing their gear.

The SDV's usual mode of delivery was to be attached to a U.S. Navy submarine that could bring it in close to a coastline or a ship, after which the SEAL team could enter the SDV and use it to approach their target undetected. However, the current mission required them to be dropped very close to the USS Tennessee and to then quickly make their way to the SDV dry-dock hangar on top of the Tennessee. This initial task had to be completed within minutes of entering the water, and for this reason, it had been decided that the vehicle would be dropped with the team already inside it.

The mission had been in the works for several days now in an effort that was coordinated between SAS HQ in London and the U.S. Special Operations Command or SOCOM, at MacDill Airforce Base in Tampa, Florida. Under normal circumstances, it would have been a SEAL team operating the SDV. However, due to the extreme urgency of the current situation, the joint task force had decided to instead pursue a different avenue. The plan was to use an SAS team that had just completed an anti-piracy mission off the coast of Ethiopia and that was now at RAF Akrotiri on their way back to the UK. The Akrotiri airbase is just a few hundred kilometres from what the intelligence community had determined with a very high probability would be the position from which the USS Tennessee would attempt to launch its missiles. The SDV vehicle about to be used for this mission had been flown over from Florida earlier that year to allow various NATO armies to send teams of special forces soldiers to train on it. Everything was now ready, and the large network of hydrophones operated by NATO in the Mediterranean along with airdropped sonar buoys had picked up faint signs of what was likely to be the Tennessee. Analysts had estimated that the submarine would arrive at the launch coordinates within less than an hour.

McGregor and his team jogged up the ramp and into the back of the Hercules where they quickly found their seats by the side of the fuselage. Here they strapped themselves in facing the hulking black SDV. The submersible was pointing forward inside the cargo hold, and the plan was for it to slide out of the back of the plane and then enter a barely-controlled dive towards the sea below using a large parachute to reduce its speed as much as possible during the final phase of the descent.

When the C130K stopped at the end of the runway with its engines spun up waiting to be cleared for take-off, McGregor looked to his side at the faces of his team members. There was recon specialist Logan, also known as *Ghost*. The explosives expert Dunn, and also Grant and Thompson whose usual role was to provide fire support. The last team member was the sniper Wilks, who had looked decidedly unhappy about leaving his sniper rifle behind. All five of them were carrying the short but powerful Heckler & Koch HK53A3 assault rifle which packs a substantially heavier punch than the MP5, at the cost of increased recoil and a slower rate of fire.

They all looked calm, focused and ready to execute their mission, and McGregor couldn't help but produce a wry smile. He would be happy to put his life in the hands of these men any day of the week.

Suddenly the pilot released the breaks and the bulky-looking aircraft accelerated along the runway at a steady rate until the nose pitched up and it lifted off amid the roar of the four powerful Allison T56 turboprop engines. Since it is a military cargo aircraft, the C130K has no internal noise suppression the way commercial aircraft do, so the noise was deafening inside the cargo hold. Soon, however, the aircraft headed west and reached its cruising altitude after which the pilot reduced the engine RPMs and the noise level abated slightly.

The team settled in for the journey, and, as was usually the case en route to a drop-zone, Wilks fell asleep. When they finally reached the area around the launch coordinates, the co-pilot received an encrypted data package containing the latest readings and inferences from the network of hydrophones and the large teams of analysts that were now working on locating the Tennessee, both in London and at the Office of Naval Intelligence in Suitland, Maryland. None of the teams had been able to arrive at a precise location, simply because the Tennessee was built to evade detection and did a very good job of doing so, but employing multiple sets of hydrophones and using triangulation between them they had been able to pin down her rough location to within a circular area roughly one mile across. Refining the final waypoint using this updated data the pilot then descended and slowed the aircraft to a few tens of kilometres per hour above stall speed. The slower the speed when the SDV was dropped the lower the risk of unforeseen events or accidents.

An alarm began blaring inside the cargo hold and a red light above the cargo door began to flash. McGregor's team unbuckled themselves and rose, filing into a neat line behind McGregor without a word. Then they mounted the SDV with McGregor at the helm and the others in the seats behind him. Once inside, they strapped themselves in tightly and put on their underwater breathing kits. The co-pilot had come down from the flight deck to oversee the procedure and release the SDV.

As the cargo door opened and the ramp lowered itself, the fresh sea air whirled violently and noisily into the cargo compartment so the co-pilot was having to use hand signals to communicate with McGregor.

Inside McGregor's helmet, the voice of the pilot came on.

'Alright chaps,' he said. 'Coming up on the drop point in forty seconds. All set?'

'All set,' replied McGregor in his thick Scottish accent. 'Ready to release. Let's go for a swim.'

Shortly thereafter the co-pilot released the locking mechanism and the SDV began to slide backwards on a specially designed set of rails towards the open ramp at the back of the aircraft. McGregor and his team were strapped in but still held on tightly to the handlebars inside the vehicle as it left the aircraft and was instantly enveloped by a torrent of air rushing past it. They had all trained with the SEALs on this type of vehicle a couple of times, but none of them had ever experienced an airdrop quite like this.

Looking like a giant nuclear bomb as it began plummeting towards the ocean below, its sleek shape and tailfins ensured that it was aerodynamically stable, and as it picked up speed the team inside it could feel the air rushing past then faster and faster through the exposed sides of the vehicle. Hurtling towards the ocean below, the vehicle shuddered and rattled as the wind tore at it as it plummeted through the air, getting closer and closer to the sea. McGregor was about to conclude that the altimeter on the automatic chute-deployment mechanism had failed and that he would have to trigger it manually, when there was a brief judder throughout the body of the SDV as the drogue chute deployed. About a second later the main chute shot out of the back and unfurled, causing a sudden and violent deceleration of the vehicle around two hundred metres above the water. The team were thrust forward hard into their harnesses as the SDV's speed continued to bleed off over the next several seconds. Eventually, it gradually settled into a gentle descent, swaying slightly from side to side as its fifteen tonnes of weight dangled lazily underneath the large canopy.

When it was less than five metres from the surface, McGregor released the parachute and then the SDV dropped like a stone into the water with a huge splash. The SDV was immediately enveloped by air bubbles, but after a few seconds they had all dissipated back up to the surface, and McGregor was then able to grip the control and manoeuvre the small vessel to a horizontal orientation. Next to him, Logan was operating the small passive sonar that had been attached to the bottom of the hull especially for this mission.

Turning his head towards McGregor, he brought up his hand and pointed to their ten o'clock to indicate the direction of the USS Tennessee. They did not have visual contact yet but she was close, and on the visual display it looked to Logan like she was stationary.

McGregor engaged the propeller which quickly began driving the SDV quietly forward through the water, and then he adjusted their heading slightly to their left in the direction Logan had indicated. Moments later the enormous dark shape of the 170-metre-long and almost nineteen thousand tonnes heavy USS Tennessee loomed into view ahead of them.

They were approaching from the rear on the starboard side, and McGregor could immediately see that the propeller was not turning. But what was more significant and concerning was that the outer hull hatches for all of the 24 Trident II launch tubes had been swung to their vertical open position. This meant that Vandenberg was in the process of spinning up the nuclear missiles and getting ready to launch.

As the huge submarine sat motionless in the water in front of them, it seemed almost otherworldly. As if it was a giant creature with spikes running down its spine and languidly floating just below the surface of some alien ocean. But this creation was not alive. It was made from steel by human beings, with the sole and perverse purpose of killing millions of other human beings or at least representing a credible threat of being capable of doing so.

As they passed by the immobile propeller with its five-metre-long curved scimitar-like blades that were designed to reduce cavitation noise and then approached the SDV hangar on top of the submarine's main hull, the vessel seemed to grow in size. Sitting alone and immobile in the water like this, the six-storey height from its keel to the top of its sail made the SDV feel like a small gnat that could easily be swatted.

However, this steel beast was unaware of the small submersible that was now approaching, and as McGregor steered the submersible right up to the SDV hangar, Logan slipped out and swam ahead to the hangar door. The hangar itself was just a three-metre-wide tube fixed to the top of the submarine that was fitted with pressure pumps. It was connected to the USS Tennessee with a hatch that could only be opened once the hangar was sealed, the water had been expelled and it had been pressurised to just above 1 atmosphere.

The hangar door was a large circular hatch fixed with two large hinges on one side, and it had an exterior mechanical lock which Logan quickly disengaged. The hangar was kept full of water for neutral buoyancy when submerged, so when Logan slowly swung the door open, only a few air bubbles came out and there was no noisy rush of air or water that might have alerted the crew on the bridge to their attempt to board the submarine.

Giving McGregor the OK-sign, Logan then directed the SDV slowly forward toward the hangar. On the one hand they had to work fast in case the Tennessee suddenly began moving, but on the other hand they could not risk moving so fast that they ended up making noise that would betray their presence. He waved slowly for McGregor to keep moving forward as he himself moved backwards into the hangar. After about a minute when the SDV was finally all the way inside, he quickly swam to the open end of the hangar, swung the hangar door back to its closed position and then locked it. As soon as it was locked, Logan turned and signalled McGregor who had climbed out of the pilot's seat and moved to the wall of the hangar next to the hatch to the submarine's interior airlock. Here he flipped open a plastic cover and used both hands to press two buttons that were arranged next to each other. After holding them in for three seconds, the pumps on the hangar module fired up and began pumping air into the hangar, thereby expelling the water that was inside it. Within less than a minute, the hangar was emptied of water and the team of five SAS soldiers wearing wetsuits converged silently on the hatch to the submarine's interior.

Twenty-Eight

Captain Vandenberg had made his way down to the torpedo room with his sidearm strapped to his belt along with a junior officer who was also armed. He had told the bridge that he would perform a damage assessment after the fire himself, in order to ensure that the Tennessee was still seaworthy. His real reason was quite different. He had always had this contingency plan ready in case it should become necessary, but he had never actually believed that it would come to this.

Walking around inside the blackened room with the long torpedoes on one side and the launch tubes extending forward to the bow on the other, he pondered the old axiom about how no war plan survives contact with the enemy. Conflict is a fluid and dynamic thing, and it invariably ends up becoming more about improvisation than planning.

The original plan had been for himself and Chisholm to take the boat to the launch coordinates and then launch all twenty-four nuclear missiles in batches of three over a period of about ten minutes. They were then intending to head to Egyptian territorial waters and sail through the Suez Canal, and then spend the next two weeks covering the roughly eleven thousand kilometres to the South Island of New Zealand, where a specially selected team from the ARK would meet then and ferry them by helicopter to Mount Taylor. At that point, the majority of the crew would have to be eliminated, except for those of the junior officers who he thought had proven themselves sufficiently loyal to him.

Initially, everything had gone smoothly and exactly according to schedule, not least the complex and long-planned deception in the North Atlantic which had allowed the Tennessee to slip away from the fleet despite being attempted tracked by the most extensive and sensitive hydrophone network in the world. Vandenberg had also anticipated the scenario where attack submarines were ordered to find and destroy the Tennessee, but using his superior skill, cunning and experience he had managed to negate that threat too. What he had never envisioned was to almost lose control of the mission because of a few saboteurs among his own crew.

Precisely how Payne, Martinez and Jackson had worked out what was going on and then been able to see through the fake EAM messages, he still did not fully understand. Now, he was burning with rage at the way those three men had managed to partially sabotage the plan. At least Payne was now dead, but the fact that the two others were still hiding somewhere on the huge submarine made him furious. He was reminded of a time several years ago when he had arrived in his log cabin in the mountains after a tour at sea, only to find that it was riddled with hundreds of rats that were chewing through everything. The little bastards were hiding everywhere. They were in the attic, under the floorboards and inside the walls. Pest control had told him they would be able to easily cleanse the cabin of the infestation, but instead, Vandenberg had decided to burn the whole thing to the ground.

A few minutes earlier he had sent out two teams to find the miscreants, each with two armed junior officers, but they had both come back empty-handed. Instead, Vandenberg had ordered those two teams to guard the only two access points to the bridge, guns loaded and drawn at all times. There was still a chance for him to complete the mission, and he wasn't about to let two cowardly rodents ruin it. All he had ever done in his whole professional life was to successfully complete his missions, and he was not about to fail now.

Having finished his inspection of the torpedo room, Vandenberg ordered the junior officer to return to the bridge, telling him that he would come back up a few minutes later. The junior officer looked puzzled, but he knew better than to question the captain's decisions so he headed out and back upstairs, leaving Vandenberg alone with the torpedoes.

Once he was by himself, Vandenberg opened one of the two torpedo launch tubes that had an MK-48 torpedo inside, ready to be fired. He then placed a small explosive charge inside the tube, activated the radio receiver and re-sealed the launch tube.

A couple of minutes later he re-emerged on the bridge where Chisholm had been left in charge.

'Captain has the conn,' said Chisholm as soon as he spotted Vandenberg entering. 'What are your orders, Captain?'

Vandenberg walked to his chair and sat down.

'Initiate launch sequence,' he replied. 'Load target package and prepare to fire missiles 1 through 3 on my command.'

'Ay-ay, Captain,' said Chisholm and began issuing a set of orders to the junior officers that would allow the submarine to ready itself for the release of the first batch of nuclear missiles.

After a couple of minutes, Chisholm turned to Vandenberg.

'Captain,' he said. 'Missiles 1 through 3 are spun up and ready for launch.'

Vandenberg joined him, and the two of them then walked to the weapons officer and inserted their launch keys into their respective keyholes in the control panel.

'On my mark, turn your key,' said Vandenberg and looked at Chisholm, a hint of tension in his voice.

'Ready, Captain,' replied Chisholm after inserting his key.

Vandenberg nodded.

'Three. Two. One. Mark'

Both men simultaneously turned their launch keys clockwise a quarter turn, and a usually dormant panel above the weapons operator lit up. In front of

Vandenberg, a thick transparent plastic cover over a large red button popped open. Next to it was a digital count-down timer indicating that there were 500 seconds remaining before the rocket engines of the three missiles were spun up, the coolant was loaded and the guidance systems were initialised and calibrated, after which the missiles would finally be ready to launch.

Once the timer reached zero, the red button would light up and the launch of the first three MIRVed Trident II missiles with 36 warheads would be just a single button press away.

★ ★ ★

Inside the SDV access tube in the missile compartment on board the USS Tennessee, Jackson pushed past Martinez to unlock and turn the wheel on the hatch to the SDV hangar. They had both heard the three firm knocks on the hatch from the outside that signalled the arrival of the special forces team. However, Martinez had been unable to make the wheel budge because of the slight pressure differential between the submarine's interior and the SDV hangar, which made the hatch lock stick. Jackson grimaced as he strained to turn the wheel, but it finally came loose and then there was a loud hissing noise for a moment as the air pressure equalised.

When the hatch finally swung open, Martinez and Jackson were met by a terrifying sight. Standing above them and wearing intimidating futuristic full-body combat suits and masks, dripping with water and glistening in the red low-level lighting of the SDV hangar's interior, were three large soldiers with powerful-looking stocky weapons pointing down at the two enlisted sailors. The only sound they could hear was the eerie rhythmic wheezing of their breathing apparatuses. One of them reached up to his face and removed his mask.

'Evening lads', he said in a heavy Scottish accent. 'We're the cavalry. Which one of you is the radio operator? And which way to the bridge, please?'

★   ★   ★

Back on the bridge, Vandenberg was about to step up to the control panel and initiate the launch of the first three nuclear missiles, when at that moment there was a distant but audible metallic clonk somewhere on the submarine's hull, and a very slight but noticeable judder throughout the vessel.

'What the hell was that?' said Vandenberg, turning to his left. 'Sonar. Anything on the scopes?'

'Negative, Captain,' replied the sonar operator. 'I'm not picking up anything. Scopes are all clean.'

Then they all suddenly heard the unmistakable sound from the pumps connected to the SDV hangar.

'Captain,' said Chisholm. 'That's the SDV…'

'I fucking know what it is!' spat Vandenberg angrily. 'We've got visitors.'

The sound of the pumps stopped, and then there were three dull metallic clangs that reverberated throughout the submarine's outer hull.

'Crew of the USS Tennessee,' said Vandenberg loudly in an authoritative voice. 'We are being boarded by Russian special forces. There is a real risk that they may have already sabotaged our launch capability. I want everyone to arm themselves and take up positions between the bridge and the missile compartment. Shoot to kill.'

Some of the junior officers exchanged nervous glances as they got up and a couple of them suddenly appeared reticent of what was happening, but Vandenberg's mention of Russians had been enough to motivate them to defend the boat. They quickly filed out of the bridge and hurried down the stairs to where Chisholm had unlocked another weapons locker and was now handing out shotguns and more ammunition for their pistols.

The group, led by Chisholm, then spread out along the corridor leading to the missile compartment and each man took cover behind whatever solid object they could find, some of them simply standing behind a doorway and leaning out whilst aiming in the direction of the solid steel pressure door. The idea was simply to lie in wait and attack the intruders as soon as they attempted to make their way towards the bridge.

A few tense and silent minutes passed when suddenly the junior officer nearest the door heard movement on the other side and then spotted the handle moving. He signalled to the rest of the improvised fireteam, and as one, they raised their weapons ready to open fire on what they expected to be a team of Russian Spetsnaz soldiers.

'Hold your fire,' said Chisholm in a hushed and tense tone of voice. 'Wait for them to come through.'

After the door handle had moved fully to the unlocked position, the door began to open very slowly, as if the person opening it was trying to sneak through and gauge whether anyone was on the other side. A scared and sweating junior officer who was hiding on the other side of a doorway with his pistol aimed at the pressure door suddenly felt a salty bead of sweat run down into his eye. He blinked and quickly brought up one hand to wipe the sweat away, but as he did so he accidentally squeezed the trigger enough for a shot to go off. The noise was loud inside the narrow corridor, and immediately the other officers frantically opened fire thinking that the Spetsnaz team was about to come through the pressure door.

A hail of bullets smacked into the door and the area around it, several of them hitting pipes and wires to cause small electrical sparks to fly and the light in the corridor to flicker and dim slightly. Those that impacted the solid steel pressure door pinged off harmlessly and a few of them ricocheted off noisily in random directions.

After a few seconds, the firing stopped and small clouds of gunpowder smoke now wafted through the air in the corridor. The pressure door had been opened just a few centimetres, but no one had attempted to come through and there was only silence coming from the other side. Some of the junior officers were looking at each other nervously and reloading their weapons, while other were nodding each to each other believing that they had held off the Russian special forces assault.

Suddenly two grey cylindrical canisters that were roughly the size of beer cans dropped through the door and onto the floor, and then the pressure door was pulled shut. Before anyone could react, the canisters popped and plumes of dark grey smoke started billowing out violently amid a loud hissing sound, and making the canisters spin and move around on the metal floor of the corridor. Within seconds the entire corridor was so full of smoke that visibility was less than a metre, which meant that suddenly none of them could see the door. The thick smoke was also making several of the junior officers cough as they inhaled it.

'Open fire!' shouted one of them, clearly believing that the Russians would now be coming through.

A hail of bullets erupted from their guns, and those that had also carried shotguns began firing those as well. It was a deafening staccato cacophony of gunshots mixed with the metallic impact noises as the bullets smacked into the pressure door once more. It lasted at least twenty seconds before it gradually petered out. Chisholm had moved towards the back at that point, keeping his distance from the pressure door. Throughout the entire planning phase of this mission, the crew had always been regarded as expendable, and he was not about to play hero at this late stage. He was only partially inside the cloud of smoke, and in front of him, the fog was so thick that he could no longer see the pressure door. Most of the junior officers were now completely enveloped by the smoke. Chisholm backed up a few more steps. He was beginning to get a bad feeling about the situation.

At that moment the intruders opened the door silently, tossed through a flashbang and then closed the door again. The ear-splitting noise of the flashbang in such a small enclosed space was enough to stun every last one of the junior officers, and at that moment somewhere behind the thick veil of smoke, the pressure door swung open and McGregor's team came through. They were all wearing state-of-the-art night-vision goggles that can see through smoke. Unlike conventional night-vision goggles, the ones worn by McGregor's team used infrared thermal imaging technology. This meant that they were able to display a crisp image to the wearer of what the goggles see, even in the middle of the smoke from the smoke grenades.

At that moment, Chisholm turned on his heels and ran away down the corridor towards the nearest stairway. His own limited special forces training told him that this position was about to be overrun and that he needed to get back to the bridge and attempt to barricade it somehow. All he and Vandenberg needed were a few more seconds, and he was hoping the junior officers would be able to provide that.

Through ringing ears and blinded eyes from the flashbang, some of the disorientated junior officers began firing wildly at where they thought the intruders might be. Moving swiftly and as a coherent unit, McGregor's team came through the door and immediately opened fire with their suppressed HK53A3's taking down each of the hapless junior officers one by one within a matter of seconds. None of them took any pleasure in doing so, but it was a case of kill or be killed, and the stakes were simply too high. McGregor knew that there was no time to waste and that they would almost certainly be unable to convince these officers of who they were and what was really going on. The only thing that mattered was getting to the bridge as soon as possible and preventing Vandenberg from launching the missiles.

★   ★   ★

As the elevator came to a stop and its doors began to open, Andrew and Fiona were greeted by the loud whine of a turboshaft helicopter engine as well as the characteristic noise of rotor blades thudding rapidly through the air. When the doors opened fully, they realised that they were by the edge of a large circular hangar that was around fifty metres across and that had two small helicopters parked inside it. The two choppers were identical, but one of them on the far side of the hangar was spinning up its rotor blades and it had only one occupant inside. It was Dietrich, and he was sitting in the pilot's seat with a helmet on busily flicking switches and preparing the helicopter for take-off.

About five metres above them, the huge circular ceiling had split down the middle, and its two semi-circular halves were now parting and retracting into the sides of the hangar's walls. They looked to be at least three metres thick and made from reinforced concrete, and even through the noise from the helicopter engine, Andrew could hear the hydraulics systems straining to move their immense weight.

Dietrich's helicopter was almost ready for take-off, and the rotor blades were now spinning so fast that the individual blades became a blur of motion. A torrent of air was being whipped around inside the confined circular hangar space, and it was tugging at Andrew and Fiona's clothes as they stepped out of the elevator.

'We have to stop him!' shouted Fiona over the noise.

Andrew advanced towards the helicopter which was around thirty metres away, raising his MP5. Firing off short three-round bursts he was aiming at the glass canopy surrounding the pilot's seat, but the bullets smacked into the toughed glass and ricocheted off. Fiona also fired her pistol several times.

'No use!' shouted Fiona. 'Bulletproof glass.'

'I know! Shoot then engine!' shouted Andrew.

He aimed at a small grille high on the side of the helicopter which he guessed was an auxiliary air intake. He fired several bursts but the bullets did not penetrate the fuselage, which must also have been made of a toughened metal designed to be able to deal with small calibre bullets. The whine of the turboshaft engine increased significantly in pitch and volume, and then the helicopter lifted off from the pad.

As it took to the air and began to lift itself up and out of the hangar, Andrew ran forward switching his submachine gun to automatic. As he ran, he aimed up at the belly of the chopper and emptied his magazine, but it was no use. Dietrich had clearly had this helicopter fitted with enough protective plating to make it completely immune to small arms fire.

As the helicopter lifted clear of the hangar opening, it stopped ascending and entered a brief hover. Peering up at the cockpit, Andrew could see Dietrich reaching behind the pilot's seat to the passenger cabin, where he appeared to pick up something large. Then the door to the pilot's seat swung open, and immediately Dietrich extended an arm holding a small assault rifle and aiming it down at Andrew and Fiona.

'Take cover!' shouted Andrew and barged into Fiona, dragged her behind a small black and yellow-painted forklift used for handling cargo.

They both fell heavily in a heap onto the concrete floor as a hail of bullets peppered the area around the forklift, slamming into its engine and tyres and shattering the glass of its small cabin. Then the firing stopped, and the noise and pitch from the helicopter engine began to increase again. Wrestling free of Andrew with an incensed look on her face, Fiona moved up into a crouch and took cover behind the forklift while poking her head out to see what was happening. Dietrich had closed the door and the helicopter had resumed its ascent and was now slowly turning to a northerly heading.

The last thing Fiona saw before the helicopter pitched forward and began to accelerate away from the small hangar near the top of the mountain, was Dietrich giving her a small wave, a sickening smirk spread across his face. Fiona shrieked in fury, aimed her pistol and kept firing at the helicopter until the gun clicked several times. Then she looked back towards Andrew who was loading a fresh magazine into his submachine gun.

'Can you fly that thing?' shouted Fiona and pointed at the other helicopter parked around ten metres away.

Andrew didn't reply, and Fiona didn't bother to wait for him to do so. Instead, they both bolted for the chopper. Andrew quickly climbed into the pilot's seat and glanced at the dizzying array of controls on the panel above his head.

'Right,' he said. 'How hard can this be?'

★   ★   ★

The SAS team had taken no casualties in the fight with the junior officer crew of the USS Tennessee, and moving forward through the smoke with speed and momentum they had quickly made their way up a stairway towards the bridge whilst moving and covering each other as the well-trained and coherent unit they were.

Soon they found themselves at a closed and locked door to the bridge. The door was not a pressure door like the one leading to the missile compartment, but it was still designed to be able to withstand a complete flooding of the sail caused by a malfunctioning top hatch during a dive. Without hesitation and with no need for orders to be given, Dunn moved up and began fixing a breaching charge to the door. It only took a few seconds and then the team moved back a few metres and hugged the walls.

The detonation of the directed charge was thunderous inside the small space and it reverberated through the long corridors of the submarine, but the result of the explosion was instant. The door was blown off its hinges and flew into the room with such force that when it slammed into a terminal, it instantly flipped over and cartwheeled a couple of times whilst crashing noisily into the ceiling and one of the walls.

Almost instantly, Captain Vandenberg, Chisholm and two lieutenants called Hodges and Richards who had remained on the bridge, opened fire. They were crouched behind the improvised cover of the control consoles and the raised captain's chair, but their handguns would be no match for the heavily armed SAS team who had kept back a short distance in anticipation of the breaching charge detonating.

Suddenly a grenade landed with a metallic clonk at the feet of the SAS team. Using fragmentation grenades inside a submerged submarine was, for obvious reasons, an extremely risky thing to do. Even if the grenade did not have enough power to damage the hull, it could easily damage the vital systems of the submarine which could then compromise the crew's ability to control it.

As soon as he saw the grenade roll towards them, McGregor leapt forward onto the floor where it had come to a stop, grabbed it in his right hand and rolled once with his momentum carrying him forward. Then he hurled it back inside the bridge and scrambled for cover behind the doorway just as it hit the floor and exploded about a metre from Lieutenant Richards who had been crouching behind a terminal. Shrapnel tore through him, and one of the fragments shot through his head making him collapse in a heap on to the floor, small wisps of smoke rising from his body.

Dunn tossed a flashbang inside the bridge, and immediately after it detonated in a flash of brilliant white light, the SAS team swarmed through the doorway and rushed towards the remnants of the submarine's crew. Grant and Thompson had barely entered before they were across the room with their assault rifles up and ready to fire, descending on the temporarily stunned and blinded captain, XO and Lieutenant Hodges. Vandenberg and Chisholm were next to each other near the sonar console, and Hodges had been taking cover next to a doorway a couple of metres away.

'Drop your weapons!' shouted McGregor.

All three men were staggering slightly and looking disorientated as they dropped their guns onto the floor, having instinctively closed their eyes after the deafening and blinding detonation of the flashbang.

'Keep your hands where I can see them,' continued McGregor sternly.

Grant, Thompson and Wilks swarmed the small group and kept their weapons trained on them as McGregor spoke, ready to react if one of them decided to try to be clever.

After a few seconds, Captain Vandenberg was the first to open his eyes and scowl at the SAS team.

'Smart move,' he said blinking a couple of times, a hint of genuine admiration in his voice. 'This was the only contingency we never planned for.'

Lieutenant Hodges, still with his hands above his head, squinted and looked at the black-clad soldiers. He couldn't place the accent of their leader, but it didn't sound Russian. Then he noticed that the soldiers were carrying HK53s which are only used by NATO forces. Finally, he spotted the small Union Jack on their shoulders, just beneath an insignia with a winged dagger and a motto written in capital letters that said, *Who Dares Wins*.

Hodges, who was a stocky but athletic young man, instantly spun to his left to face Vandenberg and Chisholm with a furious look on his face. Grant, who had been restraining him by holding his arms, had to tighten his grip to keep him under control.

'These guys ain't Russians!' he yelled angrily. 'You fuckers lied to us. Why?'

An angry dark cloud seemed to form across Vandenberg's face. He was not used to being addressed in such a disrespectful way by a junior officer. He tilted his head to one side and pressed his lips together, and he was just on the cusp of saying something when McGregor interjected.

'Everyone, calm down!' he said sternly, raising his voice.

'You fucking bastard!' screamed the junior officer, ignoring McGregor and taking a step towards his two senior officers, rage burning in his eyes. 'All my guys are dead because of you. What the fuck is wrong with you two?'

Unable to contain his rage, Hodges suddenly wrestled himself free from Grant's grip and launched himself towards Vandenberg and Chisholm, looking as if he was about to tear into them barehanded.

In an instant, Chisholm had reached behind his back and pulled out another pistol that had been concealed there in his belt.

'Gun!' shouted Grant instinctively as he brought his weapon up again, but before he could fire, Chisholm had already shot Hodges twice, once in the neck and once in the head.

The body of the dead lieutenant had barely hit the metal floor before Grant and Thompson had opened fire, peppering Chisholm with bullets. As each bullet slammed into his torso he jerked and spasmed, staggering backwards with his arms flailing uncontrollably as the large calibre ammunition tore through him.

In the confusion, Vandenberg threw himself away from Chisholm through the air towards a console where a large red button had just lit up. While he was still airborne, McGregor brought up his assault rifle and fired two shots at the captain in quick succession, one hitting his shoulder and the other smacking into his abdomen.

However, the momentum of Vandenberg's body kept carrying him forward through the air, and with one arm outstretched he managed to reach the lit-up button and slam his hand down onto it forcefully.

As Chisholm's ruined body slumped to the floor in an unnatural heap, Vandenberg crashed into the console, dropped to the floor with a thump and lay still, breathing heavily and wincing from the pain of his gunshot wounds.

McGregor, still aiming his assault rifle at the captain, managed to take two rapid steps towards him when the whole submarine suddenly shuddered, and a distant but powerful rumbling sound reverberated through the bridge. After a couple of seconds, there was another shudder and then a third. Then there was silence.

'The missiles,' said McGregor stunned. 'You launched them!'

50 feet above the USS Tennessee, the calm waters of the Ionian Sea were suddenly broken by a huge four-storey tall missile that seemed to leap out of the water amid a violent gush of vapour and water. Having been expelled from its launch tube by a large volume of highly pressurised gas, the 59-tonne missile had shot to the surface in just over a second. As it penetrated the surface and continued up into the air it quickly lost almost all of its initial momentum, seemingly hovering in the air for a brief moment. Then the missile's rocket engine ignited, directing a powerful blast out of its nozzles which lifted the missile further up into the air and quickly accelerating it away from the roiling and steaming surface of the water.

Seconds later another missile appeared, and a couple of seconds later a third. The first missile quickly arced almost due west, the second made its way north and the third began a long journey towards the northeast.

As the three SLBMs accelerated and streaked inexorably upwards in slightly curved trajectories towards space, they quickly built up so much speed that a wispy white pressure wave formed at their tips, and just as they punched through a thin layer of cloud several thousand metres above the ocean, they went super-sonic and three powerful sonic booms could be heard rolling across the ocean like thunder.

Initially, the missiles would use their onboard inertial guidance systems to direct themselves in the right direction towards their intended targets, but once above the atmosphere and powering themselves further into space several hundred kilometres above the Earth, they would switch to their celestial guidance system. This system registers the positions of the stars in the sky and then determines a missile's precise location, after which it calculates the optimal flight path and adjusts the trajectory accordingly. GPS data is also used to refine the trajectory. Using this system, an intercontinental ballistic missile can hit a target as much as twelve thousand kilometres away with an accuracy of less than 100 metres.

Down inside the bridge of the USS Tennessee, McGregor rushed over to Vandenberg, grabbed his shirt with one hand and yanked him violently to a sitting position against the console.

'You crazy bastard!' yelled McGregor. 'Do you have any fucking idea what you've just done?'

Vandenberg winced and produced a wry, almost condescending smile.

'I am the commander of an Ohio-class submarine, son,' he said slowly with a pained expression on his face, clearly having to make an effort to say each word. 'Of course, I fucking know what I have done.'

He inhaled slowly and deeply a couple of times before continuing. 'I have given the world a chance to right itself.'

Then he slowly brought his right hand up to his chest, and only too late did McGregor see that he was holding a small black plastic transmitter with a button on it. Vandenberg looked up into McGregor's eyes with a stony look.

'Time to end this,' he said and pressed the button.

The explosive device he had placed next to the Mark 48 torpedo instantly detonated, and within a fraction of a second it triggered the torpedo's own

450-kilogram warhead. The blast ripped open the torpedo tube and then tore a giant gaping hole in both the inner and outer hull of the USS Tennessee.

The entire vessel shook violently, almost causing the members of the SAS team to lose their balance, forcing them to brace themselves against walls and the control consoles.

McGregor bared his teeth and gripped Vandenberg's shirt even more firmly, slamming him hard into the console.

'You're not taking me alive,' said Vandenberg with a defiant snarling grin on his face, his shirt now soaked in his own blood. 'I am not leaving. This is my boat.'

McGregor hesitated briefly but then gave Vandenberg an icy glare.

'You sick bastard,' he said coldly.

Then he jumped up and pointed behind him towards the doorway as violent hissing noises could be heard from two decks below where the air was rushing out and seawater was gushing into the submarine.

'Everybody out!' he shouted, swiftly backing away from Vandenberg. 'Back to the DSV. We are leaving!'

As his team began rushing out of the doorway and back towards the launch tube compartment, the floor began to tilt down slightly towards the front of the vessel. The USS Tennessee was sinking.

Twenty-Nine

'Have you ever flown one of these things,' asked Fiona as they opened the side doors and got into the small black Eurocopter EC120, Andrew in the pilot's seat and Fiona next to him in the co-pilot's seat.

'Kind of,' replied Andrew as he strapped himself in and looked up at the banks of switches on the panel above his head.

'That doesn't give me a lot of confidence,' said Fiona haltingly, glancing at him. 'What does that mean, exactly?'

Andrew flicked two switches, turned a dial and then pressed and held a button above him, after which the turboshaft engine fired up with a loud whine. At first, the rotors began spinning very slowly, but they quickly picked up speed to make the entire chopper vibrate.

'Once in Afghanistan I was part of a recon team waiting for extraction in a small valley,' said Andrew, checking the telemetry on the various dials to see if anything looked anomalous. 'The operation went south pretty quickly when the pilot was hit by incoming fire as he came in to land, so I had to take his place. But that was years ago and back then I had him in the co-pilot seat to instruct me.'

'Well, I guess we have no choice,' said Fiona resolutely as she strapped in. 'I hope you know what you're doing.'

They both donned the helmets that were hanging on hooks next to their seats, and Andrew opened up the communications channel to allow them to talk to each other. Even with the doors now closed, the noise from the engine was so loud that without the microphones and the headsets inside the helmets, they would have had to shout to each other to be heard.

Andrew went over the telemetry one more time as the main rotor reached its take-off revolution of around 450 RPMs. Everything looked nominal, so he leaned back in the seat and with his left hand grabbed the collective stick which controls the pitch angle of the rotor blades and thereby their lift. With his right hand, he gripped the cyclic which in a conventional aircraft would be called the flight stick. This controls the pitch of the helicopter, making it move forwards, backwards or to the side.

He pulled up gently on the collective, and immediately the helicopter lifted from the hangar floor and began to slowly ascend. Andrew was watching the instruments and trying to get a feel for the controls as the helicopter hovered above the hangar floor for a few seconds.

'Andrew!' yelled Fiona suddenly, her voice filled with panic. 'The hangar doors are closing!'

Having spent the past couple of minutes focused on the helicopter's instruments, Andrew's attention was immediately directed outside and up above him, where he could see the huge semi-circular hangar doors slowly begin to close. Unless he was able to get the helicopter up and out of the hangar quickly, the rotor blades would clip the closing concrete doors and send the chopper and the two of them crashing to the floor in a violent uncontrollable spin which they would be unlikely to survive.

Andrew pulled up hard on the collective and immediately he and Fiona were pushed down into their seats as the small chopper shot straight up into the air at the chopper's maximum climb rate of six metres per second. As they exited the hangar, they just missed the huge concrete doors as they slid out of their recesses and eventually sealed the hangar back up beneath them.

'Keep going straight up,' said Fiona. 'Look out for Dietrich's helicopter. He can't have gone far.'

As they ascended further, Andrew applied slight pressure to the left of the two pedals that control the tail rotor, making the helicopter spin slowly counter-clockwise as it rose higher and higher above the mountain. This allowed them both to scan the peaks and ridges around them to try to spot what would by now be a small dot several kilometres away.

'There!' shouted Fiona and pointed out to her side. 'Two o'clock. Just passing over that ridge.'

Andrew peered to where she was pointing, and he just caught sight of Dietrich's helicopter as it slipped up and over a snow-covered ridge a couple of kilometres to the northwest. Then it dipped down behind the ridge and disappeared. Dietrich already had a good head start, but now that they knew his heading, they could begin to guess what his intended destination was.

Andrew pitched the helicopter forward and increased the collective again, causing it to accelerate rapidly towards the ridge behind which Dietrich's chopper had just disappeared.

'He must be going for Greymouth Airfield,' he said. 'It's about a hundred kilometres north of here. He can make that run in just under thirty minutes.'

The small airfield services the town of Greymouth on the west coast of the South Island where the Grey River comes down from the valleys to the northeast and meets the Tasman Sea.

'He probably has an aircraft ready and waiting there,' said Fiona. 'If we don't get to it before he does, he will fly off in a jet and we won't be able to follow. And then we will probably never see or hear from him again.'

'Unless…' said Andrew pensively, and then he suddenly unbuckled his seatbelt. 'Take the controls!'

'What?' exclaimed Fiona. 'I can't fly this thing!'

'Just hold the collective up in this position,' said Andrew looking down at his left hand, 'and then use this stick to keep the nose pointing slightly down to maintain speed. The speed indicator is there. And this over here is the altimeter. Nudge the stick left or right to adjust our heading. It's easy once you get the hang of it.'

Fiona scowled at him for a moment, but then she relented.

'Alright, fine,' she said. 'What are you doing?'

'Just having a look in the back,' said Andrew and clambered out of his seat. 'I bet Dietrich has equipment in here for all eventualities.'

He squeezed between the two front seats and past Fiona, causing the helicopter to wriggle slightly to one side as he accidentally nudged her shoulder making his way past her.

'Sorry!' he shouted. 'It is a bit cramped in here.'

'Just get moving,' shouted Fiona. 'I might be able to keep flying straight for a bit, but if I have to land this thing then we'll both meet a fiery death.'

'You might not have to,' said Andrew as he headed into the passenger cabin which had just two seats.

He looked around inside it and discovered that beneath each of the seats were metal handles. He pulled hard on the one to the left and out came a deep drawer-like compartment full of different types of weapons all neatly inset into hard foam that perfectly fit their individual shapes. There were several pistols, revolvers, two combat shotguns and two assault rifles, as well as a large box of ammunition. Andrew almost grabbed the assault rifle, but then decided instead to pull at the handle underneath the other seat.

'Bingo!' he said to himself.

'What did you say?' asked Fiona.

Andrew looked back over his shoulder to where Fiona was sitting

'How are we doing?' he said. 'How far away is he now?'

'I think we're gaining on him,' replied Fiona. 'I don't think he realises we are trailing him. We might even catch up with him soon.'

'Good,' said Andrew. 'Keep it up. I think I've found something back here that we can use.'

He reached into the second compartment and pulled out an FIM-92 Stinger missile launcher. Next to it were three missiles neatly packed into the cut-out foam. He extracted one of them and inserted it into the launcher from the back. Then he extracted the cylindrical argon gas cooling unit from its foam compartment under the seat and slotted it up into the launcher.

'Fiona,' he shouted. 'Things are about to become slightly unorthodox.'

'I don't like the sound of that,' said Fiona, quickly glancing behind her. 'What do you mean?'

'There's an anti-aircraft launcher back here,' he replied. 'A Stinger. It uses an infrared targeting system, so I think I can take down Dietrich's helicopter with it. But there's a catch.'

'There always is,' said Fiona. 'What?'

'We need to get close,' replied Andrew, 'and then I will need to open the door.'

'Ok?' responded Fiona, not quite able to imagine what Andrew had in mind. 'Is that a problem?'

'Well,' said Andrew. 'The doors are hinged at the front, so I can't open them in flight. The force of the wind will slam them shut again. I will need to find a way to remove the door somehow. Things might get noisy back here.'

'Can't you just smash the window?' asked Fiona.

'Huh,' responded Andrew, sounding impressed and a little bit surprised. 'That's not a bad idea.'

He reached for one of the two SPAS-12 shotguns. Manufactured by the Italian company Franchi, the black folding stock all metal and rubber weapon fires 12-gauge ammunition and can hold six shells in its internal magazine plus one in the chamber. It is capable of being used both as a classic pump-action shotgun as well as a semi-automatic weapon.

Andrew loaded the magazine with shells, and then he placed himself on the seat behind Fiona pointing the shotgun across the other passenger seat towards the door.

'I am shooting out the window,' said Andrew. 'It's going to be loud.'

'Ok,' replied Fiona. 'Just do what you…'

The powerful shotgun going off was like a small controlled explosion inside the cabin, and Fiona jumped in her seat making the helicopter momentarily swerve to one side. Instantly, cold mountain air whirled inside the cabin, and through the cyclic, she could sense the helicopter now feeling slightly different because of the subtle change in its aerodynamics.

'Jesus!' she shouted and looked over her shoulder to see a gaping hole where one of the passenger windows had been. 'Are you done?'

'Yup,' said Andrew and slotted the shotgun back into its foam cut-out. 'That should do it. Now we just need to get close.'

'I seem to have lost a bit of speed now,' said Fiona. 'Should I be worried?'

'No,' replied Andrew. 'There is increased drag on the chopper now that the window is missing, but she is still perfectly airworthy. Just keep closing the distance. How far away is he now?'

'Maybe six or seven hundred metres,' said Fiona. 'I am not great with distances, but we're a lot closer now than we were a few minutes ago.'

'Alright,' said Andrew. 'Once we get to within five hundred metres, I want you to keep this heading, but press down slightly on the right tail rotor pedal. This should make us fly slightly sideways and give me a clear shot at him.'

'Alright,' replied Fiona. 'I'll try.'

Andrew sat back on the seat and placed the Stinger on his lap, prepping and disarming it and switching on the infrared target acquisition system. Then he slid over to the other seat next to where the small window had been.

'Almost there,' shouted Fiona after another couple of minutes. 'We're about to leave the mountains so he might start to descend soon.'

'That's fine,' said Andrew. 'Just stay on him.'

'Ok,' said Fiona. 'Ready?'

'Ready,' replied Andrew and brought the launcher up onto his right shoulder and poked the end of it through the window where the onrushing air immediately began tugging at it. 'Oh, and one more thing.'

'What?' she asked.

'There's going to be a lot of smoke in here when I fire.'

'Great,' replied Fiona sarcastically. 'Just don't miss, ok?'

'I'll do my best,' replied Andrew.

Just then Dietrich's helicopter crested a ridge and began dropping down through a rocky snow-covered valley. Fiona pitched the helicopter forward even further and it soon followed Dietrich's trajectory into the valley, but unlike Dietrich, Fiona did not let up on the cyclic and so she kept gaining on him.

'Three seconds,' she shouted.

'Ok,' replied Andrew and engaged the target acquisition system, which produced a rapidly pulsing single tone.

'Now!' shouted Fiona and began pressing down firmly on the left pedal.

The tail of the helicopter immediately stepped out to the left, causing the chopper to keep flying forward but partly side-on. This gave Andrew the opportunity to look through the sight and allow the Stinger to acquire its target. The pulsing sound from the launcher became a constant high-pitched tone, and through the target acquisition optics, Andrew was shown a flashing X overlaid on the enlarged image of Dietrich's helicopter. The missile was now locked on.

He squeezed the trigger and amid a loud and violent rush of air and smoke, the Stinger shot out of the launcher and almost instantly accelerated away towards its target, leaving Andrew and Fiona in a cloud of smoke inside the cabin.

The smoke quickly dissipated, and a couple of hundred metres away they could see the small but deadly missile streaking through the air at several hundred metres per second, leaving a neat trail of smoke from its small rocket engine behind it.

Almost as soon as they spotted it out of the front of the helicopter, the missile slammed into the tail rotor of Dietrich's helicopter and exploded with the force of about five hand grenades. The tail rotor immediately disintegrated with pieces of it flying off in all directions. The tail rotor's only purpose is to counteract the natural torque effect of the main rotor which constantly wants to try to spin the body of the helicopter in the opposite direction, so as soon as Dietrich's helicopter lost its tail rotor it began turning left. As it did so it rapidly lost speed which in turn allowed it to turn faster, and within a few seconds, it was spinning uncontrollably and losing altitude. The engine was now on fire and thick black smoke was billowing out of the back.

'Look,' shouted Fiona. 'He's getting out.'

Ahead of them less than a hundred metres away now, they could see Dietrich trying to open the door next to the pilot's seat.

'He might have a parachute,' said Andrew.

The cockpit of the stricken chopper was now full of thick smoke. As it kept losing altitude faster and faster, they watched as Dietrich managed to push the door open and get out of the cockpit to stand on the helicopter's metal landing struts. He looked like he was about to leap off when suddenly the fuel tank must have ruptured because in an instant Dietrich and the chopper were enveloped in a huge fireball. The force of the explosion threw Dietrich's flaming body out and away from the helicopter, and he continued to be enveloped by fire as he plummeted towards the ground where he eventually impacted among the rocks with such force that it produced a small cloud of smoke and dust.

As the thundering noise from the explosion rolled through the valley, the burning debris from the now almost completely disintegrated helicopter began falling all over the small ravine where Dietrich had landed, and a couple of seconds later the mangled and flaming main body of the chopper slammed down onto the rocks, producing a large plume of smoke as it continued to burn.

Andrew slipped back to the pilot's seat and strapped back in. Then he took control of the helicopter again. None of them said anything as he circled the impact site a couple of times, watching the smoke rising up into the crisp mountain air.

'Let's head to Greymouth,' Andrew finally said.

'Good idea,' replied Fiona, looking slightly shell-shocked at what had transpired. 'Perhaps we can refuel there and then make it back to Auckland via Wellington.'

'I just hope Strickland's plan worked out,' said Andrew grimly. 'This might not be over yet.'

★ ★ ★

The GEO-4 satellite is part of the Space-Based Infrared System or SBIRS, which is operated by the United States Space Force. Holding a fixed position relative to Earth in its geosynchronous orbit 35,786 kilometres above Europe, it is on permanent watch looking down on the European continent.

The SBIRS network of satellites covers the entire surface of the Earth and is able to instantly pinpoint missile launches by using its extremely sensitive infra-red sensors to recognise and track the distinct heat signature of a missile being launched. This includes standard cruise missiles, hypersonic missiles and ICBMs, and the system is able to detect missiles regardless of whether they have been launched from aircraft, ground-based launch systems, or naval platforms such as submarines.

As soon as the sensors picked up the three heat signatures blooming up inside Greek territorial waters, the infra-red sensors fed the data via highly encrypted channels to the early warning command centre inside of NORAD, aka the North American Aerospace Defence Command at Peterson Space Force Base in Colorado.

On the computer display in front of one of the 6 junior watch officers manning the monitoring stations, a small bright diamond-shaped symbol was lighting up 75 kilometres southwest of Greece amid an insistent-sounding electronic warning. Two seconds later another appeared and then another.

'Sir,' said the officer urgently to the Space Force Major who was in charge of the command centre that day. 'We have a possible launch of three SLBMs from a location in the Ionian Sea, 75 kilometres from the Greek coast.'

The major hurried over and leaned in towards the display.

'On screen,' he said, and immediately the junior officer mirrored the image on his display onto the large screen occupying the entire wall in front of them.

'Additional information is starting to come in,' said the junior officer.

'Speed of those missiles?' asked the major as he stepped back and looked up intently at the huge map of Europe where the three small glowing diamonds were moving slowly along their trajectories.

'Accelerating past Mach 2 already,' replied the junior officer. 'They've entered boost phase.'

'Alert CentCom,' said the major tensely to another officer sitting next to him. 'What else do we know so far?'

'Naval assets in the area observed the launch, and indications are that it was the USS Tennessee. This is corroborated by the acceleration profiles. It looks like three Trident II missiles.'

'Jesus!' breathed the major tensely. 'Targets?'

'Running trajectory analysis now,' replied the junior officer, now beginning to perspire as the realisation of what was unfolding was beginning to hit him. 'Preliminary estimates indicate intended targets are Washington DC, Moscow and Beijing.'

'Get the Russians on the deconfliction line asap!' he said urgently. 'Tell them this is a rogue launch. Same with the Chinese.'

Then he brought his hand up and wiped the sweat from his brow.

'They'd better not retaliate,' he said to no one in particular, 'or we'll all be burnt to ashes in about thirty minutes. ETA?'

'Estimate 9 minutes, sir.'

The major exhaled heavily.

'Sir,' said the junior officer, now sounding anxious. 'We have detected a missile launch from the Russian Federation.'

The major's face turned white as he looked up at the wall display to watch as a small red diamond appear near the Russian border with Belorussia.

Is this the end? He thought and swallowed hard.

'Target?' he said, trying to remain calm.

'Unclear,' said the junior officer, a perplexed look on his face. 'It looks like it might be on an intercept course with the Trident missile heading towards Moscow. It is accelerating at an extremely fast rate. Hypersonic. Intercept in less than one minute.'

'Sir,' said another officer. 'CentCom are activating missile defence assets along the Eastern Seaboard. The Navy's ballistic missile defence systems are also spun up and ready to intercept.'

'And the missile heading for Beijing?' asked the major.

'Now over Turkish territory,' replied the junior officer. '600 kilometres down-range. Mach 6. Going exo-atmospheric now.'

'Twenty seconds to intercept of the missile heading for Moscow,' said the other junior officer nervously.

The entire room watched as the red diamond and one of the white diamonds converged somewhere over northern Romania. The major pressed his lips together as the two met, and then he felt sick to his stomach as he watched them both continue on their trajectories past each other.

'Russian interceptor failed,' the junior officer called out, his voice trembling slightly.

'Oh god,' breathed the major and closed his eyes. 'They missed.'

★   ★   ★

Near the town of Zhukovka in Bryansk Oblast in western Russia about 60 kilometres from Belorussia and almost 400 kilometres southwest of Moscow, a concrete structure built in the middle of a large clearing inside a forest suddenly came to life having seemed completely dormant for several years. Surrounded by tall barbed-wire fences and minefields, the only access to the building was through a heavily guarded gate, but no one ever entered or exited the concrete structure. It was remotely operated by the ballistic missile defence directorate of the Army of the Russian Federation and housed a new top secret anti-ICBM system.

Amid the loud noise from a klaxon, the roof of the concrete structure seemed to split down the middle and the two halves retracted. Then a large dark grey turreted contraption the size of a bus emerged and continued moving upwards on a platform that eventually positioned it just above the top of the trees.

Within seconds the whole machine rotated, making the turret swing around and point towards the southwest. The stocky-looking turret itself was around ten metres long and did not resemble any type of conventional weapon. It was the result of a highly classified project to develop an electromagnetic railgun, and during its testing phase, it had demonstrated its ability to shoot down incoming missiles travelling at many times the speed of sound.

It worked by using electromagnets to accelerate projectiles to Mach 14, or more than seventeen thousand kilometres per hour. Activating a series of extremely powerful magnets in a rapid and perfectly timed sequence along the rail, the elongated aerodynamic projectile would be pulled ever faster along and thereby be accelerated rapidly to incredible speeds, without the need for rocket engines as is the case with most conventional weapons.

Amid the whirring sound of hydraulic actuators, the turret began moving slowly as it tracked slightly ahead of the incoming Trident II missile which at this point was just over the horizon. As soon as the railgun had a line of sight on the missile, the turret shuddered violently and produced a loud metallic-sounding twang as the first projectile was accelerated along the rail in an instant. Less than half a second later the railgun fired again, and so it continued with the gun hurtling metal projectiles up towards the incoming missile at such speeds that they became super-heated at their tips. As it fired, the turret began to arc gradually upwards as the missile approached on its exo-atmospheric trajectory. However, the closer the missile got to the weapon, the less the turret had to compensate for its movement, making it increasingly likely that one of the projectiles would hit it.

After thirty projectiles had been fired, the turret was pointing upwards at an angle of about 65 degrees, and it was about to begin swivelling to keep tracking the missile when a bright flash appeared overhead some 80 kilometres above the forest. One of the projectiles had impacted the body of the missile just before the MIRVed warheads were about to separate from it.

Because of the almost unimaginable speeds involved, the kinetic energy of the metal projectile was of such a magnitude that it evaporated instantly in a cloud of superheated gas when it impacted the missile above the atmosphere. The missile, which itself had been travelling at almost thirty thousand kilometres per hour, was ripped to pieces and what remained of it spun wildly out of control. It began to disintegrate increasingly rapidly as it re-entered the atmosphere where it experienced more and more drag, causing so much friction that it began to burn up as it decelerated.

The warhead housing had split open and separated from the missile, but the guidance system was no longer being fed location data from the sensor suite. This meant that it was now unable to ascertain its position and so none of the individual warheads would now be able to separate from the missile and detonate.

Roughly three minutes later the warhead housing slammed into the boggy ground about a hundred metres from a herd of grazing cows where it buried itself five metres into the soft soil making the cows jump with fright. As pieces of mud rained down and steam began to rise from the impact site, the cows glared at the strange phenomenon for a few seconds. Then they continued chewing their grass.

* * *

170 kilometres southwest of Ireland, the sleek Arleigh Burke-class guided-missile destroyer USS Bainbridge had been cutting its way through the waves and steaming east towards the United States when it had received the missile tracking data for the Washington-bound missile from NORAD in Colorado. The destroyer was equipped with a large arsenal of different weapons to combat threats from the air and the sea, and it had been part of the same naval exercise as the USS Tennessee a couple of weeks earlier. It had been on its way back towards Naval Station Norfolk in Virginia when the high-priority message from CentCom had arrived, and immediately the captain had ordered all hands to battle stations.

Now, at the fire control console inside the ship's tactical command centre, the weapons operator was preparing for the order to launch. The target, the Trident II missile launched from the USS Tennessee, would be passing overhead some 230 kilometres to the south of the Bainbridge's current position, as it made its way above the atmosphere towards Washington DC at Mach 24.

'Fire control,' said the Tactical Weapons Officer. 'Select SM-3. VLT number 6.'

The weapons operator selected the RIM-161 Standard Missile 3 sitting in Vertical Launch Tube 6, and loaded the flight path that had been calculated based on the observed trajectory of the Trident II missile. The SM-3 is specifically designed to shoot down ICBMs during the midcourse stage of their flight.

'SM-3 selected,' said the weapons operator. 'Target locked. Ready to fire.'

Outside on the front deck of the ship, the roughly one-square-metre hatch for VLT 6 popped open with the tip of the missile just visible inside the launch tube.

'On my command,' said the Tactical Weapons Officer, waiting until the SLBM had entered the optimal window for launch of the SM-3. 'Launch!'

The weapons operator pressed the launch button, and instantly a virtual geyser of orange flames and grey smoke billowed violently up and out of the launch tube on the front deck as the SM-3's rocket engine ignited. A split second later the 1.5 tonne, 6-metre-long missile shot out of the launch tube and instantly tilted slightly to the south as it accelerated upwards towards its maximum speed of Mach 18 or around 5 kilometres per second. It soon left a thick trail of grey exhaust as it arced gradually, manoeuvring itself towards the intended interception point which was over a thousand kilometres ahead of where the Trident II missile was currently located. As the SM-3 missile continued upwards, it established a link with the USS Bainbridge and was then continuously fed updated data about the exact location of the Trident II missile, adjusting its course constantly to ensure that it would end up being in the exact same location at the exact same time as the Trident II.

The objective of shooting down a missile with a missile has been likened to trying to hit a bullet with another bullet. The difference in this case was that the missiles were both travelling around ten times faster than a bullet, and that the target was following a parabolic trajectory around the Earth as opposed to a straight line. Another important difference was that the intercepting missile had the ability to continue to adjust its course almost until the moment of impact.

At an altitude of just over one thousand kilometres when the two missiles were approaching the intercept point at just over forty thousand kilometres per hour, the tip of the SM-3 missile split open and the two payload fairings folded outwards to reveal a spherical cluster of small metal cubes packed tightly together. This was the so-called 'kill vehicle'. At this point the distance to the Trident II was around 350 kilometres, which meant that the SM-3 was less than thirty seconds from the intercept point.

A couple of seconds later the kill vehicle detached from the missile and another two seconds later the sphere seemed to disintegrate as the cluster of small metal cubes moved out slowly from its centre to form an expanding spherical cloud of metal cubes. Over the next twenty seconds the sphere kept expanding until its diameter was roughly fifty metres across.

Each cube weighed less than one hundred grams, but when the Trident II rammed through the cloud it collided with two of them. Because of the extreme amount of kinetic energy involved, the solid form of the metal cubes instantly converted into gas as they made contact with the tip of the Trident, and a few millionths of a second later they tore through the missile, making it rip open and explode in a huge fireball travelling at almost thirty thousand kilometres per hour. Another cloud of super-heated gases shot out in the direction the SM-3 had been travelling, as that missile's booster ripped through the metal and gas cloud at Mach 18.

'Kill confirmed,' exclaimed the weapons operator on board the USS Bainbridge. 'Fuck yeah!'

He then looked apologetically at the tactical weapons officer. 'Sorry about the language, sir,' he said sheepishly. 'I got carried away.'

The officer placed his hand on the weapons officer's shoulder and smiled.

'That's alright, son,' he said empathetically. 'We just saved the lives of two million people. I think we can allow ourselves a few cuss words today.'

THIRTY

On an arid desert plain near the town of Xinhaote in Inner Mongolia some 450 kilometres north of Beijing, the secluded and secret base belonging to the People's Liberation Army had sudden sprung to life. At any given time, it was manned by less than twenty people, most of them service personnel, and on most days anyone arriving there along the 20-kilometre dirt road that led to the facility would have been able to see virtually no activity behind the multiple layers of barbed wire fences and armed guard posts. Nondescript featureless buildings and what appeared to be a huge spherical radar dome was all that was visible at the dusty windswept site, and whoever operated the facility were always ensconced inside the main building which contained living quarters, restaurants, leisure facilities and the control centre.

What happened next had only happened twice before in the history of the facility, and both of those occasions had been tests. The radar dome split open and the sides folded back partially, origami-style, to reveal what appeared very similar to the astronomical telescopes that are placed on mountaintops throughout the world and that are designed to peer up into the night sky at stars and galaxies many light years away.

But this was no telescope. This was a directed energy weapon developed in secret by the PLA, and designed to eliminate aerial threats at long ranges and high speeds such as ICBMs. The stocky twelve-metre cylinder that constituted the main body of the device was painted white and sat on a circular platform which rotated. Amid the loud whirring of electric high-precision actuators, the platform began rotating the cylinder towards the northwest and at the same time the cylinder itself began slowly tracking an object that was 700 kilometres away but approaching at nearly twenty-four times the speed of sound. Beneath the facility, an enormous high-energy capacitor bank was gradually being spooled up from an equally impressive array of batteries that in turn was powered by a small nuclear reactor inside an underground bunker nearby.

Using targeting data from multiple sources, including ground-based radar stations, airborne surveillance aircraft and a number of military satellites, the weapon's targeting system gradually refined the orientation of the electromagnetic emitter inside the large white cylinder. Suddenly it produced an extremely loud warbling noise that lasted for just under two seconds, and which seemed to reverberate around the entire facility and rush out across the desert plain. After a pause of around one second, the capacitors were ready to deliver another burst of energy which the emitter again converted into an electromagnetic pulse which shot out of the cylinder in a highly concentrated and directed beam travelling at the speed of light.

Around 460 kilometres away, the invisible but highly energetic electromagnetic pulse slammed into the Trident II missile instantly overwhelming the warhead's EM shielding and overloading the electronic circuits inside the guidance system. Its small electronic capacitors and transistors exploded and its circuit boards melted. After a barrage of three bursts from the directed energy weapon, the Trident II had been reduced to an inert collection of metal and fried electronic components, but with a MIRV still sitting inside the missile housing. As it began its re-entry into the atmosphere without a guidance system, it quickly spun out of control and disintegrated, breaking up somewhere over the border with Mongolia and plummeting towards the enormous and virtually unpopulated desert plains below. Here, after several minutes, the MIRV smacked into the ground, creating a huge cloud of yellow dust and sand. The impact was powerful but nowhere near enough to trigger a nuclear explosion. Only a controlled detonation of a nuclear warhead will cause a chain reaction, so none of the 12 MIRVed warheads exploded. As the dust settled, two military helicopters with specialist teams were already in the air and en route to recover the remnants of the missile for study by PLA researchers.

★   ★   ★

Aboard the USS Tennessee, McGregor, Dunn, Wilks, Grant and Thompson were sprinting along the corridor to the missile tube compartment, the sound of their heavy boots hitting the metal floor echoing along the corridor. As they went, they had the distinct sensation of running increasingly upwards on a slight incline. They barged through the pressure door and scrambled up the rungs of handles inside the false launch tube that led to the DSV hangar where Martinez and Jackson were waiting anxiously, wide-eyed with looks of near-panic on their faces.

'What the hell is happening?' shouted Martinez.

'Close the hatch!' ordered McGregor quickly, ignoring the question. 'Grant. Thompson. Provide breathers for these two gentlemen. Dunn, get to the door and prepare to open. The Tennessee is sinking, so time is against us.'

McGregor switched on the pump system and the hangar compartment immediately began to flood as cold seawater was pumped in and air was vented out. Grant and Thompson pulled out small short-duration underwater re-breathers that would allow them to breathe under water for up to five minutes and handed them to Martinez and Jackson. Dunn quickly made his way to the large circular door at the end of the SDV hangar and waited for McGregor's signal. On the pressure gauge next to the pump controls, McGregor watched as the pressure increased beyond 1 atmosphere and kept climbing. At their current depth, the 30-metre water column bearing down on the Tennessee created a pressure outside of the hangar of almost 3 atmospheres, but with the torpedo room now flooded and the submarine beginning to sink, the outside water pressure was steadily increasing and therefore pressing in on the hangar door making it impossible for Dunn to push it open.

'Almost 4 atmospheres now,' shouted McGregor towards Dunn. 'Try it.'

Dunn pushed as hard as he could but the door didn't budge. Then Grant and Thompson rushed over to help try to push the door open. Dunn turned to McGregor and shook his head.

McGregor increased the pump speed to maximum, and through the sound of the water rushing into the hangar compartment, he could hear the pumps straining to try to outrun the speed with which the submarine was sinking. Unless the pumps could catch up and increase the internal pressure beyond that of the outside so that the door could be opened, they would be dragged down with the submarine to a watery grave.

McGregor then decided to hit the switch to close the hangar valves and thereby stop air from being expelled in tandem with the water coming in. He hoped that this would more rapidly increase the pressure inside the hangar. However, it would have the downside of the hangar being only half full when the doors opened, but at this point that was of no concern. All that mattered now was to get that door open.

Indicating to Martinez and Jackson to help the team push against the door, McGregor glanced again at the pressure gauge. It was reading over five bars, which meant that the submarine now had to be below fifty metres. Putting the regulator in his mouth as the last of the team to do so, he waded over to the door and joined the others who were already straining against the large metal door. It still would not budge.

Putting his shoulder against the door, McGregor saw Jackson out of the corner of his eye place one large hand on the end of the DSV and using it as fixed support, and the other hand on the metal door. Then he pushed with all his strength against both. Grimacing to the point where McGregor thought the big man was about to bite through the mouthpiece of his rebreather, Jackson's bulging arm muscles strained and looked as if they were about to make the sleeves of his shirt burst open. Behind them, the noise from the ever more strained pumps continued to increase in pitch as they attempted to match the internal pressure with that of the outside.

Suddenly the door burst open, and all of them were pulled out into the cold water of the ocean along with the DSV and the air that had occupied roughly twenty percent of the hangar's interior by the time the pressure finally equalised. Temporarily at the mercy of the rush of air and water, the team quickly re-orientated themselves, and Grant and Thompson grabbed hold of Martinez and Jackson and began pulling them towards the surface some 65 metres above them.

McGregor remained in place for a few seconds to make sure that everyone was well underway to the surface, and that none of them was in any sort of trouble. Before he began making his way to the surface himself, he looked down.

Against a dark blue background, the giant nuclear submarine continued its gradual descent. It looked almost calm and serene, but McGregor understood what awaited the submarine and its one occupant now that it was sinking. Below it was a drop of more than five thousand metres to the seabed. They were currently over the Vavilov Hole, which at its maximum depth is 5272 metres below the surface, where the pressure is over five hundred times that at the ocean's surface. The USS Tennessee was doomed, and so was its captain.

★ ★ ★

On the bridge of the USS Tennessee, Captain Vandenberg had crawled along the tilting floor to his captain's seat and dragged himself up. Gripping the armrests and with a resolute look on his face, he was staring straight ahead, but his eyes registered nothing. He had managed to engage the multiple automatic pressure doors between the now flooded torpedo room and the rest of the ship, theoretically maintaining the internal hull's integrity, at least up to a point. He looked around the bridge for a few moments, in his mind's eye able to see the familiar sight of it being manned by his submariners.

A loud metallic noise of the hull straining and creaking under the increasing pressure sounded through the submarine. It had been fifteen minutes since the SAS team had dashed for the DSV tube, and the submarine was rapidly approaching the limit of its ability to resist the mounting crush of the deep ocean.

The creaking grew louder and more rapid and urgent, and Vandenberg now sensed that this was the end. This was now as much as the Tennessee would be able to take. He closed his eyes for a few moments, taking a deep breath and then he exhaled slowly.

'Carrie,' he whispered. 'I'm coming.'

At that moment the structural integrity of the already damaged submarine finally failed and the internal hull collapsed in a powerful and almost instant implosion. The crush could be heard for hundreds of miles and was picked up by the network of hydrophones spread across the Mediterranean. Then followed the sounds of the submarine's individual compartment buckling and the noise from various parts of the vessel being squeezed until they gave way to the irresistible pressure.

It took the mangled remains of the USS Tennessee just over forty minutes to travel the more than five kilometres straight down until it finally reached the pitch-black bottom of the Vavilov Hole. Here it impacted the seabed slowly but heavily, and then it slumped down lazily into its final resting place and moved no more.

★ ★ ★

Three days later, Andrew and Fiona were sitting in the Orbit restaurant at the top of Sky Tower in Auckland. As it rotated slowly, it gave them a full 360-degree view of New Zealand's capital and its surrounding suburbs. They had booked a table by the window intending to have an early dinner before their late-night flight back to London, and enjoy the view of the capital from 328 metres above street level. Every ten seconds the restaurant would rotate almost imperceptibly one degree clockwise, affording them a complete view of the entire city and the horizon beyond it every hour.

Fiona was looking out of the slightly tilted floor-to-ceiling windows with her elbows on the edge of the table and her head resting in the palms of her hands seemingly lost in thought.

'Are you ok?' asked Andrew gently. 'What are you thinking?'

Fiona blinked a couple of times, shaking her head slightly as if to pull herself back to reality.

'Oh,' she said, smiling at him and gesturing to the scenery outside the window. 'It just seems completely surreal to me that if Dietrich's plan had actually been carried out, this right here would have been ground zero for his new civilisation, pardon the expression.'

'Well, we stopped him,' replied Andrew. 'Us, Lynch, McGregor and his team, and everyone else who stepped up and did what needed to be done.'

'Is McGregor alright?' asked Fiona. 'What happened with them?'

'They're back at Hereford,' nodded Andrew. 'They only just managed to escape from the submarine, and then they were picked up by one of the NATO ships in the area and taken to the mainland.'

'And Lynch?' she asked.

'He's fine,' replied Andrew. 'Still sounds a bit croaky on the phone, but the doctors say he will make a full recovery.'

'And what about all the people who were in on this whole thing?' asked Fiona. 'People like that Hurley character. There are hundreds of people who understood full well what the ultimate goal of Dietrich's insane project was.'

'We are already in the process of beginning to round them up,' replied Andrew. 'Both we and the Americans believe that we have rooted out Dietrich's network within our intelligence services, armed forces and police forces. Once we obtained all the data from the ARK including long and detailed lists of people who were affiliated with him, it was straightforward to unravel the whole thing. There were a lot of them though. We might have to build a couple more prisons to house them all. It is terrifying how deep this conspiracy ran. They almost pulled it off.'

'It was close,' nodded Fiona. 'Too close.'

'Yes, but it's over now,' said Andrew, taking a sip of his wine.

'This time perhaps,' said Fiona, somewhat ruefully. 'In the long arc of history, there have been countless men like Dietrich who have tried to take power and been completely ruthless in their pursuit, with calamitous consequences for thousands or even millions of people. Julius Caesar was such a man, Dietrich more or less tried to emulate him and there is no doubt in my mind that it is a question of time before someone else tries to do it again.'

'Perhaps you are right,' said Andrew, leaning back in his chair. 'All we can do is fight back, and try to prevent that much power from ending up in the hands of one or two individuals like that again. I am pretty sure the U.S. Navy is going to overhaul its nuclear launch command procedures after this, and other countries will be following suit, I am sure. This will be a case study for decades in how *not* to do things.'

'Well, yes,' said Fiona dubiously, 'But eventually there will be some new super weapon which will be open to the same type of abuse from the same kinds of people. Nuclear weapons are just one of many with that potential, and who knows what humans will invent in the future?'

'In my line of work, I know that better than anyone,' said Andrew. 'But let's cross that bridge when we get to it.'

'You know,' said Fiona after a brief pause. 'I read quite a chilling anecdote from the Trinity Test in 1945. Apparently, Enrico Fermi the nuclear physicist who later invented the world's first nuclear reactor, and who was present that day, along with a number of other prominent physicists, offered wagers to a group of scientists about whether the nuclear chain reaction caused by the Trinity Test would ignite the atmosphere of the Earth and incinerate the entire planet. Apparently, at the time it was believed to have a very small likelihood of actually happening, but no one knew for certain whether that might actually occur. I think that gives us a glimpse into how uncertain the future is for our species. For as long as our best minds employ their abilities in that fashion, I am not sure there is much reason to be optimistic for our collective future in the very long term. Of course, the ultimate irony in that story is that this was the man who later gave name to the so-called Fermi-paradox. As you might know, it basically poses the question: If there is intelligent life in the universe, where is everyone? And I think that one of the most obvious answers could be that as soon as a civilisation becomes sufficiently technologically advanced, it quickly ends up wiping itself out, quite possibly with nuclear weapons.'

Andrew smiled at Fiona before replying.

'I suppose it has been possible to employ that line of thinking throughout human history,' he said. 'Every new invention carries with it the potential for abuse. But we can't let ourselves be ruled by fear of the future. Death is coming for us all eventually.'

He paused.

'That reminds me of something a former platoon commander of mine used to say. *"You can't outrun death forever, but you can make the bastard work for it."*'

Fiona smiled.

'Very funny,' she said. 'But I suppose there is a lot of truth in that. I guess all we can do is try to make the most of the time we have, and perhaps not worry so much about a future that might never even happen.'

'I think we agree there,' smiled Andrew and looked out over Auckland Harbour. 'The sun is about to go down. In another couple of rotations, we should be able to see it set over there to the northwest beyond the harbour.'

Fiona lifted her wine glass calmly off the table, swirled the red wine around a couple of times and looked at Andrew.

'Well,' she smiled. 'I'm not going anywhere.'

THE END

Epilogue

The U.S. Navy ROV was stationary just metres above the mangled wreck of the USS Tennessee. In the ink-black darkness, a bright cone of light from the submersible's floodlights was illuminating a section of the sail that had remained more or less intact. The ROV had been launched from a U.S. Navy ship whose mission was to ascertain the levels of damage to the critical systems of the USS Tennessee. Specifically, it had been tasked with measuring radioactivity levels around the reactor compartment, in order to determine whether the reactor had ruptured during the implosion of the submarine, and might now be in the process of leaking radioactive material into the sea at the bottom of the Vavilov Hole.

This was part of the initial stages of a wider effort to secure and salvage as much of the submarine as possible, not least to ensure the recovery of the remaining 21 Trident II missiles that were still on board the vessel, lest they fall into the hands of adversaries or terrorists.

At this depth, a given volume of air was one-fifth of one percent of what it would have been at the surface more than five kilometres above, so any sealed compartment or container on board the submarine had imploded at various points during the long descent towards the seabed. For this reason, there were large amounts of debris strewn across a huge area surrounding the sunken submarine, most of it mangled metal and parts of machinery. However, here and there, objects that had belonged to human beings lay scattered. Clothes, books, tools and a couple of chairs and pieces of wooden lockers and beds.

Over the course of around fifteen minutes, the ROV completed almost a full orbit around the wreckage performing a visual inspection and carefully tracking the reading on the onboard Geiger counter. Suddenly, the operator spotted something that stood out against the dark grey and silty seabed. He twisted the control stick in his right hand which pushed the ROV's rudder out and slewed the vehicle to one side. With his left hand, he pulled back slightly on the throttle to slow it down. As it slowly turned, the ROV followed a gradual curve until it was close to the object. Then the operator shut down the thrusters altogether and hit the 'Hover' button, which caused the ROV's onboard gyroscopic navigation system to kick in and make micro-adjustments to all the propellers to ensure that the vessel stayed in the same place, even with ocean currents trying to push it along.

The operator pushed the tiny red hat stick on top of the control stick to the right and down to focus the ROV's powerful spotlights on the object. He could clearly see what it resembled, but he did not understand what he was looking at. Having settled gently in the powdery grey silt near the wreckage of the USS Tennessee was a small off-white marble bust. This had clearly belonged to one of the crewmembers. For a brief moment, he considered using the ROV's manipulator arms to retrieve it, but then he decided against it. It somehow felt right that the bust should remain where it was. It seemed to belong down here with the submarine.

After several more hours and multiple radioactivity measurements, the ROV finally headed back upwards and began its long journey towards the surface and the light, leaving the imploded wreckage of the once-proud USS Tennessee behind in the darkness.

NOTE FROM THE AUTHOR.

Thank you very much for reading this book. I really hope you enjoyed it. If you did, I would be very grateful if you would give it a star rating on Amazon and perhaps even write a review.

I am always trying to improve my writing, and the best way to do that is to receive feedback from my readers. Reviews really do help me a lot. They are an excellent way for me to understand the reader's experience, and they will also help me to write better books in the future.

Thank you.

Lex Faulkner

Printed in Great Britain
by Amazon